LEGALLY
Charming

LAUREN SMITH

OTHER TITLES BY LAUREN SMITH

Historical
The League of Rogues Series
Wicked Designs
His Wicked Seduction
Her Wicked Proposal
Wicked Rivals
His Wicked Secret (coming soon)
The Seduction Series
The Duelist's Seduction
The Rakehell's Seduction
The Rogue's Seduction (Coming soon)
Standalone Stories
Tempted by A Rogue

Contemporary
The Surrender Series
The Gilded Cuff
The Gilded Cage
The Gilded Chain
Her British Stepbrother
Forbidden: Her British Stepbrother
Seduction: Her British Stepbrother
Climax: Her British Stepbrother

Paranormal
Dark Seductions Series
The Shadows of Stormclyffe Hall
The Love Bites Series
The Bite of Winter
Brotherhood of the Blood Moon Series
Blood Moon on the Rise

Sci-Fi Romance
Cyborg Genesis Series
Across the Stars (coming 2017)

DEDICATION

To my father, a true gentleman lawyer and to baby Hayley, a beautiful gummy bear. I also have to thank my friends Jennifer H. Liz M. and Kerri H. for their love and support!

TABLE OF CONTENTS

CHAPTER ONE

A man wearing only the bottom half of a *Star Wars* stormtrooper outfit streaked past Felicity Hart. She ducked out of the way as the half-naked frat boy whooped and bounced to the music, heading straight for a group of girls wearing white bunny ears who were gathered by the kitchen bar.

So this is what grad student parties are like.

Drinking, dancing, and insanity. Felicity shook her head, trying not to laugh. After growing up in a small town in Nebraska, she hadn't been prepared for college life in Chicago. Talk about culture shock. She was used to everyone in town knowing not just her name, but far too much about her personal life. Even after six years of living here, being surrounded by thousands of strangers who knew absolutely nothing about her, it was still both completely unsettling and oddly liberating.

For the first four years of college and the past two years of her master's, she'd hidden in her little shell. But a few months ago she'd met Layla Russo, a graduate student just like her, and they'd hit it off. Layla was the only reason Felicity had pulled a Cinderella and come to the ball. She would have laughed at the thought, but she was dead tired and stifled a yawn instead. At this rate, she'd turn into a pumpkin before midnight.

Happy Birthday to me, she thought and fisted her hands in the voluminous skirts of her Tudor gown. She stood out too much at this party—which happened when you skipped over the sexy cat costumes and zeroed in on the classy Anne Boleyn Tudor ball gown. Felicity should have worn some cheap costume, but she just couldn't do it. Halloween was her favorite holiday. She'd scrimped and saved to buy a good costume, one that meant something to her. She'd been lucky enough to find this gown on a deep-discount rack at a costume warehouse. Hence the beautiful, elegant, yet still sexy gown she wore at that moment. At least it had been sexy in the sixteenth century.

I am such a nerd.

She had gotten her share of raised eyebrows and smothered laughs when she'd entered the apartment with her friends, but she didn't care. She was ready to celebrate her entrance into adulthood at a normal party. Even if it had taken her until graduate school to be brave enough to attend a social gathering like this.

And why shouldn't she? She'd worked hard—late-night study sessions, endless art exhibit submissions—all in the hope of attaining grades that would be good enough to take her from a small Nebraska town to the hip art communities of Chicago. She *deserved* a party. And going to one at Layla's boyfriend's fancy apartment was safe enough since it was close to the school and the gallery where she worked.

Several laughing girls bumped into her, plastic cups brimming with alcohol. She danced back a step, narrowly avoiding drenching her gown in cheap beer as one of the girls stumbled in her heels, sending her cup flying through the air.

"Shit!" the girl hissed, then started giggling with her friends as she bent over to clean up the mess.

The entire night had been one near miss after another. The last thing Felicity needed was her costume smelling like beer.

She glanced at the group of pretty girls in the bunny ears and the gathering of boys around them.

Why didn't I think of wearing something like that? She glanced at the girls with their perfect bikini bodies, and she blushed. There was no way she could run around in something skimpy like that and feel confident. She just didn't look good in tight clothes...or revealing clothes. She was a size twelve, which was just a little too plump to look good in a skintight costume. She shuddered at the thought of being so exposed.

The crowd of people thinned out as she headed toward the room she sought. She took a moment to pause, one hand resting on the wall as she tried to suck in a breath. Maybe the corset was a bad idea.

"Hey!" A familiar feminine voice cut through the noise, and Felicity looked over her shoulder.

Layla was the official hostess of the party even though the apartment belonged to her boyfriend, Tanner, and she certainly acted like it as she strode toward her. She was a sight —five foot, curvy, and completely rocking her zombie stripper costume. Amazingly, Layla managed to look both scary and cute as she crossed the room in her four-inch stilettos. Felicity knew without a doubt that she'd break her neck in shoes like that, which was why she'd opted for red silk slippers that matched her gown.

"Hey, you okay?" Layla reached her and linked her arm through Felicity's. "I saw you yawning from across the room."

Felicity wrinkled her nose. "Just tired. Been up since

dawn, have a midterm paper due tomorrow, and I feel every minute of a year older." Felicity wrinkled her nose. "Is it still all right to crash in Tanner's brother's bedroom?"

"Of course! I don't want you having to travel across half the city tonight to get back to that little hole in the wall you live in." Layla linked her arm through Felicity's. "I really wish you'd just move in with me." Her friend pouted dramatically, but Felicity stiffened her spine in an attempt resist Layla's begging.

"As much as I love your apartment, Layla, it's out my budget at the moment." It was double what her tiny place was, and Felicity's budget was already stretched thin. "You sure Tanner's brother won't mind?" It still felt weird to be sleeping in a guy's bed whether he was there or not.

"Yeah. Jared won't be back till Sunday night, so you're welcome to stay the whole weekend," Layla said. "Besides, even if he wasn't spending the entire weekend working, he'd never be caught dead anywhere near a party like this. That workaholic wouldn't know fun if it bit him in the ass." She snorted as though picturing just that. "Are you sure you're just tired, birthday girl?"

With her classes and her part-time job, Felicity was grateful for early nights where she could find them—and the prospect of staying up into the wee hours and endangering her beloved dress didn't hold much appeal. No, the sweet song of a comfy bed and a few hours of oblivion was calling to her.

"I'm good!" she insisted. "Go have more fun and don't worry about me. Go find Tanner before he realizes you've ditched him." Felicity pointed to Layla's boyfriend, who was politely escaping the group of bunnies and searching about for Layla.

Tanner Redmond and Layla had hooked up the first day of classes five years ago and had been together ever since. He was hot, smart, and totally nice, not at all like some of the entitled jerks she had to deal with when she handled rich clients at the gallery where she worked, which was a shocker given that he was a rich kid. He and his older brother, Jared, shared this beautiful apartment. She'd never met Jared. Even though she'd spent the last three months around Tanner and Layla, the mysterious older brother had never once shown up.

Layla's dark eyes ran up and down Felicity with concern. "You sure you don't want to stay out here? You don't have to crash now. Unless you're not feeling well?" Layla cocked one hip, her hand perched there as she continued to study Felicity. Felicity swallowed down the flutter of nerves that always came whenever her friend tried to make her participate more in the student culture, but she shook her head. She wasn't good at being fun and spontaneous or wild. Graduate student life seemed to be built on those three things when one wasn't studying or writing papers. It was just her luck that she was too shy to be bold in life like Layla.

It never ceased to amaze Felicity how much of a mother hen her friend could be.

"I'm good," she answered Layla, her voice firm. Sometimes she had to use a "parent voice" in order to get Layla to stop mothering her. "Go and have fun. You said the bedroom is the last on the left?"

"Yup. And seriously, stay the weekend. Just come back here after your midterm, and we can hang out." Layla's offer was tempting, and Felicity found herself more than considering it. It sure would be nice to crash here for a few days. "I still can't believe you have a term paper due on the Saturday after Halloween," Layla muttered. "Ugh." Layla wrinkled her nose. "Some teachers are jerks. I'd be happy to make a voodoo doll of him, and we can shove pins in him." Her friend was grinning wickedly as she suggested this.

Felicity bit back a laugh. "If I didn't like Professor

Willoughby as much as I do, I might take you up on that."

Layla escorted her all the way to the door and then curved her arms around Felicity in a hug. Her throat tightened as she fought off the fierce happiness that came over her whenever her friend hugged her.

Layla didn't hug by halves—she gripped you hard, squeezed the air out of your lungs, and made you feel loved.

Felicity just wasn't used to that—unlike Layla with her sprawling and loud family that found it natural to hug and kiss constantly, Felicity's parents were not overtly affectionate. They were sweet, and she knew they loved her, but they didn't put their affection on display like Layla—unbridled and consuming.

"Just do me a favor. Get some rest and kick butt on your research tomorrow."

"Yes, *Mom*." Felicity stuck her tongue out, and they both giggled.

As Layla turned back to the party, Felicity slipped into the sanctuary and relative quiet of the dark bedroom. Her breath caught as she took in the view of the city through the tall windows. The skyline of downtown Chicago was a man-made mountain range of lights twinkling in a sea of black. The sky behind the buildings was a soft purple, cutting a contrast against the silhouettes of the buildings. It was one amazing view, and it always made her breathless when she caught a glimpse of the monolithic buildings. Her hands ached to sketch the sight, but she hadn't brought her pad with her.

Fifteen stories up, none of the city sounds that kept her up at night could be heard from Jared's bedroom. She liked that. She wandered over to the window, wanting to sate herself on the sight of glittering lights and an endless glowing horizon. When she'd had her fill of the view, she turned back to investigate just what sort of room she would be spending the night in.

A massive bed against one wall with a cherrywood headboard and a deep crimson comforter looked soft and inviting. The scent of aftershave and an enticing masculine aroma made her all too aware again that this was a man's domain. She scanned the rest of the room. A large desk was laden with files and paperwork. If he was such a workaholic, why didn't he spend more time at this desk and enjoy the view? If she had this to look at all day, she could see the appeal of working from home. But as a lawyer, maybe he didn't get that option, and had to be in the office all day.

It suddenly bothered her that she had no idea what Jared looked like. Being in his personal space like this was oddly intimate, and it felt strange seeing so much of the man without ever having seen his face. As an artist, all she did was think about what things and people looked like. Not being able to see the features or the build of the man who lived here was unsettling.

Layla had said he was thirty and panty-melting hot—but not as hot as Tanner, of course. Layla wasn't the type of girl to really eye another man when she was happily in love, but she did appreciate beauty of the masculine variety. Felicity had laughed at the thought. She'd never seen any guy worth calling panty-melting hot, at least none outside of the movies. Layla said that Jared could give Jamie Dornan a run for his money on hotness and intensity.

Layla's words came back to her, and she smiled as she could hear her friend's voice so clearly in her head. "You know what I'm talking about. Tanner is all sorts of brooding and intense. He can just look at you and you go all wet and melty, you know? Like he'd fuck you so good you'd break the bed and ask for more. Jared's like that, too." Felicity hadn't been able to get that out of her mind. Layla had said Tanner was just like Jared, only younger. It explained everything.

Tanner's intensity was tempered by his youth and sweetness, but his older brother had that jaded, hot bad-boy thing going on, according to Layla.

Now she stood in said panty-melter's room and couldn't help but picture a gorgeous, sexy man walking through the room, putting on a suit, critically eyeing his appearance in the mirror over the dresser.

Unable to resist and knowing it was completely inappropriate, she opened the top drawer of the beautiful dark dresser. Neatly rolled ties of a dozen different colors and patterns decorated the drawer, and a set of different styles of watches with leather and metal bands sat next to a box filled with cufflinks that glinted like jewels beneath the glass lid.

"Wow." She trailed her fingertips over the watches. A man with refined, expensive tastes.

Felicity watched the shadows play across the room, accenting the bed where Jared slept. What would it be like to share a bed with a man like him? To be the focus of all that raw masculinity and sexual energy? Her body hummed at the fantasy her mind seemed determined to play out. Her skin burned at the thought of what could happen if he came here tonight and found her in his bedroom. What if he just stood there, blocking the door, staring down at her? What if he told her to strip off her clothes and get into bed?

God, I need to get laid. Felicity shook her head. Even though she was a virgin, her fantasies could get wild. She struggled to get her libido under control.

Felicity sighed as she leaned against the bed, relishing the moment to bask in such luxury. She smoothed a hand over the red comforter. Satin? No, silk. She was tempted to lie down, just for a bit, but she knew she should change into her PJ's before getting in. She tried the nearest door, only to discover a large walk-in-closet with dozens of suits and a tall rack of expensive leather shoes. Not the bathroom. Her bag was supposed to be in the bathroom where Layla had said she'd put it. She approached the last door she hadn't opened. Felicity flicked on the light, found her bag sitting on the marble floor, and then searched through her clothes. When she didn't immediately find them, she dumped her gym bag over, muttering as she dug through the contents on the bed.

"Damn!" No pajamas. She'd left them at home.

All she had was her change of clothes for tomorrow. She wouldn't sleep in those. Returning to the bed, she put a hand to her stomach. The corset dug deep into her. How the heck did women live like this back in the day? Sure, it was fun to wear for a couple of hours, but spend her life in one of these? No way.

Gathering her skirts, she tucked her legs up on the bed and rested her head on the pillow.

So soft. Her mind started to drift in that hazy place between being awake and being asleep. What would it be like to live in a place like this? Surrounded by beauty, success, wealth? She'd likely never know. Her dream was to be an artist and a curator of a museum. Not much money in either of those dreams, but they were her passions.

Passion.

The word made her smile. The man who slept in this room definitely had passion, workaholic or not. He appreciated the finer things, and his taste was impeccable. Her fingers tapped along the bedding. It really was a pity she'd never meet the owner. A yawn escaped her, and she stuck a balled fist against her mouth. Her thoughts drifted, and she let them wander into dreams of the sexy man whose bed she was currently in and what would happen if he returned.

Jared Redmond stumbled from the taxicab, his brown leather briefcase smacking his back as he struggled to stay on his feet. He swallowed a growl of frustration. This was the last time he let the senior partners of his firm keep him out late to celebrate. He'd only had one drink, since he was dead tired from the last few months of overtime at the office. Having to smile, laugh, and socialize all night with the partners left him edgy and desperate to get home and crawl into bed.

God forbid he just do his job and do it well enough to earn respect. No, he had to spend hours at one of the most expensive restaurants with them, watching them pat each other on the back when he'd done all the heavy lifting in their multi-million-dollar transaction.

Big fucking mistake.

Now he was completely drained, and his body was determined to go to sleep on him right there on the street. His vision was fine, but his motor skills seemed to have abandoned him. He reached the glass doors of his apartment building lobby, leaning a little too heavily against the glass. Fishing around in his pocket for his keycard, he muttered a string of curses when his hand came up empty. He glanced up and rapped his knuckles. Thank God, the guard recognized him and buzzed him inside.

"Mr. Redmond." The security guard nodded, a knowing smile on the older man's lips.

"Hey, Randy," he greeted, wincing at the slur of his words.

A few more steps and he reached the elevator. After much effort focusing on the series of floor buttons on the panel, he pressed the button to the fifteenth floor and it lit up. He leaned his head back on the mirrored walls, resting. Jesus, it was like he was drunk, but he knew it was sheer exhaustion.

It had been a hell of a day. After two months of

negotiations, sleepless nights, long hours, and no chance of reviving his obsolete social life, he'd closed the massive real estate deal, and closed it earlier than he'd anticipated. Everyone demanded they go out and celebrate. He just wanted to crash and sleep off all of the stress pent up inside him.

He was going to walk into his bedroom and face-plant on his bed and not move all weekend from that spot.

Tanner would be out with his girlfriend, Layla, celebrating. It was Halloween, wasn't it? A little grin tugged at his lips. The apartment would be empty and *quiet*. The perfect benefit of arriving home early. He'd told Tanner he wouldn't be back until Sunday, and it was only Friday now. He expected his little brother and girlfriend would be out partying the night away, giving him total silence and a soft bed to crash on without any disturbances.

The second the elevator doors slid open with a soft hiss, he heard the music and the erratic noises of a party. Laughter, voices, all coming from their apartment.

Fucking hell.

"Tanner," he growled, fists clenched.

So the partying tonight was *in*, not *out*.

Jared contemplated turning around and finding a hotel, or worse, calling Shana. No, bad idea. They'd dated on and off during law school and after, but they'd never been exclusive. Currently he and Shana were off. *Definitely off.*

Lousy timing for Tanner to throw a damn party.

That was the main problem with letting his twenty-four-year-old brother live with him. He'd thought it would be nice to spend some time with his little brother, but with his work schedule he barely saw Tanner. The one night they might have hung out, he was too tired to care. He was not in the mood to dodge drunken graduate students all night and try to drown out all the racket they were making. Luck wasn't with him tonight. Fuck, he was turning into a crotchety old man if he was going to let a party piss him off.

The door to their place was unlocked, and when he swung the door open, a wave of fresh sound engulfed him. His eardrums throbbed, and he winced at the explosion of the music that drilled into his skull like nails. Scantily-dressed girls bounced about to the pounding rhythm of the music along with guys who were watching with giddy-schoolboy expressions. Some of them cheered and smiled, drunkenly overjoyed that a new person had shown up to the party. Several familiar faces, Tanner's friends, waved at him or nodded as he walked past them.

"Jared! I thought you weren't coming home till tomorrow?" A zombie stripper stepped in front of him, hands on her hips. Through the gory makeup he thought he recognized her.

"Layla?"

Tanner's girlfriend was dressed as a zombie stripper. Only Layla could manage to pull off that look.

"Layla, what the hell is going on?" he demanded, gesturing to the insanity. A girl in a sexy *Lara Croft* costume was singing a bad karaoke cover of "Somebody's Watching Me." Holy fuck. He was going to need some noise-cancelling headphones to survive this shit. For a brief second he considered tossing everyone out on their damn asses, but this place was half Tanner's and he'd told Tanner he wouldn't be here tonight. Brother code demanded he suffer through this bullshit.

Layla didn't look chagrined in the least. "It's Halloween. Oh, and Felicity's birthday, obviously."

"Who is Felicity?" He'd never met anyone named Felicity. Not that it was surprising, because he was never around when his brother was hanging out with Layla and their friends. He didn't really remember what it was like to be that carefree. Law school and work had a way of consuming a person's good memories.

"Scratch that, I don't care. Is this thing"—he waved a hand around—"ending anytime soon?" He shifted his briefcase strap over his shoulder. His suit was starting to suffocate him, and as much as he liked the particular steel-gray tie he wore at the moment, he was desperate enough to cut it right off his neck if he couldn't get to his room fast enough.

"Uh…" She licked her lips. "Don't know. But you said you weren't coming back until Sunday."

"Well, here I am and tired as fuck. So I'm going to bed. Try to keep it down," he growled.

"Uh, Jared." She dodged around him, trying to prevent him from getting past her.

"What did you do?" He arched a brow, sensing by the way her eyes widened and she shifted in her stilettos that something was wrong.

"I might have given your bed away." Layla bit her lip, yet she was brave enough to still meet his eyes.

"What do you mean you gave my bed away?"

She attempted to smile. "You were *supposed* to be gone until Sunday, and Felicity needed a place to stay tonight. It's late, and I didn't want her to go home alone. She lives in a sketchy part of town—so I told her she could crash in your bed since *you* weren't going to be here." She glared at him, accusing him of something he wasn't entirely sure was his fault. "So she's in your room tonight." She ended with a finality that did not entirely make sense to his tired brain.

"Let me get this straight. Some girl is in my bed…right now?"

Layla swallowed, her eyes darting away before coming back to him. "Um…yeah?"

"No," he stated and stalked toward his room, Layla at his

heels. Whoever this Felicity person was, she was in his bed, and since it was *his* bed, whatever Layla and this girl had seemed to think otherwise, he'd have her out of it.

Reaching his bedroom door, he crashed it open and strode in, prepared for all the hell and fury that came with drunk, twenty-something females—and instead, as his eyes adjusted, he found a princess in his bed.

Layla clattered behind on her too-tall stilettos. "Jared, wait—"

He pushed the door open, and a yellow beam of light from the hallway cut across the dark room, revealing a figure lying across his bed.

A princess. There was a princess in his bed.

The burgundy-and-gold gown was draped over his comforter with pearls glowing like tiny moons on the bodice of her gown.

What the fuck?

"Please don't wake her," Layla begged.

Wake her? Jared shook his head. *What nonsense.* He wasn't a romantic. Even though she was certainly a fantasy. All luscious curves and mystery. Her dark auburn hair cascading over the pillow looked soft. His hands ached to reach out and fist in the strands. She looked like the kind of woman a young man dreamed about and ruined his sheets over, the kind of woman he'd stopped dreaming about a long time ago because he was convinced they didn't exist.

He didn't turn to look at Layla as he spoke. "Who is that?"

"Felicity Hart. Birthday girl and, more importantly, my best friend." The threat was heavily implied. Don't screw with Layla or her friends. Her loyalty in that respect was one of the things he admired most about his brother's girlfriend.

Layla's fingers curled around his biceps and squeezed, getting his attention.

"I told her she could sleep in your room since you weren't supposed to be here. It's the only place available for her to sleep."

"I'm not giving up *my* bed. I worked seventy hours this week. I'm going to sleep." He got one step inside his room before Layla practically tackled him, climbing up his back like a spider monkey.

"You. Will. Not. Wake. Her. Up," Layla growled, nails digging into his arms. "She has a really important research paper due tomorrow, and she needs to sleep."

"She can stay, but I'm sharing my bed with her. End of discussion. Go back to your party." With a little shove, he made sure Layla couldn't get back in before he shut the door in her face.

When he turned back around, he studied the girl in his bed. Without the hallway light he could barely make out her features. Just a silhouette, really, of a princess. Arousal slammed into him. He felt like an idiot. He never dated anyone who was still in school. They were too young. A year ago he'd tried to date a girl who was twenty-four, but she'd gotten pissed every time he'd had to work late. She didn't get the pressures of his job. None of the girls younger than him seemed to understand that. Layla was all right, but she was still a kid. He needed someone mature who was at the same point in her life as him, an adult.

The hot little princess was the last thing he needed to be thinking about.

Don't think about her or how much fun it would be to wake her up and kiss her. Just be a gentleman and go to bed.

His inner voice was a goddamn control freak, but he was thankful someone was still responsible.

Turning away, he started to strip out of his work clothes. He kicked his shoes off and then slipped a pair of pajama bottoms on. He didn't bother with a shirt. He always got a little hot at night anyway. As he moved deeper into the room, he caught his foot on a chair. It screeched as it slid across the wood, and he winced, catching himself against the back of it. He glanced at the bed, but the girl hadn't woken. A few quick steps and then he hit the bed, landing on his stomach and bouncing a little. The princess next to him didn't stir. He shifted a couple of inches and slid one arm beneath his pillow to puff it up as he laid his head down. The toll of the night's celebrations dragged him to the edge of the abyss of sleep. He was so close...

A little gasp and a half-strangled whimper pulled him to the surface again. "Whah?" He groaned and rolled onto his side facing the girl.

She was thrashing and whimpering beside him. Her hands clawed at the bodice of her dress, as though trying to escape it.

"Damn it!" He sat up and flicked on the lamp by his side of the bed. The wash of color in the room showed how flushed the girl was. She still shifted and kicked, moaning as if in pain. Jared leaned over and gently jostled her shoulder.

"Hey, kid, wake up."

She jolted awake. Bright gray eyes like liquid mercury flashed in shock and fear as her gaze fell on him.

"Hi," he said.

The princess blinked, her eyes darting around the room, then back to him, focusing on his bare chest. Her pupils dilated.

"Did we...um...who—" She shook her head as though to clear it. "Who are you, and what are you doing here?"

Jared let out a raspy chuckle. "I'm the one who should be asking questions. But it's been a long day and I'm beat. I'm Jared, and you are in *my* bed."

He stood and walked back to his cherrywood dresser. His fingers curled around the brass handle, and he opened the top drawer.

"You're Tanner's brother?" Her voice was soft, husky. It rolled over him, soothing his irritation.

He selected a silk striped button-down nightshirt and a pair of boxers from his drawer and then returned to the bed. "Here." He held the clothes out to her.

"What are those for?" she asked. One elegant brow rose.

"You. You woke up clawing at your dress. Looks like it's too tight around your chest and it's restricting your breathing. Unless you have clothes of your own, you're changing into these so we can both get some sleep. Layla said you had some paper due tomorrow."

When she opened her mouth, he could see the protest in her eyes and it amused him. *Feisty little thing.* And damned if he didn't picture all the things he'd like to do to that little mouth.

"Take the clothes and change in the bathroom. *Now.*" He deepened his voice, and she hopped out of bed, snatching the clothes as she darted into the bathroom. She froze, then slowly looked over her shoulder at him.

"What?"

"My dress...it's the laces in the back. I can't reach them."

A sigh escaped him. "Come here." He crooked a finger and sat farther back on his bed. She sidled up to him, bashfulness in her every movement.

There was something sinful and suggestive about the way she nibbled her bottom lip. He twirled a finger, indicating for her to spin around. She offered her back to him. The silk ribbons on the back of her gown came undone easily enough, but he was surprised to see the second set of laces beneath, which belonged to a corset. It was black with embroidered red roses that set off the color of the loose tangles of her hair. The strands teased the back of his hands as he unlaced the corset. The creamy skin of her lower back made his mouth go dry.

The princess was trying to kill him with these temptations.

All too soon the view disappeared as she rushed into the adjoining bathroom to change.

He fell back onto the bed, staring up at the ceiling. His fingers tapped a rhythm on his stomach as he waited. This was not at all how he'd predicted his night would go. He wasn't complaining—not exactly.

The princess emerged, gown gone. She looked so young, standing there dwarfed in his button-down shirt and a hint of his boxers beneath the hem at her mid-thighs. Her gorgeous hair was wild and long, and it looked like she'd been well loved in bed. He didn't miss the swell of her full breasts against the thin, expensive silk. The top button was low down her chest, exposing a wealth of creamy skin. Damn.

He was about to say something bad, something that his exhausted mind would probably get him slapped for, when his bedroom door burst open and light from the hallway illuminated them both.

"Dude...found a bed." A man wearing the bottom half of a stormtrooper costume stumbled toward Jared's bed. Behind him trailed a girl in a Playboy Bunny outfit.

Jared glanced at Felicity, who'd frozen in shock, her hands pulling the button-up shirt closed against her throat, her cheeks a bright pink in the dim light.

"Oh...hey..." The stormtrooper finally noticed Jared as Jared got to his feet, scowling. "Do you mind if we—"

"Get the fucking hell out of my room," Jared growled. "*Now.*" He may have been almost half-dead with fatigue, but he could still throw a punch if he needed to.

"But come on, man, I want to get laid..." the boy whispered too loudly, and the bunny behind him giggled.

"I'll lay you flat on your goddamn ass if you don't get lost." Jared took a menacing step toward the inebriated pair, and they stumbled back into the hall. Jared didn't hesitate.

He slammed his bedroom door in the wooden frame and clicked the lock into place before he turned back to face Felicity. Her hand was covering her mouth, and her eyes were wide.

"Sorry about that, princess. I locked the door. No one else will stumble in—I promise."

She blinked, dropped her hand, and then her eyes drifted from the door to his face as though debating whether she was safe with him in a locked room.

"Come on. I don't bite." *Hard,* he silently added, and flashed what he knew was a wolfish grin.

"I could sleep elsewhere," she hedged, playing with the collar of the button-down shirt. "Layla said you'd be gone all weekend."

"It's fine. This thing is a California king. Plenty of room for both of us. It's just one night."

He waited for her to pad on little bare feet to her side of the bed. It dipped slightly as she got in under the covers. She tensed when he crawled beneath the blankets, but after a moment, when he didn't move toward her, she blew out a breath. He rolled away to turn off the lamp by his bedside, then settled back, puffing his pillow again as he lay on his back and closed his eyes. A sweet, subtle scent filled his nose, like vanilla and fresh rain. When the princess shifted, trying to get comfortable, the scent grew stronger. Her scent.

"Thanks for letting me stay. I'm Felicity, by the way."

He could hear the yawn in her voice, and it made him grin.

"Good night, princess," he murmured.

She didn't respond. The soft little sound of her faint breaths did something funny to his chest. It tightened, and he sucked in a deep breath, hoping to ease the tension.

Now was not the time to be having a soft spot for a woman. He had so much to worry about at work, especially with Shana and her father. There wasn't time to seduce a sweet little princess, even if he wanted to. She really was a cute little thing, though.

Not for me. He sighed and let his body crash.

CHAPTER TWO

The cell phone alarm buzzed, a light musical chime accompanying the vibrations. Felicity fumbled on the nightstand for the phone and silenced it.

6:00 a.m. Two and a half hours until her American Colonial Art paper was due. The urge to get up and get moving just wasn't there. The bed was warm, and she felt safe. The last thing she wanted to do was get up and think about a bunch of colonists and loyalists duking it out in the seventeen hundreds and how that had affected painting styles in Colonial America. Right now she wanted to stay where she was, cocooned in heat, and drift back to that pleasant place between being awake and dreaming.

It was then she noticed the long, muscled arm curled around her waist, tucking her back against a hard, warm body.

What the—

Another rattling buzz. This time it came from the other side of the bed. She rolled over, careful not to wake the man in bed next to her. A wall of muscled male chest met her face.

Her gaze raked up the bare torso of the man to his face where it rested on his pillow.

Jared Redmond.

She was sharing a bed with Tanner's brother. Had she really let him untie her dress and corset last night? Her eyes closed for a brief instant as she pushed back her shyness. He was still asleep, and she took advantage of it to study his face. It was a nice face, not too handsome, yet somehow sexy and incredibly attractive. Strong jaw, aquiline nose, too-long dark eyelashes fanned over slightly tanned skin. Dark brows winged over eyes that she knew had to be dark brown like his brother's. He was the sort of man who wasn't a pretty boy, yet he had some serious animal magnetism even while he slept.

Her fingers tingled as she resisted the urge to reach out and trace his lips. The bottom lip was slightly fuller than the top. His hair was a rich chocolate, long enough to tunnel her fingers through. Would it be silky or slightly rough in texture? She nibbled her bottom lip.

This was the closest she'd ever been to a man before—at least in bed—and it was fascinating and a little unnerving. A shadow of a beard made him look older, a little rugged. The pit of her stomach dropped, and she shivered with excitement. He was only thirty, but that felt so much older than her at the moment. He was a man.

Jared had the body of a man, unlike the graduate student guys in her classes. He was hot and dangerous looking, and every time she thought about that, her stomach quivered. She was in *his* bed, as he'd said the night before. She'd been helpless to resist when he'd gently commanded her to undress with that deep baritone voice of his. She glanced down at herself. His shirt and boxers were large and comfortable on her, and the intimacy of wearing his clothes had her heart thrumming like a hummingbird's wings.

That other phone was buzzing again on his side of the bed. Suddenly he jerked, rolling away as he picked up the phone.

Had he been awake this whole time? Did he know she'd been just staring at him? Had he meant to be holding her so close when she'd woken up?

God, I'm such an idiot.

"Hell," Jared muttered and fell back on his bed, eyes closed, his phone silenced. Two breaths more, and then he spoke again. "So you getting up? I'll let you shower first."

"What?" He was offering her his shower? Before she wouldn't have thought twice about using it, but now that its owner was here, she'd figured she'd skip it until after her test. The idea of her being naked with just a door between them sent a little shiver through her.

"The shower. It's yours. I'm still waking up." He twisted to face her, propping his head on his hand to stare at her.

"Get moving, princess. Or else I might give in to my desire to kiss you. A man can only stand so much temptation." He chuckled.

Felicity shot out of the bed like she'd been fired out of a cannon. Kiss her? Was he serious?

"I'm a good kisser," he called out after her.

He was still laughing, probably because of the look she knew he must be seeing on her face. His grin hit her right behind the knees. She retreated, her back hitting his dresser.

"I...um...have a term paper due." That was stupid. She was making it worse by opening her mouth. She mentally smacked herself and ran to the shower. Cranking the nozzle to hot, she picked up her bag from the bathroom floor and searched for her toiletries.

The water burned her skin, and she sighed. Her own apartment had hot water only when the water heater thought it could handle the building's demands, which wasn't often.

And when it did bother to work, the pipes rocked inside the walls, creating a banging noise that drove her crazy.

Staying here at Jared's apartment was like staying in a four-star hotel. Scrubbing her face in her hands, she let the water pour over her. The tension in her shoulders eased. Not once last night had she woken up. Where she'd grown up, she'd fallen asleep to the melody of crickets and other country sounds. But here in Chicago, with her apartment's paper-thin walls, all she heard were the violent sounds of the city outside. Ambulances, shouting neighbors, banging pipes, slamming stairwell doors, and the endless creaks and groans as the elevator ground through its gears. Felicity was lucky to get even an hour or two of uninterrupted sleep. Last night had been amazing. Just silence and warmth. Ironically, sleeping with a total stranger—and a man, at that—had been one of the most restful nights of sleep she'd had in a long time.

Felicity's skin tingled as she remembered the way it felt to roll over and see him so close. Shock aside, it had been nice. Layla must *never* find out. She'd try to hook her up with Jared. It would be a bad idea. Between school and work, she didn't have time. Not to mention she and Jared were nothing alike and had nothing in common. He was a hotshot lawyer, and she was an art student. She doubted he'd even be interested in her, his jokes about kisses aside.

Rinsing the last bit of soap and conditioner away, she slipped out of the shower and pulled one of the large fluffy white towels off the shelf next to the shower. The towel fit around her body perfectly, and she was able to tuck the corner of it in near the tops of her breasts to keep it on so she could rummage around the drawers of the bathroom counter. There had to be a hairdryer in here somewhere. She hadn't thought to pack one since Layla had said she could borrow one, but it wasn't as though she could go parading past Jared in nothing but a towel to find Layla's hairdryer.

"What do you need?"

Jared's deep voice made her freeze as she bent over the drawer, her bottom in the air.

"I can help you find whatever you need...although I do love this angle, if you want to keep looking for whatever it is."

"Oh!" She whirled around, hands clutching her towel so it wouldn't drop.

When she raised her gaze, she found him standing in the open bathroom door, wearing only pajama pants. He leaned one shoulder against the doorjamb. His body was lightly tan, the muscles lean but impressive now that she could see them at a better angle. His pants hung on his narrow hips, and she gulped at the visible V-shaped line of muscles at his hips that seemed to point farther south to places hidden from her eyes. A perfect six-pack. How did a guy get those? They looked too good to be true. She certainly didn't look like she lived in the gym. Her fingers went white-knuckled on the towel. The last thing she wanted was for him to see her fuller figure. No matter how many diets she tried or how much she exercised, she could never get down to anything below a size twelve.

"What are you looking for?" he asked again. His gaze lazily drifted from her face down the length of her body. Was that approval in his eyes? Why did she suddenly want him to approve of her?

"I...uh...hairdryer, please?" She was usually more articulate. The man had the ability to destroy her control over her own mouth.

He pointed to below the sink. "Should be there."

"Thanks."

"Coffee or tea?" he asked.

"Tea," she replied without thinking.

"I'll make some in the kitchen. Come out when you're done." He didn't give her a chance to protest. The bathroom door closed, and he was gone.

Felicity scrambled through her morning routine, and in fifteen minutes she was dressed in jeans and a comfortable navy-blue sweater with a gray anchor on it. Sitting back on Jared's bed, she tugged on her worn pair of leather ankle boots. The bedroom was empty, so she headed to the kitchen. A few lone plastic cups lay on surfaces around the apartment, the only remnants of the wild party from the night before. Other than that, the place was surprisingly clean. Out of habit, she collected the few cups and walked into the kitchen to throw them away.

"Over here, sailor." Jared was at the other end of the kitchen, where the table was set for two.

He looked more delicious than the breakfast he'd prepared. He stood there in his pajama pants and shirtless, making her mouth water. His feet were bare, and for some reason that made her smile. She tried not to look at his chest, but it was pretty hard not to admire its muscled perfection. It reminded her of the times she and Layla would spend a night eating pizza and drooling over the gorgeous hunks in *Men's Health* magazine. Jared could have been posing for an article on six-pack abs.

Even though he was the one half-dressed, it made her feel strangely naked. The half-smile that hovered around his lips told her he knew she was uncomfortable and a little flushed.

Waffles, scrambled eggs, and bacon were already on the plates, and two cups of tea were waiting, steam coiling up in the air in milky tendrils. Her mind blanked. He was feeding her, too? What sort of man did that? Take care of a woman? Definitely none she knew. He fed her, clothed her…without threats, without demanding she accept what he offered. Something about that made her chest ache. She needed to regain control of her emotions.

"Sailor?" she asked.

"Your sweater." His lips twitched as he sat down at the

table.

She glanced down at the anchor. "Oh, right." What was with him and the nicknames? Kid, princess, sailor...

She dropped into the seat across from him and reached for her cup of tea. The porcelain cup burned her fingers—not quite to the point of pain, but enough to make the rest of her warm. She loved that about tea, the way even holding it in her hands could erase a bone-deep chill.

Jared watched her. The weight of his gaze was an almost tangible touch. Felicity shifted in her chair as she wriggled under his scrutiny.

"What paper do you have this morning?" he asked after a moment of painfully awkward silence.

"It's an analysis of the changing artistic painting styles in Colonial America during the Revolutionary War." She sipped her tea. Irish Breakfast. Her favorite.

Jared dug into his waffle, chewing thoughtfully. "You pick that by choice or force?"

She didn't understand his question. "I picked it. I'm an art history major."

"Ah...that explains the costume. You, princess, are a nerd." His judgmental smirk made her want to punch him, yet she still also found it infuriatingly attractive.

A prickle of indignation buried beneath her skin. *Nerd? Nerd!*

"I am *not*. Appreciating history isn't bad," she countered.

With a scrape of a fork over the plate he continued to eat, his whiskey brown eyes fixed on her every few seconds.

"Never said it was bad."

Okay. Felicity wasn't sure how to respond to that, so she decided to eat in silence. After a few bites—delicious ones— she realized she had relaxed a little more around him. She'd slept with Jared. Well, not *slept* with him, but being around him and not making a fool of herself by being too awkward was impressive when she'd rarely spent time alone with any guys back home. Instead, her heart beat a little quicker, her mouth was desert-dry, and her hands trembled with excitement.

"So...Layla said you're an attorney?" She decided to try small talk again. Her plate was wiped clean and so was his. He leaned back in his chair and put his hands behind his head, fingers laced as he studied her.

"Yeah. I focus on real estate transactions. I'm an associate attorney at Pimms & Associates LLP."

The name didn't sound familiar, not that it should have. She and Jared moved in very different circles. She was a graduate student with no connections to any big companies in the city, especially not law firms. And she wasn't from Omaha like Jared. She was just a small-town girl, but he didn't make her feel that way.

For the last couple of months of being around Tanner, she'd learned the Redmonds were wealthy, but they had earned it through hard work. More than once Layla had confessed it was one of the things she loved about Tanner. He wasn't a spoiled playboy. He played hard, sure, but he worked hard, too. He was an engineering major. Those students had an intense curriculum. Felicity and Layla joked that one look at Tanner's textbooks gave them headaches.

"Want another waffle?" Jared's voice cut through her thoughts. He was standing right beside her. *When had he moved?*

"No thanks." She patted her stomach. "Quite full."

"Okay. Just make sure you eat enough to fuel your brain for your research paper." He ruffled a hand over her hair, messing up the artful windblown look she'd spent several minutes that morning perfecting.

"Hey!" she said, swatting his hand away. When he caught her hand and tugged her body against his, she closed her eyes, praying for a kiss.

Gentle fingers cupped her chin and lifted her face. "Look at me, princess."

She pried one eye open, her heart beating wildly. To her surprise, Jared was studying her, but only kindness and curiosity shone in his warm brown eyes. Like rich maple syrup... She blinked.

"There you are," he murmured more to himself than to her. "Welcome back." He grinned and patted her cheek.

She couldn't escape the crushing disappointment. Why hadn't he kissed her? Was there something wrong with her?

The gesture was patronizing, yet Felicity couldn't summon any anger. No one had ever been playful with her or treated her like a kid, or maybe like a sister. But the look in his eyes—there was something dark and wild there, something that did funny things to her insides. Her lips pursed in a tight line.

"Don't frown, princess." He laughed, his back still to her.

She shot him a scathing look, hot enough to melt steel.

He was already walking back to the sink, whistling a tune under his breath.

"Better get going if you're going to make it to your class." He joined her back at the table and held out a wad of cash. "Cab money." He set the money in her hand and then walked back to the sink, apparently oblivious to her standing there gaping. The water ran as he scrubbed pots. A lawyer who did his own dishes? What next?

"I have money." She attempted to put the money on the counter next to him, but he caught her wrist. The warmth of his hand, slightly slick with dish soap, made her heart skip a beat. She met his gaze, steel determination forcing her not to mentally cower.

"Consider it an apology for whatever I may have said or

done last night and for disrupting your sleep. I really wasn't supposed to come back last night, but we closed our sale on time without any issues, so I was able to come back early."

Apology? Was he serious? He'd saved her from a drunken stormtrooper and a Playboy Bunny. She'd felt completely safe with him, like she had her very own knight in shining armor guarding her while she slept. That wasn't the sort of thing a girl like her would forget. She'd never been the damsel-in-distress type, but she had to admit she liked knowing someone had her back, that she wasn't alone. But it wasn't meant to be. She was hoping her boss at her art gallery was going to give her a personal recommendation for a position at the Los Angeles County Museum of Arts, or LACMA as it was called. If she got that job, she'd be leaving Chicago at the end of the school year when she graduated. That meant no dating, no love—not here, not with him.

"Look, this is really—" She pulled out of his grasp, unnerved by how unafraid of his touch she was.

"Let a man be chivalrous once in a while. We like it. Makes us feel needed." He dried his hands off and tucked the money in the front of her jeans.

Heat exploded through her in an almost violent rush as he invaded her space yet again. Why was she letting him affect her like that?

"No argument?" he teased.

She shook her head, her mind a little blank as she got lost in the splinters of gold and the flecks of green in his eyes. She hadn't seen that before. They weren't hazel, but the brown had a myriad of subtle colors in it. His eyes made her think of summer sun and lazy afternoons, the few in her life she'd been able to enjoy. She licked her lips, trying to erase the cotton-dry feeling in her mouth.

"Go get your stuff and get out of here. I don't want you to miss out on the colonial artwork." He winked.

Felicity finally found control of her body, and she hastily left the kitchen to pack her things. She left her change of clothes in her gym bag in Jared's room, even though she wanted to leave it with Layla. There was no way she was interrupting Layla and Tanner in bed. Right now she had to focus on her term paper. She couldn't afford to jeopardize her scholarship. Not even to linger one more minute in the presence of a handsome man who was just a little too sexy and a little too dangerous. Not scary dangerous, but the sort of dangerous that, if she wasn't careful, she might fall hopelessly in love with him. She'd had her heart broken already, and trust wasn't easy for her. The last thing she needed was Jared destroying her carefully-constructed fortress.

Yeah, he was dangerous all right.

CHAPTER THREE

Felicity haunted his thoughts. A flicker of light against the windows reminded him of her flashing gray eyes. God, she was something else. Jared grinned. It had been a long time since he'd had so much fun teasing a girl. The look on her face when he'd tucked the cab money back in her pocket—she'd been all flushed and wide-eyed. *Damn.* He'd gotten hard as a rock imagining how else he could have made her all pink and hot. But she was young. A graduate student.

So why did he keep reliving last night like some teenager in a fantasy? There was more to it than a warm body in bed beside him. It was the way she'd fallen asleep almost instantly, showing complete trust. Sharing a bed for the night with another person was more intimate than sex. You let your guard down, had no ready defenses. Most people refused to let themselves become that vulnerable. He was one of them.

But last night, he could have stayed next to her forever. The sweet smell of her, the rhythm of her light breathing, and the way she'd curled up against him until just before dawn.

Jared doubted she remembered that part of the night. He'd have to remind her later, just to see a blush creep across her cheeks.

There couldn't be a later, though.

Suddenly gripped by a bad mood, he stalked down the hall to his bedroom. Even though he kept his windows fairly tinted against the sun, the bold rays lit up the room. A streak of gold and burgundy caught his eye.

A wolfish grin tugged his lips back up.

The princess had left her gown.

Walking over to his bed, he reached out and touched the silk, which gleamed in the light. A hint of heat from the sun warmed his fingers as he picked up the gown. His eyes closed as he remembered the way she'd offered her back to him, so shy and yet completely trusting him. His hands tangling in the laces as he sought to undo them. The whisper of silk against skin.

Arousal slammed into him. His eyes flew open, and he forced himself to let go of the gown. Since when had he become so sentimental?

"Morning, Jared," Layla greeted him from his doorway, dressed in Tanner's shirt and boxers. Her long dark hair was sexy and rumpled. No doubt she and Tanner had partied well into the night.

"Layla," he answered and shifted slightly to block the view of Felicity's gown on his bed.

Her eyes tracked the movement like a cat sensing the darting shadow of a mouse.

"What's that?" She was instantly alert as she padded across his room.

"Nothing," he growled, taking a step toward her. Layla had no sense of boundaries, the result of too many siblings growing up, he supposed.

"Oh yeah? Sure doesn't look like nothing." She winkled

her nose as she giggled. Then without warning, she dove around him and snatched up the gown. "This is Felicity's costume. Why do you have it?"

Jared licked his lips. It never ceased to amaze him how she could intimidate him, despite her small size. He stood nearly a foot taller than her, but when she got that look in her eyes, it made even him want to retreat.

"She left it here when she took off for her class." He attempted to wrestle the dress back from Layla's hands, but the young woman kept a possessive grip on the fabric, and he didn't want to tear it.

"Uh-huh." She didn't sound all that convinced. "I'll just take this, if you don't mind. It's not like you need it." With a saucy little wink she started for the door, then stopped to look over her shoulder. "Oh, Jared, how was last night, by the way?" She paused in the doorway, her gaze on him assessing.

"Fine." That was all she was going to get.

He waited until Layla had disappeared before he shut the door and headed for the shower. Technically, he didn't have to work today. The sale for their client, the buyer, had gone through yesterday. After this sale, things at the office would settle down. At least for a few days.

Jared cranked the shower nozzle on and stripped out of his pajama bottoms. When he stepped inside, a sweet vanilla scent hit him hard. Felicity. Her body wash? Or maybe her shampoo? He reached for his own shampoo, a minty-scented bottle. Disappointment prickled inside him at the way the spearmint covered the vanilla. One more trace of last night's encounter was gone. With a frustrated growl, he scrubbed his scalp, lathering the shampoo into a thick froth before he rinsed.

A whole day. He had a whole day to burn and do whatever he wanted. Part of him was tempted to crash on his bed and sleep the rest of the day away. But that would only screw up his sleep schedule. He got so little as it was. It would have been worth it if he could have slept in with Felicity in his arms, although if she was there, he'd likely be tempted to do other things than sleep.

How is Felicity doing on her research? It had been six years since he'd been in college. Seemed more like a hundred. Law school and college were nothing alike. Undergrad had been fun. He'd worked hard and played hard. He didn't know what getting a master's degree was like compared to law school, though. Law school—that was the equivalent of joining the army and, rather than going to boot camp for training, just being dropped into the middle of a war zone with a water gun. He had barely gotten out of that experience alive. If it hadn't been for Shana—and more importantly, her father—he might never have landed his current associate position.

He scowled. These were never thoughts he liked to linger on, the possibility that he'd only been hired because he'd dated a partner's daughter. Yeah, really bruising to his ego.

Jared was tempted to linger in the shower, relishing the way the water soothed his tense muscles. But he couldn't avoid the inevitable. With a heavy sigh, he shut the water off and exited the shower. He reached for a fresh towel and saw the one that Felicity had used dangling over one peg. It was impossible to forget the look on her face when he'd caught her searching his bathroom. The puffy white towel had hugged her full figure, making her look soft and cuddly. He'd been torn between the desire to hug her to him, stripping the towel away to lick the crystalline droplets from her skin, or to just drag her to bed to make love the rest of the day.

His cock twitched in a silent salute at the idea. Damn. He needed to get his mind off the little princess. Princess. She'd left her gown. Surely she'd want it back, right? The pearl-encrusted bodice and silk fabric looked pricey.

It would be rude of him not to return the dress. He had no other plans today. Might be fun to tease her again. Striding over to the chest, he grabbed jeans and a black T-shirt. No suit today, thank God. As much as he loved dressing well, sometimes a man just needed jeans. Once he was dressed, he went in search of Layla and the costume.

His brother's girlfriend was in the kitchen, perched on the counter, bare legs swinging as she texted someone and sipped coffee from one of the black mugs he and Tanner had in their cupboards.

"Where's Felicity's costume?"

She didn't pause in her texting. "My room. Why?"

"I'm not working today, and I'd like to return it to her."

This made Layla's fingers freeze above her phone's screen. Her dark eyes drew a slow line up from her phone to his face. A glint of mischief peeked out from beneath her lashes.

"Mmmkay. Do you need her phone number and address? I wouldn't call for at least an hour. She has to finish the paper and turn it in to the professor around eleven a.m."

"Good point." He pulled his phone out of his pocket and waited for Layla to give him Felicity's info. When she was done, he pocketed the phone and returned to his room. He unloaded his briefcase on his desk and happily turned his mind off work, an event that rarely happened.

"You should take her bag, too." Layla was in his doorway again, pointing to the blue gym bag half-hidden behind his door. He'd missed that somehow. Layla hadn't.

"Okay. Thanks." He retrieved the bag and set it on his bed.

"So what happened last night?" Layla asked, her tone neutral as she walked over to his bed and plopped down on it like she owned the place.

"Kid, it's none of your business."

She kicked one leg off his bed, grinning like a Cheshire

cat. "She's my best friend. It's definitely my business."

"You only met her like a few months ago, right?" He wanted to know more about his bed partner, but he didn't want Layla getting any crazy ideas in her head.

"Sometimes how long you've known a person doesn't matter." Layla fixed him with a catlike gaze full of intentions he couldn't read clearly. "She and I just clicked."

He understood that. Sometimes you met someone and they just fit into place, like an intricate puzzle. You fit, no questions, no doubts. Something about Felicity made him feel like that. He'd never felt that way about a girl before, and frankly, it was a little unnerving.

"If you like her, Jared, be careful. You break her heart, I break your balls." Layla mimicked a karate chop motion.

He chuckled. "You don't need to worry. She's sweet but way too young for me. I just feel like I owe her after last night. I should have taken the couch."

Layla bit her bottom lip but didn't bother him further. "Uh-huh." She slid off his bed and walked to the door, only pausing once to motion with two fingers pointing at her eyes, then to his face. She would be watching him.

He grinned and picked up his phone and Felicity's things. He wanted to be ready the moment she turned her paper in. He thought about surprising her. Would that be weird? To show up at her place? No, it wasn't like he was some creep. He was just giving her bag back.

With a tenderness that shocked even himself, he folded her gown and then tucked it into her bag. A flash of bright red caught his attention deep in the bag. Using his finger, he extricated the item.

Red silk panties. Not a thong, just a normal pair, but the way the silk caught the light and slid smoothly against his skin… God, was the girl determined to drive him insane with lust?

"Damn it." Guilt nipped at his insides as he tucked the red silk underwear back into the bag. He checked his watch again. Half an hour to go before he could text her. Excitement jittered inside him, a strange feeling he hadn't felt in a long time. He couldn't wait to see his princess again, make her blush again, make her smile.

At a quarter till eleven, Felicity printed off the last page of her term paper from the library computer system and hastily stapled it and her resource list as well as her painting examples to the back. Then she slipped it into a clean, crisp black binder.

She was done. The relief of finishing such an intense research project was immense. She'd been working on this paper for two months, and now she could start on something new for next semester. Felicity left the library and headed toward the classroom building across the narrow sidewalk, tugging her coat up to keep out the cold wind. Her professor always preferred to collect term papers in person in his classroom rather than at his office. She had a sneaking suspicion he enjoyed heightening the tension by making everyone wait in line to hand it to him.

When she arrived at the classroom, a group of students were standing in a small circle showing their papers to each other and muttering as they examined each other's work. Felicity wasn't going to let herself get dragged into that potential drama and let them make her second-guess herself. So she stepped up to the front of the line, her binder ready.

Eyes locked on her as she walked up to Professor Willoughby to hand him her term paper. The middle-aged man leaned back in his chair, feet propped on one corner of the teacher's desk at the front of the classroom.

He was fine-boned, with a rather unremarkable face, except for the way his sudden grins seemed a touch sarcastic. His eyes were always assessing everything around him and reflected back on her with a cleverness that often matched his words. His lectures were actually fun. He cracked historical jokes with a straight face, and only she and a few others seemed to realize that not everything he said was true. Not everyone had figured Professor Willoughby out, but Felicity was pretty sure she had.

"You're sure it's ready?" he challenged, a little smile hovering about his mouth, making the faint laugh lines in his cheeks reveal themselves temporarily.

"Yes. I think I'm okay." She smiled. He was always trying to tease the students and keep them on their toes, but she felt confident of her research. As she left the class, she could almost hear her professor's silent laughter.

Halfway out of the classroom building, her cell phone vibrated. She paused, dug the phone out of her pocket, and checked it.

One new message.

Unknown number: *Hey, princess, you left your gown on my bed.*

Princess? It had to be Jared. How in the heck...? *Layla.* She growled. Her best friend had betrayed her. Wasn't that against the girl code? No giving of one's number without permission. Layla was in serious trouble, but she'd deal with her later.

What was she going to do now? Text him back? What could she say? God, she wished she'd done this whole "interact with the male species" before now. If Felicity wasn't so pissed at Layla, she would have texted her and gotten her advice, but that would be such a bad idea to let Layla anywhere near whatever this…thing was between her and Jared.

Her fingers hesitated above the screen. Why was he texting her, anyway? Layla could have easily gotten her dress back to her.

Unknown number: *Don't get shy on me now, princess. We did SLEEP together.*

She saved his number to her contacts and typed a reply.

Felicity: *Is this always going to come up between us?*

Jared: *You didn't just say that, did you? There are lots of things that can come up between us.*

Felicity: *I can't believe you just texted that!*

Jared: *HAHA. I can't believe your mind went there, princess.*

Laughter bubbled up from her, and she couldn't contain it, nor did she want to.

Felicity: *Is Layla still at your apartment?*

Jared: *Yeah…why?*

Felicity: *Tell her she's dead. I'm gonna kill her for giving you my number.*

Jared: *Haha. Will do. Did you get your paper turned in?*

She paused. Her heart skipped a few beats, then rushed to catch up. He wanted to know how her day was? A guy like him was taking time out of his day to ask her if she got her paper completed?

Felicity: *It was good, I think. My research and assertions were well thought out.*

Jared: *I'm sure you nailed it.*

The text made her smile, bite her lip, and then she smiled again. He thought she did great. Just thinking about that made her feel good. She didn't dwell on how pathetic it was that she responded so much to his praise.

Jared: *You're still a nerd, btw.*

The smile on her lips stretched even wider. She would

have been offended by anyone else calling her that. But after this morning she could only grin.

Jared: *What? No witty comeback?*

Felicity: *Give a girl time to come up with one.*

She tucked her phone in her jeans pocket and headed toward the street so she could hail a cab. It was too cold to make the long walk back to her place. Jared's money still filled her pocket. She hadn't used it, even though she'd been tempted. Boy, had she been tempted. At the curb, she stepped off a step and raised a hand. One of the many yellow cabs waiting for fares skidded into place in front of her. Climbing in, she settled her backpack on her lap and gave the driver her address.

Her phone buzzed again. Another message.

Jared: *You have lunch plans?*

She rolled her eyes and tapped her phone's keyboard.

Felicity: *Don't you have work or something, Mr. Big Shot Lawyer?*

Jared: *Mr. Big Shot Lawyer. That's your comeback? I gave you plenty of time to think of a good one.*

She snickered and then typed.

Felicity: *Seriously?*

Jared: *Seriously. I'm a lawyer. I'm dead serious. And you didn't answer my question.*

Felicity: *What question?*

Jared: *Do you have lunch plans?*

Why was he asking her that? Did he want her to come over and get her costume during lunch? Probably would be easier for her to do that so he could make it to his own important lawyer lunch or whatever it was lawyers did during lunch.

Jared: *Still waiting...*

Felicity: *No plans. Why?*

Jared: *Good.*

She waited for him to explain. No more texts came through. Disappointment slithered into her, bit by bit. The strange elation she'd experienced during their brief and very odd conversation deflated. It was the first real interaction she'd had with a guy her age—well, close to her age. Jared was a *little* older, but in a good kind of way.

The cab ride was fifteen minutes long, and yet Felicity was so lost in her thoughts that she only noticed they'd stopped when the cabbie tapped his fare machine and coughed loudly. She handed him her money, even though she was tempted to give him Jared's. They were even, though. And she didn't like taking handouts.

As she got out of the cab, she stared at the eyesore of an apartment complex in front of her. The red brick was chipped and crumbling, and the plaster in the halls was peeling. Inside she knew aromas of urine and booze would linger in the halls. The cracked sidewalk leading up to the building was a clear reflection of the tenants inside.

Home sweet home. After leaving Jared and Tanner's apartment, she felt like a mortal returning from a brief night on Mount Olympus. *Back to reality.* Her steps slowed when she reached the elevator. A "Broken" sign was taped to the orange-painted metal doors. Three months and the thing had yet to be fixed. She climbed the three flights of stairs to her floor. The overhead lights flickered, buzzing like enraged bees in a low hum.

A tall figure leaned against the wall next to her door at the end of the hall, his back to her. A pool of shadows formed by the lack of hall lights above him made it impossible to see him clearly.

Crap, that wasn't good. Last week the man who lived two doors down from her had gotten jumped by a guy who'd followed him into his apartment and knocked him out. The man had robbed her neighbor and left him bleeding from a nasty head wound for two hours before someone found him and called the police. Ever since then Felicity had been sleeping with one eye open and her cell phone at the ready.

Please, please don't be here to rob me...

CHAPTER FOUR

The figure at the end of the hall turned to face her, the flickering lights revealing half of his features as he moved toward her. Terror spiked through Felicity, and she swallowed down a wave of panic. Her feet and legs refused to move in sync, and she fell flat on her backside, backpack flying and cell phone smacking the hard carpet.

"Princess? What are you doing on the floor?"

Jared. Thank God, it was Jared. She sucked in a breath as her lungs expanded again. It was Jared.

"What are you doing here?" she growled as she scrambled to her feet and then went to pick up her phone and backpack.

"Lunch." He held up the flat box he'd been holding with one hand and her gym bag in his other hand. She hadn't noticed it in her terror.

"Gino's Pizza?" She licked her lips. Best pizza in the city. She'd only had it once. They didn't deliver to her place because it was too far away.

"You okay? I didn't mean to scare you."

"I'm fine. It's just that a neighbor got assaulted and robbed last week. Made me a little jumpy," she admitted softly. Mortification made a pit drop in her stomach. She was acting silly, thinking she'd been in danger.

"What?" Jared barked. "God, I don't like you staying in a place like this." He glanced around, a dark frown tugging his full lips down. "But we'll talk about that later. First you need to eat."

Jared moved back so she could unlock the door. Her eyes focused on his face. The rich brown of his eyes made her think of coffee with a touch of cream. She'd never been one for coffee, but after gazing into his eyes, she wanted to run to the nearest Starbucks and order a cup.

"Pizza's getting cold." He stepped closer, his height impressive and a little intimidating. It threw her off balance every time he got too close.

"Right. Pizza." She fished her keys out of her backpack and then unlocked the door. They both stepped inside, and when he moved close enough for her to feel his body heat, she shivered. Every part of her in that moment wanted to be back in his bed, his body curled around hers, warm and safe. This morning seemed like a lifetime ago, and she had to remind herself it wouldn't happen again, no matter how much she might wish it to.

Focusing on the present, she tried not to look at him. Jared Redmond, Mr. Big Shot Lawyer, was in her apartment. Why did that make her feel suddenly self-conscious?

"Stay there," she begged and hastily attempted a quick cleanup, throwing laundry in her basket, then gathering her textbooks into one corner. She wasn't messy, but she wasn't ready for guests, either. If only he'd had the decency to warn her he'd be coming over. Yet again, Felicity silently vowed revenge on her friend, since it seemed Layla's loose lips had effectively given away Felicity's address in addition to her phone number.

"Am I allowed to move now?" Jared asked, lips twitching.

"Yes. Sorry, my place is—" She tripped over the corner of her couch and toppled straight into him. His reflexes were so swift that she barely had time to squeak in surprise before she crashed into his chest. He'd dropped her gym bag and swung the pizza away just in time to keep her from crashing into it.

"Your place is fine." The softness in his tone melted her bones, and she relaxed against him, for only an instant. Then she shoved herself away, muttering an apology.

He headed toward the kitchen. When he was gone, she took her sketchbooks and slid them under her brown leather couch. She drew and painted, but the scenes were private. She didn't want Jared seeing her exposed through pencil and paper.

The sounds of cupboards opening and closing and plates being set on the counter drew her into the small kitchen. Jared had removed his long black coat and tossed it over the back of one of the two chairs placed on either side of her table. He popped open the lid of the pizza box, and the smell of the special Gino's sauce hit her nose. The low gurgle of her stomach made him laugh, the sound rich and deep.

"How many slices?" he asked.

"Two, please." Her face heated as she realized she still felt shy. Maybe he wouldn't notice.

Jared offered her a plate. He looked just as enticing as the pizza, maybe more so. In jeans that hugged his lean hips and the fitted black T-shirt that highlighted his muscular physique, he was a girl's dream.

"Here, kid." He chuckled and held her plate out farther. With a jolt she reached for it and darted around him to the table.

She eyed her plate with unrepressed joy. Pizza. God, she loved pizza. The slices were loaded with sausage. Her favorite.

"Hope the toppings are okay." Jared was filling his own plate. "I should have asked—sorry." Sliding into the seat next to her, he lifted a slice and took a bite. His eyes closed, and he moaned. "Damn, this is good."

His reaction had her stifling a giggle. "It is." She nibbled on her own slice, then finally asked what she'd been wanting to since she'd realized it was him leaning by her door.

"Jared, why are you here?"

Without pausing in his eating, he nodded his head toward her gym bag resting by the door. "Thought I'd return your clothes. Layla and Tanner are enjoying their afternoon. It's a little...distracting."

"Distracting?"

"Yeah, you know." He grinned and nodded toward her bedroom.

"Oh!" *Sex.* He meant sex. If her face hadn't been red before, it had to be fire-truck red now.

A rumbling laugh escaped him. "I definitely didn't want to spend my day off in the next room. Some things you just can't unhear, you know?"

Felicity snickered, then covered her mouth in embarrassment. Jared reached over and pulled her hand down. "Don't. I like your laugh."

"So a day off, huh? What on earth are you going to do?" she asked, surprised and delighted that she could actually tease him.

"I thought I might bring pizza to a girl I know." As he spoke, he smiled, but it was a strangely boyish, almost bashful smile that knocked her right behind the knees. Her face heated as she realized the power this man had over her. He could turn her to jelly with just a curve of his lips.

"It's only noon. What are you going to do the rest of the

day?" She reached for a napkin at the same time he did, and their fingers touched. Heat blossomed in the wake of that simple connection, and their gazes locked. For a second his eyes darkened to a rich chocolate, and she shivered. Was that desire she saw? Or was it wishful thinking taking over?

"Don't know. What are you going to do? No more papers I hope."

She shook her head. "No, luckily it was just the one. I can enjoy my weekend now. I might go see the John Singer Sargent exhibit at the Art Institute." The words were out of her mouth before she could take them back. She hadn't meant to share that with him, but something about him made her open up. It was dangerous.

Jared shifted in his seat, his knees bumping into hers under the small rickety table, and the plates rattled. This weekend she really should fix the table legs. He was too big, his frame too tall and his legs too long, to fit at her tiny card table currently serving as a dining table.

"I haven't been to see anything there in a while. Sounds fun. Want to go after we're done with lunch?" He pressed his palms on the table, seeming to notice the way it tilted at his touch. A distracted look captured his face as he made the table rock back and forth, clearly displaying the uneven legs.

"Wait...you're coming with me?" Surely he wasn't serious?

Shoving his chair back, he got down on his hands and knees, disappearing from her view as he studied the table legs.

"Hey....um...Jared. You don't have to come."

"I want to," his muffled reply came from beneath the table.

This conversation required a face-to-face interaction, she decided, and therefore, she had to resort to getting down on the floor with him. He had one table leg slightly lifted as he shoved a folded business card under the stubby leg.

"Jared." When she said his name, he finally looked up. Their faces were so close, and for a second she had the wild urge to close the distance and kiss him. The absurdity of the thought had her balking, and she reared back.

Crack!

Pain exploded through her skull, and she crumpled, clutching her head. "Ow!"

"Easy there, princess. Sounds like that hurt." Gentle hands clasped her face, his thumbs slightly rough as they stroked her cheeks.

"Yikes," she moaned. "That *really* hurt." She finally opened her eyes to meet his gaze.

"Deep breaths," he encouraged.

Dark hair fell across his forehead. She was enchanted by its silky appearance and wanted to touch it more than anything in that moment. If her head hadn't been pounding, she might have succumbed to the temptation and stroked his hair out of his eyes.

Can't. He's not yours. She scolded herself for the foolish thought. A guy like Jared was probably into tall, leggy blondes who were armed with fancy school degrees and trust funds. He definitely didn't date grad student artists.

"Let's get you out from under here and settled on the couch." He moved so she could get out from under the table and then escorted her over to the worn leather sofa.

She dropped back onto the cushions and shut her eyes, trying to dispel the throbbing ache on the top of her head. The sounds of ice cubes cracking and the rustle of paper towels drew her attention. When she opened her eyes, Jared was standing in front of her. Without a word, he sat down on the couch next to her and placed a plastic bag of ice wrapped in a paper towel on her head over the tender spot.

"Hmmm." She winced, and he grimaced at her reaction. "This is so humiliating." Her eyes darted away from his. The last thing she wanted to see was pity in his gaze.

"You seem to be having a bit of a rough day." He kept one hand on her head, holding the ice there while his other hand patted her knee. A soft pat, then his hand remained there, his fingers stroking her thigh soothingly.

Shivers of arousal and heat licked their way up her leg to her center, making the blood pound a little harder in her head.

"I'm not a klutz or anything," she grumbled, shying away, but he didn't allow her to retreat.

"I'll believe that when you've gone a whole day without injury."

"So says the lawyer," she laughed.

"No laughing." His tone was almost stern, but she didn't miss the flash of humor in his eyes. "It makes it worse." And that only had her giggling, then wincing all over again.

"Is bossiness a family trait or a professional trait?" she asked him, lips kicking into a grin as she relished the way he laughed.

"Keep teasing me and you'll find out." His husky words were a sensual threat that sent her mind and body spinning in dizzying circles.

They were so close again, his hand still on her thigh, but she didn't feel the cold wetness anymore. The ice bag lay forgotten on the floor.

So close.

If she just leaned in one more inch, their lips might…

His warm breath fanned her face, and little shivers trekked up and down her body.

Jared's eyes consumed her, a burning flame that rippled along her skin in heated tendrils. His gaze dropped to her lips. And a second later, he was gone, striding away to the kitchen. He rummaged in the cupboards again. This time when he came back, it was with a glass of water and two aspirin.

"Here."

She took the pills, popped them into her mouth, and then put the glass to her lips. Taking a big gulp, she watched him over the rim of the glass. Her focus was intense, and she felt cornered between him and the couch.

Licking her lips, she ignored the little rush of nervousness as she gave him back the glass. His fingers curled around the glass, brushing hers. He walked into her kitchen and set the glass in her sink and then turned around to look at her, leaning back on the counter, elbows propped on the edge.

"So, you still up for Sargent?" he asked.

Felicity picked up the bag of ice from the floor and stood. "Yeah, I think so. Looking at art will make my headache go away."

One of his brows lifted, doubt shadowing his lips in a faint frown.

"I promise. I'm *fine*."

He pushed away from the counter and walked over to her. "Okay, princess. Art it is." He took the ice bag from her and then tossed it in the sink.

"Thanks for everything." She meant it. The man had taken care of her. She'd always taken care of herself and sometimes, to a small extent, her parents. They'd all had to work hard, and she knew she couldn't ask her parents to support her when they had it rough.

"You seem surprised." Jared's deep baritone was smooth.

She *loved* his voice. If she closed her eyes, it would pour over her like rich red wine. Sink into her skin, seduce her heart, her mind, her body. Like honey and silk, almost hypnotic. She'd be tempted to do anything he asked with that voice.

"I'm used to taking care of myself. It's just nice, what you did, I mean."

He took two long strides to the couch and sat beside her, caging her against the other side. Cupping her cheeks in his hands, he just stared down at her, eyes as dark as cocoa and heavy with concern.

"No one takes care of you?" The words were a low growl, and anger sparked like summer lightning in his eyes.

She managed a quick shake of her head, relieved he wasn't angry at her.

For a long second, neither of them moved or spoke. He just held her face in his hands and gazed at her. Time seemed to slide away in a silken stream, untouchable, unstoppable, save for his hands on her skin, his eyes holding hers. She'd never wanted anyone to touch her, not like this. Dating and men hadn't been part of the plan. But Jared... Like a spring rain washing away the dust from winter, she felt free, blessedly free to just be herself.

He broke the spell at last and moved away from her. He bent over the couch and retrieved his coat and slid it on, then held hers out. She stood, legs trembling slightly, as she let him help her into her coat. Such a gentleman. It shouldn't have surprised her. A smile played upon her lips as her heart gave a funny flip in her chest.

After they were both decked out in scarves and gloves, they left the apartment and caught a cab. When the driver pulled up in front of the Art Institute, Felicity handed Jared the cab money from this morning. He quirked a brow again, lips twitching as he shook his head at her in silent reproach and then paid the fare. She slid out of the seat, and he followed, his body bumping into hers from behind when she didn't move fast enough. His hands settled on her shoulders with a slight amount of pressure as he caught his balance.

"Sorry," he murmured in her ear, and then released her.

She couldn't move right away. Her feet were rooted to the ground. Something about him behind her, whispering in her ear…a quiver of longing and hunger rippled through her. With a little shake she started up the steps after him, dodging the flocks of tourists who posed for pictures. Two bronze lions stood as stalwart guardians of the masterpieces inside. She'd always liked the lions. Something about their noble yet ferocious appearance made her feel safe. Protectors of art, of artists. Like her.

She and Jared were halfway up the stairs when Jared's gloved hand reached for hers. She paused for a second, shocked and delighted, before she hastily masked her joy. He acted casual, as though he hadn't just reached for her hand.

Why? She wanted to know why he was doing this, holding her hand, spending time with her, but she was also terrified of what his answer might be. Pity? He'd seen her tiny apartment, the neighborhood she lived in. God, she hoped it wasn't pity, but why else would he be taking care of her?

He paid for their tickets, only shaking his head when she attempted to pay for herself. It was a silent but physical way to show a mixture of displeasure and amusement at her paying her own way.

Her lips parted on a protest, but he only snorted. "No, princess. Don't even start. You've already wounded my male pride." Flattening a palm on his chest over his heart, he closed his eyes for a second as though he'd been stabbed.

The main galleries were familiar to Felicity as they studied the map of the institute. Each painting hanging on the white walls was like an old friend. She came as often as she could, whenever she felt like she had to escape. The worlds painted on the canvases were a comfort, a promise, like the sounds of birds chattering in the wake of a storm. Seeing the paintings was her birdsong. The reassurance that life could survive even when times were tough.

"Do you want to go straight to Sargent?" Jared asked. His voice pulled her back to him, and like a dewdrop on a finely-spun web, she trickled back to him like he was gravity itself.

"Yes, let's do it first." She let him lead her in the direction of the tall banners of a distant gallery that showed the familiar figure of one of Sargent's portraits. There were skylights above that afforded the galleries a wash of gold that softened into warm yellows as it slid down the white walls.

The exhibit was a collection of his more famous portraits of women in high society. He'd created over nine hundred oil paintings, but this particular exhibit had about sixty. Excitement had her tugging Jared's hand as she collected an exhibit booklet for each of them and approached the first piece. A lady in a white gown, half-turned as though someone had called her name. The part of the painting that caught everyone's attention was the long black satin sash that trailed down her back. It cut through the white gown and drew attention to the woman's willowy figure.

"She's beautiful." Jared's voice was slightly soft and low as though speaking in a church. Reverent.

"She is. Sargent had the ability to make any woman beautiful, mysterious. He paints a story, even though it's supposed to be a simple portrait. See how it looks like she's turning around?" Felicity gestured to the lady's movement, then looked at Jared.

His analytical eyes moved over the canvas, taking in every detail. "I'd say it looks like she's twirling, almost preparing to dance, the way her hand holds the train of her gown. She might not lift it up if she was merely turning." He glanced at her and grinned.

She focused on the painting again and then realized he could be right. How had she missed it?

"What of the next one?" Jared's long legs ate up the floor as he led her to the next painting.

The portrait of Lady Helen Vincent. A lovely young

woman in a black silk dress was posed before a balcony. Crimson curtains fell behind her, setting off the alabaster of her skin. The gown hung low, well below her breasts, which were cupped by a filmy white chemise.

"Rather risqué," Jared noted. "Her dress is hanging really low." He waggled eyebrows at Felicity, and she stifled a giggle. Why on earth was he making her act like a silly girl? She *was not* a giggler.

All too soon, though, she forgot self-consciousness and lost herself in seeing the way the long strand of pearls hung on the painted lady's fingertips and over the dark gown. What had it been like for Sargent to gaze upon such beauty and try to capture it on a canvas? How incredible that must have been, to hear the whisper of silks, the soft click-click of pearls colliding as slender white fingers played with them in muted firelight.

"He was incredibly talented. I think I like his style more than that modern art people always rave over," Jared said as they proceeded down the line to the next work. Their hands were still linked. Like a lifeline, she clung to him and the feeling of safety that his touch gave her.

Why did she have to meet him? Why now when she couldn't afford to fall head over heels for someone? It would be so easy. He made it easy. *Damn him.*

Afternoon sunlight sparked and smoldered in the gold flecks that splintered through his eyes. Eyes that saw too much, saw right through her.

She swallowed hard and avoided his gaze.

I don't want to fall in love. I can't.

CHAPTER FIVE

Art was stimulating. Who knew? Jared hid a smile as he approached the next portrait. Watching Felicity take in the exhibit was fascinating. He had never really given art much thought before. Now he was appreciating each painting and Felicity's reactions. She was almost quivering with excitement, her eyes bright and her lips slightly parted. Like a woman on the verge of climax.

He swallowed a groan as his body responded to the mental image his thoughts created. Jared shook his head, trying to get rid of all thoughts of Felicity in bed beneath him.

This is just a day off with a nice girl. Nothing more.

It couldn't be anything more. He had no time for dating. Come Monday it was back to real life, back to his office and the mountain of work he always had. His father's voice, a cool reminder of his failures, echoed inside his head. *"Don't work so much that one day you wake up and can't recognize yourself in the mirror."*

But his father had already earned his way in the world.

Jared had only just begun to earn his. He couldn't stop now if he was going to get anywhere, even if that meant long hours and killer workloads.

"What's with the frown, Mr. Big Shot Lawyer?" Felicity's rich, husky voice was a punch to the stomach, and his body jolted awake.

His companion was studying him as seriously as she did her paintings. Was he frowning?

"Sorry. I was just thinking I've missed out on a lot of art. I didn't ever think I'd enjoy it as much as I am." A rueful smile curved his lips as she drew closer to him.

"You haven't seen much art? But aren't you..." She seemed to swallow whatever she'd planned to say, and two pink dots blossomed on her cheeks.

"Aren't I what?" He nudged her arm gently with one elbow to encourage her.

"Well, you're...well off. I thought everyone with money had a lot of exposure to art. I know it doesn't mean they have good taste, but they at least have been exposed to it, right?" She glanced up at him, as though expecting him to confirm her theory.

"Huh, so rich people and art are supposed to go together? Well, I can tell you it's not true. My family is wealthy, but we aren't much for art. Omaha doesn't have much in the way of good museums or exhibits, not like Chicago or New York, anyway. Our summer home in Colorado and our winter home in the Bahamas aren't near galleries or museums, either. My mom likes it well enough, but you say art to my father and he runs the other way. And Tanner, well, his idea of art is body art. I know Layla has spent the last two years talking him out of tattoos." He chuckled. "No, we definitely aren't an artistic or even art-appreciative family, and I'm just now realizing what we're missing out on." He nodded at the paintings.

"Wait a sec," Felicity said with a gasp. "You have summer *and* winter homes?"

When he looked her way again, he noticed her cute little gray eyes were as wide as saucers and she'd paled.

"Yeah. We own a house in Steamboat Springs and a little place on the coast in the Bahamas."

Felicity took a step back, her lips parting as she breathed a little heavier.

"Hey, are you okay?" He curled an arm around her and cupped her chin, lifting her face up so he could see her eyes more clearly. "What did I say?" It was obvious that whatever had upset his princess had come out of his own damn mouth.

She tried to escape his gaze, but he wouldn't let her. With a resigned little sigh, she finally raised her eyes to his. "We're so different, Jared. This whole thing is...I just feel like we're doing something crazy because we have nothing in common. I've never left Nebraska except to come to college here in Illinois. I worked all through high school just to afford my piece-of-junk clunker car, and you've got two vacation homes?"

The way she spoke, the words coming out a ragged whisper as though she was torn between mortification and shame, broke his heart.

"There is nothing wrong with the fact that you worked hard to get where you are. Hell, it's a turn-on for me, sweetheart." He chuckled and tucked a lock of her hair behind her ear. "I *love* that you earned everything in your life. I didn't earn my parents' vacation homes. So trust me when I say I admire how hard you worked to get here."

"Really?" She sounded so hopeful that it stung him to think she'd been worried he'd judge her for her lack of money.

"Absolutely. I think you're fucking amazing," he whispered before he bent to press a tender kiss to her lips. She shivered and leaned into him.

It would be so easy to get lost in kissing her, but a cough from a security guard made Jared pull back reluctantly. He looked over Felicity's head to see the guard looking the other way, but clearly the man was hiding a smile.

"Come on, let's look at some more paintings before we get too carried away. The last thing I need is to get thrown out of a museum." When he saw her smiling again, he tugged her along to the next painting. "What's the story behind this?" He gestured with a nod to the painting in front of them. The plaque read "Portrait of Madame X." Felicity's entire face lit up like a child on Christmas morning scampering down the stairs and catching that first glimpse of a mound of presents beneath a tree bathed in winter morning light.

"This one"—she gestured at Madame X—"is scandalous. The subject is an American expatriate who was married to a French banker. She was known for her beauty and her infidelities in Parisian society."

Impressed, Jared studied the painting. A woman stood facing the painter, but her face was turned, offering only the profile. She wore a wisp of a black gown that clung to her hourglass figure, held up only by two gold straps that glittered from her shoulders. Most of her chest, arms, and neck were exposed, yet the dress was understated and elegant.

"What was scandalous? The painting, or the subject?" He crossed his arms, examining the woman from head to toe critically.

"Well," Felicity said, her voice growing breathless as she leaned closer to him to whisper, "in the original version, her gown straps were falling off her shoulders. The subject's mother was horrified when Sargent presented it at the Paris Salon in 1884. Sargent refused to withdraw the work from the exhibition, but he did paint the straps to look more secure, and he also renamed the painting to call her Madame X to return some anonymity to her."

Jared chuckled. "Sounds like the damage was already done."

"True," Felicity agreed.

They moved from painting to painting after that, a delightful and incredibly insightful discussion accompanying each one. It amazed him how much she knew about art. She had a firm grasp on the subject she was passionate about.

When he wasn't overworked he felt the same about real estate transactions. It was fascinating to take a piece of land and transition it through a sale to a new owner. It was akin to taking a watch or an old radio apart and seeing the gears and cogs at work. He'd done that so often as a child that his mother had often wondered aloud if he'd be an engineer. Jared liked to know how a thing worked, no matter what that thing was. Understanding something and how it operated was crucial, whether it was a company, a machine, or a person. In his job, he saw the insides of the companies of the buyers and sellers as he drafted purchase and sale agreements.

Felicity came to a stop, and he instantly halted too. There were no more paintings to view. His head dropped a little as disappointment weighed him down.

"We're done?" He glanced about, noticing they had come full circle, back to the entrance of the gallery.

A little wistful smile twisted Felicity's lips. "You've paid your dues, Mr. Lawyer." She nudged him in the ribs with her elbow.

Surprise fluttered through him. "We don't have to leave. There are other galleries." He wanted to stay here with her and bask in the afternoon sun, taking in the worlds created on the canvases.

She pulled her coat sleeve back on her left hand and peeked at her watch. "It's been three hours. It's nearly dinnertime."

He jumped at the opportunity. "Dinner it is, then. What are you in the mood for?"

Her lips parted, and her gray eyes widened. "Dinner?" she mouthed as though she didn't quite believe he'd said it. It had been four hours since they'd had lunch.

"Yeah. You're not ditching me yet, princess." He leaned toward her, intending to cage her against the gallery wall, but an institute employee lingered nearby—watching them closely as though worried Jared might pin the girl against a priceless painting—and made a motion with his hand for Jared and Felicity to get away from the wall.

"Come on, princess, looks like we're wearing out our welcome."

Felicity's breath quickened as a little rosy flush stole across her creamy skin. She narrowed her eyes and shoved him back a step. "You have to stop calling me that." A flash of humor streaked across her eyes before she tried to bury it. She liked it when he teased her.

He reacted before thinking and slid his arms around her waist, tugging her close to him. "I like making you flustered," he whispered.

Her lips parted, and the tip of her pink tongue peeped out as she licked her lips. Her long dark-brown lashes fluttered like the wings of a startled butterfly. Jared would have given anything in that moment to lean down and kiss her, but something held him back, kept his body from acting on its desires. He blew out a slow, barely controlled breath and then let go of her. Wounded shadows hung in her eyes, and he knew, just knew, she'd wanted him to keep holding her. Hurting her, even by putting a necessary distance between them, was like having an arrow plunged into his chest.

"We should go and find a place to eat before it gets too

crowded." He took her hand in his. The need to keep attached to her had become an almost vital one now.

The brisk November winds bit into his skin as they hurried down the front steps of the Art Institute toward the row of waiting taxis. Jared flagged one down, and it pulled up to the curb.

"After you." He guided Felicity into the cab and climbed in after her. He had the perfect place in mind for dinner.

"The Italian Village restaurant, please," he instructed the cabdriver.

He grinned at Felicity's mixture of delight and frustration.

"You don't have to have dinner with me," she insisted.

"If you think I'm going back to my place where my brother and his girlfriend are playing house, think again."

She wrinkled her nose and laughed. "Are they really that bad?"

"Honestly? I don't know. I sure as hell don't want to find out." It wasn't exactly the truth. He really doubted Layla and Tanner were that bad, but it was an excellent excuse to spend the day with Felicity. He didn't want to think about why being with her mattered so much, but it did.

The man was a walking temptation.

Italian? She loved Italian. If she didn't know better, she would have sworn he was reading her mind. Their gloved hands were still touching, and that single contact grounded her when she was on the verge of floating away. Everything inside of her was excitement and light, like waking on a Saturday in early May. Sunlight pouring over her, heating the bed, birds whistling soft songs to their mates. She had something in the world to look forward to that wasn't class or work. Jared was offering her life and a chance to live it. She'd missed out on so much the last six years, and now that she had him, even if it was temporary, she wanted to make the most of it.

Today at the gallery, she had exposed herself, her passion, and he hadn't shunned her, hadn't mocked her. Not like some of the guys who'd been in her art history classes. They'd assumed it would be an easy class to pass and had attempted to get to know her so they'd get to copy her assignments. Jared was so different from those guys. In every comment, he'd challenged her, but in a way that made her think and analyze paintings from a different angle. It had been fun, but so had been just being around him. Jared had made her wish she had the time to have a relationship with a man. Who knew a man could be around her and show her all the things in life she might miss?

The taxi jerked to a halt half a block from the restaurant, and the early evening was broken by the sounds of honking and the bright flashes of blue-and-red lights.

"What's going on?" she asked.

The driver glanced back at them. "Looks like a fender bender. I'll be stuck here for a while." He nodded at the meter at the front of his car.

"Right," Jared muttered and reached for his billfold, slipping the driver a few bills to cover the fare. "We can walk the rest of the way."

Unfortunately, they had to walk in the direction of the police. People were thick on the sidewalk, watching whatever was happening ahead of them. Cameras flashed and the crowd parted as the policemen hauled a man in cuffs toward a police car. He was shouting rudely at the driver of the car he'd hit. Felicity flinched. Things like this didn't happen at home. The worst that she'd seen was the mailman blow through a stop sign and get a lecture from one of the four cops who made up her hometown's local police department.

Jared wrapped one arm around Felicity and tucked her into his side, the gesture protective. It felt too good, and she hated that she wanted him to keep holding her.

"Why don't we get food to go and head back to my place? It's a great night for watching a movie."

They entered the Italian Village, and Felicity hesitated at the crush of people just inside the door. Tourists flooded the stairway, but Jared kept walking up the stairs, ignoring the line. At the reception desk he smiled at the girl holding the menus and taking names.

"Maria, tell Angelo that Jared Redmond wants double his usual order to go."

Maria, a curvy caramel-skinned girl, winked and trotted off toward the kitchen.

"Angelo?" Felicity asked.

"A buddy of mine. We both went to University of Nebraska. He got into the Culinary Institute of America before moving here, and I went off to Creighton for law. We kept in touch."

"Redmond! *Tu cane! Non hai detto che saresti dovuto venire da stasera!*" A booming masculine voice reverberated around them as a handsome man, definitely Italian, strode toward them from a swinging door that led back to the kitchen. Dressed in a white double-breasted jacket and black pants, the man, Angelo, removed his white toque hat and tucked it under one arm. The man was gorgeous, like a Roman god, but he didn't make her stomach flutter like Jared did. Angelo did, however, make her instantly smile when he grinned at her and Jared.

"*Spiacente, Angelo, non avevo programmato su. Ma è stato un giorno speciale e volevo portare un amico qui,*" Jared replied, grinning wickedly.

Angelo turned to Felicity. "Jared usually calls ahead, but he said it was a special day, and when I see you, I completely agree, *bella*."

Felicity stared at Jared. "You speak Italian?"

He lifted up one hand and pinched his thumb and forefinger. "*Un po.* A little."

Angelo snickered. "You speak a fair amount." Angelo nudged him laughed and slapped Jared's back in a one-armed hug.

"Special night," he replied, his head angled toward Felicity.

Angelo swung his gaze over her, appraising, then appreciative.

"Ah, *bella*," he purred in Italian and captured her hand in his, kissing it.

"This is Felicity, a good friend."

Was that it? She wasn't sure if that was a compliment or not. She'd only known the man for one day, yet she wanted to mean more to him than that.

"A good friend?" Angelo's dark brows rose, and his lips twitched. "You bring her here for dinner. That's a smart thing. I can put the sous chef in charge while I grab a bottle of your favorite Chianti. The private room in the back is open." Angelo winked.

Jared shook his head, but he smiled. "Thanks, normally I'd love to, but I think Felicity and I are going to dine in at my place. *Just the two of us.*"

"Ah well, that's good too." Angelo smirked knowingly and pointed to a bench in the corner. "Wait there and I'll get you what you need and a little extra." Then he bent and captured Felicity's hand to press a kiss to the backs of her knuckles.

"Thanks, man." Jared shook Angelo's hand, and then he

led Felicity over to the bench Angelo had indicated.

She glanced about, taking in the restaurant and marveling at the interior design. Every wall was painted with evening scenes of distant villas. The dim lighting made her feel as though she stood on a hill in Tuscany and could spin in a circle, viewing rolling hills. Tall trees pointed like green needles toward the full moon. Small pinpricks of electric lights winked in the cobalt-blue painted sky like stars. She was moved by the beauty of it, a simple artistic creation that had the effect of sending her across the ocean to a place she'd never been, a place she'd likely never go, no matter how she might wish to.

"What are you thinking about?" Jared's lips brushed her right ear as he whispered to her.

She could hear him, despite the low rumble of the crowd of waiting guests. A little tingle, like the touch of butterfly wings on her skin, shot down her spine, and she turned to see his face. Their noses touched, but she didn't move back.

"I was thinking how much this place feels like Italy. I've never been, but I know this is how it feels." She would have felt foolish confessing something like that to anyone else, but not with Jared.

"I've been, and it is just like this. Maybe someday I could take you there."

Italy. *With Jared.* Why did everything he said have to be so wonderful? So irresistible? He had to be a dream. No man like this was real.

"Don't," she begged, blinking away the burn of tears.

"Don't what?" he asked, still smiling.

"You're too nice. Stop being perfect." He could never know what she really was thinking. That he was temptation enough to make her want to consider leaving her dreams of working at the Los Angeles County Art Museum behind to stay here with him.

His lips kicked up in a crooked grin. "Too bad." His gaze dropped to her lips, and her heart skittered to a stop.

He's going to kiss me. He's going to...kiss me. Her lashes fluttered shut, but he didn't kiss her, not on the lips. She nearly moaned in frustration but stopped herself. The soft pressure of his mouth settled on her cheek. A brief kiss. Her eyes opened and she stared up at him, a little sigh of disappointment escaping her.

"Your food is ready." Maria carried over a large bag and then handed it to Jared.

"Thanks." He started to reach for his wallet, but she shook her head and held up a hand to stop him.

"Angelo said it's on the house." She shooed them toward the stairs, giggling.

Felicity didn't resist the bubble of laughter that came out as she turned to Jared. "Your friends are awesome."

Jared curled an arm around her waist. "I agree."

The cab ride back to Jared's apartment was quick. He talked about Angelo and how they used to get in trouble on campus. Neither of them had rushed in a fraternity and had instead formed their own fraternity of sorts.

"Besides me and Angelo, there's Thad. He's here in Chicago too, works as a partner in his dad's real estate company. They buy and sell lots of property all the time."

"Thad?" she queried, wondering what this other friend was like and if he was just as different from Jared as Angelo was, and yet somehow alike.

"Thad Worthington. Rich-as-hell real estate tycoon along with his father. Smart, too."

The respect Jared had for this mysterious Thad was obvious.

"So you, Angelo, and Thad?" She smiled, thinking of Layla, hoping that she would be close to Layla in the coming years after they'd graduated.

"Yeah. I'm lucky. Good guys, both of them." He ducked his head, looking slightly away from her as though the admission was something to be ashamed of. But this was one of the many things she was learning about him that made her adore him all the more. His loyalty, his friendship, his respect for his relationships on all levels.

Curling her fingers around his arm, she leaned into him a little. "I think it's wonderful that you're still so close to them." She hoped he would understand the tone underlying her words. Don't be ashamed of friendship.

"Yeah. I suppose it is." He raked a hand through his dark hair, and it fell into his eyes almost immediately. When he looked her way, his eyes were lit with a fire and life, his cool lawyer exterior melting away. Everything around her seemed to shrink into that one moment, with just the two of them. Something had changed between them yet again, like two stars in the same galaxy spinning closer and closer together.

"Today was nice," he said.

"It was." She had to agree. How long had it been since she'd allowed herself to enjoy something? She couldn't remember. And she didn't want it to end. She could see by the way he shifted that he didn't want it to end after dinner, either.

"I can't believe I didn't worry about work once today. You don't know how rare that is."

His words filled her with a fuzzy warmth. He'd been able to relax and escape his worries because he'd spent a day with her. A little bit of her puffed up with pride at the thought. She didn't dare let herself think about the other women who might help him forget his worries. She had this moment, right now. It was all she could afford.

CHAPTER SIX

As they reached Jared's luxurious apartment building, he took the bag of food from her and they headed inside. It never failed to amaze her how beautiful the building was. It was one of those old hotels whose exterior was art deco, but inside everything was sleek and modern with leather couches, subtle décor, and glittering chandeliers.

"Do you suppose Layla and your brother are still…" She didn't finish.

"Probably. If he's anything like me, he can go for hours."

She sucked in a breath and stumbled. With a low laugh, he wrapped an arm around her, catching her before she face-planted on the nice marble floor of the lobby. What was it about this man that made her lose all control of her body? She was *not* a klutz. Luckily it was dark enough outside that he wouldn't see the blush burning a path across her face.

Can go for hours. Her mouth dried up, and her tongue scraped like sandpaper as she licked her lips. As a virgin, she should have been terrified at the idea of hours in bed with a virile man like Jared, but…she wasn't. It had the opposite effect. Her legs turned to jelly, and a strange quiver started up in her abdomen. *Desire. Jared.* That word and his name seemed forever linked.

"I should stop teasing you." He laughed softly, the rich sound warming her from her head to her toes. "But it's just too much fun."

She didn't dare reply to that. Her mind was still caught on the idea of being in his bed again and seeing just how long he could go. She hadn't let herself think about the sort of man she'd lose her virginity with. But now she couldn't stop thinking about *it*…or Jared.

When they opened the apartment door, she glimpsed Layla and Tanner, fully clothed and squabbling like children in the kitchen. What a relief! She'd been a little afraid that she and Jared would stumble upon the two lovebirds in a less-than-flattering situation.

"We had pizza last night." Layla stood arms akimbo, attempting to corner Tanner against the wall by the pantry. "We're not eating it again tonight."

Tanner was a foot taller than Layla, and his lean muscled body towered over hers, a resolute expression on his features as he stood his ground.

"I'm not cooking tonight, babe. You wore me out. Whatever we eat is gonna be takeout or something."

"I wore you out?" Layla's voice was a little shrill, but Felicity swore she detected a barely restrained giggle hidden beneath the tension.

Tanner wrapped his arms around his girlfriend's body and pulled her to him. "Babe, you sure did, and I meant that as a compliment." Tanner smiled, a smile that was an echo of Jared's. Her heart tightened like invisible strings were lightly squeezing it.

"I smell food…" Her back to Felicity and Jared, Layla

sniffed the air.

Over the top of her head, Tanner looked at them, noticing their arrival and the bag of food from the Italian Village.

"I don't smell anything," he lied and then kissed the tip of her nose and grinned in a comically evil fashion.

"Yes, you do, you liar. Smells like—" Layla spun around and gasped. "Felicity!" Squealing like she hadn't seen Felicity in years, she ran over to her, hugging her.

Braced for the contact, Felicity accepted the hug and returned it. Jared dodged around them, food in his arms as he headed for the kitchen.

"So…" Layla bit her lip for a second. "I know you want to kill me right now. But I bet you had fun today, didn't you?" She pulled back from the hug but left her hands on Felicity's shoulders as she studied her.

Feeling a bit impish, Felicity cocked one brow. "I am going to kill you. He showed up on my doorstep, Layla. On. My. Doorstep. Like a lost puppy."

Her friend scoffed. "I doubt that. No guy that hot has to play the lost puppy card. So tell me everything that happened, and I mean *everything*." Layla tugged Felicity over to the huge L-shaped couch facing the sixty-five-inch flat-screen.

Jared and Tanner were in the kitchen, talking softly as they set out plates and food.

"Well…he brought me pizza."

With a low groan, Layla rolled her eyes. "Those Redmond boys have an obsession with pizza. Seriously, you have no idea how long we argued today over *not* having pizza for dinner."

"I believe it."

Felicity shot a glance at Tanner. He mouthed, "Hey, Felicity," and winked at her.

God, he was such a nice guy. Really. Never in the three

months that she'd known him and Layla had he ever made her feel like the odd one out whenever she hung around them.

"Okay, so pizza, then what? Hot sex? I know there was hot sex."

"What? No!" Felicity hissed.

Layla bit her lip for a moment, looking pensive. "No hot sex?" She huffed out a breath. "Huh…when he left today, he had that look Tanner gets when he's going to take me to bed and bang me hard enough to see stars."

A flash of heat exploded through Felicity at the thought of Jared on top of her, his hands gripping the headboard as he…

Whoa…for a second she couldn't breathe. "No. Definitely nothing like that. We went to see the Sargent exhibit at the Art Institute."

Layla sighed heavily as though the weight of an entire world had settled on her shoulders. "I would have sworn he was into you. Still…" Her eyes flicked to Jared and Tanner. "Maybe he's playing it slow."

"He's just being nice." Felicity tucked her legs up and wrapped her arms around her knees and sighed.

"Dinner's ready, princess," Jared called out.

Layla's face lit up like it was Christmas. "*Princess?*" She whispered the word at Felicity and looked like she was about three seconds away from squealing.

"Don't even go there," Felicity warned.

"Layla, get over here and eat." Tanner sniggered. "Quit making trouble."

Felicity mouthed back "Thank you!" to him, and he merely nodded as if he'd only done his duty.

The four of them dug into the rich Italian food.

"So, Felicity," Tanner said and reached for his wine, "Jared said you went to the Art Institute. I can't believe you got my brother into an art museum." He elbowed Jared and shot a wicked grin his way.

"I enjoy the finer things, like art." Jared glowered at his younger brother, completely unamused at Tanner's teasing.

"It was a great exhibit. A lot of pieces were on loan from other museums and private collections." She knew that this didn't mean anything to the others, but it meant a lot to her. Museums held paintings and other forms of art and artifacts as assets. Private collectors hoarded their own pieces like dragons their gold, and rightly so. If high-end thieves ever got wind of their locations, they'd steal them. For the institute to have so many Sargent works together in one place was the equivalent of finding the Holy Grail for an art student.

Layla sipped her wine, and then with a smile at Felicity, she focused on Jared. "Did you know that Felicity wants to be a curator of a museum someday?"

Felicity aimed a kick at Layla from under the table, but Layla was prepared. After years of living with siblings, she'd learned the art of dodging under-the-table kick moves.

Jared leaned back in his chair, hands resting on his thighs. "I didn't know that." He paused, then spoke more softly, as though she and Jared were the only ones in the room. "I think you would make a great curator. You have the passion and the knowledge required." His eyes were almost a honey brown, warm and melting.

God, she loved it when he looked at her like that, as though she could do anything, be anything, all because he believed in her. She'd only known him a day, but he'd glanced at her so often that she felt like he'd been looking at her like that forever.

"Thank you." Her reply came out a little husky, and she drank a few gulps of wine to moisten her dry throat.

"So, Layla, what did you and Tanner do all day?"

Bold, brash Layla only showed her teeth liked a cornered

fox. "What *didn't* we do might be the better question."

At her reply, Tanner choked, dropping his pasta with a splat as he desperately chugged wine like it was water. As he continued to cough, Layla whacked him on the back.

"Don't forget to chew, *big boy*." She snickered.

"Christ, Layla." Tanner laughed. "Give me some warning before you go announcing our private business."

She rounded on him. "If you think this is business, honey, we must not be doing it right."

Jared shoved back from the table as he burst out laughing. "Okay, you two, enough. Go back to your bedroom before you drive me crazy."

His brother, grinning like a jackal, scooped Layla up out of her chair and into his arms. "Hope you ate enough, babe, because I'm ready for another round."

And with that, Layla and Tanner were once more closeted away in their room.

"Guess this is what I miss when I work on the weekends." Jared shook his head, lips curved in a sexy smile.

"No wonder you work a lot. It's tough to be around them when they get into bunny mode," Felicity said with a giggle.

"Bunny mode?" His lips quirked. "Do I even want to know what that is?" Jared stood and collected his dishes and hers before heading over to the sink.

"You know...busy as bunnies," she added. For some reason she couldn't say "humping" to Jared. Talking about sex around him made her body heat up like a firecracker.

Busy scrubbing the plates, he only froze after a second, as though her words sank in. "You mean...humping like bunnies, don't you, princess?" His jaw clenched slightly, not from anger but from his attempt to hold in a laugh.

"Yeah, that." She bit her lip and looked away, her face hot.

"Well, I vote that you stay a little longer, help me ignore what sounds might come from their room."

Stay? Could she? She wanted to, but staying later meant leaving for her apartment in the dark, something she wanted to avoid.

"I...uh...I really need to get back to my place before it gets too dark."

Jared wiped his wet hands on a dish towel and then curled a finger under her chin, angling her face in his direction.

"Sounds dangerous. I don't want you to do anything risky. Stay the night then. *Please*. We can watch a movie, I'll crash on the couch, and you can take the bed. Sound fair?"

With him touching her, anything sounded fair. A girl couldn't think when he was offering such an opportunity.

"But I don't have any clothes or even a toothbrush."

His hands slid down from her chin to wrap his fingers around her throat, the hold possessive but not threatening.

"You looked good in my clothes. I wouldn't mind loaning them out again. And with all the hotels I visit, I always leave my brushes behind, so I keep a bunch of new unopened packages of them in the drawer to the left of the sink. You are welcome to one."

He effectively destroyed any argument she would have had, and finally she had to concede with a nod.

"Okay, I'll stay."

He took a step closer, their bodies almost touching, and his head dipped a few inches as though he was going to kiss her.

Please, please kiss me. Her silent prayer went unanswered. Instead, he swept the pad of his thumb over her lips, as though trying to memorize their shape and feel.

The man was going to kill her. All these near-kisses and no...kisses. If she didn't get control of herself, she was going to grab him and kiss him herself.

"Good. Let's change, and then we'll get a movie going."

Ten minutes later, Felicity was sitting on one end of the couch in the center of the L-shape, wearing Jared's black boxers and a large red T-shirt. Jared wore pajama bottoms, blue-and-black plaid with a blue sweatshirt that said "Creighton Law" across the chest.

"Creighton?" She pointed at his faded sweatshirt as he collected several thick blankets and pushed the large leather ottoman toward her so she could prop her feet up.

"Yeah. Been out six years, but I love this sweatshirt too much to give it away." He tossed her a fleece blanket, and she settled into it, relishing the way the soft fabric soothed and warmed her.

"You like old movies?" Jared held up two DVD cases. *Suspicion* and *Notorious*.

"Tough choice...um...*Suspicion*." She nodded at the Cary Grant and Joan Fontaine flick.

He popped the movie into the player and turned the TV on. Once the huge flat-screen was filled with the credits, he joined her on the couch. Rather than sit a few feet away, he lifted up her blanket, eased in beside her, and curled an arm around her waist, tucking her firmly against his side. The sudden intimacy had her entire body tensing, both with apprehension and excitement.

"It's just a movie," he murmured in her ear and feathered a kiss on her temple, as though assuring her that she didn't have to go any farther physically than she was with him right now.

How did he seem to know what to say? He was perfect and too damned tempting.

His scent, that wonderful woodsy scent mixed with fresh rain, was an endless comfort. It reminded her of home. When spring showers washed through the town and she'd leave her windows open. The scent and sounds of rain were a soothing enticement.

"I'm glad I went to see Sargent with you." His chest rumbled with his low murmur.

"Me, too. It sounds like you don't get enough time to enjoy life." She winced. "I'm sorry, that sounded rude. I didn't mean it like that." She lifted her head and leaned into his touch when he brushed the hair back from her face.

"I know you didn't. You don't have a mean bone in your body, princess." He tapped her cheek playfully with his index finger.

"Hey! I can so be mean. You don't know me." She bristled, irritated at the increasing amusement at his face. Tiny lines crinkled around the corners of his eyes and mouth. A sexy mouth, one she'd fantasized about kissing most of the day.

"I am getting to know you." He was tracing her lips, his brow furrowed in thought. She sucked in a breath, wondering, waiting to see what he'd do next.

"You, Felicity, are a kitten, sweet, soft..."

Struck by an impish impulse, she bit his thumb.

"Why you little—" He tackled her back on the couch, laughing as she squealed. He pinned her down with the weight of his body and started tickling her.

"Oh! Quit that!" She was laughing too hard for the threat to be taken seriously. The blankets fell off them and onto the floor, and in the midst of their playful struggles, Jared's hips slid into the cradle of her thighs. The intimate press of his body to hers made them suck in a shared breath. Faces close, both of them panting, Felicity dared not move except to wriggle her hips under his. He captured her wrists, pressing them down into the soft, worn leather of the couch on either side of her head. She licked her lips, rocked her hips again in a silent invitation, a plea for something she needed but feared to ask for.

"Not a kitten," he murmured moving a few inches closer, enough that his nose brushed the tip of hers. "More like a tiger. Fire, spirit, beauty."

For a man who claimed he knew little of art, he painted with his words.

"Please, Jared." She didn't know what she wanted him to do, only that he had to do something.

"Shouldn't…" he breathed.

"Have to…" she begged.

"Yeah," he agreed and dipped his head toward her.

The velvet press of his lips to hers melted in a slow-burning fire. Feathery, teasing, his tongue sought hers, and she gasped against his lips in erotic delight. The kiss hardened, turned possessive, and it thrilled her. Her body was on fire, the way he gently restrained her, took his kisses slowly, deeply, a banked eagerness one thread away from losing the control he held as he taught her how to kiss.

Open-mouthed, raw, persistent yet tender. He demanded everything and conquered her kiss by kiss, sigh by sigh. When his hold on her wrists vanished, she slid her hands up his body, fingers dipping and rising over the contours of his muscled back. They settled on his shoulders and her fingers dug in, clinging as he assaulted her senses and destroyed everything she thought she knew about him, about herself.

Their bodies rocked together, an ancient rhythm hindered only by clothes. The leather of the couch was soft and whispered beneath her as she tried to shift, to find some way to ease the pangs of desire exploding like fire in her womb. Fear tinged each kiss, fear of the climbing heights, the pounding blood and the flashbangs of heat along her skin whenever he touched her. Felicity had never felt this way before.

Jared's kisses cast her into the fire, molded her into something new, never to be undone by any man's kiss but his.

She slid her hands under his shirt, and the warmth his skin radiated made her toes curl and her back arch. His hips rolled into hers again, and she hissed sharply as arousal and need shot through her. Her nails raked his back, desperate for another taste of the endless bliss each movement of his body promised. Was this what the poets and songwriters meant? This steady yet frantic race toward an unknown length of time when only pleasure could exist? White-hot stars shot across her eyes.

Jared nibbled her lips, licked the seam of her mouth, and then plunged his tongue inside again and again, until she felt like she was free-falling. The room went black around her, and she drifted in the clouds, not a breath left in her as she let go. After an eternity she came back down, bit by bit, to realize where she was…and what she'd done. With Jared.

"You are so fucking beautiful when you come," his gruff voice murmured close to her ear, tickling her, sending delicious little shivers through her.

A new tingle licked like warm little flames up and down her spine, and her womb clenched again with a new riot of small aftershocks. It was the first time she'd heard him curse, and somehow the way he'd said it made her body spasm. Embarrassed, she ducked her head into his shoulder and neck, hiding from him.

"So shy? Don't be, sweetheart. Not after that."

A kiss, so faint she wondered if she'd dreamed it, tickled her ear.

"We'll just sleep here, together," he suggested gently. She couldn't resist snuggling deeper into him. Jared embraced her, completely wrapping himself around her.

It sounded so simple, but she'd never be able to just drift off…

Jared knew the moment she fell asleep. So quick, so sweet, she curled into him like a sleepy kitten, and almost purred before drifting off. He gently shifted her body so he lay lengthwise against the back of the couch and she lay in front, spooned against him.

The tumble of her hair teased his nose with those hints of vanilla, and the sweet scent of her skin was alluring. She tasted like heaven, had kissed like it, too. Wild, innocent, passionate. There was no casual seduction or feigned interest. Felicity poured her heart and soul into her lips. Each kiss was imbued with the power of her soul.

And when she'd come apart beneath him? Jared swallowed a moan, trying to ignore his body's hungry demands for more. This had been for her, to show her what she had to look forward to. He couldn't give her everything he ought to—but he could give her that. And it had been something for him as well, sinking into her mouth, feeling her unwind beneath him and let go. Their chemistry was palpable, scorching his body in ways he'd not felt for years. But he knew a girl like Felicity deserved chocolates and dancing and moonlit serenades—and he just wasn't in the position to give her those things right now. He'd have to let her go so she could find another man to be her prince, another man to make her happy...

Still, the thought of someone else, another man touching her, holding her, kissing her... He tightened his grip and held on, afraid she'd vanish like mist after sunrise.

Please, let me have this, let me have her, just for one more night.

He was a good Catholic boy, but it had been years since

he'd prayed for anything. Reaching over Felicity's body, he retrieved the blanket from the floor and settled it around their bodies. A soft click from down the hall made him lift his head.

Tanner padded toward them in the direction of the kitchen, wearing only pajama bottoms. He froze when he saw Jared holding Felicity on the couch. Jared held a finger up to his lips to indicate silence, and then he turned his attention back to the movie that still played on the flat-screen. Tanner could think whatever he wanted, and Jared knew he would hear about it tomorrow, but he didn't want to think about it right now. And he didn't want to wake Felicity. She was smart enough and shy enough that she'd try to pull away. He couldn't allow that. Not yet. He had to have her for just one more day if he could. Then he would let her go.

CHAPTER SEVEN

Heat. Searing kisses. The melding of bodies and the twining of limbs… Felicity moaned and shifted in bed. A sharp ache grew inside her, filling her with desperation.

"Jared!" Her own gasp woke her up.

She jerked and blinked several times as she realized where she was. In Jared's bed. Again. Only this time she was alone. Was he on the couch where he said he'd be? For some reason, she hoped he hadn't kept his promise. Being in bed with him, surrounded by his warmth and strength, was better than feeling alone in bed. Chivalry be damned. After what had happened between them last night, he should have stayed here with her.

The mere memory of last night had her blushing and burying her face in her hands with a little sigh. She'd come apart in his arms. But he hadn't—they'd still been fully clothed. Mortification churned her stomach and made her hands shake. This was just what she needed, to show an older guy how much of a virgin she was, that she couldn't even wait before they...

With a little shake of her head, she sat up and took stock of her situation. The sounds of water running, splashes against marble, caught her attention. The bathroom door was open a crack, allowing a beam of light to cut a thin blade's edge of illumination across the room. Jared must be in the shower, she realized. Felicity glanced at the clock on the nightstand.

7:45 a.m. Sunday.

"Shit!" She threw back the covers and dove off the bed, scrambling to find her clothes. She needed to be at Sabine's art gallery in fifteen minutes to start work.

As soon as she found her clothes, she frantically stripped and redressed. The shower still ran, so she took a moment to steal a blank piece of paper from Jared's desk and write a quick note. Then she grabbed her purse and exited the bedroom. Tanner was in the living room, sprawled on the couch, fully dressed and showered. There was no sign of Layla. Tanner lifted a cup of coffee to his lips as he studied the screen of his laptop. National news was on the TV. The sound was muted, but Tanner was more distracted by his computer as Felicity passed by him.

"Where are you off to?" he asked, a little twist of his lips hinting at the smile he held back.

"Work. I completely forgot! I'm running late." She retrieved her coat and started toward the door.

"Does Jared know you're leaving?" Tanner's eyes flicked to the hallway in the direction of his brother's room.

"He's in the shower. I left a note," she called over her shoulder before she closed the door behind her.

A wave of melancholy hit her instantly, crashing through her and ravaging her like the sea against a craggy cliff face.

It was all a dream. A lovely one. But it's over now.

Jared would go back to his life and she to hers. Even though she knew it was the truth, it still stung like salt in a fresh wound. Her eyes burned, and she clenched her fists. It wasn't meant to be.

She focused instead on work. Sabine's art gallery was a high-end art dealer that also offered clients an avenue for interior design options on a large scale or a small scale. As a part-time job, it was ideal for Felicity. The gallery itself was located just off Michigan Avenue, close to the expensive clothing and retail stores.

Her cab stopped in front of the Burberry store when she got out. The massive glass windows of the designer store were full of oversized photos of beautiful, elegant women and handsome men sporting the latest fashions. Clothes she could only dream about wearing since the price tags were well out of her scholarship student budget. One mannequin in the store window wore a navy-blue suit, and suddenly she was seeing Jared. His dark hair, long enough to thread her fingers through. Soft, warm eyes that hypnotized rather than pierced.

Felicity gave herself a little shake and quickly trotted past the store and down the side street. A sleek black-and-white sign read, "Sabine's." Across the street, tourists were already lining up to wait for Garrett's, the famous popcorn store, to open up. By mid-afternoon, Sabine's would receive a fair amount of customers toting popcorn tins as they perused the art and furniture at the gallery. Excellent business, as Sabine often said.

Sabine's gallery was a mixture of modern antiques and furniture, with pieces of unique art for sale. The prices were surprisingly affordable for a majority of the items in the store. When Felicity was left alone to run the gallery while Sabine was meeting with clients on site for a design job, Felicity secretly imagined it as a miniature museum.

"You are late," a feminine voice teased.

Felicity blinked and realized her boss, Sabine, was leaning against the doorjamb of her office, watching her, a little smile hovering about her lips.

"I'm so sorry," she apologized hastily.

Sabine shook her head, her long black hair and fringe of bangs rippling sleekly. "You're fine, Felicity. I'm only teasing." Her eyes, like polished turquoise, shimmered. "Come on, we've got loads of work to do."

Unable to resist, Felicity grinned back at her boss. The woman always had something fun and exciting to do, which made this job refreshing, and a nice change of pace from school. Sabine was a thirty-five-year-old, self-made businesswoman who had museum and gallery contacts in every major city in the United States. Working with wealthy clients, she often was able to arrange that pieces were donated to museums upon the deaths of the owners, which naturally made Sabine a favorite with curators.

With beautiful caramel-colored skin, long rich black hair, and those blue-green eyes, she was gorgeous. Her clothes were an added bonus. With a black pencil skirt, leopard-print pumps, and a white blouse, she gave off a sense of natural flair.

Felicity hoped one day she'd be able to wear something sexy, yet elegant like that with confidence. Something a man like Jared would find attractive. Suddenly self-conscious, she glanced down at her jeans and sweater, wincing. Oh well, it wasn't like she had time to change, and they didn't have any client appointments today.

Hanging her purse on the hat rack by the door, she followed Sabine into the conference room and then froze. Two good-looking men, one young and one middle-aged, were seated next to each other at the small conference table. Massive design booklets with patterns and photos of furniture selections were spread out around them.

"Felicity, I'd like you to meet Mr. Tim Worthington and his son, Mr. Thad Worthington."

Felicity's mind blanked, and then in the next instant flashes of the day before exploded through her. Thad! Jared's friend. What was he doing here? Thad was tall and fair-haired with hazel-green eyes that rooted her to the spot with their piercing intensity. He was too intense, like Jared.

"It's a pleasure to meet you," Thad murmured, and his father stood and held out a hand, which Felicity shook, still in a daze. What were the odds that Jared's best friend would be here at Sabine's?

"Felicity," Sabine whispered in her ear and nudged her in the back.

"So nice to meet you both. Would anyone like coffee?" she asked.

The older Worthington politely answered, "Black, please."

She backed out of the room and headed for the small kitchen down the hall. If she could just have a few minutes to compose herself... She'd expected to have a day to bury herself in work and not think about Jared, but it was impossible now that Jared's friend would be right in front of her for the next few hours.

Her shaking hands rattled the coffeepot as she tried to put it on the hot plate, and she cursed under her breath.

"Everything okay?" A deep voice made her jump and nearly drop the pot.

Thad rested one shoulder against the doorjamb of the kitchen, his arms crossed. He wore a crisp black suit and a thin silver-and-blue striped tie. His brown hair was a little shorter than Jared's and artfully styled to look like he'd just crawled out of a woman's bed.

"I'm sorry, I left before I asked if you wanted anything. Do you?" she asked, hoping her voice didn't shake. She didn't know how to act around one of Jared's best friends. He had no idea who she was, and she'd spent a good part of yesterday learning about him. He was good-looking, in that frightening sort of way that scared someone like her out of her wits. A man could be a little too handsome, she decided. Jared, though…he was different, too good-looking but never frightening, only enticing, irresistible—warm and safe yet sexy as hell. Her heart clenched as she had to face the fact that she'd ended whatever she and Jared might have had.

"The name's Thad. You're Felicity, right?"

She nodded, shaking his hand. The grip was firm, perhaps a little tight. He was powerful but tense, whereas when Jared held her hand, it was powerful but relaxed.

"I'm Felicity Hart." Jared's name was on the tip of her tongue as she longed to mention that she knew him, if only to justify a reason to talk about him to someone. But she didn't say his name. He might not want her talking to his friends. Maybe he wouldn't care, but she had no way of knowing for sure. She'd only spent one day and two nights with the guy. It wasn't the same as really knowing him.

She waited for the coffee to begin brewing, and Thad lingered by her, his blue eyes studying her from head to toe.

"So you and your father are hiring Sabine? What sort of project is it for?"

"We're going to be buying an old hotel from the 1920s, and it badly needs an overhaul and a revamped interior design scheme."

Distracted by that, she gasped. "That would be a huge project!" Sabine would make a huge profit, and Felicity would hopefully be a part of it.

Thad's lips quirked. "It's going to be. Do you work for Sabine full-time?"

"Uh, no. Just part-time. I'm a working on my master's at the University of Chicago."

"Are you now?" Thad's gaze sharpened. "What's your line of study?"

"Art history."

"And you've gotten a job here? That's serious. Most art history majors I knew when I was in college were using it as a blow-off major. But I'm betting you're serious about this art business." He winked at her. "Good for you. And what do you plan to do when you graduate?"

The coffee machine beeped, indicating it was done. She reached past Thad to fetch an empty white ceramic cup. He didn't move back even an inch, and she had to brush against him.

"Well?" he asked, voice softer than before.

She drew back, trying to put distance between them. "Hopefully I'll be a museum curator."

"Ah, that's why you're working with Sabine. She's got the best connections in the country to the major museums, especially the Art Institute here in Chicago." The gleam of triumph in his eyes told her he was a man who thrived on unraveling puzzles, especially puzzles that were also people. Felicity knew she'd have to be careful around him.

"Um, yeah. Sabine's great to work for, and it's nice to know she's connected."

She picked up Thad's father's coffee, and Thad trailed behind her as they returned to the conference room. Sabine and Mr. Worthington were discussing the art deco style of the twenties and how they planned to integrate updated Roaring Twenties styles into the old hotel. They didn't even seem to notice she had returned.

"They'll be at that for hours." Thad chuckled from behind her.

She glanced over her shoulder and met his gaze. He nodded his head in the direction of his father and her boss. "You should join them. I've got to make a quick call." He touched her lower back, gently pushing her so she would go inside the room. Before she could say anything else, he was already turning away, his cell phone to his ear as he stepped outside.

She watched him through the shop windows pacing outside the shop. He moved like Jared, a slow panther-like grace that entranced and warned her.

"Felicity, what do you think of the color schemes Mr. Worthington and I have been discussing?" Sabine drew her attention to the task, and she quickly lost herself in the project. She likely wouldn't see Jared again, and the pain her chest was sharp, but she had to ignore it. What other choice did she have?

Jared felt like singing. He wanted to belt out songs in the shower, but he wisely resisted the urge. Felicity was still asleep in his bed, and it might wake her up. He didn't want that. The pleasure of waking her up was something he wanted to do himself. As he got out of the shower and wrapped a towel around his waist, he whistled softly.

It was an irresistible temptation to go to his bed, climb in, and curl his body around hers. The passion simmering inside him demanded action, preferably through breathless kisses and slow, teasing caresses. Last night with her had been mind-blowing. Jared had had sex before, lots of sex, with a fair amount of women, but nothing compared to what he'd done with Felicity last night. He hadn't even gotten off, and it hadn't mattered. Only her pleasure had.

He'd held her for an hour on the couch, making sure she was deeply asleep when he finally lifted her in his arms and carried her to his bed. The promise to stay on the couch had seemed irrelevant by then, and he'd just gotten in bed beside her, pulling her back into his arms. Her body was fast becoming an addiction, a craving he didn't understand, only knew he wanted and had to have.

Opening his bathroom door with a wicked grin, he said, "Good morning—" His words died on his lips as he took in the sight of the empty bed, the empty room.

"Felicity?" Why he said her name he didn't know. She wasn't there.

A small slip of paper lay on top of his pillow. The sight of it made his muscles tense. He crossed the room and snatched it up. A scrawling, delicate hand filled the paper.

Jared,

Thank you for the wonderful day yesterday. It meant so much to me.

—Felicity

For a long second he didn't move. His breathing became harsh through his nose and mouth as his heart beat rapidly. Her words felt like a goodbye, but why? She wanted to walk away from what they'd shared. Logically he knew it was for the best, but damn it, he wasn't ready to let go of her. It was too late, though. She'd walked away, and he hadn't been there to stop her. Rage and pain exploded inside him, so powerful and shocking, but he swallowed it down and crumpled the note in his fist. She was just a kid, someone he'd met only twenty-four hours ago. Her being gone shouldn't mean anything to him, didn't mean anything to him.

What was the phrase? Ships passing in the night? He had to view it that way—there wasn't any other option.

Still... He tossed the note in the trash bin by his desk and glared at it for a long second before he bent, retrieved the crumpled paper, and smoothed it flat again. With a heavy sigh, he tucked the paper in the top drawer of his dresser. It was then he noticed the carefully folded shirt and boxers. The ones she'd worn. He picked them up and grimaced. They still held a lingering sweet vanilla scent. Hers. How could he come to miss that scent, to feel the loss of its owner so deeply in so short a time? Felicity had turned him sentimental.

He dressed hastily, not that he had any reason to. There was nowhere to go, nothing to do. No art exhibits to view with her. He had to stop thinking about Felicity or he'd go crazy.

His phone buzzed in his pocket, and he pulled it out. Thad's name flashed across the screen.

"Yeah?"

"You busy today?" Thad sounded amused, and for some reason that pissed Jared off.

"Maybe I am," he snapped, then regretted it. "Why?"

"I'm meeting with the interior designer for the new hotel we're buying. I want you to look over the contracts before we sign them. It'd only take a couple of hours," Thad said.

A couple of hours. Not like he was going to do anything today anyway. He might as well work. Especially since this deal could make his career. Thad's father had promised Jared that if the hotel deal went well, they'd start using Pimms & Associates for their legal work. Jared would be a partner by Christmas. Six years of hard work would finally pay off.

"Fine, but I'm charging double my hourly fee." He knew Thad would pay without question. His friend was exploding with money and never had an issue paying extra for weekend work.

Thad chuckled. "I'm happy to pay that. Besides, it's worth it. There is the hottest girl at this little gallery. She's... interesting. I'm planning on taking her out tonight. You ought to see her. It might inspire you to get back into the game."

Jared scoffed. "Game? You don't play, Thad. You sleep with women for a night and move on. That's not even a game." He slid his jacket on and headed for the door.

"I might make an exception. This girl is…well, you'll see when you get here. It's been a long time since I've gone after a sweet, innocent little thing. I bet she's a firecracker in bed." Thad was laughing. "I need a good challenge. This will be it."

With a shake of his head, Jared rubbed his eyes with his thumb and forefinger. "Whoever she is, leave her alone. Find more willing prey."

"Not on your life." Thad hung up.

Great. Now he had to go and intervene before Thad broke some innocent girl's heart. With a low growl he stalked out into the main room and looked about for Tanner, but his brother was nowhere to be seen. Either he had a class or he'd gotten back into bed with Layla.

Half an hour later he was in front of the address Thad had texted him. A chic looking little gallery faced him. He opened the glass door and followed the sound of voices. Thad, his father, and a beautiful olive-skinned woman were seated around a conference table poring over sketches and design books. Thad glanced up, saw him, and winked.

What the—

Someone bumped into him from behind, and he stumbled forward.

"Oh, sorry!" A feminine gasp came from somewhere in the hallway just a foot behind him.

"It's fine." He spun and caught the woman from behind him, and his heart stopped.

Felicity. She's here. In my arms. The sheer rush of joy and excitement short-circuited his brain for a full five seconds.

Startled gray eyes met his, and her lips, those luscious lips he'd loved tasting last night, parted in surprise in a little *O* shape. His fingers curled around her upper arms, and in that moment all he could think was how much he wanted to kiss her.

"Ahem." Thad's cough broke through the haze of his desire, and just like that, he remembered the empty bed, the note she'd left. An invisible layer of ice washed over him, and he dropped his hands from her body and stepped back.

"Ah, Jared, you've met Felicity. She's Sabine's young protégé." Thad joined him by the door and turned his attention to the olive-skinned woman poring over the books. "This is Sabine."

Sabine raised stunning turquoise eyes to meet his. Beautiful, of course, but they lacked the heat and passion that a certain pair of silvery eyes had. Sabine's lips twitched, and she nodded in silent greeting before returning to her work and speaking to Mr. Worthington. He turned back to Thad and Felicity, seeking her face instantly.

Felicity continued to stare at him with a deer-in-the-headlights look that made him feel strangely satisfied. What was the right thing to do? Pretend they'd never met? No, he couldn't do that.

"We...uh, have met. She's a friend of Tanner's," Jared finally said.

"You have?" Thad somehow worked his way between them, one shoulder blocking her from Jared's direct view. The possessive and somewhat protective move made him want to growl.

"Yeah, at one of Tanner's parties," Jared added. It took all of his power to focus on his friend. "You mentioned contracts? I'm ready to review whatever you have."

"Good." Thad pointed to the table and glanced over at Felicity, who was still gaping at Jared.

It was a wicked thought, but he was glad she was still stunned. After her disappearing act, he was happy she was the one off balance and not him. Clenching his jaw, he slid into a seat at the table next to Mr. Worthington, and after a quick greeting to the older man, he took the contract paperwork

and glared at the first page.
        He didn't read a single word.

CHAPTER EIGHT

She couldn't breathe.

Jared was somehow at Sabine's. And he was angry. At her. Why else would he act as if they were just acquaintances? Was he upset because she'd left? Because of the note? Surely that wasn't it. He had to understand why she'd left, why she hadn't said goodbye. But she looked at his face, and he was glowering and raking one hand through his dark hair.

Maybe he didn't understand why she'd left after all.

Sabine looked up from her pattern books and sketches, winged brows raised in concern.

"I'll just put some more coffee on," Felicity muttered, then spun out of the conference room.

She took refuge in the small part of the gallery just off the hallway where several paintings hung and a nice couch offered a place for her to collapse. Which she did, immediately sinking into its pillowy depths. Leaning forward, she braced her elbows on her knees and buried her face in her hands. A tiny tremor worked its way through her.

She hadn't expected to see him so soon after last night. She'd had to leave while he was in the shower and had felt guilty for slipping away like that and now here they were stuck together with clearly unresolved issues, since he was angry with her. Was he mad she'd left? Or was he mad she was here, in the middle of his work life? Neither of them had time to commit to each other, and that was assuming he was interested. One mind-blowing orgasm on the couch did not mean he was seriously into her or that he wanted more to happen between them.

She wished she had dated more in high school. She might understand men more if she had. Of course, she'd been too busy trying to survive school and working nights at the only restaurant they'd had in town. Jared was so worldly, and she felt so out of sync with his world that it scared her. He was a lawyer with a high-pressure job and demanding hours, and she was just a girl still in grad school, playing at being an artist.

Maybe he was used to taking a girl out on the weekends and having a good time, and then going back to work. She didn't know. That was the problem. There was so much she didn't know about Jared, except that when he kissed her it made her feel like she was the only person in the universe who mattered, and when he looked at her with those soft bedroom eyes, it unraveled her entire being.

We're still worlds apart, though. He's the kind of guy who vacations in Italy and has silk sheets on his bed. I'm the girl who can't even afford an apartment with a working hot water heater. The only place they made sense together was in the tiny world of his apartment when they were inches from kissing. That was the only thing that made sense about this.

God, I'm an idiot, thinking for a second he and I could work long term.

She couldn't explain it, but everything about this

moment made her feel wildly out of control, like being on a train headed for a broken bridge. Her job was supposed to be a place of tranquility where she could bury her other worries. But now Jared was here, and all she could think about was him and how much she wanted to be back in his bed and in his arms, not thinking about what tomorrow would bring. If she was too focused on him, she could screw up and Sabine might not give her the recommendation for the LACMA job she so desperately wanted in California. Tears sparked in the corners of her eyes.

"Felicity?" Sabine's soft, husky voice made her look up and drop her hands from her face. The air cooled the wet path that tears had taken on her face. Using the backs of her hands, she rubbed her cheeks and tried to smile.

"Sorry, Sabine."

The woman swept a hand through her hair, pushing it over her shoulder as she plopped down next to Felicity on the couch.

"Sweetie, what's going on with you?" She held up a hand when Felicity started to shake her head. "Huh-uh, you tell me the truth. Come on now." Sabine patted her knee and leaned closer, her bright eyes pinned Felicity in place.

"I..." She hesitated only a second before telling Sabine the truth. The woman was like an older sister to her and wouldn't judge her. "I spent the last two nights in Jared's bed. Mr. Redmond, I mean," she confessed in a barely audible whisper.

Sabine's almond-shaped eyes widened. "You and that gorgeous man in there? Now why would that make you cry? You're young, he's young, love is a beautiful thing at your age. As long as it doesn't interfere with your work here or his, you shouldn't let it worry you."

Easier said than done. I'm already freaking out about him being here. Felicity sniffed. "He's mad at me. He looks mad anyway." She sat up a little straighter, feeling honestly quite stupid for crying. She had *no reason* to cry. It wasn't like he had any right to be mad at her, and it wasn't like they'd been dating and broken up.

It's time for me to grow up.

Her boss waved a hand in apparent unconcern. "Oh, he's probably mad because the Worthingtons called him in to work on the weekend. Most lawyers I know hate working weekends. Having met some of their clients, I don't blame them." Sabine winked at her.

Felicity laughed, but her heart wasn't in it. "He's a workaholic. Trust me, this is normal for him. That's why I know that if he's mad, it has to do with me."

Sabine pursed her lips and tapped a finger on her lips thoughtfully. "Okay, so why do you think he's mad at you? What happened when you were together?"

"Well, we weren't actually together, if you know what I mean. We just shared his bed twice to sleep..." She blushed again. "Though there was a pretty heavy make-out session on the couch." She couldn't believe she was confiding to her boss, but Sabine had a way of making Felicity feel like she was talking to an older sister who wouldn't judge her. As an only child, she'd always felt lonely, but Sabine had taken her under her wing ever since she'd arrived and had applied for the job at the gallery.

"And you think he's mad at you for that? Trust me, he isn't. Getting a girl hot and bothered would be something to be proud of. I know a thing or two about men. He'd relish the effect he had on you. What else happened?"

Felicity quickly relayed the note she'd left and its contents when Sabine questioned her further.

"So you just ran out on him while he was in the shower?" Sabine's tone was thick with disapproval.

Felicity gasped. "I couldn't just walk in on him while he

was in there, and I couldn't wait till he was out because I would have been late getting here."

Her boss grimaced. "Since when do I care about what time you show up? Half the time you beat me here, which is why I had the extra key made for you. Being a little late one day wouldn't kill you, or me." She hugged Felicity's shoulders in a gentle squeeze. "You work too hard. Take a break now and then. You're young. Take advantage of the nights you could be spending in bed with a gorgeous man who looks like he walked out of a Burberry ad, okay?"

Felicity sniffled and then laughed. "He does, doesn't he?"

Both women dissolved into a fit of barely stifled giggles. When they quieted, Sabine grew serious again.

"You should tell him the real reason why you left this morning. He might be fine with it if you tell him the truth. If you care about him, even as a friend, he deserves honesty. Besides, I need you to be on your game. This could help influence my recommendation for the LACMA job you want."

"You're right." Felicity wiped her eyes again, removing the last evidence of her tears.

Sabine brushed a hand over her hair, a sisterly touch that was comforting. "Good. Now, tell me you can work with him and it won't be a problem. I need your help on this project. It's going to be huge, and you'll make a lot of money helping me out."

A lot of money. She could sure use the commission this would give her and Sabine. She might be able to afford renting another apartment for half a year, or maybe even split the cost of Layla's place. No more late nights spent worrying about the robberies that kept happening in her building, or the drunks who wandered into the lobby in the evenings, or the police busting up domestic violence fights. Yeah, this was huge. She had to get herself together.

She stiffened her spine and met Sabine's gaze. "I can do this."

Her boss patted her shoulder again. "That's what I want to hear. Now let's go talk contracts with the men."

Felicity squared her shoulders, wiped at her eyes, and nodded. "Right." She followed Sabine back into the conference room, and when she met Jared's intense gaze, she didn't flinch. It was time to focus on work, and she had to put thoughts of him aside until the job was done.

Four hours later, with a lunch break in between, the design scheme was settled, the contracts adjusted, and hands were shaken all around. It had been easier than Felicity had expected to put aside worries about Jared and dive into the project with Sabine. Halfway through the meeting, she'd abandoned her "observe and assist" attitude and found herself engaging Mr. Worthington and Thad equally with her ideas on the nouveau art deco themes she came up with.

Her boss had eased back in her chair and let Felicity take charge of the rest of the negotiations and strategizing. By the end of the meeting, she was full to bursting with confidence. Even Jared had stopped looking mad and had been participating fully.

"It seems like Ms. Hart has quite an eye for Roaring Twenties art deco themes," Mr. Worthington announced with some pleasure, directing a fatherly gaze of approval Felicity's way.

"She does," Sabine agreed with pride.

"I agree, Felicity has quite an eye for beauty." Thad was staring at her, his chin resting in one hand, the perfect picture of masculine ease. Jared went rigid next to him, and suddenly Thad winced and looked at something beneath the table before he shot Jared a dirty look.

Mr. Worthington cleared his throat and stood. "Right. Well, Thad, we ought to get back to the office and hammer out some of the details. Thank you, ladies, for an enjoyable morning. I believe this redecoration will be quite an adventure for us all." A hint of a smile played upon the older man's lips.

Both Thad and his father were ready to leave for their office, and Sabine went with them to the door to show them out.

Jared remained behind in the conference room with Felicity as he gathered up the contracts he had revised during negotiations.

"Your boss drives a stiff bargain for her design fees," Jared mused softly as he ruffled the papers before slipping them into his briefcase.

Felicity raised a brow, feeling her temperature rise as she sensed he was challenging her somehow. Not in a bad way, but he was…testing her.

"Sabine is one of the best interior designers in the country, and with her master's in the arts, she is unparalleled in her profession."

His lips twitched. "I'm not disputing that, sweetheart, but she's expensive, and a good lawyer always tries to trim costs for his clients." He sidled a step closer to her, and her entire body tensed with anticipation. They weren't arguing, not quite, but the way he said "sweetheart" in that dark, soft, seductive voice while disagreeing with her… Felicity had the sudden desire to drag him into the nearest coat closet and shred his clothes to get to him. But this was work; she couldn't be caught with Jared. She'd promised Sabine she would keep things professional.

"You could hire someone else, but you'd sacrifice quality," Felicity replied.

"We could, but the Worthingtons want the best, and I believe Sabine is it."

She tried not to look his way, but it was impossible to

resist. When she peeped at him from beneath her lashes, he was watching her, a narrow-eyed expression hardening his features. For a long second Felicity feared neither of them would speak. A thousand things to say came to her lips, but never left them as she struggled to find the right words. Would they talk about last night? Did he feel the tension of working together like this, too? The tightness in her chest eased as he opened his mouth.

"What was with the note this morning?" He gripped the back of one of the conference chairs, knuckles white as he leaned on it.

Damn, Layla should have warned her that Jared had a scary lawyer-style scowl. Was this how he was at all business meetings when he wanted answers? His intensity was sucking up in all the air in the room.

She swallowed hard. "I...I'm sorry about the note." She shored up her confidence, knowing she had to own up to the fact that she had run this morning. "I had to leave because I was running late to get here. There wasn't time for—"

"For goodbye?" He cut her off, and the way he whispered the word, she heard the hurt in his voice, the wounded acceptance of what they'd shared coming to an end. He shrugged, as though trying to rid himself of a great weight that rested there.

"Yes." It felt like she was sinking into the floor. She'd just left him without an explanation, yet it felt as though they were talking about something deeper, a more permanent issue that lay between them. It was scary as hell to think about.

"It's just one little word, Felicity." His tone was still soft, hurt, and it shocked her. Her leaving *really* had upset him.

It was supposed to be this way, this goodbye...but suddenly the idea was unbearable.

"I'm sorry," she replied, her voice shaking. "We both know that this thing...whatever it is...won't work out in the long run. I'm not staying in Chicago, not if I get the job I want in Los Angeles, and you've built your career here. The deeper we go, we can't..." She struggled with the words. "So I thought I'd just make a clean break." There, she'd said it.

"You never even gave us a chance. You don't know what it would have been like between us." Jared released his grip on the chair and raked a furious gaze over the room before settling on her.

"What would have been the point of that? I'll be leaving next year. This isn't permanent for me." Each word hurt as she spoke, but it was the truth. She'd never planned on staying here, no matter how much she'd fallen in love with the city and the friends she'd made. She hadn't found any museums willing to take her on here, or she would have stayed.

"What's the point? When you have feelings for someone, there's always a point, Felicity. You don't walk away from the chemistry we have. When I touch you? It makes my entire body burn. I've never felt that way about anyone else." He spoke so desperately, a quiet rage in his eyes as though he fought to hide how much he was hurting. "Shouldn't we have at least given it a shot? Hell, we might have been terrible together, but I wanted to take that chance." His jaw clenched as he swallowed whatever else he had planned to say.

"You really wanted me?" She couldn't believe it. A guy like him could have anyone. Why did he want someone like her? She wasn't good enough for him. She was... Dark voices from her past slithered through her. Hateful words she knew couldn't be true, yet she still believed them anyway. She wasn't good enough for him. Just a mousy little girl from a small town in Nebraska. She'd been a waitress at an Applebee's in high school while he'd probably been studying in law school. It just didn't...fit. *They* didn't fit.

His eyes darkened. "There you go again, with that look

on your face."

"What look?" she demanded, irritation and pain prickling her inside like deep-rooted thorns digging into flesh.

Jared walked around the table to stand in front of her. She'd almost forgotten how tall he was, but as he towered over her, forcing her to tilt her head back, she remembered the way his long, lean body had curled around hers in bed. Protective, warm, seductive. A combination that was fatal to her heart.

He cupped her chin and turned her face to the right where a gilt-framed mirror hung on the wall. Embarrassment hollowed her out inside as she saw her face. Eyes wide, lips trembling, a heavy sadness painted its broad brush across her features, which now flamed red with shame.

"That look," he breathed in a disappointed sigh. "Like you can't believe that anyone would want you." Anger snapped and burned in his eyes like hungry flames devouring tinder. He didn't unleash it though, didn't hurt her. He only muttered a strangled curse before his fingers dropped from her chin to the back of her head, his fingers fisting into her hair as he dragged her into his arms.

Mouth open in shock, Felicity was unprepared for his punishing kiss. The edge of violent desperation that sparked from his lips and the way he savaged her heart and soul with the pain she tasted in that kiss. His pain and hers. She had hurt him. But she couldn't take it back, could not turn back the clock to undo this morning. Her hands rested on his chest, feeling the faint thump-thump of his heartbeat beneath her palms. Her own heartbeat echoed his, like a dove cooing to its mate.

Whenever he kissed her, she lost all sense of self and time. She found herself swept into a secret place where only sensations and emotions reigned. It wasn't something she could fight, nor did she want to. If only she could stay like this in his arms forever and not have to face reality.

Jared brushed his lips back and forth over hers, and she tried to press close again. He shook his head and stepped back. "You're killing me, princess." His words were husky and a little rough. He licked his lips and then tilted his head back and sucked in a deep breath.

Felicity watched him, her body shaking with need, her chest squeezing her heart in its iron fist.

"You're afraid," he said. "You're so young. I keep forgetting that. Just a kid in some ways."

She started to protest, but he held up his hand.

"You don't know how to make a leap of faith. I get that. It's scary as hell. We probably aren't right for each other. Trust me, I know that. We'd never have time to be together between my work and your school. I get that, too." He dragged his fingers through his hair and reached for his coat. As he slid his coat on, he stepped away from her, and the feeling of that distance cut her soul deep. How could someone she'd only known a few days make her feel like this? Like her heart couldn't beat if he walked out that door?

"Jared—"

"I like you." A rueful smile twisted his lips. "You made me...feel. It's been a long time since anyone's done that. But if you aren't ready, I'm not going to push you."

His words were destroying her as much as they saved her. She couldn't have anyone in her life, not anyone she loved. In a way he was right. She was afraid he'd be too perfect, and once he left her, no other man would ever measure up. The idea of spending the rest of her life someday with another man...it left a sour taste upon her lips.

A thousand words hung on her lips, yet she couldn't say a single one. He seemed to read her silence as affirmation of his accusations.

"Thank you for yesterday. It was nice." He stepped

toward her again and pressed his lips to her forehead in a light kiss. "Goodbye, princess." He lingered, his warm breath fanning her cheeks and his hands on her upper arms as he held her close just one moment longer. Her heart beat hard against her ribs, and she couldn't speak past the slicing pain in her tight throat as it constricted.

And with that he left.

Felicity crumpled into the nearest conference chair, staring blinding ahead of her. Jared Redmond had cut out her heart and walked away with it. She'd practically challenged him to do it, and he had.

It was better this way.

Yet it felt as though she'd betrayed herself by not running after him. He had wanted her, but was he right about what he'd said? She believed she didn't belong with a guy like him or his glittering world. Even if she could convince herself she and Jared could be together, it was crazy to think it could work. When would she ever get to see him? Their schedules were impossible to match, so what was the point? She would leave Chicago and any relationships she had behind. Just let it go. A terrible hollowness filled her until her entire body echoed with its emptiness. She hadn't known how full of happiness she'd been until she'd lost it all, when she'd lost Jared.

CHAPTER NINE

*M*ondays were shit.

Jared had never thought otherwise, but now more than ever, he *hated* Mondays. The brief but explosive beginning to his weekend had rocked his world to the core, and yet the thing that had spun his world on its axis had pushed him away.

She had pushed him away.

And losing a chance to be with a woman like Felicity, it made him fucking hate today. Fucking Mondays.

He walked into his office at Pimms & Associates and dropped his leather briefcase into one of the two black armchairs facing his large desk. Then he stripped off his gray mélange virgin wool suit jacket and flung it over the back of one chair before he studied the surface of his desk.

It was a battlefield littered with paper bodies. Contracts, sales agreements, licenses, and everything else related to his work was all here, a ready distraction. But for the first time his heart wasn't in it. He'd spent the rest of Sunday in a foul mood. Alone. Tanner and Layla had tiptoed around him after he'd all but snarled like a beast at the first mention of Felicity. He'd told himself to let it go, that focusing on her wasn't productive or healthy.

She was a kid. Too young for him to date seriously. She had a life ahead of her, decisions about her career that could take her far away from Illinois, far from him. He shouldn't be so…attached. Attached, God, he sounded pathetic, but he was somehow *connected* to her.

That kiss on the couch and the one in Sabine's conference room had bound him to Felicity with invisible strings. He knew he should want to shake them off, enjoy being single, but it didn't feel right. He wasn't like Thad or Angelo. He didn't play the field. He was a one-woman kind of guy when it came to dating. What the hell was he supposed to do if his one woman was running from him and running from herself? The memory of seeing her doubt and pain, so stark and sharp in her eyes, as though her life was at risk, knifed his heart. Why was she so afraid to trust him? Why didn't she think she was good enough?

"Jared." A feminine voice pulled him from his thoughts. He glanced up to see Shana Pimms, his ex, standing in his doorway. Her long blond hair was pulled into a sleek chignon, and she wore a black suit jacket and matching pencil skirt. He knew her enough to know she preferred pantsuits, but her father insisted female attorneys wear skirts in the office.

"Hey," he greeted, offering her a smile he didn't even remotely feel.

Her brows drew together in concern. "Are you okay? You look awful." She blushed and glanced at the floor as though embarrassed she'd said that. They'd been so close…once. Before her father and their jobs had driven a chasm between them.

When her words finally registered, he looked down at

himself. His clothes were freshly pressed and clean, but there was something unkempt about him, probably the fact that his hair was a mess, and he felt like shit. Dressing well and looking sharp had always been natural to him, but the last few days he'd been too distracted to focus on little things like shaving.

"I had a rough weekend. What's up?" He rose from his chair.

Shana only shook her head, a troubled expression on her face. "It's nothing. We're having a meeting in five minutes in the main conference room. Just wanted you to know." She tucked a strand of loose hair behind her right ear and returned a smile just as melancholy as his before she left. Pity for her filled him.

When they'd been together in law school, she'd been so wild, so free and fun. It was what had drawn him to her when they first met. They'd connected as friends more than lovers. However, with the weight of her parents' expectations that she become a Super Lawyer—especially her father's expectations in the last few years—any fire in Shana had been extinguished. She wasn't in love with real estate law, not like Jared was. Her passion lay with adoptions and family law, but her father refused to let her practice that. Getting a job in Chicago without his help and influence was impossible, so she'd resigned herself to practicing in an area she wasn't passionate about.

Jared rummaged around his desk until he found a yellow legal pad and a pen before he headed for the conference room. Pimms & Associates was on the twelfth floor of their building and housed about forty attorneys, six of whom were partners and the rest associates. The modern-style offices were cool and impressive, from the gold letters of the firm name hanging on the wall behind the receptionist's desk, to the huge conference room with flat screens and expensive teleconference and video conference technology.

Shana's father, Matthew Pimms, was already seated at the head of the table. His secretary, Alice, a pretty young woman, hovered behind him, her pen flying across a notepad as he told her what he needed to be prepared for the meeting. Shana sat in a seat as far away from her father as possible, apparently on purpose. Her own legal pad and pen were in front of her untouched. She brightened a little when Jared walked in, but then she seemed to catch herself, and grimaced when she realized her father noticed. Other attorneys were soon crawling into the conference room, legal pads and coffee in their hands.

"Redmond, over here." Pimms pointed at the chair to the left of his.

He did that a lot, singling Jared out for favoritism. For as long as he'd worked here, Pimms had allowed him to participate in most of the heavy billable transactions. But with that privilege and the stressful workload there were the comments Pimms made, the little references to Shana and his future, always together in the same conversation. A future he had no intention of bringing about.

Once all of the attorneys recruited for the assignment were in their seats, Pimms passed around copies of a document. Jared took his paper and scanned it. A basic letter of intent for the sale of the art deco era hotel that Thad and his father were interested in purchasing, and the same project he would be working with Felicity on.

Pimms ran through the facts relayed to him by their clients and the brokers on the deal. Jared was only half listening.

"Redmond, you'll be in charge of drafting the purchase and sale agreement. The letter of intent will set out the terms. Work with Shana on this and get in touch with the seller's counsel immediately. The rest of you will be covering the other aspects, such as the hotel income and other pertinent information we'll need to know when restructuring the hotel ownership. I'll spend the rest of the meeting discussing the Worthingtons' strategy for the purchase and the general idea behind the relaunch of the hotel."

Jared's phone vibrated, and he slid it out of his trouser pocket, glancing at the screen for a second, praying it would be Felicity. It was Thad.

Thad: *What did you think of Felicity? I am planning to ask her out tonight. Sabine gave me her number.*

Like hell! Jared swallowed the vicious growl. He had to remember where he was: in the middle of an attorney meeting. For a short time today he'd thought he could put Felicity behind him. *Fucking Thad. Shit.* How was he supposed to handle this?

Thad was competitive. Maybe if Jared downplayed his interest, Thad would lose interest. With a careful glance at the lawyers around him, he typed his reply.

Jared: *She's too young, no challenge. Poker night instead?*

"Come on, Thad, take the bait." His mutter drew some curious looks from the other attorneys.

Thad: *Naw. Why don't you come and bring a date. 4 of us can go to Club Amazon. 9:00 p.m., my room in VIP area.*

Jared nearly crushed the phone in his hand before rationality returned. *Fuck.* The last thing Felicity would want would be to be trapped in a private room with Thad. Hell, she was barely twenty-four. That wouldn't matter to Thad.

He texted Layla and told her that she needed to make plans with Felicity tonight and that it was important that Felicity was too busy if anyone else called. She irritatingly texted back within seconds.

Layla: *Why?*

He all but groaned in frustration. Was everyone determined to piss him off today?

Jared: *A friend of mine wants to ask her out to a club tonight. She can't go.*

Layla: *Who? Do I know this guy?*

Jared: *It's Thad. You met him a few months ago.*

Saying Thad's name was apparently the only warning he'd needed to give. Layla's next text was almost an audible scream.

Layla: *OH HELL NO. She's not getting anywhere near him. He's too much for her. She can't handle a man like that. Why aren't you two going out?*

Jared: *Because she's scared of dating me. I'm pissed off, Layla. But I can't help her. So can you spend tonight with her?*

Layla: *I'll see what I can do.*

He breathed a sigh of relief, and when he looked up from his phone's screen, he found every eye in the conference room on him.

"Something more important than this sale, Redmond?" Pimms's steely tone was the only warning he had that he was on thin ice.

"Sorry." He shoved the phone his pocket, snatched up his legal pad, and scribbled some random notes that meant absolutely nothing, but Pimms wouldn't know the difference.

His boss continued to talk for a few more minutes before he ended the meeting. Jared leaped from his seat and headed for his office. If he was going to go out tonight, he was going to need to get a head start on the purchase and sale agreement.

He was just easing into his desk chair when Shana came in after him, smiling broadly.

"I just heard from Thad. He said we're all meeting at Club Amazon at nine. He said you needed a plus-one to even out his numbers." Shana's grin made his heart sink.

He hadn't invited her, hadn't even thought to.

"Uh, right, well, I won't be there a long time, just an

hour or so," he answered carefully. Shana didn't seem to pick up on his hesitancy.

"That's fine. I could just use an hour of fun. Dad's been running me ragged these last few weeks," she admitted with a grimace. "Some music and dancing would be good for me."

How could he deny Shana a little fun? Thad was her friend just as much as he was Jared's. He tried to ignore the impending disaster of having his ex and the girl he was currently fascinated with in the same place at the same time. That could only be trouble.

"Great, well, see you at nine." He reached for the nearest group of files and attempted to look busy. He didn't miss the way her smile faltered, but she nodded and left.

Damn, he was being an asshole today. First with Felicity and now with Shana.

Jared pulled his phone out of his pocket and called Layla.

"Yeah?" she answered, sounding distracted.

"I'm serious about tonight. Don't let her go, okay?"

"You're not her father, Jared, so quit acting like it."

"Fuck, Layla, listen to me," he almost snarled. "You know what Thad is like. Do you honestly trust him not to seduce her out of her dress? She'd be much safer with someone else. Got it?"

Layla had the audacity to laugh. "Maybe we feel like dancing tonight. Guess we'll see you there."

"What the fu—" She hung up before he could finish. He thought she was going to help him. What the hell had changed in the last ten minutes?

"Son of a bit—" He choked down the curse. It wasn't like him to lose his cool. He dialed Tanner's phone and got his voicemail.

"Tanner, don't let Layla and Felicity go out tonight. They need to stay home. Tie your woman to your bed if you have to." He ended the call and slapped his phone on his desk. It hit a huge stack of papers, and the *thump* was less gratifying than if he had smashed it on the wood. Why had Layla changed her mind? What game was she playing?

And more importantly, how was he going to handle a night of watching Felicity getting hit on by Thad without it ending in a fistfight with his best friend?

CHAPTER TEN

Felicity snuggled into her couch, an Egyptian history book propped on her slightly bent legs. She held a highlighter between her index and middle finger, flicking it back and forth as she perused the chapter on the upper and lower kingdoms. Survey of Egyptian History was one of the most interesting classes she was taking this semester. Lust, power struggles, betrayals, rising and falling empires—it was a history major's dream.

She uncapped her highlighter and marked a passage that explained how the Nile flowed from south to north. Flipping to the next page in her textbook, she found a picture of Elizabeth Taylor from the classic movie *Cleopatra*. She was lying on a thin purple couch, one hand raised in a seductive come hither gesture. The queen of Egypt certainly had confidence in spades. Felicity envied her for that.

Felicity shut her eyes. It wasn't Elizabeth Taylor on the couch, but her. Eyes darkened by kohl, almost catlike in her steady gaze, she gestured for Marc Antony to come to her. Only it wasn't Richard Burton playing Marc Antony, but

Jared. His skin was golden from hours in the sun, and his hair was a little longer, enough to thread her fingers through and grasp the silky strands.

His eyes were hot like the desert sand when the sun was at its zenith in the sky, burning and inescapable. He strode to her in slow, sure steps, his body shielded in armor that molded to his chest and a burgundy-red tunic beneath the leather waist flaps that covered his hips. Leather wrist bands wider than her palms covered his arms, adding a lethal look to him. He put one knee on the couch by her hip and braced one hand next to her head at the base of the couch where she leaned back against a pillow. Felicity skimmed her palms up the shaped silver muscles of the armor. The metal was cool beneath her fingertips as she traced his pectorals before she lifted her gaze to his. She was caged against the couch by his body, and the thrill of her captivity made the blood burn in her veins.

"So beautiful." His voice was soft and dark, like a heady sip of red wine.

He stroked her cheek with his knuckles, then moved them down over her neck and breasts. Her nipples pebbled beneath the thin silk of her dress. His dark lashes fanned down as he watched her flush and arch into his touch. As Jared cupped one of her breasts and then gently squeezed, a bolt of heat and desire drew a gasp from her. Ashamed of her own wanton reaction, she bit her lip and angled her face away from him.

"Never hide from me, never," he growled at her, and turned her face back. He lowered his head, and she tipped hers back, her entire body aching, her soul crying out for his

—

Wump! Her textbook hit the carpet with a thud, and she bolted upright. The book was facedown, pages bent at odd angles, and her highlighter had rolled several feet away.

Had she fallen asleep? Or had the daydream been too intense? She shifted and then flushed as she realized her body was hot and definitely bothered...and wet. God, how embarrassing. She rubbed her face with her hands. What did it say about her that she couldn't even read about ancient Egypt without thinking about Jared, about kissing him, about his hands on her body?

Leaning over her couch, she hooked her fingers around her hidden sketchbook and slid it out. Whenever she needed to clear her head she always reached for her pad and pencil. She flipped through the other sketches until she got to a blank page. She smoothed her fingers over its surface, listening to the way the paper whispered beneath her caress. Then she picked up one of her medium graphite pencils and started to draw.

An hour later she stared at the finished sketch, pleasure and embarrassment mingling within her to the point that her face was hot and she was biting back a smile. A man leaned over a woman on a couch, distinctive Roman and Egyptian clothing identifying it as the image of her fantasy. Maybe she should start calling Jared "Gladiator." A snort escaped. He'd love that. Yeah, right. Besides, she wasn't going to be around him again, at least not by choice and not alone where she could call him a nickname. The thought was oddly depressing. She would have loved to see his face if she did call him that.

Her phone vibrated on the arm of the couch, and she picked it up to answer.

"Hey, it's me."

Felicity rolled her eyes. Only Layla would say that, as if there was no doubt in the world who "me" was.

"What's up?" She tucked the phone in the crook of her neck and shoulder as she bent over to slide the sketchbook back under the couch.

"Word is Thad Worthington is going to ask you to go out to a club tonight."

Her phone slid from her hand and hit the floor.

"Hello? Hell—oh?" Layla's shout was still audible from the floor. Felicity scrambled to pick it up.

"How do you know Thad Worthington, and what do you mean he's going to ask me out?"

Layla scoffed. "You're kidding, right? I don't reveal my secret sources. That's why they're called secret."

Sometimes Felicity wanted to strangle her friend. "Okay, so if this is all secret or something, why did you even call me?"

"Uh, to make sure you say yes when Thad calls. I thought that was fairly obvious." Irritation oozed out of Layla's tone, the tone she used on her younger sisters when they pestered her. Rather than upset Felicity, it made her feel a little warm and fuzzy inside. Layla often treated her more like a sister than a friend.

Felicity closed her eyes and sighed. "No way. I'm not going out with Thad. If I went out with anyone, I'd—" She bit her tongue to keep from saying she'd go out with Jared.

"I know he's not your kind of guy. Trust me. I know you, Felicity. But if you go out with him, it will make the one guy you *do* want go crazy."

"What?" She shook her head as confusion filled her. Layla wasn't making any sense.

"Look, don't you want to make Jared jealous? He's into you but won't make a move unless he's crazy jealous."

Felicity's eyes flew open, and she scowled. "Layla, I don't want to make Jared jealous. He's not into me, not really." Even if he had said he liked her and wanted her, she didn't believe him. She *couldn't* believe him.

The answering giggle from her friend might as well have been a doomsday bell ringing out.

"What?" she demanded sharply.

It took a few seconds for Layla to get control of herself before she replied. "Jared called me and was all like, 'She's mine! Don't let her go to the club with Thad, blah blah blah.' Don't you see? Crazy jealous. We've got to work that until he's so desperate he makes a move."

Little did Layla know about the moves he'd already made and how Felicity had come undone. Her cheeks flamed at the rush of memories.

"I really don't want to do that, okay? I'm not ready for a relationship, and—"

"I know you're busy and you have no time, but you can't let it hold you back. You are missing out on life. As your best friend, I'm not going to let you do that. So get your best dress out and be ready for me and Tanner to pick you up, okay?"

There was no arguing with Layla, she knew that. "Fine."

"Good." Layla hung up.

A split second later her phone rang. Was she going to have a minute alone tonight without Layla hounding her? She answered without looking at the screen. "I said I'd go tonight —you don't have to make me swear it or anything."

"Oh?" Thad's rich voice came through the phone speaker. "That's excellent. You've read my mind."

Even though she expected Thad to call, it was still a shock.

"Um, Mr. Worthington?"

"Please, call me Thad." His chuckle was soft and full of amusement, as though that happened at all the time.

"Sorry. I thought you were someone else when I answered," she explained as she climbed off the couch and headed into the kitchen for a glass of water.

"Ah, that makes sense. Well, I had a nice time at the gallery yesterday, and I wanted to know if you'd like to come out with me tonight. I have a VIP area at Club Amazon downtown."

There it was, the question. How did she answer?

"Oh, well I was actually already going. My friend Layla invited me. I suppose I could meet you there?" She clenched her free hand on her thigh and hoped he'd accept that. It wouldn't be a date, at least not in the normal sense. She wouldn't be betraying Jared. Still, they weren't together, so even a date wouldn't technically be a betrayal. She just didn't want to do that to him.

"All right..." Thad seemed puzzled. "I could pick you up," he suggested.

"That's not necessary. My friend said she was already on her way to get me." Not the truth, but it would have to work. She didn't want Thad anywhere near her apartment. She knew the sort of man he was, the kind she didn't want to have anywhere near her bed. He was trouble. It wasn't that she was afraid he'd force her to do anything; she just had a sense he was a man who would talk a woman right out of her clothes before she realized it. She'd much rather have a man she trusted in her apartment, someone like Jared. Not that Jared would ever be in her apartment again.

"Well, then I'll see you at nine?" Thad asked in that smooth, liquid voice. Strangely it made her miss the way Jared sounded when he talked to her with a whiskey-rough rumble when he was close to kissing her.

"Yeah. See you then." She waited for the line to disconnect, and then she poured herself a glass of water and took a long, slow drink. How was she going to get through tonight?

Jared read through the purchase and sale agreement for the fifth time that evening. There were still a few clauses he needed to tinker with a bit before he sent it off to the seller's counsel. It was crucial that he covered the due diligence and inspection periods and other areas of the contract that would protect Thad's company. Every good real estate lawyer knew that when you represented the buyer, you had to stay on top of the seller and their counsel, and hold their feet to the fire on the contract they signed in order to make sure everything was done.

More times than he could count, Jared had seen ill-drafted purchase agreements dissolve into litigation when sellers abandoned their duties after they'd been paid by the buyers and no longer considered themselves responsible for the property, even though the deal hadn't been fully closed.

The entire afternoon, Jared had worked undisturbed on the agreement. He saved the document on his computer and then shut it down. He spun in his chair to glance over at the horizon and the Chicago skyline. The sun had set, leaving only a ruby-red halo just above the buildings. The evening lights of offices and buildings were starting to wink on in a slow, gradual wave as he watched the view darken. It was beautiful. Funny, he wouldn't have noticed that before.

The last couple of years he had been so focused on his career, so bent on proving himself, that he rarely stopped, and he sure as hell didn't notice sunsets. Before last Friday night, he wouldn't have appreciated what he was seeing now. He wished Felicity was here. She could explain the different colors to him and how some of the famous artists might use their different styles to paint the same view.

God, she was so brilliant, and she didn't even seem to know it. She absorbed information, especially on subjects she loved, and made great use of it to educate others. She also appreciated what she was learning and loved to share her passion when she talked about art. She would be one hell of a curator someday. Jared wished things between them hadn't been so awkward. He'd *never* been awkward with women before. It was probably because he hadn't cared before, hadn't felt as unsure of himself as he did around her. She made him feel like he was fifteen years old asking a girl to dance at a school formal and he had two left feet to dance with. He hadn't been that boy in a long time.

He closed his eyes and rubbed his temples as he recalled what he'd shouted at Layla: *"She's mine!"* He wanted it to be true, yet he already knew enough about Felicity to know she wasn't someone to be owned. How could he make a girl like her fall for him? It was like chasing rainbows. You see them from afar, see the beauty and the colors, but no matter how hard you work to catch them, they always dissolve when you get to where they are supposed to be. He didn't want to be standing there soaked and cold with the passing rains as he waited for the colorful vision to return. It was no way for a man to live.

Even if I can't have her, I still have to protect her. Thad was too serious, too experienced. He'd scare her if she went out with him. Felicity needed a gentle lover, one who would introduce her to the world of passion with the utmost tenderness and respect. She was too innocent, and Thad was attracted to that for all of the wrong reasons.

His phone rang, and Layla's name flashed on the screen. "Yeah?"

"Hey, so Felicity needs a ride. I said I'd pick her up, but I'm running late. You know where she lives. Can you bring her to Club Amazon tonight?"

"No," he answered instantly.

"Fine. I'll hire a cab for her." Layla called his bluff.

"Don't. I'll take her," he snapped.

"Thanks! You better hurry. It's eight thirty."

Jared slid his suit coat sleeve back from his wrist and hissed a curse.

"Shit!" Time had gotten away from him faster than he'd realized. After hanging up on Layla, he shoved the documents back into the file for the hotel and then bolted for the office door.

The cab ride took too damn long. What the hell was he going to say when she opened the door?

Maybe I shouldn't say anything. I can just grab her and kiss her. She can't argue with me or send me away if I'm kissing her, right?

By the time he was striding down the half-lit hall to Felicity's apartment, he was thinking up a hundred ways to talk her into moving out of this building. He was pretty sure he saw a drug deal go down in the lobby before he caught the elevator up to her floor.

God, he had to get her out of this place. It was falling apart and in the worst part of town with bad shit happening all around her. But he couldn't force that, wasn't even sure how to start that conversation. She was probably here because she couldn't afford something better. Pride would prevent her from accepting any help, so he'd have to get creative. He rapped his knuckles on her door and waited.

"Just a sec!" Felicity's call was a bit muffled, but still audible. A second later the door swung open and Felicity stood there, a black pump hanging on her index finger as she bent to slide it on her foot. A silver dress with tiny sequins clung to her curves, glinting softly as she shifted.

"You're late, Layla," she added, then looked up as she secured her shoe on her foot and set it down.

Jared bit back an amused grin as she gave a little gasp and promptly tripped as she tried to retreat from him. He dove forward and caught her.

"I still think you're a bit of a klutz." He couldn't resist

the tease, but he made sure she was steady on her feet before he let her go.

"I was expecting Layla." Felicity's cheeks warmed to a delicate pink. "And I'm only a klutz around you." She muttered this with a furious blush to her cheeks.

"She was the one who called me. *I'm* taking you to Club Amazon."

Her brows rose, and she chewed on her bottom lip. That same hunger he always felt for her spiked in his blood like expensive scotch. What he wouldn't give in that moment to just kiss her and make her forget all about the club and Thad.

"So you're going with me on my date with Thad?" A glimmer of light flashed in her eyes, like a ripple of quicksilver. Was that anger? Interest? Whatever it was vanished so quickly he couldn't read it.

Jared crowded into the room, bristling as he replied, "It's not a date. Thad doesn't date. It's just a night out, for everyone as a *group*." He emphasized the last part, and she narrowed her cute little eyes at him. He didn't want to even start on the fact that she seemed ready to date Thad but not him. That was an argument for another night, one when he had a bottle of bourbon at the ready.

"Okay." She didn't act at all convinced. "I am almost ready to go. Make yourself comfortable." She waved in the direction of her couch. Then she headed for her bedroom.

He noticed the back of her dress was unzipped, giving him a glimpse of that beautiful back. Not a hint of a bra, either. He swallowed a groan as he sat down on the couch to wait. He wasn't exactly dressed for clubbing, but the suit was better than nothing. Club Amazon was a top private venue, and Thad loved to take girls there and impress them with his private room, which cost a small fortune. Unlike Thad, he wasn't really into the club scene. He preferred to put his money into his clothes and his investments.

The club had natural-looking waterfalls, exotic decor, wild colorful plants, and trees built into the space around the dance floors and the private rooms. Each room inside was designed per the patron's specific requests and didn't have to correspond with the jungle theme.

He shifted on the couch, and the heel of his black dress shoe hit something. Bending over, he slid the object out. It was a sketchbook, already open to a drawing. His heart flipped and his mouth went dry as he studied the work. A very provocative piece of a woman stretched out on a fainting couch covered the page. Jared settled the pad on his lap, then angled the sketch for closer inspection. The woman wore a white gown that hung over her curvaceous body. The short chin-length cropped hair was severe, yet exotic. The woman's eyes were outlined with dark lines, making her look Egyptian.

A man was also in the picture, wearing chest armor and a thick sword hanging from his hip. It reminded him of Russell Crowe from *Gladiator*. Only… He peered at the faces of the man and woman. They resembled Felicity and…*him*.

She'd sketched him? Felicity wasn't just interested in art. She was a real artist. With a rapid beat of his heart, he realized that he was holding a piece of Felicity's fantasies in his hands. Like a glimpse of her soul.

And fuck, she's fantasizing about me.

With a guilty glance over his shoulder, he slipped his cell phone out and positioned it above the drawing and snapped a shot of it.

There was something about this sketch—it fascinated him. Like peeking into her soul and catching sight of one of her fantasies. So this was what ran through her head when she daydreamed. He grinned and then tucked the sketchbook back under the couch and pocketed his cell phone. *Role playing*. It hadn't interested him before, but if Felicity was fantasizing about Cleopatra, then he was all for it. He'd start looking for a costume tomorrow. The thought made him chuckle.

The click of heels on wood drew his attention as Felicity came into view in the bathroom. She twisted around, her dress only half-zipped as she attempted to pull her hair up. He was on his feet instantly and moving to stand behind her.

"Leave it down," he murmured in her ear.

She looked at his reflection in the mirror. Her eyes wide, her lips parted as she sucked in a breath. He brushed the coils of her hair over her shoulder and out of the way as he zipped up the back of her dress. The thousands of tiny sequins on the dress reminded him of the luminescent scales of a mermaid's fins. With her auburn hair in long beautiful waves, Felicity could have been the tragic heroine in Hans Christian Andersen's tale. What was it about this woman that had him dwelling on fairy-tale fantasies?

"Thank you," she whispered. A little shiver rippled through her, visible to his eyes. She blinked as she seemed to fight for control over herself. They were both battling themselves and their desire. It was the only consolation his taut body could have in that moment. They would both be suffering until she overcame whatever fear was holding her back.

"You ready?" he asked.

"Uh-huh." She reached for the small red satin clutch purse. His mind flashed to the red panties he'd seen in her gym bag, and he bit the inside of his cheek to keep himself in check. Still, he couldn't resist the temptation of checking out her perfect ass as she walked toward the door. He wanted to get his hands on it—and a lot of other places on her body.

Forbidden. It was all forbidden until she banished her fears. *Be brave.* He silently prayed she'd conquer her demons and let him inside her walls.

CHAPTER ELEVEN

Club Amazon was packed with writhing bodies. Electronic dance music boomed loudly enough that it reverberated inside Felicity's own body. The heady scent of expensive perfumes and the flashing strobe lights were overwhelming. Silver chandeliers hung from the ceiling, with beads glinting from the flashing lights, and surrounding the dance floor were areas with satin couches and bartenders offering drinks in crystal glasses. Everywhere around her was decadence and luxury.

Felicity swallowed hard and took an instinctive step back into Jared's body. His arms wrapped around her from behind as she turned, pressing against him. Startled at her own actions, she tried to recover her control and put distance between them again, but he didn't release her right away. She had to tug herself from his embrace.

"You okay?" His voice reached her ears, even through the shouting of the crowds. She knew that no matter how loud it got, she'd always be able to pick out the sound of his voice in a crowd, and knowing that was frightening. How could he affect her so much that she'd be *too* aware of him?

"Yeah, I just don't like crowds," she confessed.

Jared studied her, then held out his hand. She hesitated, knowing that if she touched him again, it would remind her how much she loved being close to him.

"I don't want you to trip in this place—it's a bit wild," he explained, and curled his fingers in invitation. She took it, her palm fitting perfectly into his.

"Come on, I know where we can go."

He led her to the back of the club where several private areas were cordoned off with glass doors that, when closed, would fog up to give the room privacy. Felicity would have balked if not for the trust she had in Jared. She'd always been a bit panicky in crowds and small spaces, but while Jared was there, holding her hand, she felt safe. He stepped up to the door of a private room and placed his hand on a glassy black panel, glancing back toward her with a wink. A small green light illuminated the pad under his palm, scanning it before the locked clicked. Jared pulled on the handle and it opened.

"Whoa!" she whispered. Her reaction made Jared chuckle.

"Thad doesn't want anyone he doesn't trust to use his VIP suite."

Suite? She'd been expecting a cheesy booth roped off with a velvet cord, not a handprint-accessible, fog-glassed room.

When they stepped inside Felicity gaped. The air inside here was cooler than the heated room of the club, and she instantly relaxed. The room was beautiful. Cobalt-blue wallpaper with a dark-brown wooden base around the room set a seductive mood. Expensive white couches and armchairs were placed throughout the suite to accommodate several people. The ceiling had several modern glass chandeliers that lit the entire room with a seductive glow. At the back of the room, a small bar was waiting for them with bottles of champagne resting in an ice bucket and glasses ready. But it was the art that caught her attention, modern masterpieces that were splashes of vivid color in shapes that reminded her of the jungle themes.

"You made it." Thad stood from a chair on the left side of the room.

Felicity had been so distracted by the room and the art that she hadn't noticed Thad or the woman beside him.

A woman in a ruby-red silk dress that ended mid-thigh rose as well. A little tremor of jealousy passed through Felicity when the blond woman flashed Jared a brilliant, perfect smile. But when Jared merely nodded back at the woman, to Felicity's dismay she felt a ripple of satisfaction that the woman's smile faltered and then faded.

"I was wondering where you were, Jared, but now I'm wondering why you're with my date?" Thad asked the question politely and with a hint of humor, but Felicity heard the edge to his voice.

"She needed a ride," Jared answered slowly, but the answering hard stare he sent his friend's way was unsettling. The air seemed to crackle with sudden animosity.

Thad focused on Felicity, his hazel-green eyes sparkling with curiosity, and yet she glimpsed a tinge of wounded pride behind them.

"I thought you said you were coming with Layla."

"Uh...right." Felicity bit the inside of her cheek before replying. "She had to cancel, so she called Jared, and he just showed up."

Felicity had to step back when Jared and Thad stood almost toe to toe, sizing each other up in that macho way men did sometimes.

The woman in the red dress sighed and rolled her eyes. "Either get over it, guys, or get to measuring."

Measuring? Felicity shot a glance at the woman, and she winked at Felicity and mouthed "male egos" before rolling her eyes again.

Thad was the first to blink, but Felicity knew it wasn't any sort of concession in the silent battle of glares. He smoothed a hand down his dress shirt and then walked around Jared to get to Felicity.

"Come on, let's go dance." He stepped between her and Jared, effectively separating them and forcing Jared to move away. Taking Felicity's red clutch purse, he smacked it into Jared's chest, forcing his friend to take it, and then he grasped Felicity's hand and led her from the room. She nearly balked at the thought of leaving the sanctuary of the room and Jared to go back out into the wild part of the club.

Throwing a glance over her shoulder, she saw Jared follow them to the door of the suite, eyes dark and brows lowered. His lips were pursed in a thin line, and a tic worked in his jaw, but he didn't come after her. Something in her chest clenched, and her eyes burned. She *wanted* him to come after her, but she had pushed him away too often. He wouldn't rescue her. Not this time.

She was supposed to be here with Thad, and she should focus on that.

He curled an arm around her waist as they stepped out onto the dance floor. Beams of light shot around their heads as they started to dance. Thad could really move, with a seductive roll of his hips against hers, and the way he could guide her around to the music, but she couldn't stop thinking about the fact that she'd left Jared and a woman back in the suite.

"Who was that woman in the suite?" She practically had to shout to be heard.

"That's Shana, Jared's old flame. They dated through law school and work together at the firm. It's just a matter of time before they get back together. Everyone knows they'd make a killer lawyer duo if they got married. He's not stupid. His promotion to partner pretty much depends on getting back with Shana since her dad's Jared's boss."

For a second Felicity couldn't breathe. Jared and Shana had been a couple and his promotion to partner depended on his dating Shana? Why hadn't he mentioned that when he'd been declaring at Sabine's that he wanted her? That seemed like something a guy should have mentioned before he demanded she take a chance on him and date him. Her stomach roiled, and she struggled to speak past the nausea.

"She's his ex?" Surely they weren't still an item. He'd never mentioned her before, hadn't said he was still in a relationship. He couldn't have lied about that, not after they'd... No. Jared wasn't that kind of guy. Then again, what did she *really* know of him? He was sexy and charming, but she didn't *know* him. Maybe he was the type of guy to lie about his relationships. But Layla knew him because of Tanner, and she would not have let Felicity get anywhere near a guy who wasn't decent. Why hadn't Layla mentioned Jared's history with Shana?

"They're always on-again, off-again, those two." Thad didn't say anything else, just pulled her out onto the dance floor and settled his hands on her hips.

"But—" She had to know more, but Thad pressed a finger to her lips, silencing her.

"This is *our* date, Felicity. You and me."

He was right. She'd agreed to come here to meet him. Albeit she'd done it because Layla had made her, and she secretly hoped Layla would be right and Jared would be jealous. That hadn't worked out well at all. How did other girls do this? Play the field with men and get them to be jealous and fight for them? She didn't have a clue.

Heck, she hadn't even wanted Jared to be jealous—she

only wanted him to want her. She'd only pushed him away because she had to protect herself.

I can't make up my damn mind. I want him, but I know I can't have him because I can't juggle a relationship and work and school. The thought of trying to do just that made her feel even worse. A headache began to throb just behind her eyes.

Playing games with him wasn't fair to either of them. She just had to let him go, leave him alone. No more listening to Layla and being convinced to do these stupid, selfish things.

Trying to put her concerns aside, she focused on Thad and the way he danced. Her heart rate sped up with each touch, each caress of his hands on her body as they moved to the beat, but the fire beneath her skin simmered rather than erupted the way it did with Jared. Would anyone else ever make her feel the way he did? Was he making Shana feel that way right now? Were they at that moment rekindling their romance in the suite? The beautiful, poised Shana, who seemed to be everything Felicity was not.

Despite Thad's excellent dance moves, Felicity was not enjoying herself. She was miserable. After a couple of songs, Thad seemed to notice his lack of effect on her. They both stopped moving on the dance floor. Panels of light burst through the darkness between them, painting his face with blues and reds, before vanishing and bursting back into existence a few feet behind them. Everywhere there were people moving, laughing, dancing, enjoying themselves. Thad curled one finger under her chin and lifted her face so he could look down at her.

"Come with me—this way." He led her away from the main floor and into an alcove where the noise was muted by the position of the walls.

"Are we done?" Felicity tried not to sound hopeful.

"I guess I am." He sighed, and his little disappointed smile made guilt twinge sharp in her stomach. "You're not having any fun, are you?" He bent his head down a little, not to kiss her as she thought at first, but to get a better look at her face. Like Jared, he was easily a head taller than her. Such a gorgeous man, but not her type—he wasn't Jared.

"I'm sorry. This really isn't my thing." She looked around, taking in the world of life and excitement, the other young men and women having a good time. Unlike her. If she could have been anywhere in that instant, she wanted to be back on Jared's couch, his arms around her, his lips on hers, the quiet sounds of an old movie in the background.

"Why did you agree to come?" he asked. "You didn't have to, you know."

She ducked her head. "I know. Layla said—"

"Layla Russo? Christ, I should have known. Honey, don't ever listen to Layla, okay? If you aren't into a guy, don't agree to go with him. Layla can play the game, but you...you aren't that kind of girl. Understand?"

For some reason his words made her want to cry. She bit her lip and blinked back the burn of tears. Now was not the time to cry. He didn't know her, didn't know what kind of girl she was, but he was right, she wasn't into games and didn't know how to play them.

"You and Jared...are you...?" He made a vague motion of connecting his fingers as though to imply they were together.

"Uh, I really don't know. He and I aren't really, well, we're at different times in our lives. He's got his work, and I've got school, and we just don't...But I want..." *Him.* She couldn't finish the thought aloud.

Thad shook his head, then shot her a wicked grin. "Trust me, honey, if a man wants you, work won't matter."

Work won't matter? Jared was a workaholic, and his job didn't seem the type to give him a spare moment for himself, let alone someone else, just like her.

"I'm sorry this wasn't a fun night for you. I didn't mean to lead you on." She tried to change the subject, and he let her. She could see it in his face, the barely hidden amusement.

"Let's go back to the suite and relax before you go home. I'll find Jared." He looped his fingers through hers and led her away from the alcove.

When they stepped back out onto the dance floor, the wave of sound engulfed them, and it hit her like a passing L-train. Too many people around, too many sounds. Before she'd been so focused on Jared, she hadn't let herself get bothered by the crowds and the lack of air. But now that she was feeling better about Thad and her non-date, that old claustrophobia and fear of crowds kicked in. The music pressed into her skull, the bass thudding at the back of her eyes and the base of her spine. Nausea struck her hard and without warning was quickly followed by a dizzy spell.

"Thad, wait, I need to sit down..." The world tilted wildly around her as she tugged on his hand.

"Hey!" Thad leaped to catch her just as everything went black.

CHAPTER TWELVE

"So…who is she?" Shana asked as Jared continued to pace in the small suite. He didn't want to go outside and see Thad putting his hands on Felicity. It would be too much. He'd lose it.

"What?" He was barely paying attention to anything around him.

"The girl. The one you brought here." Shana's accusatory tone was laced with hurt. That, and nothing else, got his attention. He stopped pacing. His feet were rooted to the expensive white carpet. He was hurting Shana, his ex-girlfriend, his *friend*. This was not who he was. He didn't hurt people.

"Shana, she's…Felicity," he said. There weren't words to describe what she was, and as a lawyer if he was at a loss for words, it meant something.

Shana smoothed her red satin dress and looked away as she eased into one of the chairs by the door. For a long moment, her gaze was distant, seeing things he could not. A rueful smile finally played with the corners of her mouth.

"You're with her?"

"No...yes—I don't know." He flung himself into the chair beside her and raked his hands through his hair, tugging madly at the strands.

"I think you want to be," Shana said as she moved to face him directly.

"Even if I do, it doesn't matter. She's afraid, Shana. Afraid to be with me, afraid of a relationship. I don't know why. She's young, maybe that's it."

Shana frowned, tilting her head, and he knew she wasn't pleased with him. How had he managed to upset the two women in his life he cared about outside of his own family?

"So you let Thad waltz in and steal her while you play it safe? Don't do that. If you do, then you're a coward." She'd buried her own pain and was forcing him to face his own. God, what a friend she was, and he'd done nothing to deserve it. She was always brave for others, never herself.

"I'm not a coward. I won't force her to be with me. Not when she's agreeing to go out with Thad. I think that's an obvious message she's sending, don't you think?" He nearly snarled, but he controlled himself at the last minute.

"Or she's testing you. Women do that sometimes." Shana placed her hand on his arm and made him look at her. "Sometimes a girl wants to know if a man will fight for her. So if you want her bad enough, fight for her." Shana's eyes shimmered, and that flash of pain, so sharp, so clear, was a knife to his own heart.

"Shana..." he whispered.

"Don't." She shook her head. "Just don't, okay? I need a drink." She stood, picked up her purse and coat, and left the suite.

There was no point in going after Shana. She needed him to leave her alone. It was for the best. He'd ruined her night because he was a selfish bastard, and he had no right to push her further. But she was right about Felicity. He couldn't let her push him away, not when it was only her fear of the future that made her hesitant to be with him.

He had to go find Felicity. He abandoned the suite and started pushing his way through the dancers and partiers. He caught a flash of silver, a hint of sequins, and he bolted in the direction he'd seen it. No one else had been wearing a dress like hers.

A booming song took over, and the DJ encouraged the dancers to jump in sync, which made it nearly impossible to see over the bouncing bodies.

Where is she? Panic flashed through him, and he jerked to a halt when the crowd parted and he saw Thad holding Felicity. Was he too late? They were embracing passionately. The sight made his stomach turn. Fury and despair welled up inside him. He needed to get away from them before he did something he'd regret, like deck his best friend in the face when Thad had done nothing wrong. Jared nearly turned to leave, but then he saw Thad glance around, his lips parted and his eyes wide. Thad had never looked like that in all the years he and Jared had been friends. He looked...afraid.

"Thad!" he shouted, and his friend turned his way, relief brightening his eyes.

Felicity went limp, practically dangling from Thad's arms, her head falling back. Jared reacted instantly, shoving bodies aside as he fought to get to them.

"What happened?" he demanded as he reached them. Thad cradled the girl in his arms, but when Jared got close enough, he held Felicity out and Jared took her from him.

"Take her back to the suite. I'm going to call an ambulance." His friend reached for his phone once he was sure that Jared had a secure grip on Felicity. Then he started clearing a path back to his private room as he called 911. Jared shifted his burden in his arms, lifting her up so he held her behind her knees and her back. Her head rolled inward to touch his chest. She was completely unconscious, but breathing. Other than that, he couldn't tell if she was okay or not.

For a second he was rooted to the spot, panicking inside as a thousand terrible thoughts shot through him with a force that almost knocked him flat. What if she wasn't okay? What if…?

No! He snapped himself out of that dark spiral. If he fell apart now, he'd never be man enough to take care of her, and that's what mattered most.

The moment he got her inside the suite, he laid her across the couch and lifted her chin. When he placed two fingers against her throat, her heartbeat was slow but steady beneath his touch. He counted the beats while keeping time on his watch. Slow, but not too slow. That was a small relief.

The suite door flew open, and the burst of noise made him jump, and his entire body grew rigid. It was only Thad, and he took one look at Jared before shutting the door, sealing them off from the sound.

"How is she?" He crouched down by her head, studying her.

"She's breathing. Her heart rate is okay, a little slow. What did you do?" He didn't even try to hide the accusation. Felicity had been his to watch over, but Thad had put her in danger. Jared was only able to tamp down his fury by focusing on the terror that thrashed inside him like a wounded beast.

Thad sighed and ran a hand over his jaw. "We were dancing, talking, and then she just collapsed."

"She didn't drink anything, right?" Jared asked. It wouldn't be the first time some asshole had tried to roofie a girl at a dance club in Chicago.

"No. I wouldn't have let her. You know my rule about

that. It's why I keep bottled water in the suite."

Jared did know. Thad was a player, but he wasn't an asshole.

"I'm going to go wait for the paramedics. You stay with her." Thad left the suite. Jared was flooded with relief that Thad had gone to get help, but being left alone with Felicity and unsure of what to do made him feel helpless...adrift.

"Hurry up, Thad," he muttered.

Jared forced himself to remain calm, but every muscle in him was tense, and a headache thrummed just behind his eyes. She had to wake up. She had to be okay. He would not accept anything else. His heart couldn't take it if anything happened to her.

"Come on, princess, wake up. Let me see those beautiful gray eyes," he pleaded as he   tucked a strand of her hair behind her ear.

As though his words or perhaps his touch awakened something in her, her lips parted and her lashes fluttered. He clung to that small movement like a tiny boat in a vast storm. Fingers digging into the wood of the boat, sucking in breaths between the pounding waves of the sea, he prayed she was okay. That flutter of her lashes was his only hope. She had to be okay.

Two paramedics rushed into the room followed by Thad just as Felicity came fully around.

"Jared..." Her lips formed his name, and he swallowed the lump in his throat as he tried to remain close as the suite filled up with people.

"I'm here, sweetheart. *I'm here*," he promised softly, stroking her cheek.

"Please give us some room," one of the emergency medical staff instructed.

Jared stepped back, allowing the man and woman in the medical jumpsuits to kneel by Felicity. She blinked, then struggled to sit up as she took in the scene. The female paramedic set her bag down and was digging through it for a stethoscope.

"Can you tell us what happened, miss? We received a call that you fainted." The man clicked a small pen flashlight and pointed it at her face. "Follow my finger, please" He moved his index finger back and forth, and Felicity's beautiful eyes tracked it without problems. The man shined the light more fully into her eyes, and she blinked again, turning her face away from the brightness.

"I'm sorry. I sometimes get dizzy in crowds and I can't breathe. One minute I was dancing, and then..." Her shoulders rose and then slumped in a helpless shrug.

When the male paramedic took out a blood pressure cuff, Felicity's gaze locked on Jared's. Another swell of relief moved through him. He hadn't realized until that second how much he needed her to look at him, to show him she was okay. He was stepping in her direction before he even realized his feet were moving. Abruptly, he forced himself to stay back.

"BP is a little elevated." The man removed the cuff from her arm.

"How are you feeling right now?" the woman asked.

"Okay. Just light-headed. It helps when I get away from the crowds." Felicity glanced at Jared again, her gray eyes shadowed with anxiety and her cheeks red with mortification.

Screw it. Jared abandoned his plan to stay back and walked quickly over to the back of the couch and leaned over it to touch her cheek and then stroke her hair. He wanted to say it was to comfort her, but it was more of a comfort to him.

"Do you have episodes like this frequently?" The woman put the stethoscope back and waited for Felicity to answer.

"Not that often. Never so bad before. I think the music

made it worse." Felicity licked her lips, and her hands were clasped together in her lap in a white-knuckled grip. "I usually can get somewhere quiet and get myself together. Not this time, I guess."

The two paramedics got to their feet, and the man reached for her. "We should take you to the hospital and get you checked out by a doctor."

"No!" Felicity lurched up from the couch.

Jared reached over and caught her by the waist. "Easy," he murmured softly in her ear.

She didn't seem to hear him. "No hospitals. I'm fine. Really. I just need to eat something and rest in a quiet place. I'm sorry, I just hate hospitals," she added.

The medical team exchanged looks, but when Thad coughed politely, they looked his way. "I'm sure she'll be fine. I promise we'll watch over her the rest of the night, and if we think she needs medical help, we'll bring her in to the hospital immediately."

Jared could see that the two medical personnel were reluctant to agree, but all it took was a glance at Felicity's terrified face and they didn't press her to go with them.

They packed up their gear and let Thad escort them out. When Jared was alone with her, he came around to the front of the couch and pulled her down to sit beside him. He wrapped his right arm around her body and cupped her face with his other hand.

"Are you really okay? You scared the shit out me, princess."

A weak laugh bubbled forth as she closed her eyes and curled into his embrace. That single act of trust eased the last bit of tension in his muscles.

"I just have these attacks sometimes. Too many people and too much noise usually brings them on."

Jared bristled protectively. "So you decided to go

clubbing? This is the worst place for noise and crowds." He didn't mean to sound admonishing, but he heard it in his voice too late to be stopped. "Why did you come out here, anyway?"

"It's a long, stupid story. I really don't want to talk about it. Can you take me home? *Please?*"

He would have to get the story later, when she didn't have those damned defensive walls up, but not tonight.

"Sure. I'll take you home." He picked up her clutch purse and helped her stand, holding her a little too long against him as she stood. She tried to tug her dress down, but her hands shook. She lifted her face up to his, and he couldn't breathe for a second. He lost himself in the depths of her gray eyes, so dark and heavy with worries and embarrassment.

"I'm so glad you're okay." His voice was a little rough as emotions choked him.

"I—"

Thad entered the suite, silencing whatever she might have said.

"You taking her home?" Thad asked.

Jared nodded. "Yeah. I'll watch over her tonight."

"Good. Let me know if you need anything." Thad took Felicity's hand and kissed the back of her knuckles. "Sorry this night didn't go as planned." His eyes flicked from her to Jared, a flash of knowing in their depths.

"No, *I'm* sorry. I ruined your night. It's my fault," she said. Her pale face was now tinged with a rosy blush.

"Nonsense. Go home and rest so I don't have to worry about you." He patted her hand, and then with a cocky grin he opened the suite door. "The night isn't over for me yet." With a nod at Jared, he walked off toward a group of young women who cooed and shrieked with excitement when they saw him. Thad would be just fine. Too bad Felicity didn't know him like Jared did.

As he led Felicity toward the club exit, she slipped her arm through his, her fingers digging slightly into the fabric of his coat. The simple connection, the reliance she had on him in that moment, filled him with a rush of relief. She wasn't a weak woman, nor was she some damsel who needing rescuing, but she was leaning on him, trusting him to support her when she'd always had to look out for herself in the past. He wouldn't let her down.

She's still mine. The caveman thought was foreign but not unwelcome. Something about Felicity brought out primal urges Jared hadn't thought he was capable of. Urges to claim and protect. His relationships with women before had always been good and the sex hot. With Felicity, though, his every thought, every desire was keyed in to her and what she needed.

Anything she needed, he wanted to be the one to provide it. Pleasure, protection, happiness. He didn't want to think about why that mattered so much. Hell, the idea of wanting and needing this one woman was terrifying. Was that what Felicity felt for him? Was that why she was scared to be with him? If it was, it made perfect sense, and he couldn't be angry with her for running. But perhaps he could convince her that all of this—the two of them—would be worth the risk. It was worth it to him. She made him feel alive, real, and that was worth fighting for.

CHAPTER THIRTEEN

Felicity sighed and dropped her clutch on her bed. What an awful, embarrassing night. She was going to kill Layla for this.

But I was dumb enough to think I could go to a dance club where I knew I'd get stuck in crowds. She had to own up to her own idiocy. She just wished Jared hadn't seen her pass out like that.

She covered her face with her hands. Her fingers were icy from being gloveless in the cold, but they felt good on her flushed face.

Large masculine hands settled on her shoulders, then slid under her collar as they removed her coat.

"Let's get you into bed," Jared murmured, his warm breath fanned over her left cheek. How could he do that? Make her feel so safe and warm and yet desperate for more of what his hot gazes promised? Maybe it was time to stop fighting her desires and just surrender to them?

"Bed?" A little shiver rippled through her, but it wasn't from the cold.

He chuckled. "So you can rest."

Something wild and completely unlike her took over. "No reason you can't join me." She started to turn around, but his hands gripped her waist and held her still. She'd been trying not to think about it for the last few days, but the truth was...she wanted to be with him. She wanted to experience making love, and for the first time in her life, she knew who she wanted to be with. After going out with Thad tonight and failing miserably at a casual date, it was obvious what her choices were. To stay alone...or to be brave and go after what she wanted. *Jared.*

"Felicity, I'm not a saint. Please, don't tempt me, not when I want you as bad as I do." His voice was ragged, a breathless whisper. His fingers dug into her waist a little as he begged.

There it was, that glimmer of hope, that single silver star in her night sky that reassured her that life hadn't sucked her into a black hole. She rested her hands on his wrists and squeezed in response.

"Stay the night. Nothing else has to happen." A silent prayer for more went unheard by him, but the feeling of it rang through her body like a clear bell. If she kept gently nudging him toward sex, she'd get what she wanted.

He laughed, the sound rich with amusement. "Princess, you really don't know a thing about men."

Her breathing quickened with irritation, and she knocked his hands away from her body as she turned on him. Why did he always have to make this about her age? She was twenty-four, she wasn't a child, and it wasn't like he was ancient. He was only thirty—they weren't that far apart in age.

"I may not know a lot, but you don't have to make me feel like a kid," she snapped.

His eyes narrowed, their focus falling to her lips. "I don't you think of you as a kid. Trust me, that's exactly the problem."

"Then why are you being such a jerk?" Her entire body was tense, and her muscles were screaming for some release of the energy that filled her from head to toe.

He stepped closer, their bodies almost touching. "If I don't remind myself to stay away, I'll end up doing things to you I shouldn't, princess, starting on that bed behind you and probably moving on to any other flat surface in the next several hours. You aren't ready for that. Trust me."

"You don't know that—you don't know *me.*" *But I want you to.* She lifted her chin and gazed up at him from beneath her lashes, hoping he'd still want her enough to take a chance on her. He stepped closer, that single decisive action jolting her heartbeat into a wild gallop.

The art of breathing was forgotten. There was only this moment, this connection of gazes. Then he reached out to tip her chin up. She let him, knowing he would see the silent invitation to take something more. Caught between that single feather-light touch and the heavy promise of wild passion in his gaze, she was torn asunder.

Please, Jared. Don't let me shut you out. Make me open up. Fight for me.

"Fuck," he growled and captured her mouth.

The kiss was dark and thick with sensuality. She wrapped her arms around his neck and then squeaked in shock as he lifted her up in the air. She was flying with him, and then they hit the bed and bounced. He covered her body with his, the weight of him enticing and exciting. The small smile on his lips between kisses made her heart jump and skip in her chest. His hands swept up her outer thighs, pushing her dress toward her waist. Her legs clenched together as her body panicked out of sheer instinct.

"Easy," he coaxed as his hands abandoned her thighs and

moved back to her waist, holding her as he plundered her mouth with sweet, intoxicating kisses. Her head spun as the world tilted on its axis, everything around her cartwheeling in dizzying glory until it settled on him.

He paused in his kiss and stared at her, his bold gaze softened by the slight crinkling at the corners of his eyes in a hidden smile.

"Shouldn't we get out of our clothes?" she asked, puzzled. Her body hummed with a delightful daze like bees in summer, dancing from flower to flower. She felt light and ready to fly with the approaching pleasure they'd soon share.

"If we're going to do this, princess, we're going slow and we're going to savor it." A full smile burst on his face as he trailed a fingertip down the bridge of her nose and over her lips. "We have all night."

A mischievous merriment stole through her as she replied, "You did say you could go for hours."

"Minx." He bit her bottom lip and then licked away the sting.

This time her thighs squeezed together to repress the sudden burst of need that swept through her. She was empty and yet parts of her throbbed and burned, demanding things she didn't quite understand, things she had felt only for brief seconds in her life before now.

"Jared, I haven't done this before…" She had to tell him the truth, in case it mattered. It seemed important for him to know, in case she wasn't good in bed.

"You're a virgin?" his brows lifted.

She nodded, her lungs burning as she held her breath. His silence terrified her.

"I'm sorry, I should have told you sooner—" She started to tug her dress down. Apparently they weren't going to make love after all.

"No." His hands cupped her face, and he kissed her

softly, sweetly, almost chastely. "You told me at the right time. I'm glad you said something. This is big, Felicity. As long as you are sure you want this, then I am honored to be your first." He pressed a finger to her lips when she tried to respond. "If you want to stop at any time, you just say it. We don't have to do this tonight, or ever if you don't want to, all right?"

Tears stung her eyes, and she blinked rapidly, feeling so emotional.

"What is it? Talk to me, sweetheart." He wrapped his body around hers, holding her.

"It's you. Why do you have to be so...perfect?" She swallowed down the sob she held back and embraced the happiness that she felt sharing this secret part of herself with him. He was the right man to be with, the right man to do this with tonight. She didn't want to wait. Jared was the right one.

"I've been called many things, but perfect isn't one of them." He laughed, and her body shook with his rumbling response. It made her smile.

"Well, you are to me."

Jared held her, their bodies pressed close, and he met her with a suddenly solemn gaze.

"Thank you, Felicity. For this, for *tonight*, for opening my eyes."

He smoothed his hands over her back, warming her even more. This was all so intimate, full of a myriad of emotions she'd been scared to feel before. Tonight she was letting go of that and embracing this pure joy of being with him and being happy.

"Now can we get out of our clothes?" she asked again.

"Why do I have a feeling your eagerness is going to rush this?" He sat up and pulled her to sit up with him. "Face the wall," he instructed.

She kicked her legs over the side of the bed so she was sitting on the edge with her back to him. His hands grasped her dress zipper, dragging it down. The whirring sound was the only noise in the room apart from their slightly rough breaths. He didn't tug her dress down or try to rush the moment. He simply waited. It heightened the vulnerable, exposed, and blatantly sensual act of waiting for him to undress her. She had to resist the urge to squirm.

"Can we turn off the lights?" She blushed. Something about being totally naked with him in bright light was a little frightening. It might be smarter to ease into all of this.

"Sure." He bent forward to press his lips on the center of her back between her shoulder blades. Sharp shivers of desire shot straight to her clit, and her abdomen clenched. She curled her fingers into the bedding beside her hips as he got up from the bed and flicked off the overhead light. He walked over to the bedside table and turned on the small lamp, which only cut into the dimness with a heavy glow of gold light.

Jared didn't come back to the bed. He removed his jacket and tossed it to the floor, unbuttoned his shirt and removed his tie, then dropped them on top of his clothes. He toed off his shoes and removed his socks. Felicity watched all of this in fascination. His movements were so calm, so controlled, while she sat there, fully dressed and trembling. The man was too beautiful, his bare chest, the rippling muscles, the V-shape half-hidden by his trousers... Her mouth was dry, and she tried to swallow but found it nearly impossible.

"Like what you see?" His mouth kicked up in a playful grin.

"Uh-huh," was the only answer she could get out. This was happening. She was going to *sleep* with Jared. Her heart beat against her chest hard enough that she feared it would shatter her ribs trying to break free.

Jared walked over to stand in front of her, and then he knelt on one knee and reached for her feet. He took off one black pump and then the next, pressing kisses on the inside of her ankles before setting her feet back down.

"You still want to do this, princess? You don't have to." He meant it. She could see that clearly enough. Despite the way his hands trembled as he took her hands in his and the desire that was flaring between them like fourth of July sparklers, he would stop if she asked. He was that kind of man. A good one.

"Yes. I'm sure." She took a deep breath and reached for his waist. She hooked her fingers in the front of his trousers and pulled him closer. Felicity met his eyes as she unbuttoned the waistband of his pants, her hands fumbling with the zipper as the smooth texture of his trousers slipped against the pads of her fingers.

"Better let me do that." He finished unzipping them, and then he shrugged out of his pants. He took a moment to dig through the pockets and pulled out a shiny foil packet before he kicked his trousers away. He held it up with a cocky grin.

"Always be prepared." He chuckled.

"How very Boy Scout of you," she teased before her gaze dropped down to his practically naked body. It stole her breath, how beautiful he was.

He tugged his briefs off, and she stopped feeling stupid altogether. The sight of his erection erased all thoughts she'd just had. He was large, very large. She'd never seen a man naked before, outside of the occasional piece of art or R-rated movie. Curiosity got the better of her, and she was reaching for him before she realized it. When her fingers closed around his length, she marveled at the way it felt silky yet hard.

"Ah," he hissed softly, and his hips jerked in her direction. Her grip loosened, but he took her hand and made her squeeze him again. "That felt so damn good. Don't stop," he encouraged in a ragged whisper.

"You like this?" Her own body was responding to his arousal as wetness dampened her panties.

"Oh, fuck yes," he growled.

Her nipples beaded in response to his gruff utterance. She would never tell him, but she loved it when he lost enough control that he started to curse. There was something incredibly sexy about it. She tightened her grip again and moved her hand, this time down to the base of his cock and then back up. There was a tortured look on his face, but his little growls and groans showed her he liked it.

"Okay, enough teasing me, sweetheart. It's your turn." He removed her hand from his length, and then he reached for her dress, peeling it down to her waist like he was folding down the petals of a flower. Then he urged her to lie back on the bed.

"Lift your hips." After she did that, he slid her dress all the way off.

"Red panties, hell," he muttered at the sight of her red silk underwear before he reached for them and slid them off her body. She hadn't worn a bra, only the panties. Her hands shot to her bare chest as she remembered that, but it was too late. He caught her wrists and pinned them on either side of her head as he climbed between her spread legs on the bed.

"What about my red panties?" The question came out breathless.

He lifted his gaze to hers, a wicked grin on his lips. "I may have snooped through your bag while you were taking your test. I saw a pair of these." He nodded at her underwear. "It made me so fucking hot, princess."

"Really?" She couldn't picture him staring at her panties and getting hot, but...

"Oh yeah," he growled softly. "I was picturing how it would feel to peel them off your legs and drop them on the floor." As he spoke his voice was rough, and his words scraped against her ears in a delicious way that made her nipples harden into tiny points and her belly quiver.

"Are you sure we can't turn off the lamp?" she begged, suddenly terrified. What if he looked down there and she wasn't…oh God. "*Please*, Jared."

"You are beautiful. I'm going to prove just how hot and sexy you are." He released her hands and sat back on his heels as he picked up the condom package from the bed. He bit into the corner and then tore it open.

"You still okay?" He didn't put the condom on yet. She swallowed and nodded.

"Yeah," she admitted.

"Don't worry," he promised, rolling the condom on before he covered her body with his. Somehow, this full-length skin-to-skin contact soothed her. She felt protected by him.

"You looked frightened. I don't want to scare you."

"You don't. You could never scare me." She hoped he heard her unspoken words, that she felt safe with him, no matter what.

"Good. Now lie back, princess."

He kissed her throat, then worked his way down her chest with gentle kisses before he explored the tip of one breast. She gasped and arched her back, shoving her breast more firmly against his lips. He bit the tip, then sucked on it hard. The tug at her breast made sharp, stinging arousal burst to life in her womb and between her thighs. He scraped his jaw over her sensitive nipple. The slight night beard coming in rasped against the nub, and she whimpered in pleasure. By the time he turned his attention to her second breast, she was writhing and panting and clawing at his back.

Jared only smiled. "Just feel me, feel every touch," he murmured. He stroked his hands up and down her body, his fingertips tapping a light melody only he seemed to hear. The touches and teasing taps reached the back of her knees, her inner thighs, moving higher and higher. She felt like the white and black keys of an old piano, being tickled to life with a musician's touch. Right before he reached her sex, he dipped his head down to hers and kissed her.

The consuming kiss was a heady distraction, and she melted into a symphony of breathless moans before she realized his fingers were parting her folds and exploring her entrance. Like a live wire, she jolted to life when he sank one finger into her. Her channel clamped around his finger, and he growled for a second, breaking the kiss.

"God," he hissed. "You're so tight. If you do that while I'm inside you, I'll lose it." His lashes fluttered, and she saw the molten core of his gaze burning through every defensive layer she'd ever built. He was tearing her battlements down, laying siege to her soul.

He sank two fingers into her, then slid them back out before plunging them back in. With little pants, Felicity concentrated on the pleasure, not the alien feel of something pressing into her.

"That's it, sweetheart, get used to it." Then he kissed her again.

At some point in the hazy world of his kisses, she parted her legs farther and he settled deeper into her thighs, only the barest amount of space between them to allow his hands between her thighs. She reached down, trying to find his shaft, wanting to touch it and give him the same enjoyment she was receiving. His hands left her body temporarily as he sheathed himself in the condom.

"You ready?" he asked.

"Yes." She didn't even think what he meant until it was too late to turn back. He withdrew his fingers and replaced them with his cock. The blunt head nudged at her entrance, and when she started to tense, he kissed her again, and that single action made her relax enough.

"Felicity," he whispered her name like a midnight prayer and then thrust deep.

Pain lanced through her, and she gasped. If felt like a knife had just torn part of her open inside.

"Ow," she whimpered into his shoulder and then dug her fingers into his back, hoping she wasn't hurting him. The need to cling to something, to ease her pain, was primal.

"I'm sorry. Just breathe, okay? The worst is over." He held so still, she would have been worried he was the one not breathing if she hadn't been able to feel his chest expand against her aching breasts.

"Kiss me," he said.

It was an easy request, one she happily obliged. For several long seconds, he didn't move inside her. He simply spoke to her in a language of kisses. His entire body was tense with the need to finish what they'd started, and she sensed him holding back his passion until she could adjust to him without pain. Her mouth trembled against his, knowing his care and concern for her—even at this moment—was at the forefront of his mind. It filled her with a sense of awe and... love. How could she not love a man who would do this for her? Thankfully, the pain was nearly gone.

"I think I'm okay now." She nipped his ear, hoping he'd believe her.

His hips jerked in response to her love bite, and his thickness filled her, stretching her. It was a little strange and uncomfortable, and she wriggled her hips. Jared groaned and withdrew. A protest formed on her lips, but it faded as he drove back in, hard. This time there was a frightening amount of wild pleasure that exploded in the back of her head. He did it again, and again, sharp, deep thrusts that slammed them together. Her gasps turned to little shouts of encouragement as he pinned her to the bed and pounded into her until she felt the world drop out from beneath her.

Jared's roar above her was almost distant-sounding as her own pleasure swept her away on clouds. What had happened between them on the couch had been a pale imitation of this. *This*. Sex with Jared. Her thighs quivered, and she clamped her knees around his hips. Sweat dewed upon their bodies, with a slight slickness. He was still on top of her, his body warming hers like a blazing fire in winter. He was staring at her, his eyes wide, his pupils slightly dilated.

"That was—" He licked his lips.

"What?" she prompted, anxious. Surely it had been as mind-blowing for him as it was for her?

A seductive smile tugged at his mouth. "It was fucking amazing." He dropped his head to hers, letting their foreheads touch. "How are you feeling?" he asked as he rubbed one hand on her bare hip, the touch possessive yet impossibly tender.

"A little sore, but good, too." She didn't want any lies or half-truths between them. At least not when it came to something like this.

"I'm sorry. I was rough." He brushed a kiss on her lips, then very slowly lifted his body off hers. When he pulled out of her, she winced from the tenderness of her flesh, and then she flushed as she saw the streaks of red on her thighs and his shaft.

"Stay there," he commanded and went into his bathroom to dispose of the condom.

Felicity propped herself up on her elbows, enjoying the sight of his muscled bare backside. The sound of water running was followed by cabinets opening. When Jared returned, he climbed back into the bed, and before she could protest, he was wiping a cloth wet with warm water between her thighs.

She caught his wrist, startled by his actions. "You don't have to—"

"I want to." He silenced her with a dominating look, one that reminded her that despite his gentleness he was still an alpha male.

With one scorching look, her body flushed, hot and aching, yet at the same time she wanted to curl into him for the safety he promised. She'd never understood girls who clung to their boyfriends, but now? Oh, now she did. There was something about being with a man, knowing he was yours, completely and totally. You could reach out and touch him, have his body wrapped around yours whenever you wanted. It had never been something she wanted before, a man who belonged to her. Yet as she returned Jared's gaze, both of them bare-skinned and as open as two people could be, she wanted him.

He stood and walked back into the bathroom to dispose of the cloth. When he returned, he pulled back the blankets on her bed and got her to climb in.

"You're staying?" She knew it was stupid to ask, but she definitely didn't want him to leave. Was that too clingy? Would it freak him out?

In answer, he slid into bed beside her and pulled her into his embrace. He nuzzled her neck, and then with a low, raspy chuckle, he nibbled her earlobe, which made her womb clench and the sensitive parts of her newly used body quiver and twinge.

"We shared something special tonight, and you think I'm the kind of man who would get up and leave? You wound me, princess." His words were serious, but the lightness of his tone eased her fears.

"You have to stop calling me princess." She nudged his chest with her elbow.

"Nope. It's who you are to me. My walking fantasy." He

pulled the covers higher up around their bodies and puffed up the pillows beneath their heads.

"A walking fantasy?" Felicity queried, wrinkling her nose. How could she be anyone's fantasy? She was—

"Stop. Whatever you're thinking. I can see it on your face. *You* are my fantasy. Well, better than that. You're now a reality in a way I couldn't have imagined. You're sweet, sexy, smart, caring. A guy couldn't ask for more in a woman. Don't think for a second that you aren't perfect or that I don't want you." Jared expelled a slightly frustrated breath. "Hell, I tried to walk away from you, tried to stay out of your life. I lasted a day and a half. That's it." He brushed the backs of his fingers over her cheek. "If that doesn't tell you something about how I feel, then I don't know what else to say."

He was killing her with his sweetness. When she burrowed deeper into Jared's arms, he didn't push her away. Instead, he held her close, shushing her as her body trembled. She didn't want to think about what would happen when they went their separate ways. What if he went back to Shana, his ex? It would make sense. The other woman was beautiful and smart and had so much in common with Jared, not like her. Felicity swallowed thickly and didn't let the tears burning in her eyes escape. He could not see her cry.

"We can make this work. I know we can." His arms tightened around her body, holding her close.

Her tongue was like thick sandpaper, and her throat closed as emotions battled inside her like angry gods, shaking her down to the foundation of her soul.

"I hope so," she whispered.

CHAPTER FOURTEEN

For the first time in years, Jared slept deeply and without dreams. He was warm and comfortable and happy. Work stress didn't intrude on the sweet nothingness. He simply rested. The world could have ended in fiery sonic boom explosions and he wouldn't have stirred. That was what it was like to share a bed with Felicity after making love to her. He was content. Truly, blissfully content.

When he came out of his sleep at last, it was to see the late-morning sun filtering through the blinds on the small window in the bedroom. Everything he'd said the night before, everything he felt came flooding back, and he closed his eyes again. Part of him, a deep part that responded with anxiety to any signs of change, wanted him to bolt from the room and pretend he'd never revealed his weakness, his feelings for the girl in bed next to him. He hadn't held back from her, not a damn thing. It scared him shitless, like he was freefalling without a parachute. But the rush, the adrenaline-spiking, blood-pounding thrill of letting go of his barriers, was an untouchable high.

She was curled in his arms, her hair flowing about her neck and shoulders in a waterfall of color. He propped his head in his hand and watched her sleep. Her dark gold lashes were thick and curled at the ends where they rested on her cheeks. The urge to reach out and touch them was almost irresistible. The moment he gave in to temptation, her eyes opened, and she focused on him. A blush and a shy smile made his heart feel encased in a fuzzy warmth.

"Good morning," he said.

"Good morning," she whispered.

"How are you feeling?" He curled his hand around her shoulder and rubbed his thumb on her silky skin near her collarbone.

Felicity shifted her legs, and her knees bumped into his thighs.

"I'm fine." She started to sit up, but when the covers dropped, it exposed her perfect, tantalizing breasts. Jared cupped one breast before she could retrieve her shield. The little moan she made and the way her lashes fluttered shot his body straight to full arousal.

"You don't have to hide from me." He meant it. Jared wanted to explore her the way a painter learned the surface of his canvas. An intimate acquaintance. A knowledge of secret places. He wanted it all with her.

She bit her lip, indecisive for a long second before she spoke. "I'm so used to hiding. I don't like being the center of attention. I like blending into the background, you know?" Her gray eyes were ancient, the way they spoke silently of her pain and burdens.

Jared sat up and faced her fully. "I get that. I don't like the spotlight myself, but I don't want you to hide from me, just be yourself. I *like* you, Felicity. Every part of you." When she still hesitated, her gaze darting away before returning to him, she reminded him of a skittish animal.

He wrapped his arms around her waist and pulled her onto his lap. Her bare bottom settled over his cock, and he had to ignore the flare of need as his body responded. She settled in his arms and tucked her head beneath his chin.

"Talk to me, sweetheart." He nuzzled her neck, breathing in her scent like it was his own personal drug.

"I've had to work for everything in my life. It hasn't been easy. I used to work double shifts on the weekends, drink tons of caffeine to get through my schoolwork late at night. Nothing's really changed. I'm burning the candle at both ends most days." Her body shuddered, and Jared tightened his grip.

"Your parents can't help out?" he asked.

"No, my mom's a nurse at the local hospital, and my dad is a mechanic. They barely get by as it is. I can't ask them to spare anything for me. They weren't even sure I could survive college—financially, I mean. They tried to talk me out of it."

"Seriously?" The lawyer in him had a thousand questions he wanted to ask, but he knew he had to take it slow. They were building a precarious bridge of trust, and he didn't want to destroy it before he had a chance to cross over. But the thought of her having to go against her parents, who told her not to go to college, made him see red. Sure, not everyone needed a college degree, and certainly not a master's, but if someone wanted it, they should have the right to fight for it. And Felicity had, by working harder than anyone he'd ever known and by earning her scholarship. She was fucking amazing.

Jared rubbed her arms and held her, wishing she'd ask him to help. He didn't know what he could do, but if she asked for anything he'd try his best.

"I'm sorry, Felicity," he murmured and kissed the crown of her hair.

She laughed, but it sounded hollow. "It's not your fault."

"No one should have to work that hard just to get by." He kissed her neck behind her ear and shivered.

"Are you distracting me?" she asked, a breathless giggle escaping her.

With a wicked grin, he nibbled her ear, his own body keying up, his shaft swelling and hardening. God, he needed to be back inside her.

"Is it working?"

"Mmm…yes." She tilted her head back, resting it on his shoulders as she leaned back against his chest. Her breasts thrust out, and he cupped them eagerly. When he tweaked her nipples, she hissed and clawed his thighs as she reacted to the little zings of pleasure/pain he knew he was giving her.

"I was about to ask if you've ever had shower sex, but I know the answer. Want to try it out, or are you too sore from earlier?" He drew a lazy circle on her sensitive clit, and she wriggled.

"What do you think?" she demanded.

"Bossy little thing, aren't you? I'll take that as a yes." He helped her from the bed, and they went into her bathroom. She had a small tub/shower. He cranked the nozzle over to hot, and while they waited for the water to heat up, he pulled Felicity back into his arms to kiss her.

She was his drug. He had an insatiable need to touch her, kiss her, hold her close, and claim her over and over. Part of him knew he was rushing this, but he couldn't stop, couldn't turn back. His desire for her was a raging avalanche of power, an unstoppable force. He embraced it, knowing if he fought it, it would only kill him.

He was so lost in kissing her that he didn't immediately notice the thick steam filling the bathroom.

"Should we get in? My building doesn't get much hot water—we don't want to waste it."

"You don't get enough hot water?" The thought that she had to take cold showers, especially in winter...his fists clenched. That could give her a cold or pneumonia.

"Uh-huh." She blushed, but he knew it didn't have to do with her nakedness.

Jared lunged for her, and she dodged back, laughing. "I'll make sure that your water issue gets fixed."

She studied him solemnly. "You don't have to do that."

"I want to." He picked her up and set her in the shower. "But first I want to get you wet." He shot her his best wolfish grin. "In more ways than one." He climbed into the shower with her.

For a moment, he just stared at her, the way the water hit her creamy skin and beaded in lickable drops. Her arms were wrapped around her stomach as though to protect herself, from what he didn't know. She was so young, so vulnerable and afraid. A newly-made woman, and she was probably scared of him. He barely remembered what it had been like to be twenty-four.

Lucidity crashed in on him and made him feel like a barbarian at the way his cock twitched in anticipation of claiming her in the shower. With her full curves and natural shyness, the way she angled her body slightly away from his sight, it was like looking at a 1940s pinup photo of Rita Hayworth. Most guys didn't know who Rita Hayworth was, but Jared did. He'd found a stack of old magazine photos in his father's closet when he was fourteen. Rita had made him want to grow up real fast. Looking at Felicity now, with her hair in a wild tumble of auburn waves, beads of water dewing on the strands, she was gorgeous. Half-aroused, half-shy, she was a man's perfect fantasy. He was about to fucking lose his mind.

"What?" Felicity asked, and he could see the blush tinge her cheeks.

"You're amazing." He stepped into the shower with her and pulled the curtain closed.

Everything in that moment was perfect. The water rushing over them, the hungry look in her eyes, and the knowledge that she was his right now. He wouldn't think about tomorrow or the future. He reached for the bar of soap and started lathering it over his body before he turned to her. Her eyes widened as he smoothed the soap over her skin and then set it down so he could focus on washing her with his hands. She was still a little reluctant, but she couldn't retreat from him in the small confines of the shower. After a few minutes, the sexual energy between them was too much, and he was lifting her up to pin her against the shower wall. He was ready to thrust into her and relieve them both of the wild wanting when her breathless words broke through his desire.

"What about protection?" Her nails dug into his shoulders, clinging to him, making him half-crazed with need.

"Shit." He dropped her back down onto her feet and scrambled from the shower.

He had just one more condom in his pants pocket. *Just one.* He'd have to restock ASAP. Soap bubbles billowed off him in small puffs, floating away as they popped out of existence, as he left a trail of large wet footprints on the bedroom carpet. After he found his last condom, he skidded back into the bathroom. Felicity was peeping around the edge of the curtain, an impish grin animating her face. He knew he had to look ridiculous, stark naked, bubbles drifting off, him, but she'd soon stop laughing once he got inside her. He'd remind her just how serious he was about her and how much he wanted her.

"Find one?" she asked.

He held up the condom package and tore it open. "Oh yeah, you still ready for me?" Her eyes drifted down from his face to his groin. Yeah, he was still hard, and by the way she reddened and glanced away, he could tell that she noticed. She held the curtain open for him, and he nearly shouted in victory.

Jared stepped back in with her, sheathed himself in the condom, and then focused on Felicity.

"You still all right with this?" He smoothed his hand down over her back and her ass, trying to touch her gently, but his entire body hummed with desire. He'd die if she said no, but he'd find a way to hold back. This was only her second time, and she didn't deserve to be rushed into this. Exploring one's sexuality was a journey to be done safely and with someone you trusted. Felicity needed to trust him, and he needed her to trust him.

"Jared." Her palms flattened on his chest, and she stroked his pecs, lightly raking her nails over his skin. "If we do this…"She held her breath a second before finishing. "I'm terrified. Not of this." She gestured between their bodies before finishing. "I'm scared of relationships. You know I might get a job in LA and have to leave…" She shook her head and then came into his arms willingly. That small gesture lit his entire world like fireworks in the night sky.

"It's because of that you're afraid to get serious." The realization was cold enough that he half expected the hot water hitting his back to turn to ice. A job in Los Angeles? The thought of her leaving turned him ice-cold inside with fear. He could still lose her. She could walk away from him at the end of the year if she got a job on the West Coast.

"Yes. I don't want to talk about it. Let's just focus on us right now." Her whispered words were a plea he couldn't ignore. They could talk about her going to California later.

She lifted her head and kissed his chin, then his mouth, and so on. They were both lost in passion and heat.

This time when he lifted her up and pinned her to the

wall, he had no reason to stop. He thrust into her and she cried out, clinging to him. She was heaven. Hot, wet, tight. The sensation of her taking him inside her body obliterated what rational thoughts he had left. The way she gripped his shaft, her inner muscles clamping down around him as he withdrew, made him groan. Her legs wrapped around his waist, and he was able to piston his hips, ramming deeper and deeper into her.

"That's it, right there," she suddenly cried out in a strangled voice.

He slammed into her at the same angle, hitting that sweet spot over and over again.

"Oh God!" his quiet little artist screamed.

He fucking loved it. He pumped into her a few more times, his control slipping before he shouted and followed her into an explosion of pleasure.

When they both came down from the high, he realized she was shivering. He disposed of the condom, then urged her to stand beneath the hot water. Neither of them spoke for several minutes as they washed each other. Felicity was smiling almost sleepily, and every now and then he noticed her legs quivering unsteadily. His own legs shook each time she smiled at him.

"I missed the vanilla scent after you left," he suddenly confessed, then bit down on his tongue before any more stupid romantic thoughts could escape his mouth.

"What?" Her brows arched a little in confusion.

"The vanilla scent. Your shampoo." He picked up the bottle they'd both used. "I missed it in my shower when you left."

"I like vanilla." She leaned into him, almost conspiratorially. "There was a weekend when I was five. My mom made cookies, and I thought the vanilla would taste good. So she let me try it." Her eyes lit up, and Jared's body burned with warmth and hunger.

"And?" he asked, breathless, holding her waist, feeling her tremble slightly.

"You can imagine what happened. One teaspoon of vanilla extract and I figured out quick it only smelled good. It's stupid, but even now, vanilla reminds me of that weekend, the two of us, having fun." She ran her fingertips along his forearms. The touch was so innocent, but he swore he could feel it through every single cell on his arms.

He wanted to share something of himself, to show her that she could trust him. "I did something like that too. I drank a carton of buttermilk when I was six. I thought it would be awesome. Butter and milk, two of my favorite things. *It wasn't.*" He laughed at the memory and how he'd avoided normal milk for a month.

"Oh, that must have tasted terrible!" Her giggling had him wanting to tickle her and then punish her for laughing at him. Damn it. Now was not the time to be thinking of things like that. Not when he was out of condoms.

"It was bad," he agreed, then gave up resisting and kissed her. She laughed against his mouth until he deepened the kiss, teasing her tongue with his with slow small thrusts between her lips, reminding her of what they'd just done. Only when she was good and limp with desire in his arms did he try conversation again.

"Do you have classes today?" he asked as he shut the water off and reached for two towels. After he helped her get out, he took his time drying her.

"Yeah, what time is it?" A panic-stricken gaze replaced her playfulness.

"Around eight thirty," he guessed. It had been around eight when they'd gotten in the shower.

"I've got classes in half an hour!" She was suddenly scrambling around him, her towel barely covering her as she bent to retrieve her hairdryer from a bottom drawer. Jared sensed that now was not the time to tease her. He backed out of her way and searched for his clothes. They were mostly in one pile, and after a few minutes he was dressed. It was going to be obvious he was wearing yesterday's clothes to work, but at this point he was too happy to care. Hell, he didn't even care that he was an hour late already. He worked long, hard hours as it was. Being a little late today shouldn't matter. He whistled softly, replaying last night and this morning, a silly grin slapped on his face as he waited for Felicity to get ready.

CHAPTER FIFTEEN

Had it really been two hours since she'd left Jared and gone to class? It seemed like only minutes ago he'd had her pressed up against her door, keeping her trapped, kissing her senseless until sanity finally returned to them both and they'd had to part ways.

She closed her eyes for a second, reliving that last sweet kiss. The way his eyes had softened, that warm brown burning into her like embers at the edge of a healthy fire. Banked, barely controlled, yet still dangerous if touched. He was dangerous, so dangerous, and it was too late. She was falling for him—had already fallen for him if she admitted the truth. It had been pure luck she hadn't melted at his feet when he'd smiled and stroked her lips with his fingertips. The man sure knew how to break down a girl's defenses against heartbreak.

What would she do if...*when*...this came to an end? Part of her feared he'd wake from this wondrous dream and go looking for a woman more his style. A woman like Shana, all quiet elegance, rich, educated, his age. Felicity couldn't offer him any of those things. She was just a kid. Hadn't he said that more than once? She certainly felt young, like there were things she couldn't understand simply because she was younger. It was stupid to feel that way, she knew it, but it didn't stop her from feeling like she was inadequate.

Sure, she and Jared were having fun now, but it would end, wouldn't it? If she got the job in Los Angeles, it would have to. That ever-present cloud on the distant horizon made her heart sink.

Felicity flipped idly through the pages of her Impressionist art textbook, only halfway paying attention to the professor as he clicked his remote and changed slides. As her eyes halfheartedly flitted over the painting called *Woman with a Parasol* by Monet, which was projected at the front of the room, she tried to shake off her negative thoughts. She would be an adult about this…relationship, or whatever was developing between her and Jared. She would enjoy it, even if it would have an ending in the future. She would not allow the sudden negative thoughts of endings and partings eat away at all the joy she had when she was with him. Her memories of last night and this morning were something to be cherished, not examined and studied until all the fun was lost through hard analysis.

Something hard and pointy jabbed her in the ribs and she jumped.

Layla was sitting next to her on the aisle. She hadn't been there a few seconds ago.

What the heck?

"Layla? What are you doing here? This isn't your class," she whispered, hoping her professor wouldn't notice the new student among the eighty current students in the lecture hall. Her friend tended to stick out even in the midst of a crowd.

With a casual shrug of her shoulders and a flick of her hair, Layla leaned back in her seat. "It's fine," her friend hissed back. "I'm not missing any classes, so this was the perfect time to talk."

Talk? What does she want to talk about? Felicity stilled, every muscle tensing as anxiety rolled through her. Did Layla know about her and Jared? Had Jared said something to Tanner? Was he bragging about what they'd done? No, he wasn't that kind of guy. In the short time she'd known him, she knew enough of his character to know that. The question was, why did she keep letting herself start to doubt him? He'd given her no reason to.

"Quit freaking out," Layla ordered as she eased back in her chair and studied the slides at the front of the class.

"I'm not freaking out," Felicity retorted.

"Yeah, you are. Your face is all…pinched." Layla made an imitation of someone sucking on a lemon. It wasn't flattering. She leaned toward Felicity. "So Tanner wants to know why Jared didn't come home last night. I told him I'd ask you."

Felicity almost exhaled a sigh of relief. Maybe Layla and Tanner didn't know. It was still her secret. Hers and Jared's.

"Why would I know where he went?"

Layla rolled her eyes. "Because I sent him to your place last night to pick you up for the club. He did show up, didn't he?"

Felicity didn't have to tell her friend anything, did she? Surely this was her private business. Maybe a change of subject was in order. She could pull the rug out from under Layla too.

"Why weren't you at the club? I had an anxiety attack because of the crowds. They called the paramedics. It was mortifying. You said you'd be there and you *weren't*." Felicity only partially regretted her razor-sharp tone.

Her friend's face paled. "You had an attack? Why didn't anyone call me?"

Leave it to Layla to make herself the victim to escape blame. Usually that trick amused Felicity, but at that moment, she wasn't seeing anything funny about what had happened at Club Amazon.

"No one called you because we were too busy. I was unconscious, and Thad and Jared were the ones freaking out."

"Did you go to the hospital?"

Felicity picked up her pen and scribbled a few notes in her notebook, trying to ignore Layla, hoping her friend would get the hint that she didn't want to talk about last night.

"Well?" Layla pressed loudly.

The professor at the front of the class paused in his lecture to glance around the room, and Felicity ducked her head, frantically faking as though she was actually listening to him and not discussing her love life with her best friend. When he started speaking again, she leaned over to Layla to hiss out a response.

"No. I didn't. I talked the paramedics into letting me go home."

Layla's shoulders dropped, and she blew out a breath. "I'm glad you're okay," Layla said, her tone softer as she eyed Felicity in concern. Then she brightened again. "Did Jared go home with you to make sure you were okay?"

"That's none of your business." *Please let class be over so I can get out of here.* Felicity could feel the stares of the other students, their prying gazes and straining ears. This was her private life. Layla had no problems shouting her own issues out in public, but she had no right to do that with Felicity. For the first time since she'd met Layla she was frustrated with her friend. It wasn't a good feeling, but she knew it was justified.

"What's the matter?" Layla nudged her again.

If she'd been a cat, she would have arched her back and hissed.

"Nothing!"

"O-kay…" Layla lifted her hands in surrender.

It felt bad. Like she'd kicked a puppy. Something she'd never done and would never do. It was just…Jared was hers. A secret, something sacred. He belonged just to her. She didn't want to share him, at least not yet.

Layla stayed the entire class, not saying anything, but she sat there next to her, looking pensive. Thankfully, the class ended fifteen minutes after Felicity's outburst. The moment it was over, Felicity gathered her books and crammed them into her bag. Layla followed her but didn't pressure her. Guilt niggled at the back of Felicity's mind. She knew that she was making Layla suffer when her friend hadn't done anything but ask about her and Jared. It just hurt to think about the future when she knew they wouldn't last, and Layla had a way of making her feel anything was possible. She was an eternal optimist.

As they crossed the campus, Felicity halted and faced her friend.

"I'm sorry for being so cranky, Layla."

"No, you were right." Layla raised her hands in surrender. "You don't need to tell me anything, Felicity. It's your business, and if you don't want to share, that's okay. But I'm your friend, and I'm worried about you. I've never seen you on edge like this. And I just need to know that you're okay. Because if he wasn't good to you—if he wasn't Prince Fucking Charming—I will kick his ass." Layla's brown eyes were bright with a vengeful gleam as though she really meant what she said, that protecting her friend was her only motivation.

Felicity's anger deflated, and it was replaced with a bone-deep weariness of years of working too hard and making sacrifices.

"I'm sorry," she apologized, and on impulse she threw

her arms around Layla, hugging her fiercely.

"Don't apologize," her friend sniffed, eyes suddenly watery. "I forget sometimes that you aren't as open to talking about stuff as I am. Just know that I'm here to talk if you ever decide you want to."

Warmth bled between them in that embrace, a melding of two souls linked by friendship. She could trust Layla, could *always* trust Layla. That sudden resurgence of belief in that fact had her wanting to share everything.

"Okay. I'll tell you. First, let's get some lunch. I'm starved."

"Hackney's?" Layla suggested.

"Sounds good," she agreed. The pub had the best sandwiches in the city, but Felicity loved its history as much as its food.

Layla all but skipped as they headed toward the street. "I can't wait to hear all about last night."

And this morning, Felicity thought with a flush of heat. Her entire world had changed. She was tired and sore, and yet she felt absolutely wonderful. It was a feeling she wanted to enjoy since she'd rarely felt so good in her life. Talking with Layla might help her strategize on how to stay feeling good. If she was going to do this, be in a relationship, she needed to be prepared. Especially now that she was having sex, she definitely needed some pointers.

Hackney's was packed with tourists and locals alike, but Layla somehow got a table in the back where it was quieter and a little more secluded. They ordered cheeseburgers, and once their waitress was gone, Layla peeked over the rim of her iced tea as she sipped it.

"Spill," she demanded.

Felicity smoothed her cloth napkin over her lap and began to tell her best friend everything. When she was done, Layla was gaping like a startled goldfish.

"Wow...the shower? So quick? I don't think I tried that until maybe a week after Tanner and I started sleeping together."

"Is that bad?" Did it make her a slut? Panic choked her throat. She didn't want to be loose. It was just so easy to be with Jared. Last night and this morning had been intense, and yet she felt so light and full all at once. There had been so little "thinking" involved. Just passion. Beautiful, mind-blowing passion and tenderness.

A snap of fingers brought Felicity out of her daydreams. Layla's lips were curved in a knowing smile.

"When you're with someone you care about, nothing is bad. Trust me, Tanner and I have done a lot of stuff, in a lot of fun ways." A little giggle escaped Layla, and she actually blushed. "Point is, none of it's bad as long as we're safe and we care about each other."

Her friend was right. She couldn't feel any regret or shame for what she and Jared had done. It was almost sacred, the sharing of their bodies and the baring of their souls. Without words, she'd opened herself up to him in ways she'd never thought she'd be able to do, but she had. And he'd done it right back. There had been such sweet vulnerability in his eyes each time he'd made sure she had wanted to participate, as though he really cared about her and yet wanted her enough that he could barely control himself. A flutter of excitement rippled through her. That's what she wanted, for Jared to lose control and be free with her, because if he could let go, then she could let go, too, and just...live.

She leaned forward on her elbows and pinned Layla with a determined stare. "How do I get a man to lose control? I want Jared to go..." She wasn't sure what the right word was.

"Crazy?" Layla cocked a brow and grinned like a Cheshire cat.

Felicity breathed out, smiling but feeling completely

embarrassed. "Yeah, crazy for me, you know…"

Layla nodded, leaning forward with a conspiratorial grin.

"Now you're talking my language. First we need to get you some lingerie. It's uncomfortable, but once he sees you in it, you won't be in it for long. I know just the place we should go."

"Pimms wants to see you."

Jared glanced up from the purchase and sale agreement paperwork he'd been reviewing to see Sean Chapman, one of the other associates at his firm, filling his doorway.

"He does?" Jared didn't like the sound of that. Pimms was rarely in the office except to parade around and put people in their places. A summons to his office was not something any attorney wanted.

"Yeah, he's in his office. Don't keep him waiting." Sean's smile was forced.

"Thanks, Sean." Jared collected the contract paperwork and set it near his computer before he stood and grabbed his suit jacket. He slipped it around his shoulders, and a hint of vanilla teased his nose.

Felicity.

The memory of their parting heated his blood. They'd had a hard time leaving her apartment. He'd pinned her against the door, keeping her closed inside with him so he could steal more kisses. There wasn't enough time with her, nor enough kisses. She made him insatiable. In a few short hours he would allow himself to text her. He didn't want to be "that guy," the overbearing, obsessive one. But damned if he didn't want to talk to her, to tease her, to see what she was up to. They hadn't had a chance to talk about tonight, but he wanted to see her, maybe cook her dinner. He'd grasp at any excuse to be near her, to touch her. His princess was absolutely fascinating. Between her interesting conversations about history and art, and the way she responded to him with passion and sensual curiosity, he couldn't get enough.

With a little shake of his head, he tried to banish thoughts of her. No work could get finished if he started to think about Felicity more than he was at the moment. He left his office and walked down the hall to the large corner office where Pimms was waiting for him. He rapped his knuckles on the door.

"Come in," a muffled voice called out.

Jared pressed his palm flat on the door and pushed it open. The corner office of Pimms & Associates was a prime piece of real estate. With tall windows, mahogany bookshelves, and a massive desk, it was as close to a kingly throne room as a head partner could get. Pimms was seated in his plush leather office chair, his phone in his hand as he stared at the screen. The man knew how to intimidate with just a look—or even by *not* looking. Jared wasn't intimidated, but the need to earn that partnership had him nodding respectfully at his boss.

"You wanted to see me?" Jared prompted when his boss didn't immediately acknowledge his presence.

Pimms's eyes flicked up from his phone, and he pointed at one of the chairs in front of his desk.

"Have a seat."

Jared slid into the nearest chair. The luxurious office around him was littered with files and large photos of the Chicago skyline at various times of the year. His own office was bare. He'd yet to hang a single thing to claim his space. Maybe he could convince Felicity to find some unique pieces of art to put in his office. Something to remind him of her. A little smile tugged his lips. He didn't need reminding of her. She was always there, like a wash of vibrant colors in the gray landscape of his soul. Like the rising dawn, her warm glow stretched across his body and heart, making it impossible to ignore her.

"Redmond, I understand that you were out with Shana last night?" Pimms's steely stare rooted Jared to the chair he sat in. How was he supposed to respond to that?

"She and I did meet at Club Amazon last night."

His boss's mouth stretched into a smile, which was a little off-putting because Pimms was obviously more comfortable when he was glaring.

"I'm glad to see you're back together. I always had hopes that you and Shana would be a couple again. You understand how easy it would be to give the firm's reins over to you when I retire someday if I knew it stayed in the family?"

What the—

Stunned, Jared didn't know immediately what to say since everything about what Pimms had just said was shocking.

"Shana and I aren't—"

Pimms silenced him. "I would be very pleased to see you two together again. When I'm pleased, people get promoted. And when I'm not happy, well…" Pimms left the threat hanging out there. Jared wasn't stupid. He got the message loud and clear. Date Shana again and he'd get promoted, probably get a nice raise. It was everything he'd wanted and worked for the last couple of years.

"I would prefer to be happy, Redmond. You had better make that happen."

Jared swallowed. Date Shana? He couldn't. It wasn't fair to either of them. But if he didn't, the consequences could be bad. He'd be out looking for another job in a month, and in this market… Everything he had worked so hard for would be obliterated, all because some man decided he had a right to control Jared's life.

"Oh, and Redmond, if you're out late with Shana, I'll permit you being late to the office, but don't make a habit of it." The man winked as though sharing some secret with Jared.

His stomach rolled at the thought. He'd been out with Felicity, not Shana, but Pimms didn't know that. What the hell was he going to do? He couldn't be with Shana. He couldn't let go of Felicity.

"Sir, you mentioned partnership if I retained the Worthingtons as a permanent client?"

Pimms nodded. "I did. But if you and Shana get together, I'm talking about handing you the entire firm, Redmond."

The entire firm…it was a promotion he couldn't even wrap his head around. Did he want to control the entire firm someday? A part of him jumped at the idea of the power and prestige that position would hold—but the cost was too high.

"Er…" Jared didn't know what the hell to say to something like that.

"You may go now. Just think on it, Redmond." Pimms waved him off and then picked up his cell phone again. Jared, for all intents and purposes, was dismissed.

In a daze, he got up and left his boss's office. He bumped into Shana, who had just come out of her own office.

"Hey," she greeted warmly, her eyes skating over his face. When he didn't return her greeting, she paled. "You were talking to my dad?"

He nodded grimly.

"We have to talk." He gripped her arm and led her to the supply closet down the hallway. He shoved her inside, flicked on the light, and shut the door.

"What the heck, Jared?" Shana crossed her arms over her

chest.

"Your father thinks we're together again. He found out we went to Club Amazon last night," he said through gritted teeth.

Shana's eyes widened. "Shit. That's my fault. Mom found out I was going to the club. I mentioned you and Thad. She must have told dad, and he jumped to conclusions." She closed her eyes and sighed. "I'm sorry, Jared. I know we're both on the same page about our relationship—or the lack of one."

"It's worse than that," Jared confessed and raked his hands through his hair, pulling on the strands.

"What do you mean?"

"He threatened me. If we're together, I get promoted. If we aren't, I might be job hunting." The last few words came out a low growl.

Shana paled. "No, he couldn't—he wouldn't." She shook her head and turned a little away from him as though she didn't want to face the truth.

Jared's laugh was empty. "Oh, trust me, he did."

"What are we going to do?" she asked.

"How the hell am I supposed to know?" He tried to shake the building tension in his shoulders, but he failed. Every part of him was coiled tight, ready to snap.

"Maybe I could talk to him. Tell him I like someone else," Shana offered.

He leaned back against the cabinets in the closet. "He wants us to be together. Unless you can figure out a way to convince him otherwise, he'll be planning our wedding in a month. I can't do this. I...I think I'm in love with someone else, and I can't give her up."

Shana nodded, seeming not at all surprised. "It's the girl from the club, isn't it?"

He met her gaze. "Yeah. She and I... It's hard to

explain."

"Love shouldn't be hard to explain." Shana smiled, that awful sadness there, like icy rain in the spring.

He shook his head. "How can I fall in love with someone this fast?"

Shana touched his arm gently. "Sometimes it happens in an instant. Trust me, I know." That sadness still lingered there in her eyes, and it made his own heart throb in sympathy. She didn't mean she loved him, but there had been someone once who had made her feel that way.

"Maybe it's just lust. I don't know how to tell," he admitted.

"If you can't picture a happy life without her, that's your answer."

A life without Felicity—he didn't want to think about that at all.

"We have to do something," Jared said. "I just wish I knew what. Let me think on it."

He wasn't going to give Felicity up, not even if it cost him everything. She was worth fighting for. Shana was right.

Love wasn't hard to explain. Love was love, and if you loved someone, you did everything in your power to keep them.

CHAPTER SIXTEEN

"I can't wear this." Felicity stared at her reflection in the changing room mirror, eyes wide. She wore a filmy black babydoll top with bikini underwear bottoms.

"Let me see." Layla's voice came from the other side of the door.

"No!" she responded instantly. "I'm practically *naked* in this thing!"

A soft giggle echoed inches away. "That's kind of the idea."

Plucking at the lacy hem of the top, Felicity studied herself in the mirror again and swayed her hips experimentally, just to watch the way the fabric swayed. It was loose, and she liked that. Even though the fabric was sheer, the loose feel of it didn't make her as uncomfortable as she thought it might be.

The bra part that cupped her breasts was transparent enough to show the dim outline of her nipples. What would Jared think if he saw her in this? Would he want to tear it off?

The idea made her nipples pebble into hard points, and she hastily scrambled out of the bikini bottoms and slid the top off. It was too exciting and too strange. She'd never worn anything like that before.

"Well? What are you going to do? You tried on half the store. Didn't you see at least one thing you liked?" She and Layla had been shopping for the better part of an hour, but it felt like a hundred years.

Layla was right. A large pile of discarded items lay in the corner of the changing room. Half of the things she couldn't even figure out how to put on, and some of them were complicated enough that she'd needed instructions to know where to put her arms and legs. Most of them were small enough that if she crumpled them up she could close her fist around the fabric completely and not see a single piece of it outside of the clasp of her hand.

For a girl with curves, she sure as heck wasn't wearing anything that revealing. The last thing she wanted was to highlight her fuller figure. It wasn't that she didn't like her body—she did. It was just that...well, she was so new to this whole sexy thing that she wasn't comfortable with that new side of herself. Easing into it seemed the best approach.

"Pick one thing. Just one."

"None of these really feel like me," she admitted as she got dressed. Felicity welcomed the comforting feel of her jeans and sweater and, more importantly, the concealing sensible bra and underwear.

When she opened the door, Layla was waiting, a patient expression softening her usually intense features.

"Sometimes you don't know what feels like you until you try it once. Besides, you don't wear this kind of stuff all the time. You wear it for one night, and twenty bucks says Jared will be ripping it off you as soon as he can get his hands on you. It's part of the game. You get to spice it up for the guy.

Remind him how lucky he is to be with you." Layla picked up the babydoll outfit and handed it to her.

"Buy this one. It's sexy, but conservative enough to be a first try."

Felicity had to admit Layla was right. The other outfits had been...well, she couldn't buy those. But this one—it covered her, but also revealed a lot. It would have to do.

"Now, we need black heels. Ones with something provocative on the back," Layla explained as they walked over to the sales desk and Felicity set her chosen lingerie on the counter and put her prepaid debit card on top.

"Heels? I have black heels." She thought of the standard pumps she'd worn to Club Amazon the night before.

"No, no, no. Those are fine for parties and stuff. For seduction, you need something else entirely." Her friend shuffled the multiple shopping bags on her arms.

"Layla, I swear, sometimes it's like your speak another language." Felicity groaned as she collected her small red bag with the babydoll outfit and tramped after her friend. A shoe store was just across the way in the mall.

"This will do." Layla swept her hair over her shoulder and marched into the shoe store like a commanding general. Shopping was serious to her, maybe a little too serious.

They approached a display of sexy black heels. All of them had something interesting at the back part of the heels: bows, spikes, glitter, different- colored fabric like leopard print. She reached out and touched one finger to a pair that had small spikes jutting off the back.

"Ouch!" She pulled her finger back after it got pricked by one of the sharp points.

"No. Not those." Layla studied them seriously. "Once a guy throws your legs over his shoulders, you don't want to stop him, unless he's into pain." Layla glanced at her. "Jared's not into that, right?"

"Huh?" Felicity then realized what her best friend was asking. "Uh, no. At least I don't think so..." She thought back to the way they'd made love. No, he wasn't into pain, at least not on his end. He hadn't seemed to want to hurt her, either. But they'd only had sex twice, which wasn't enough to gauge someone's deeper desires.

"What is it?" Layla picked up on her hesitation.

"He takes control a little. Pins me down and holds my wrists." She flushed with mortification. Maybe she shouldn't have said that.

"Oh." Layla laughed. "A bit dominant? Do you like it when he does that?"

Felicity bit her lip and nodded. "It makes me..." She paused. "I can't explain it. I just go blank inside, in a good way. I don't think or worry, I just feel everything when he takes over, and it's so hot."

Her friend smiled. "I get that way too. Tanner is playful, but every now and then he gets into this darker side. Not bad dark, just like alpha male caveman dark. Like when I get mouthy, he'll, you know..." Layla glanced around to make sure no one was close enough to hear her. "He'll spank me. Totally hot even though it sounds crazy."

Normally the idea of anyone being hit would have sent Felicity into a spiral of panic, but she knew what Layla meant. A sensual punishment seemed different. Her body certainly reacted to it differently. The idea of Jared smacking her ass with his hand? A little shiver of longing racked her.

What's wrong with me? She wanted him to do things to her that would have shamed and embarrassed her a week ago.

"Ah, here's what we need." Layla pointed to a pair of black velvet pumps. On the back of each heel was a red satin bow. The flash of rich scarlet was sexy and provocative.

"Wow." Felicity had to admit there was something sensual about the shoes.

"I know, right? Now imagine those if you wore thigh-high hose with seams down the back of your legs that pointed toward the bows. Jared wouldn't stand a chance."

"How much are they?" she asked. Her budget had barely afforded the lingerie. There was a high probability she couldn't afford these shoes. Her heart sank to the pit of her stomach as Layla flipped the nearest shoe over and winced when they both looked at the price tag.

She and her friend stared longingly at the shoes, and then Layla gave a little whooping cry of triumph.

"You know what? I never got you a birthday present." Layla waved over a sales clerk. "Size eight, please."

Felicity placed her hand over Layla's and tried to get her to put the shoe down. "Layla, no! They're too expensive! You can't do that!"

"Yeah, I can." They struggled silently before Layla smacked Felicity's wrist and then with a whoop of victory dashed away toward the sales clerk, shoving her credit card in the poor girl's face. "Ring them up!"

"Damn it," Felicity muttered. There was nothing worse than feeling that you owed somebody something. She'd never liked it, and owing a friend felt somehow worse because she knew this particular friend would never let her make it up to her.

"Give it up, Hart," Layla taunted as she signed the receipt. "I will always out-shop you." She waggled her fingertips with a gleeful cackle of a laugh.

"I'll pay you back," Felicity threatened.

"Nope. Not happening. I won't take a dime from you. You can repay me by sexing the hell out of that workaholic boyfriend of yours."

The sales clerk, a girl their age, snorted as she tried to restrain her smile. Felicity found she was grinning too. Layla was just too damn irresistible, even to total strangers. After they were done with the shoes, her friend dragged her to a department store in search of hose. Half an hour later they were back on campus, finishing the day's classes.

Her phone buzzed in her pocket at exactly five o'clock when her last professor of the day had turned off his PowerPoint presentation and dismissed the class. She stuffed her books into her bag and pulled her phone out.

One new message.

Jared: *Dinner, my place, 6:30. I'll send a cab for you.*

Not a question. He just informed her of his plans. She found that both irritating and delightful. The man knew what he wanted, and she inwardly squealed with joy at the thought that he wanted her. She hastily typed a reply, unable to resist the urge to tease him.

Felicity: *And if I have homework?*

She was dying to see how he'd react to that. There really was a mountain of reading with her name on it.

Jared: *Bring it over. I'll cook while you read. Pack an overnight bag.*

He cooked? Was that possible? Could he be any more perfect? There was just one flaw in his plan. She wouldn't be able to concentrate if she was near him. Especially now that she'd bought the lingerie and those heels. All she could think about was putting them on and enjoying the look on his face.

Felicity: *Okay. I'll be there soon. Have to stop at my place first.*

There were clothes to pack and textbooks that she had to get before she could head over to Jared's, even though her entire body was already keyed up and almost vibrating with the need to see him.

He had changed her—or rather, wanting to be with him had made her change. She was braver, more outgoing because she wanted to be with him. In a few short days, knowing him, feeling for him, she'd started to overcome years of being that girl who hid from the world by burying her nose in her books and working. Now she was the girl who was trying on lingerie and giggling with her friend about how to seduce a man with sexy shoes.

Felicity drew in a deep, measured breath and then went to pack an overnight bag. She tucked the sexy heels and babydoll with the hose in her bag, along with her black trench coat. She'd save it for tonight, after studying and dinner. She paused when she packed her toiletries and then with nervousness and excitement tucked the new small circular disc of birth control pills into her bag. Layla had helped her get in to see a doctor this afternoon and to get a prescription picked up after class. It was a good thing to be prepared, and this way they wouldn't have to worry about condoms.

Once Felicity's bag was packed with clothes, her shower kit, and her homework, she locked her apartment and headed to the street to find the cab Jared had sent for her. Tonight shouldn't have to be about school or work. It was about her and Jared and figuring out what they meant to each other. That was what was important. Was she with him? Not with him? Were they exclusive? Could she even ask him about that? And what would they do about the future when she was ready to graduate?

God, what am I doing?

She covered her face in her hands as she waited for the taxi to get to Jared's apartment building. The simple, animal instinct to bury her face in her palms and hide from the world was so strong. But she dropped her hands when the car stopped in front of Jared's place. She didn't have to hide. Jared had shown her in their short time together that she never had to hide from him. He didn't want her to. That thought alone had her getting out of the cab, her overnight bag and backpack slung over her shoulders. This was an adventure—that was how she needed to view being with

Jared.

The security guard nodded at her warmly. "Ms. Hart. Nice to see you."

When she froze, startled, the man held his hands up apologetically. "Mr. Redmond said to expect you. I noticed you coming and going a few times. He wanted to make sure I know to let you in since you don't have an after-hours security card."

He was having the doorman watch out for her? That made her feel...*special*. The thought that he was treating her as special made her heart flip over in her chest. They were rushing into this, but she didn't want to stop.

"Uh, thanks." She smiled at the guard and headed over to the set of sleek silver elevators. This world—Jared's world —was so different from hers. He was all vacation homes in Colorado and the Bahamas. And she'd grown up in a one-story two-bedroom house in a town that had less than a hundred thousand people in it. Now she was renting a shoebox-size apartment on the bad side of Chi-town.

When she reached Jared's rooms, she thrust her shoulders back and swallowed the little flutters of nervousness back down. She rapped her knuckles on the door and waited. Within a few seconds the door opened and there he stood. Still in his expensive suit. His jacket was gone, sleeves rolled up, tie loosened, and hair falling across his eyes as he brushed it away with a flick of his hand. Temptation, seductive, wonderful, irresistible. Her heart clenched, and she smiled as a swell of pure joy hit her at the sight of him.

God, I'm so screwed...

CHAPTER SEVENTEEN

"Hey." He grinned, the expression so perfect. It was as though he'd been made for smiling. Sure, it felt like a cliché, but it was true. Smiles on Jared's face lit his eyes and made him twinkle. Not to mention it made Felicity go boneless with warmth and joy just to see him happy, even more so when it felt like he was smiling because she was here.

"Hi." She shifted on her feet, still a little unsure of this whole situation. What if this whole lingerie thing didn't work? Maybe she should stick to just dinner and not worry about seduction.

"Let me get that." He reached out and slid her overnight bag off her shoulder before she could react and set it down by the door. And then he was curling his hand around her now-empty fingers and tugging her toward him. He maneuvered her to collide with his body as he pushed against her, using their bodies to close the door so fast that her head spun and arousal shot through her like wildfire.

He closed the door and then crowded her against it.

Their bodies were pressed so close together that they fit perfectly, like two halves coming together. He nuzzled her neck and then kissed her lips, slowly, sweetly, holding her close. His roaming, exploring hands were gentle, but seductive in their caresses, making her squirm for more. Felicity shivered at the wonderful feeling of arousal and security—she felt both when she was with him. She curled her arms around his neck, arching into him.

"After a long day, seeing you made it worth it," he whispered. "You look good enough to eat," he murmured in her ear as his hands roamed down her back and over her ass. He lifted her up and pinned her against the door. A bolt of heat shot straight to her clit, and she moaned at the feel of him pressing his body against hers.

"Good enough to eat?" She laughed softly and kissed him back. *God, the man was perfect. Forget homework and dinner—I want to go straight to the bedroom.*

Another teasing kiss, a duel of tongues, and she was set back on her feet. He made a soft moan of disappointment. "Fuck, letting go of you is practically impossible, but if I don't stop now, we'll end up in bed, with me making love to you for days."

Her legs shook at the thought. "Would that be so bad?" she asked.

His wry chuckle made her smile. "It would be fucking incredible, but I made a promise not to derail you from your studies."

The heated gaze that traveled the length of her body told her he wanted her to skip the homework. But they both knew that figuring out how to work around problems like these was the only way they'd get to be together. If his work or her studies were compromised, it would destroy everything.

"Right." She sighed and skirted around him and walked over to her bag and retrieved her books. He left her alone so she could settle on his couch. Even though she had to focus on her reading, she didn't want to be too far away from him.

He walked toward the kitchen and started putting steaks in a searing pan.

The apartment was quiet—too quiet. "Where's Tanner and Layla?" She noticed her friend's absence by the silence and stillness in the apartment.

"They're staying at a hotel tonight, my treat, so we'd have some privacy." Jared leaned around the open fridge door as he spoke, grinning wolfishly, waggling his brows. "I wanted you all to myself tonight."

Her face heated and she glanced away, afraid of revealing too much of how she wanted to be alone with him. It would be so easy to get carried away and forget all about the books in her lap.

Focus, stupid, focus. You can think about the hot guy making you dinner later.

She flipped open the top book to the chapter she needed to read.

Over the next hour, she pored over her books, working through the chapters and taking detailed notes. Nothing distracted her, not even the occasional noises from the kitchen. Finally it all went quiet, and she was done with her assigned readings. She tucked the books back in her bag and looked around the room. The lamps near the couch were now on, and night had taken over outside. The dining room table was set for two, and two plates of food were set out along with two glasses of red wine. Jared was seated in one chair, his feet propped up on the chair next to him, lounging back, completely at ease. In one hand he held an old, worn paperback book. From where she sat she could just see the cover, which read *Tales of the North* by Jack London. As though sensing her focus, his eyes lifted from the page and she stilled. Their dark warm depths were hot and compelling, almost magnetic. Her pulse beat to life, and she bit her lip.

"Dinner's ready." The way he said it sounded like he meant something else entirely, something more sinful.

Felicity swallowed hard and got up from the couch. She was torn between the desire to hide and to run to him. How did he have such power over her? The ability to confuse her? She was frightened of how much she was starting to feel for him, but there was no turning back. Like a drug, he was addictive, and she couldn't walk away.

He rose from his chair and pulled out the seat next to him. When she sat down, he pushed her in, ever the gentleman. Then he took his seat again.

"Steak, grilled asparagus, and mashed potatoes. I hope you like it." The flicker of hesitation, of worry in his eyes, punched her in the gut.

"It looks and smells amazing." And it did. The scent of spices coming off her plate was mouthwatering.

"Good. I had to have Angelo walk me through the preparation. I don't usually cook." His admission had her smiling. "What?" he asked, seeming to notice that she was grinning at him.

"So you aren't perfect after all?" She couldn't resist teasing him.

"No. I rarely have occasion to cook. I can grill, but nothing special. This tonight is a first for me." The look of pride in his eyes melted her heart.

Felicity giggled, then tried to stop. "So...you gave me your cooking virginity? Sounds like a fair trade." She winked at him. The incredulous look on his face had her bursting with laughter.

"You're going to pay for that later...in bed," he promised with a dark smile that lit her inside with throbbing arousal.

"I'd be fine with that." The saucy, breathless reply was so unexpected from her, but it was completely true. She would be fine with that. She craved him, desired to be with him, especially in bed.

"Hush up and eat before I skip dinner and head straight to dessert." He licked his lips, and Felicity was sucked into a fantasy of him shoving all the dishes off the table and spreading her out instead. Her body heated, and she felt a little dizzy with sensual hunger. Maybe they could just skip to dessert… She dropped her fork. The loud clatter of silverware on ceramic jolted her back to awareness, and she focused on her food. The first bite was fantastic, almost orgasmic in her mouth, just as she expected it to be.

"It is perfect," she told him. The smug look of triumph on his face was strangely endearing, as though it was one more insecurity he'd conquered. The man didn't have many.

"So, did you get all your work done?" he asked.

"Yeah. I did. The rest of the week, I'm done for reading. I usually try to get them finished early on so I can focus on working at Sabine's over the weekend." She nibbled a piece of asparagus. He'd lightly spiced it with salt and pepper and sautéed it in butter. Simple but delicious.

"Good. I thought we could finish the movie we started last time," he said. No sex? She tried not to let her disappointment show. Maybe he was trying to take it slow? They were a little too late for that. She'd just have to use that babydoll and heels to convince him otherwise.

"So what about you? How was work?" It felt a little silly to ask. She might as well have just inquired about the weather.

A flicker of shadows trespassed across his eyes for an instant before it vanished.

"I worked on the purchase and sale agreement for Thad's new hotel. There are some issues from the other side's counsel."

"Issues?"

He chuckled and leaned back in his chair. "Oh yeah. When you buy and sell real estate, there's a lot of posturing and bluffing. Mostly on the seller's end."

Felicity slid to the edge of her seat and continued to eat and listen. "Such as what?"

His brows rose. "You really want to know?"

She actually did. He was interested in his job, and what interested him interested her. She wanted to see him filled with passion, and real estate transactions were his passions.

"Okay, well, for example, there's this thing called due diligence." Jared cut a piece of his steak, looking pensive, but also amused at her new interest.

"What's that?"

"Well, when you want to buy a property, you need to check it out before you sign on the dotted line. In case there are issues in the building that could cost your client in the future. Like mold or broken appliances or structural issues."

Felicity nodded. "It makes sense. You want to buy something without problems."

His brown eyes burned like sienna fire as excitement lit him up from within. "Exactly. When you buy something, it's always on an as-is basis." He inched his chair closer as the natural teacher in him took over. "But as a buyer, you want to make sure you don't get screwed. The due diligence period gives the buyer time to escape out of everything and figure out what might be problematic. Then it's my job to work it into the contract and try to get prices reduced or get the seller to fix the items before closing the deal. Since the hotel Thad and his father are buying is old, it's really important for them to have a longer period of due diligence. That's what I've been haggling about with the seller's counsel. Extending that period of due diligence." He finished his wine and stood up as he collected the dishes.

Felicity sat back and admired the sight of him as he put

dishes in the dishwasher. He was so smart, so passionate about his work—it was no wonder Thad and his father wanted him as their attorney.

"Are your parents lawyers? Is that where you get your passion?" She left the table and joined him in the kitchen, finishing her glass of wine. She was ready to put Operation Seduction into motion. That was what Layla had called it, anyway. Felicity nearly smiled.

"My parents, lawyers?" Jared's laugh caught her attention. He walked over to her and pinned her against the counter next to the fridge.

"So not lawyers, then," she answered. He stroked a fingertip down her chin, over her throat, then traced the shape of her collarbones where they were exposed beneath her boatneck sweater. Heat blossomed wherever his lightly questing fingertip traveled.

"Mom's in real estate, and Dad's a private wealth manager. What about your parents?"

Oh no, she wasn't going there. He didn't need to know how far apart their worlds really were. It was too embarrassing.

"Hey, princess, focus on me." His tone was a little more commanding, and it pulled her out of the creeping darkness of the past. "Share something with me. We're building trust. You can do it. Just one detail." His hand circled her throat, the possessive hold oddly comforting, not frightening.

What could she share of herself?

"My favorite color is red," she tried.

He blew out a little huff, half frustration, half amusement. "What shade of red? I know you're an artist, so what shade of red?"

She considered the question seriously. He was right. There was a multitude of reds, countless subtle changes in the tone of the color.

"A red that's somewhere between burgundy and black cherry." It was as close as she could get to describing the shade she meant.

"Sounds nice. I like red, too. More like pale pink, like your lips." This last bit was murmured as he slowly lowered his head and kissed her.

His tongue teased the seam of her mouth, enticing her to open, and she surrendered. He moaned softly against her lips right before he deepened the kiss. His hands spanned her waist, holding her to him as he explored her. It was far more innocent than some of his other kisses, but at the same time, she'd never felt more aware of his strength and the physical power he held over her—not to force her, but to seduce her.

The world began to spin a little, and Felicity clutched at Jared's shoulders, clinging to him. When he separated their mouths, she actually whimpered at the loss.

"How about that movie?" He tugged at the tie at his throat, his face flushed as he stepped away from her.

What? Her inner self was just as dazed as she was. Her entire body hummed with unfulfilled desires and longing, and he was just going to watch a movie? *No. Hell no.*

"Why don't you get changed into something comfortable, and I'll get the movie cued up," Jared suggested, the tone of his voice almost brotherly. Was he trying to piss her off? A guy didn't just give her mind-blowing sex and then put that part of their relationship on ice. If he hadn't just kissed her like that she might have given up, but he wanted her. She knew that now.

"Okay." She walked a little unsteadily out of the kitchen and grabbed her overnight bag.

Operation Seduction was a go.

CHAPTER EIGHTEEN

Jared practically sprinted to the kitchen to grab another glass of wine when Felicity left to go change. He spilled the Bordeaux on the counter in his haste to fill his glass. His princess was going to kill him. He wanted to go fast, to rush headlong into this thing between them. But Felicity was fragile, and she deserved a slow courtship. Movies, dinner, sweet kisses. Not the wild, hungry ravishing his entire body wanted to give hers.

With everything that had happened at work with Pimms, he was feeling caged and threatened. He just wanted to do his job and not worry about the fact that said job hinged on whether or not he was dating the boss's daughter. Which he wasn't, and he had no plans whatsoever to do so. Felicity was his girl, and he didn't want anyone else. Thank God for his princess. She made him forget work. Kissing her, talking with her, just looking at her, soothed the tightness in his chest.

I'm becoming too damn sentimental. We'll just watch the movie, and I'll hold her in my arms tonight.

He gulped down his second glass of wine and rinsed the

glass. Then he walked over to the entertainment center and knelt on one knee by the DVD player. He was just cueing up the movie when movement in the corner of his eye caught his attention and he turned.

Holy shit... His mind went blank at the sight of Felicity in a black trench coat, high heels, and black hose.

"Felicity, sweetheart." His voice came out hoarse. "What are you—"

She flung the trench coat open, dropped it to the ground, and then did a slow turn in a circle, hands on her luscious hips.

Holy fuck. She was a damn sex goddess. All curves, lace, and heels. He used to fantasize about women dressed like that, but he never thought he'd get to experience it for real. She looked adorable...and yet completely seductive, ready for a long, hard tumble between the sheets. That's what he wanted—to grab her, fist a hand in her hair, and drive into her until they both couldn't walk. His cock swelled against the press of his pants as he stared at her, his mouth dry. He couldn't stop from licking his lips and imagining all the places he was going to run his tongue along her skin.

Screw the movies, screw the dinner. They were going straight to bed tonight, and he was going to punish her for forcing his hand when he wanted to take things slow. Yeah, he'd punish her all night until she thought she'd die from pleasure.

Jared looked...mad. Why did he look mad?

Felicity had been so confident a few minutes before when she'd been stripping out of her clothes. As she'd donned the babydoll nightie and the hose and slipped into the heels, she'd thought for sure this night was going to be amazing. He was going to go crazy for this, right? Her own skin had flushed at the thought of a hungry, hot Jared possessing her, but instead he looked angry.

Felicity's hands dropped from her hips and she covered her chest, shying away as he stood from his crouched position by the TV and studied her. Maybe this was a mistake. It had been a risk wearing something like this at all. Her breasts were almost falling out of the top, and the hose and shoes looked too…well…maybe they were overkill? God, this was really stupid. These things only worked for girls in movies.

"I'm sorry. I'll go change." She started to slide past him toward the hallway, but he moved swiftly with long strides and blocked her from reaching the hall.

"Go stand behind the couch and face the TV," he ordered. His voice was soft, dark, and full of that domination that did funny things to her inside. Her brief hesitation earned her a dark look. In a few quick clicking steps, she was behind the couch, hands resting on the waist-high back. She glanced over her shoulder, watching him.

Jared slowly approached, hands in his trouser pockets as he studied her. The predatory gleam in his eyes set fire to every nerve ending inside her.

"So this is what you want? Or is this what you think *I* want? Be honest with me."

When he was finally close enough, standing right behind her, she tried to turn. He pressed one hand between her shoulder blades and pressed firmly, urging her to bend over the couch. She rested on bent elbows, her breath hitching in anticipation.

"Answer me, Felicity." The sharp tap to her ass made her flinch and then moan as he smoothed a hand over her barely covered bottom. She liked that tiny edge of pain. It made her wetter.

"I wanted this," she confessed. "I want you, and I want *this*—please," she begged. At this point, her old self would have shaken her head at the thought of being bent over a couch, wearing lingerie and begging to be fucked. But after everything she'd been through with Jared, this was exactly what she wanted, what she needed.

In the reflection of the TV screen in front of her, she could see him jerking his tie off. He draped it over the couch next to her before he grasped her hips, holding her still.

"Do you have any idea what you just did to me?" he growled low at the back of his throat, the guttural sound eliciting a heady, lusty series of panting breaths as she shook her head.

"Did…did you like it?" She needed to hear him say it, that he loved what she'd been brave enough to wear.

His fingers clenched her hips hard, and he ground his groin against her ass. The very obvious, very big erection was apparently his answer.

"You had me at the shoes. Those little fucking red bows. That is now my favorite shade of red." He slid his hands up her sides toward her breasts and cupped them. She arched her back, trying to give him easier access. The two slender spaghetti straps slid off her shoulders, and he peeled the lacy cups off her breasts, exposing them fully to his touch. With deft fingers, he rolled her nipples between his thumb and forefinger before he pinched them lightly.

"Ah," she hissed, shoving her bottom back against his groin. If he didn't get inside her soon…

"Not so fast." He laughed softly. "If you want to play, we play." He continued to torture her until she was nearly screaming in need and frustration, clawing the leather couch back. Suddenly he was nudging her legs wider apart and tugging those black bikini bottom panties down her thighs.

She jolted like a live wire when he ran two exploring fingers along her slit. There was something sinful about her panties still being on her body but her being exposed to his exploring touch.

"So wet, so hot," he murmured huskily before pushing two fingers into her.

"Oh God." Felicity blinked, trying to focus, to grasp at any remaining strands of self-control she was supposed to have.

"Tell me now if you don't want it hard and rough. Because I'm about to let go, princess." The clink of his belt, the whir of a zipper, and she was nodding.

"Yes, please, Jared."

The crinkle of foil, the continued strokes of his fingers— they blurred together, and there it was. The sweet torturous moment when she was empty and then he shoved his cock inside her. She rocked forward, arching up on her toes even more as his powerful pounding rhythm rammed her against the leather couch. She was pinned at a perfect angle for his furious fucking. The overwhelming sensations of him surging into her again and again, waking up nerve endings as he claimed her body and soul.

There wasn't a part of her that wasn't full with him. Jared fisted his fingers in her hair, tugging her head back a little, which gave her the perfect view of their reflection in the dark TV screen. The way he towered over her, the wild, wanton look on her dazed face, the way her breasts spilled out against the babydoll, bouncing with each jerk of her body as Jared rammed into her. The orgasm exploded through her with the force of a firebomb. A hoarse scream ripped from her lips, but it was drowned out by Jared's harsh shout and three last thrusts hard enough that her whole body snapped forward. Her head dropped onto the couch, and she exhaled a shaky breath. Her shoulders and legs twitched, and then she went fully limp. Jared's ragged breaths puffed out across her back. He rocked inside her, and she whimpered helplessly as little aftershocks rippled through her.

"You okay, sweetheart?" The gentle concern in his tone meant everything.

What they had just done was raw, hard, almost violent, but she had trusted him, and it had been worth it. He was still here, asking if she was okay and showing he cared about her. The thought made her eyes burn with treacherous tears, and she choked down a sob.

"Oh God, I'm so sorry, Felicity." Jared pulled out of her and was fixing her clothes and his. Then he scooped her up and carried her around to the other side of the couch and sat down with her in his lap. His hands smoothed up and down her back with sweet strokes.

"Talk to me. Was that too much? This is why I didn't want to—"

Felicity reached up and clamped both of her hands over his mouth, silencing him.

"No. Stop. I'm happy. So happy." She met his gaze, and when the worry darkening his eyes lifted, she removed her hands from his mouth and swiped at a few stray tears that had escaped.

"You better explain." He touched his forehead to hers, patiently waiting.

"It's just...after what we did, you...cared." How else could she explain it?

He rolled his eyes playfully. "Of course I care. I care about you. Otherwise, we wouldn't be doing any of this," he said as he waved a hand around them. "So what we did just now, that was good, right?" Jared nuzzled her nose with his and tucked her hair behind her ear.

"Mm, yes. It was *very* good. I'm sorry I sort of sprung myself on you without much warning. I felt you trying to slow things down, but I don't want to slow things down, unless..." She bit her lip. "Do *you* want to?"

"Princess, I'm up for this any day." He kissed her, nibbling almost delicately. Her body responded, and her sensitive core throbbed with renewed interest.

"But—"

He met her gaze steadily. "If we go into this at the speed we're going, you're going to have to trust me. You need to start telling me things. I don't want you to still be a stranger to me, and in a lot of ways you are. And I'm a stranger to you."

The words stung a little. If she was being honest with herself, they made her ache. She wanted to tell him everything, but she wasn't sure he'd want to hear or care. She wasn't special, and she wasn't worth knowing, at least she didn't think so. But he wanted her, despite all of that. Maybe sharing herself with him wouldn't be the end of this perfect dream. She ran her hands over his shoulders. His expensive shirt was rumpled.

"What's the worst that could happen? No matter what you tell me, I'm not going to let you out of my arms. We'll stay right here and talk."

It sounded reasonable. She continued to let her fingers trace the little furrows in the once-crisp dress shirt where it covered his beautiful pectoral muscles.

"I am so afraid you'll figure out that I'm just a nobody, and you won't want me anymore." The words came out of her barely above a whisper. There, she'd told him the worst part about herself, her self-doubt, her fear that she wasn't good enough.

Jared tilted her face up to his so they were close enough to share quiet breaths.

"I see *you*, Felicity Hart. And what I see is a beautiful, intelligent, and compassionate woman. How could I not want you? You're *my dream*." He pulled her flush against him, cradling her in his arms as he pressed a kiss to the crown of her hair.

The sincerity of his words gave her a momentary sense of peace. She could believe him. He would still want her. At least for now.

For nearly an hour and a half, Jared held Felicity in his arms on the couch. He'd tucked her up in blankets and started the movie. When the movie credits rolled on the screen, he reached for the remote and turned it off. Felicity woke up from her light sleep and wrinkled her adorable nose.

"One of these days we'll actually watch it all the way through," she muttered.

"Yeah." He chuckled and pressed a kiss to her forehead. "Let's go to bed. You wore me out, princess."

When she tried to stand up, he merely picked her up in his arms, blankets and all, and carried her to the bedroom. He set her down on his bed and then shut the door. She watched him from her nest of blankets, eyes wide and so full of emotions that tugged at his heart. Like a frightened rabbit, she seemed ready to bolt, and he guessed her instincts screamed for her to run because she was afraid to care too much.

Jared stripped out of his clothes and then walked over to stand in front of her. He uncoiled the blankets until she was lying there in nothing but the hose, babydoll, and heels. He'd completely forgotten all of that as his desire toward her had shifted from lust to the need to protect. He removed her shoes and held one up, flicking at the bows with a wicked smile.

"These are hot—real hot. You'll be wearing them a lot, but just in here." He gestured to his bedroom.

Her little smile was back, a sassy smirk. "Layla picked them out."

He dropped the shoes to the floor. "Of course she did. I bet the trench coat was her idea too." He placed his hands on her right thigh, rolling down the hose and noting with no small amount of male pride that it made her flush pink. He liked that she was shy, even with him, but she was brave enough to share herself with him.

She's mine. All mine.

When he reached for the bottoms of her lingerie, she actually sighed in relief. He cocked a brow at her unexpected reaction.

"This thing...uncomfortable. The bottoms were giving me a wedgie," she admitted, then blushed and glanced away. "That was probably too much info, wasn't it?"

He laughed and immediately stripped her out of her babydoll completely. "Princess, a man always loves to get a woman fully naked." He held up the lingerie, dangling it from one finger. "This is a fine way to start, but when I sleep with you, I want you comfortable and, if I get my way, with no clothes between us." He waggled his brows, and she giggled. He inwardly marveled at how easy it was to be with her. She could go from sex kitten in heels to a sweet little thing he wanted to cuddle with, to a woman he wanted to talk to about his job, her job, everything.

Things had been easy with Shana at the beginning before she'd lost her love of real estate law. But things between them had never been electric—they'd been comfortable, that was all. With Felicity it was a cosmic pull that he felt when he was around her. They didn't make a ton of sense together on paper, but screw that. What mattered was what he felt when he looked at her, the way she heated his blood and encased his heart in warmth at the same time. That mattered.

"Get under the covers before I revisit your punishment," he commanded, letting his lips twitch in a hint of a smile. She'd seemed okay with him spanking her—more than okay if he was watching her reactions now.

Once she was under the covers, he turned off the lights and got in bed beside her. Questions still plagued him, and he wouldn't be able to resist until he had some answers.

"Felicity?"

"Hmm?" She burrowed into him, that hesitation she'd had when they'd first shared a bed slowly vanishing.

"You would tell me if something bothered you, right?"

"Yes."

"I mean it. If I do something that scares you—"

"You won't. You haven't." She kissed his chin, his cheek, and then his lips. "Whenever I'm with you, I'm excited. I love being with you." Her lashes lowered at the admission. It was so close to saying *I love you.*

A startling pang of disappointment shot through him. He wanted to hear her say it, to have it be true. Did he want to love her back? Frightening, yeah, but he had to admit that he did. For the first time in a long while, something was more important than work. Felicity was more important than his job.

I'm in deep shit.

CHAPTER NINETEEN

Felicity was in love with Jared.

There was no doubt about it. As she woke the next morning in his arms, feeling safe, sated, and happy to the point of being ridiculous, there was no denying what she felt. She lifted her head enough to slide her chin across his naked shoulder so she could study his sleeping face. She wanted to memorize each feature—the aquiline nose, the sweep of dark lashes that graced his cheeks, the slight pout of his relaxed mouth. She wanted to paint them each upon her memory, to cherish through the rest of her life, wherever it would take her.

Looking at him was like coming home in the truest sense. It wasn't the home she'd grown up in, in a little house too small to accommodate her and her parents, but rather it was the home she'd always craved, the one she'd always hoped she would deserve someday. The one that would make her happy, nourish her, excite her.

If only she didn't have class, she could've stayed in bed all day and just cuddled with him. But the day was slipping away, she had Professor Willoughby's class, and he would be returning the scored tests. Jared stirred, rolling onto his back, exposing his bare chest. All that smooth, perfect skin was irresistible. She laid her palm on his chest, relishing the way his heartbeat thumped slow and steady.

He opened one eye and looked her way, making her jolt. She hadn't thought he was awake. Jared flashed a sleepy smile at her startled jerk.

"What if we pretended we didn't have work or class?" he mused softly.

"Hmm," she sighed softly. He had no idea how tempting that was.

"Is that a yes?" He rolled onto his side to face her, offering her a winning smile that she strove to commit to memory.

"I can't. I'm getting my exam paper scores back today for my colonial art exam. Don't you need to work?" she reminded him gently.

The smile on his lips faded, and it cut her deeply, knowing that she'd splashed them both with an unwanted wave of reality. He leaned over and kissed her, showing her just what she would miss by choosing class over him. It was a kiss that sent her heart skittering and a flush of heat beneath her skin.

"Right, I'd better get up before I talk myself out of going to work and instead just stay right here, keeping you flat on your back on my bed." Jared climbed out of bed and walked into the bathroom, closing the door behind him, creating a silent barrier between them. The sound of the shower pushed at her uneasiness, forcing her to sit up and face the day. She shoved the covers on the bed back and sat up, shivering. She retrieved a clean T-shirt from Jared's closet and padded over to the bathroom.

Felicity lifted her hand to knock, unsure of whether or

not she should do what she wanted, invade his space, give in to those baser instincts Jared had created in her.

Would it be so bad if I extended our morning just a little?

She licked her lips, her eyes catching on one high heel shoe strewn on the floor, forgotten in the heady rush of lovemaking the previous night, and her skin heated anew. Determined to get what she wanted—Jared, naked in the shower—she pushed open the door. Emboldened by her own desire, she stepped into the bathroom and made her way to the shower.

She found him in the glass shower, back to her, his head resting against the back wall, water cascading down his body. His lean muscled body was fully exposed to her gaze, the shadows playing across the planes of his body, from his shoulders to his tight buttocks. When he turned to look her way, she saw his tortured gaze.

"Jared?" she whispered. The tentative note in her voice was mixed with a husky desire she couldn't conceal.

He opened the shower door and held out a hand to her.

"Join me."

She placed her palm in his and let him tug her into the stall with him. The water was cool on her skin, soaking the shirt in seconds as he pulled her to him under the showerhead and captured her mouth with his. Fire exploded within her as his erection brushed against her abdomen, the spacious shower suddenly smaller as he crowded her toward the tiled wall. He broke their kiss, reaching between them and tugging the hem of her shirt up, his fingers trailing against her wet skin, tickling her and stoking the fires already lit, even as he lifted the shirt over her head and let it fall onto the marble floor with a smack.

They stared at each other for a long moment, the heat between them only getting stronger. Without a word, he turned her around to face the wall, and he slowly, agonizingly stroked her body with his hands. His palms massaged her shoulders, cupped her breasts, pinching the nipples lightly. He shaped her hips and teased the backs of her knees with exploring fingertips until she was shaking, her core wet and throbbing. Felicity parted her legs and arched her back, pressing her bottom into his groin, encouraging him to take her.

With a throaty growl, he gripped her hips, pulling her ass toward him even more, and then she felt one hand leave her hips. The tip of his shaft nudged her entrance, and she relaxed, letting him sink into her inch by delicious inch. He rode her slow, gentle, deep, one hand on her hip, the other on her shoulder, using it to anchor her to him. Her palms slid against the tile, and she rested her cheek there, breathing hard as sensations overwhelmed her, as *he* overwhelmed her. She was so close to coming, so close she just needed...

He moved his hand from her hip around to the front of her and feathered his fingers over her pulsing clit. She cried out, her body jerking hard with a long, powerful climax that ended with a whimper from her lips. He picked up his pace, thrusting harder into her a few more times, hard enough to make her see stars, and then he groaned and she felt his cock jerk inside her as he came.

Jared leaned over her, their bodies connected. The moment their bare bodies were flush against each other, he nuzzled her neck, kissing her softly, but she could feel the tension in every line of his body.

"What's wrong? Talk to me," she begged. They separated, and she turned around to face him.

"It's so easy to forget my job and the things I need to do when I'm with you. That's dangerous, Felicity. I could fuck up everything if I'm not careful." His words were uttered roughly, as though he truly worried about it, but as he spoke, he brushed a lock of her wet hair back.

She flinched at the sting of truth in his words. This was what she'd feared since the moment she'd met him and realized she'd wanted more than just a night in bed with him. She was a distraction to him, a burden, and couldn't be anything more to him without causing problems. No woman wanted to be a problem to the man she loved. It made her emotions raw just beneath the surface.

"Now you get why I tried to stop this before it started." She dropped her hands from his shoulders and tried to get around him to exit the shower. He caught her by the waist and pulled her back against the wall.

"I didn't say I wanted you to leave. I just…" He paused as though searching for the right words. "It's going to be hard, that's all. I want to make this work. Because I *need* you in my life." He gazed at her with ragged desperation. "Do you feel the same way about me?"

Felicity swallowed the lump in her throat. "I do. But we have to keep each other in check. I can't risk my scholarship, and you can't risk your job. I want a relationship with you, not just sex. Don't get me wrong, the sex is amazing, but if we stay together I want something more."

He closed his eyes a brief moment before he opened them again, and she caught a glimpse of that steady determination that made him a wonderful lover.

"Me too," he admitted. His voice, soft and rich now, made her tingle, and a glimmer of hope blossomed in her chest.

"Busy people date all the time. We shouldn't be any different. We can do this."

Felicity nodded, the small well of hope inside her growing into a surge of joy at knowing he wanted to make this relationship work. She curled her arms around his neck and pressed herself closer, clinging to him. Maybe they could actually do this, have a relationship and not let it ruin anything they had built in their lives before they met each other. Jared's lips brushed along the column of her throat, and she moaned softly.

"Felicity, I'm going to ask you something, and I want you to think about it before you say no. All right?"

She felt so good in his arms at that moment, and she was quite sure he could've asked her anything. "What?" she murmured and tucked her head underneath his chin.

"Would you..." He paused, and she took the moment of quiet silence to enjoy the hot water and the sexy man holding her. His heartbeat thumped against her ears when she pressed her cheek to his chest, and his muscles twitched beneath her palms as she slowly explored his arms and back and dropped kisses onto his warm skin.

"Just ask." She prodded him gently in the ribs when he didn't immediately speak.

Jared's low, throaty laugh warmed her insides. "I'm nervous, princess. But here goes. Would you think about coming home with me over Christmas? We're going skiing in Colorado and staying at our house in Steamboat Springs. I want you to come with me."

Felicity was caught between two warring factions inside her, elation and panic.

"Jared—"

He squeezed her waist gently. "Don't answer now. Think it over."

"I know, but the plane tickets..." Even if she wanted to go, there was no way she could afford it.

Jared pulled back and lifted her chin. "All that's on me, princess. I know you have this whole pay-your-own-way view of the world, and I admire that, but this trip is a gift I won't let you repay. I just want you to enjoy yourself and be with me."

"And meet your family?" she asked. His parents...Oh,

God. She was being asked to meet his family? What would they think of her? Where would she sleep? His bed, the couch, a spare room? What if they didn't like her? What if they thought she was poor and trashy and not good enough? The questions swirled around in her head, making her a little dizzy.

"Yeah. My parents, and Tanner and Layla might be there if they don't go to visit her family over the winter break."

Layla would be there? That was a huge relief. She wouldn't be completely alone with Jared's family. She'd have her best friend as backup.

"Think on it, okay? You don't need to answer for a week or so. I'll be buying plane tickets and letting my parents know then."

Felicity nibbled her lip. She'd promised to drive home to Nebraska for some part of the holiday break to see her parents, and she didn't want to miss seeing them.

She buried her face against his neck and murmured shyly, "If I go...would you...want to visit my parents for New Year's Eve? I promised I'd come home for part of the break."

"Of course. I wouldn't want you to miss seeing them. I'd love to meet your parents." He stroked the pad of one thumb over her bottom lip. "So does this mean you'll come to Colorado with me?" The look of hope in his eyes made her blush when she nodded.

"I'll go. I still can't believe were doing this. We've barely known each other a week..."

Jared grinned sheepishly. "I know. It's nuts, but how I feel when I'm with you...it's never been like that with anyone else. *Ever.*"

How was it possible that this man made her hungry for him all over again just by uttering those words? She wasn't like anyone else he'd ever been with; maybe he felt the same way about her as she did him.

And then he bent his head to kiss her. It was one of those kisses a woman dreams about. One that was a blend of carnal fire and sweet tenderness. It drove out every worry and fear, replacing it with warmth and hunger for just one more minute alone with him. It was a kiss to build hopes and dreams upon. He cupped the back of her head, holding her captive for his tender kiss.

I'm lost. There's no coming back, not after this kiss.

How could she love him after just a week? It was crazy, but she did. She loved the way he bent over his desk and kept one highlighter between his lips while he worked, and that he used an expensive ink pen to sign his letters, and the way he sang in the shower, slightly off-key, and that he knew just what movie she wanted to watch when they cuddled on the couch. And he knew just how to make her body surrender to pleasure, drugging her with potent kisses before he brought her to screaming climaxes. But it wasn't just the mind-blowing, bed-breaking sex they had. In just seven days she'd learned so much about him as a person, and she adored him. And now she was going to blow it by telling him she loved him.

"I love you." She whispered the words against his lips, and he froze, his dark lashes fanning up with startled surprise. She tensed.

"I'm sorry. I didn't mean…" She floundered and finally went silent, shutting her eyes in mortification.

His lips touched her forehead, and he curled his arms around her.

"Felicity, look at me, princess."

She opened her eyes, dreading what she'd see: pity, regret, annoyance. Instead, her whole world spun wildly as she saw a bright echo of her own emotions in his eyes.

"I love you, too."

Oh. My. God.
And then he kissed her again.

CHAPTER TWENTY

"Are you ready?" Jared asked as he parked their rental car in front of a snowy hillside house. It was a massive house, nothing like the small, cozy cabin Jared had described on the flight from Chicago to Denver.

She fidgeted in her seat. Jared's parents were inside that house, and she was going to meet them.

"Ready?" She swallowed thickly. She was *definitely* not ready to meet Jared's parents. The last month of November and part of December had flown by. She and Jared had managed to settle into a comfortable relationship. They'd gone to art galleries, Jared's favorite museums by the lakeshore, and had managed to fit in time together between work and school. There had been nights where she'd fallen asleep before Jared had gotten home, and mornings when she'd had to slip out of bed early to get to work at Sabine's, but being with him had been wonderful, a dream. But now she was at Jared's parents' home—or one of the three homes the Redmond family had. How was she going to face them?

She was a small-town girl. What would they think of her dating their son?

"I...uh..." she stammered, balking when he exited the car and came around to her side of the SUV and opened the door.

"I thought you got all your nerves out on the plane ride," he teased.

She scowled at him. "I'd never been on a plane before. Those peanuts were impossible to open." It hadn't been the packaging so much as her own jitters that had made the peanuts difficult to open, but in the end she had opened them —spraying everyone within a ten-foot radius with salty, nutty missiles as the package exploded.

Jared tugged at the edge of his black wool coat and then reached for her hand.

"Come on, princess. I swear they don't bite."

"I wish Layla and Tanner were here," she muttered and climbed out of the car to join him.

Unfortunately, Layla had claimed Tanner for her own family Christmas since they'd spent Thanksgiving with the Redmonds. Jared had stayed with Felicity in Chicago, since Sabine had needed her at the gallery and Jared couldn't get off work. They hadn't had to worry about being quiet when they made love in case Tanner was in his room. Cooking and spending time together for two days, just the two of them, had been wonderful.

"What are you thinking about?" he asked as he played with a lock of her hair.

She peeped up at him through her lashes. "Thanksgiving, when it was just the two of us."

He chuckled. "No scary parents. I know. I promise my parents will behave. Don't let them worry you. We have plenty of other things to worry about." This time his smile was rueful, as though he was plagued with thoughts of just what those worries were.

"I know." *Work. Always work.* Not just for him, but for her, too.

They were so close to finishing the hotel transaction and remodel job. The closing for Jared would be in the middle of January, and then she and Sabine would take over. It would be huge for both of them. She tried not to think about how that would bring her one step closer to the job in Los Angeles —a job far away from Jared. And if he made partner, he wouldn't leave Chicago, not to start over in California with her. The thought of leaving him made her sick. She suddenly couldn't stop the churning in her stomach.

"Jared, I don't feel so good." She clutched her stomach and rushed over to the snowbank by the car and bent over, dry-heaving.

"Felicity!" Jared gently grabbed her shoulders, as though unsure what to do. She gasped, wiped a gloved hand over her mouth, and moaned.

"Oh, my God, I'm so sorry," she whispered.

"It's probably the change in altitude. You're not used to the plane and the drive over the mountains. Besides, we spent several hours in the car. Let's just get you inside and get some water in you." He handed her purse to her, and Felicity dug around inside for a stick of gum and thankfully found one.

"This is *not* how I pictured meeting your parents."

He had the audacity to laugh. "Princess, I'm sure something will happen to me when we meet your parents in a week."

"Jared?" A woman's voice intruded on their conversation as they headed toward the house.

Felicity glanced up and saw a beautiful woman in her late fifties standing in the doorway. Her brown hair was cut fashionably short, and she wore jeans and a warm sweater. Her eyes were warm and bright, so like Jared's.

"Mom!" Jared squeezed Felicity's hand and led her up the steps.

"Hello, sweetheart." She kissed Jared's cheek before turning to Felicity, her warmth flooding into her. "And you must be Felicity."

Felicity held out a hand, but Jared's mother grasped her in a hug before she could even think to resist. It reminded her of Layla. She relaxed, letting the warm and fuzzy feeling of comfort sweep over her. Maybe she'd gotten scared over nothing.

Maybe they will like me after all.

"What took you so long, boy? I know that drive is four hours, but it took you five to get here," a deep voice boomed from inside the house.

"Oh, Gerald, hush. Come in, kids." Jared's mother smiled as she released Felicity. "I'm Nancy."

"It's nice to meet you, Nancy." Felicity curled her arm around Jared's as they entered the house, and she caught a glimpse of a fit, handsome man in his early sixties standing on a ladder before a twelve-foot Christmas tree, a shiny star in one hand as he stretched to reach the top of the tree. When he was done, he climbed down the ladder and walked over to them. It shocked Felicity to see such a strong resemblance between father and son. Jared was a youthful version of his father with the clear-cut, strong masculine features. But he had his mother's eyes.

"You must be Felicity," Gerald greeted her, with a warm smile and a handshake. "How was your flight?"

She shot Jared a look to silence him when he opened his mouth. The last thing she needed was for him to tease her about the peanuts in front of his parents. She wanted to look poised and elegant, not like a nutcase who spilled peanuts on a dozen people because she'd never been on a plane before.

"It was fine. Thank you so much for letting me stay here

over the holidays."

Nancy beamed at her. "Of course, dear, you're the first girlfriend Jared's ever brought home for Christmas. We're thrilled to meet you."

"Mom," Jared warned softly.

Nancy raised a brow. "What? It's the truth. She's the first. That's a big deal, honey."

Felicity bit her lip to keep from laughing at the look on Jared's face. His cheeks turned a little ruddy. It was nice for him to be the victim of teasing for a change.

"I'm the first?" She nudged him with an elbow. His full lips twitched, and there was a mischievous glint in his eyes.

"You are." He leaned down to kiss her cheek and then whispered in her ear softly enough that his parents couldn't hear. "The first in my bed...the first I plan to do a lot of deliciously bad things to that will make you moan once we're alone." When he lifted his head away from her face, she didn't miss the searing heat in his eyes as he promised her silently just how hungry he was to take her to bed. She wanted that too, so much, but she didn't want his parents to think poorly of her.

"Gerald, go get the bags," Nancy muttered. "I'll take them upstairs so they can settle in."

"Right," Gerald said. "I'll get your bags. Nancy will show you to your rooms."

Felicity didn't miss the shared smile between Nancy and Gerald, as though they were having a secret conversation that only people who'd been happily married for a long time could achieve. It was a language of twinkling eyes, smiles, and subtle nods.

Jared and I won't ever have that. The sobering thought fractured her heart. She was still planning to leave for Los Angeles, and he wouldn't be coming with her.

"Rooms?" Jared asked. "Dad, we'll be sharing *a*

bedroom."

Oh God. Felicity ducked her head and tried to use sheer willpower to drive away the heat that flooded her face. He was making this so awkward. Why didn't he just tell his parents they would be having sex tonight?

"Stop embarrassing her, Gerald," Nancy whispered, swatting her husband's shoulder as he passed by her to get to the door. "It's just the one room. He was kidding." Nancy nodded at the stairs. "Let me take you up."

The Redmond Colorado home was stunning. Felicity was mesmerized by the dark wood timber of the mountain cabin—style architecture and the gray craggy stones of the walls. It was warm and rustic while also being open and spacious. The walls, Felicity noted, lacked art and only had the occasional family portrait on the walls. She itched to contact Sabine and find some pieces to put in the noticeable blank spaces.

"I know that look," Jared murmured. "You're envisioning decorating the place, aren't you?" He raked a hand through his dark hair and glanced about as though attempting to see the home from her point of view. "We could use some art, couldn't we?"

"What's that, dear?" Nancy asked, turning to look at them as they reached the top of the stairs.

"Mom, we need to put some cool art on the walls of this place. It's a bit bare."

With a curious gaze between Felicity and Jared, Nancy nodded. "I could certainly do that, if I had someone to help me figure out what would look good. I assume you'd be willing to help me, Felicity?"

"I'd love to." She knew she shouldn't start chatting art, because it was so easy to get lost in talking about it, but she had to share her vision of the place.

"You need warm tones, rustic pieces. I'm seeing cowboy photography and paintings of rivers and streams. There are several great modern artists who paint nature pieces, and I think they'd be perfect. I'd be happy to get you connected with them."

"I'd like that," Nancy said. "Jared, I figured you'd want to stay in your usual room," Nancy explained as they reached the door at the end of the hall at the top of the stairs. "Gerald and I are downstairs at the back of house if you need anything."

I survived. She nearly grinned.

"Thanks, Mom."

"You're welcome, sweetheart. Oh, the Maxwells are in town, and your father and I are dining out with them in an hour. You have the house to yourselves for a few hours."

"Perfect," Jared replied with a broad grin.

His mother chuckled. "Felicity, you better make him behave." His mother laughed, and then she left them alone.

Jared held on to Felicity's hand, and she was strengthened by that point of connection. Meeting the parents hadn't been that bad. They were wonderful, and any awkwardness had come from her.

"Come on. I want you to lie down and rest until dinner. You still look a little pale." He tugged her into their shared room, and she gasped.

The bedroom was as big as her entire apartment back in Chicago. A massive sleigh bed was against one wall, with a deep-blue comforter and white pillows. A red-and-white Nordic quilt was folded over the bottom of the bed. The Redmonds had made something luxurious seem cozy. A small fireplace was opposite the bed, with gas logs. On the far side opposite the door, a balcony opened up to a view of the ski slopes.

"This is incredible," she whispered.

"I'm glad you like it." He had his hands tucked into his jeans pockets and was watching her intently, as though trying to see how she was taking it all in.

She followed Jared deeper into the room and smiled when she saw a wall of photos nearby. She couldn't resist looking. He didn't have a ton of pictures of his family back in his apartment, and she wanted to see what his life had been like as a boy.

There were pictures of Jared and Tanner in the pool as boys, Jared dressed as an Eagle Scout holding a pinewood box car and standing proudly next to his father. A college-age Jared stood next to his mother dressed in ski gear and facing up a steep, snowy mountain. He looked so happy, so content.

The warm press of Jared's body behind hers put her at ease.

"You must've had a wonderful childhood," she whispered.

"I did. I was blessed." He slid his arms around her waist and rested his chin on the top of her head, holding her against him. "But I lost that happiness somewhere between leaving for college and meeting you."

It took a moment for his words to register with her.

"You're happy now?" she asked softly, her heart beating faster than it had seconds ago.

"I am." He rubbed his cheek against hers, and the quiet affection of that moment captured her, weaving spells of happiness about her heart.

"Are you happy?" he asked as he turned her around in his arms so she faced him.

The answer was already on her lips. "I am. So happy." *And so afraid to lose this.*

"So, dinner tonight?" He slid his hands into her back jean pockets.

"And then...maybe..." She nodded toward the king-size bed behind her.

"And then..." He waggled his eyebrows playfully, but

the heat in his gaze set fire to her blood. "Make yourself comfortable. I'm going to help my dad with the bags."

"I can help," Felicity insisted, but he guided her to the bed and sat her down.

"You are staying right here to rest. If you don't, neither of us will be doing anything in bed besides sleeping." He brushed a lock of her hair behind her ear and then left her alone in the room. She waited until she heard his feet descending the stairs before she got off the bed. She walked only a few paces before nausea struck again. Covering her mouth, she bolted for the door that looked like the bathroom. She collapsed on her knees in front of the toilet and gasped, trying to keep her stomach under control. Ever since they'd boarded the plane she hadn't felt right.

Maybe the peanuts had done her in. She rested her forehead against the arm that she'd braced on the toilet seat. She closed her eyes, breathing slowly and trying to swallow.

I am so not flying after this trip. Never again.

"Princess?" Jared appeared in the doorway of the bathroom, and she waved him away.

"I'm fine, just need to have a minute to sit here."

He joined her on the floor, and one of his hands settled on her back, rubbing lightly.

"I'm sorry. I'm really ruining your vacation." She groaned and reached for a Kleenex to wipe her mouth.

"Honey, you aren't ruining anything. I'd rather be right here with you on the floor of my bathroom than back in Chicago." His gentle chuckle was a balm to her, and she exhaled slowly. The nausea was fading bit by bit.

"You need water?" His brows drew together as he watched her carefully.

"That would be nice," she murmured, focusing on her breathing.

He pressed a glass of water into her hands, and at first

she took small sips, but then she began to gulp it down. Her stomach finally settled, and she climbed to her feet. He was there, gripping her waist as she got up, and she was grateful for the support. Jared was always there for her when she needed him most.

"Why don't we take you downstairs and you can rest by the fire and watch some TV. I think I'll order us a pizza."

Felicity followed him out of the bathroom. She took one look at the thick snow clouds outside and shivered.

"Won't it be dangerous for the delivery guy to drive up the hill to the house?"

He chuckled. "This is Colorado. The delivery guys have snow tires. It won't be a problem."

Jared curled an arm around her waist as they left his bedroom and walked toward the stairs. She loved it when he did that, when he held her or touched her as though they'd been together for years, not a month and a half. She'd never forget that night in his bedroom when she'd woken up next to him and how his touch had soothed her. That night had changed her life. *Jared* had changed her life.

"What are you thinking about?" he asked when they entered the large, cozy living room. A fire was crackling and popping over a stack of logs, and through a large doorway she caught a glimpse of Nancy and Gerald in the kitchen, talking and smiling. She wasn't sure what she'd expected when she'd thought a hundred times about meeting them on the plane flight over. They were warm and sweet, just like Jared. They were not at all like the rich clients she'd been forced to deal with while working at Sabine's. The Redmonds had heart.

"I was thinking how wonderful everything has been since I met you." Heat built in her cheeks, but she couldn't help it.

Jared's eyes softened, and his sensual lips curved in a half smile.

"I'm so glad you're mine, princess." He dipped his head

and cupped her face in his hands as he kissed her. The press of his lips was heaven, and she could have let him kiss her for hours, days even.

"Ahem." Gerald's voice came from behind them. "Let her have a chance to breathe, boy." That broke them apart, and they both laughed, completely embarrassed.

"Gerald!" Nancy admonished her husband from the kitchen. "Don't tease them."

Jared didn't acknowledge either of his parents. He kept his gaze on Felicity. "Sit down and rest."

Felicity let him guide her to the large dark-brown leather couch, and she watched him over the back of the couch as he joined his mother in the kitchen.

"Mind if I sit?" Gerald pointed to a space at the opposite end of the couch.

"Of course," Felicity replied.

Gerald sat down and stared at her for very long moment, his focus not unfriendly.

"So Jared tells me you're finishing up a master's at the University of Chicago. You're focusing on art history, right?"

"Yes." Felicity turned her attention from Jared to his father.

"Art history…what do you want to do with a degree like that?"

It was a question she'd faced before, and thankfully she was prepared. "Museum curation. I've been working at an exclusive art and design studio called Sabine's, and the owner is well connected to all the major museums around the country. She'll give me a reference and help me with interviews."

"So you'll stay in Chicago and work at the Art Institute?"

"I'll probably move out to Los Angeles next year. I'm applying for a job there in a few months at the Los Angeles County Museum of Art once I get my fall grades on the record."

"Los Angeles?" Gerald's eyes widened. "Does Jared know?"

"Yes, but..." She paused. "We haven't really talked about it." *Because neither of us can face the future we won't be together in.*

"Ah..." The dawning comprehension on his face made her heart sink. No doubt he was mentally checking a box on her that labeled her as a fling for Jared, not someone who would be with their son permanently. It hurt, even if it was the truth.

"Gerald, honey, we need to leave if we're going to be at the restaurant in time for dinner," Nancy called out. Felicity watched her kiss Jared's cheek before she left the kitchen.

"Have a good evening, Felicity." Gerald's smile was still warm, but she sensed that he had put distance between them.

"Good night," she called out, feeling completely wretched. If only this wasn't temporary...

She folded her arms on the back of the couch and watched Jared call for a pizza.

He leaned back against the marble countertop, his legs crossed at his ankles, his lean, muscular body so beautiful.

And he's mine...for now.

She didn't want to think about what it would be like when she moved to Los Angeles and he moved on to a new girl.

Jared ended the call and strolled over to the back of the couch, leaned down, and covered her startled mouth with his. The kiss sparked with eager heat, but a tenderness simmered below all that. It never ceased to amaze her how she'd found such a wonderful, sexy god of a man.

"We're all alone now." He gave her those bedroom eyes that made everything else around them fade away. All she could think about was their bare bodies entwined between the sheets.

"We are," she agreed against his lips.

"The pizza will be here in an hour. Do you want to sit in the hot tub?" Jared suggested as he massaged her neck and shoulders, their faces still close enough that she detected his slightly quicker breathing.

"A hot tub in the snow? Are you sure?" It sounded insane. They'd freeze to death.

"Oh yeah, princess. You haven't lived until you sit in a hot tub while it snows."

"Okay." She arched up for one more kiss before she got off the couch. "I'll go change into my suit."

"Good, I've got my suit down here. I'll throw on my trunks and uncover the tub. It's just outside there." He pointed to a pair of doors just off the living room.

Felicity rushed up the stairs to where Jared had put her suitcase. It was a hideous, beaten-up old duffel, but she had no other bag. Jared's own elegant black roller suitcase was tucked by the door. It made her wince when she looked at her own bag. She shoved the rush of negative thoughts aside and searched for the suit she'd packed, and then she cursed. The tasteful one-piece navy-blue bathing suit wasn't there. In its place was a two-piece white-and-black polka-dot suit. The top and bottoms each had some creative ruffles that...well, they would look cute, but Felicity had never worn a suit like this.

"Layla..." she said with a growl and stomped all the way to the bathroom, cursing her best friend's craftiness.

What would Jared think when he saw her in this itsy-bitsy, teenie-weenie, polka-dot bikini?

CHAPTER TWENTY-ONE

Jared hummed as he leaned over the hot tub, peeling away the cover. Fluffy white snow that had been sitting on the top of the cover showered down on his bare feet as he peeled the cover off the hot tub. Then he tested the water with his fingertips. Nice and hot. He walked over to the control panel and crouched down to search for the knob that would turn on the jets. Bubbles burst forth and filled the big hot tub.

"*Yes.*" He grinned and rested his hands on his hips. This was going to be so good. He'd get his little princess hot and wet in more ways than one. It was a perfect night with the barest breeze drifting through ice-dusted pine trees. There was a natural calm and quiet isolation to the night that made Jared forget about the bustle and noise of Chicago. The sky was a light purple, and the snow-filled clouds were drifting closer. It might even snow tonight. He hoped it did so he could see Felicity's face light up with joy.

The soft click of the patio door opening made him glance away from the skies. Felicity stood in the doorway, a fluffy white towel wrapped around her body, reminding him of that first morning she showered at his apartment. Her shoulders were bare.

"God, please tell me you forgot a suit and you're naked beneath the towel."

Her cheeks reddened, but she smiled. "You're determined to get me naked, aren't you?"

Jared chuckled and raised his palms in surrender. "I won't deny it. I'm desperate for you. I just hope you want me too, because sex in a hot tub is one of my fantasies."

Her eyes twinkled. "I always want you."

"Then drop that towel and get over here, princess."

She crept on bare feet across the snowy deck and reached the hot tub. Only then did she drop the towel away from her body.

His heart stopped.

She wore a two-piece polka-dot suit that seemed to come out of his fantasies. It looked like a suit from the 1950s, something Marilyn Monroe would have worn. It cupped her breasts and her bottom. It wasn't a strappy thing, and it covered more skin, but the way it hugged her drew his eyes to her curves. Curves he had dreamed about tracing with his hands or nipping with his teeth. The ruffles really got to him. It screamed innocent and sex kitten all at once.

"Do I look okay? Layla stole my suit and packed this instead." Her uncertainty dragged him away from his wicked thoughts. She didn't think she looked good? His cock certainly thought she looked amazing, and the rest of him was in complete agreement.

"Fuck, you look amazing, Felicity. It's not exactly manly to admit this, but I just about came in my trunks." He groaned and reached for her. He needed her body pressed to his or he might die.

She laughed, and the rich, husky sound was not helping

his painfully aroused state. When he noticed her shivering, he gripped her waist and lifted her up to sit on the edge of the tub.

"The water's hot—get in," he encouraged. As she slid into the tub, he folded her towel and set it on a chair beside his. Then he climbed up the side of the tub and eased into the bubbling water beside her. He watched in amusement as she used her hair tie to pull her long brown hair up into a cute, messy bun. The movement exposed her graceful neck, making him hot just picturing nibbling it while he seduced her out of that little bikini.

"What?" she asked when she noticed him watching.

He struggled for words. How to explain to her that she fascinated him? That everything about her made him feel funny, like he was aroused and sated and excited and calm all at once? To him she was…everything.

"You're fucking cute as hell, princess. Get over here." He patted the water near him since she was perched on the seat opposite him.

Felicity laughed again as she scooted off her spot and slid through the water over to him. He caught her and guided her into straddling his lap, facing him. The position was heaven and hell for his aching cock. Her hands settled on his shoulders, and she leaned into him, her lips curving in a sweet smile.

"This is nice." Her gaze dropped to his lips.

"It is nice." He cupped her bottom, pressing her close against his groin. She made a soft little sound the back of her throat, like a cat purring.

Fuck…

He slid his hands inside her bikini bottom to cup her bare ass cheeks. There was nothing that could stop him from torturing and teasing her until she was as desperate to be fucked as he was to fuck her. He slid his hands farther down until his fingers reached her silken folds. She jolted and gasped, and her lips parted as she stared at him in shock.

"Jared." She almost whimpered his name when he slid one finger into her. She was wet and tight, and the feel of her made him so hard and desperate for her that he was having trouble breathing.

"Ride my hand, babe," he encouraged, his voice a low growl.

"Hmmm." She rocked her hips wildly as she did as he commanded. Her hands dug into his shoulders as she clung to him.

"That's it." He rocked his own body up to meet hers, and he felt it on his fingers when she climaxed. Her body gripped him, and she dug her nails into his skin. She came so quickly, so hard, and so fucking beautifully just for him. It made him feel like a god.

When she collapsed against him, panting, he lifted her up off his lap and tugged her suit bottoms off, letting them drop outside the tub.

"Hey!" she gasped, trying to reach for the bottoms, but he kept her beneath the water.

"You don't want the neighbors to see you," he warned, laughing against her neck between hot, hungry kisses.

"Jared, you devil," she hissed, but he could hear the smile in her tone.

"I'm just getting started." He used one hand to tug his trunks off, and then he settled her back on his lap.

"Put me inside you," he whispered in her ear. "Take me, princess." He bit the lobe of her ear, and she tensed and moaned with pleasure. As she lifted her hips, she used one of her hands to grip his shaft and guide it into her. She eased down onto his cock, but he couldn't wait. He gripped her hips and pulled her down hard.

"Oh, God!" she cried out and arched her back.

Sliding into her felt like heaven. She was hot and slick, and her body gripped him as tight as a fist. She bit her bottom lip and stared at him, her gaze hazy as though buzzed with pleasure as he started to push in and out of her, possessing her, harder, faster, his hold rough. Her nails dug into him. All the while their gazes locked as though in a silent battle of wills to see who would surrender and come apart first.

"You're fucking beautiful," he growled and slid his hands from her waist to her hips, getting a firm hold on her to better jerk her down on his cock.

"Oh, God!" she cried out so loudly that he swooped in to capture her lips and stifle any further cries.

The moment their lips touched he moaned in delight and climaxed. He'd never been more thankful she'd gotten on the pill. Being skin to skin with her was like nothing else in the world. He'd never done drugs, but he imagined that making love to Felicity was like heroin. There was no coming back from that exquisite high. He'd always crave more.

Neither of them spoke, but Felicity buried her face in his neck and held on to him tight, as though she feared he'd vanish. Her body trembled, and he held her against him. He was shaking too.

"It's okay. I'm right here," Jared reassured her, unsure why he did, but something had changed between them. He could feel it pulsing beneath his skin where she touched him as though they were connected on a level too deep to comprehend.

A little strangled sound escaped Felicity's lips. She was... *crying.*

"Princess? What's wrong? Was I too rough?" he asked, worried that he might have hurt her.

After a few sniffles, she lifted her face. "We have to talk."

The words cut him and filled him with dread. "About

what?"

"Jared, I'm applying for the job in California. That means I'm leaving Chicago in the spring. Leaving you."

It was something he'd been purposely ignoring whenever he could. The thing was standing between them.

"Okay, let's talk," he replied, holding her close. It was hard to imagine her being on the West Coast, not when they were still connected right here. A cold breeze trailed up his shoulders, and he fought off the chill that came with it.

"There's no way you can stay in Chicago?" he asked.

She hesitated and shook her head. "Not if I want to work in a museum in a career path that will lead me to a curator job. It's my dream. I can't just…" She looked away from him.

"Give it up? I know." He nuzzled her cheek. "I don't want you giving up your dreams for me."

"And you, could you give up a partnership at your firm to come with me to California?"

It took him several long seconds to reply. "No. As a lawyer, transferring to a different state is complicated. I'd have to take another bar exam or try to get grandfathered in, but the pass rates for the California bar exams are extremely low. I also don't have any connections. It's not impossible, but it's complicated and difficult."

"What happens in May when I graduate?" she asked him. Her gray eyes were wide, and a dozen questions burned in the depths of her gaze.

"I don't know what will happen, princess. You don't have to decide that now. Things could change in four months." He didn't want to think about her leaving. It left him hollow inside. She nodded, but sorrow still gleamed in her gaze as she pushed off his lap. Disconnecting them.

"Hey, come on, princess. Let's enjoy your vacation. We'll face this soon enough." He curled his fingers under her chin and lifted it so she had to face him again.

"Tonight should be about us having fun," she replied solemnly. Her serious expression inspired him.

"Let's forget about everything except us, right here, right now." He cupped her face in his hands and kissed her softly at first, but soon—as always when he kissed her—he lost control. Every touch of her lips to his sparked new fire.

Something cold and wet settled on his shoulders, then his arms, and finally his nose.

He broke the kiss at the same time she did, and then he started to laugh. Thick thumb-size snowflakes were falling all around them. It was the type of snow rarely seen in Chicago, special mountain snow. The thick flakes fell into the hot tub, and Felicity wriggled against him.

"Oh my God, it's beautiful," she whispered reverently. They'd both seen plenty of snow in Chicago, but mountain snow during Christmas was magical.

"We should get inside before it gets too thick. Wait here and I'll get your bottoms." He fixed his swim trunks and climbed out of the hot tub. Felicity huddled in the water up to her chin, watching him as he bent and retrieved her ruffled polka-dot bottoms and handed them to her. With pink cheeks, she took them and they disappeared beneath the water. As much as he adored her naked, it might shock his parents if they came home to find him and Felicity skinny-dipping in the hot tub.

When she rose out of the water, he swallowed hard at the sight of her luscious body, dripping wet.

"Towel?" she asked, half giggling.

"Oh, yeah." He stumbled as he searched for the towels. She was a temptation and a distraction no man could resist.

He gripped her by the waist and helped her out of the hot tub before handing her a towel and wrapping his own around him.

"Let's get inside and warm up. We can watch a movie in

the living room." He had plans to do more than that, specifically in his bed, but he wanted her warm and cuddly.

"Okay, I like the sound of that." Felicity smiled, and it made his heart jump a few beats. She tiptoed across the snowy patio and ducked inside to turn off the jets while he recovered the tub.

By the time he'd made his way back into the house to change his clothes, he found Felicity on the couch, asleep. He couldn't blame her after the sex in the hot tub. She had taken him to a new height of pleasure tonight, and he felt almost boneless and exhausted, but for the first time in a good way. Like he'd run for miles and the aftermath of the sweet adrenaline high had made him mellow as hell. That was how good sex was supposed to be, but it'd been so long since he'd had meaningful, life-changing sex. And nothing with any woman before Felicity had felt like this.

He paused by the couch, watching her sleep. Her dark-brown lashes spread across her creamy skin, and her fists were balled as though she was clinging to something in her dreams. He braced one arm on the back of the couch and leaned over to brush his thumb across the faint worry lines on her brow. She sighed softly, and the worried look faded as she relaxed. His heart flipped inside his chest.

The distant door chime dragged him away from Felicity. It had to be the pizza. With a rueful smile he went to answer the door, knowing he didn't have the heart to wake Felicity just to eat. After the long hours they'd both been putting in at their jobs and with Felicity's classes, they both needed a real vacation with no stress or worries.

After he paid the deliveryman, he set the pizza down on the kitchen counter and helped himself to a few slices. Felicity suddenly peered over the top of the couch.

"Pizza?" she murmured and got up to come around the couch toward him. She looked adorable with her flannel PJ's, a dark-red-and-black plaid. The button-up shirt was open enough to reveal her throat and those dainty collarbones he loved to kiss and nibble. God, the woman was a walking temptation. He could never get enough of her.

"Hungry?" he asked as he offered a plate to her.

She grinned sheepishly and snagged a couple of slices. "So tomorrow we go skiing?"

"Uh-huh." He watched her closely, noticing how she looked suddenly nervous.

"You'll teach me, won't you? I've never skied."

He wrapped an arm around her waist and tugged her closer. "Of course. That will be half the fun." He couldn't wait to see her on the slopes, all bundled up and ready to go. She'd be a real snow bunny. *His* snow bunny.

Felicity grinned. "Thank you, Jared, for this, *for everything.*"

"I'm glad you came." His tongue felt thick, and he wasn't sure what else to say that didn't sound hopelessly romantic and would have him making a fool of himself.

She swallowed another bite of pizza and leaned into him.

"Just promise you won't laugh when I fall on my ass tomorrow," she demanded.

He kissed the tip of her nose. "I can make no promises, princess. It's such a fine ass." He cupped her bottom and gave it a playful squeeze.

"You better sleep with one eye open," she warned, but she dissolved into giggles when he patted her ass.

"I don't think either of us will be getting any sleep tonight." He lowered his head toward hers, stealing a kiss from her petal-soft lips.

Yeah, there would be no sleep at all.

CHAPTER TWENTY-TWO

"I'm going to die. You realize that, right?" Felicity whispered as she stared down the top of the snowy hill. Her skis were firmly entrenched in snow, and her hands had a death grip on the poles.

"You're not going to die. You just spent the last three hours doing great with your lessons on the bunny slopes. This is a blue slope. You can handle it, princess. I'll stay with you the whole way, Scout's honor." He raised his fingers in a salute, grinning.

Felicity lifted one of her poles and smacked him in the side.

"Hey!" He jumped, even though she knew it didn't hurt. They were both bundled up in ski coats and ski pants.

"Quit stalling. You can do this." He pulled his sunglasses down over his eyes, and Felicity sighed before she lowered her own. It was one more thing on a long list of what she owed him. They'd gone into town first thing that morning, and he'd bought her a complete set of ski gear. He'd tried to buy her skis too, but she'd insisted they rent skis since she couldn't fit a pair in her postage stamp—size apartment.

"Okay," she muttered to herself, and gripped the poles and faced the hill. A group of rowdy snowboarders were laughing and giving each other hell about twenty feet away from her at the top of the hill. Half a dozen other skiers were sliding down below them.

"You ready?" Jared shifted his skis, angling them slightly downhill.

"You go and I'll follow your path." It was something she could do. The instructor that morning had shown her how to ski, and she followed the man's path down several green-level bunny slopes. Once she learned the basics, like how to make a pie shape with her skis to slow down, she was less frightened, but the slope she was staring down now was much steeper.

"Off we go!" Jared called out and started to cut across the snow at a wide horizontal direction only slightly facing downhill. He'd weave like that all the way down, and she'd be able to follow him. He made skiing look sexy, with the way he leaned into the hill, masterful, in control. Like he was in bed… She bit her lip and tried to focus on the slope and not how much she wanted to skip the skiing and hop into bed with Jared.

The hot tub sex last night had been unbelievable. He'd taken her raw and a little dirty, and yet she'd never felt closer to him in her life than she had in that moment. It had broken down every last barrier in her heart toward him.

Pushing away from the uphill angle she was in, her skis moved toward the path Jared had set. Felicity focused on her form, using all of her muscles to lean into her turns, and she kept her poles up except when she needed to use them to stabilize herself.

She glanced up every few feet to admire the mountain vista. There was something about mountains that was arresting and awe-inspiring. It struck her with a sense of natural majesty. Some people found nature made them feel small and alone, but Felicity felt it was freeing. She was a small piece, a thread woven into an elaborate tapestry that made up the universe. It was a type of art, to see the beauty in things around her. Even the shapes of the distant skiers below and how they moved along in the snow in arcing patterns was all part of something big and beautiful.

Felicity tracked Jared as he made another turn. He paused and waved a pole in encouragement. She slipped her skis out of a pie shape and made them parallel so she could move faster. A snowboarder shot past her on the left, hollering wildly. Felicity's heart stopped in her chest, and she tried to twist her legs out to slow herself down.

"Hey! Watch it!" Jared shouted as the snowboarder passed him below.

Blinding pain hit Felicity from behind, and she flew headfirst into the snow below her. Something twisted in her hip, and she felt a pop. The pain tripled as she inhaled snow and struggled to breathe. Her legs felt strange, and everything in her back spasmed. It was too much, too much...blackness swallowed her up.

When she struggled back to consciousness she was momentarily confused. The world around her was white, but not from snow. Her skis were gone and so were her warm clothes. She was lying in a bed with machines beeping softly around her.

A woman in blue scrubs stood beside her bed, checking the stats of an IV drip.

"You're awake." She turned from the bed and smiled at Felicity. "How are you feeling?" the woman asked. Felicity licked her chapped lips. "Like a boulder hit me...what happened?"

The nurse chuckled. "Not far from the truth. Your

boyfriend said a snowboarder plowed into you from behind. You twisted your hip and pinched a few nerves. Nothing was broken, and you should be able to go home in an hour once we get the paperwork ready." The woman gently extricated the needle from the back of her hand and put a cotton ball and medical tape over the spot.

"I'm okay?" She couldn't believe that. If she had been hit hard enough to land in a hospital bed, it must've been serious.

"Yes. We kept you on IVs to make sure you and the baby were all right since you were a little dehydrated."

She relaxed. *I'm okay, the baby is okay…wait…baby?*

The room, which had been perfectly normal seconds before, suddenly spun as Felicity tried to replay the words the nurse had just spoken.

"Me and the…the…"

"Baby. Yes. We discovered it after we ran some blood work since we didn't want to run the risk of an X-ray on your hip if you're pregnant. We couldn't ask you because you were unconscious."

"But—" Felicity rubbed her eyes. "I can't be. I'm on the pill."

The nurse froze, her hands hovering above the heart monitor machine. "How long have you been on it?"

"About seven weeks," Felicity said. There was no way she could be pregnant.

"The blood work doesn't lie." The nurse tapped her chin thoughtfully. "Hang on. I'll be right back." She left, and Felicity stared numbly at the door and then down at her stomach.

She slowly pushed the blankets back and pulled up the hospital gown to stare at her abdomen. It didn't look like she was pregnant, but the baby would be the size of a poppy seed at this point, right?

I can't be. We've been so careful. Felicity ran over the memories of those first few days as she started the pill. The doctor had warned it would take a few weeks to start working, but Felicity had been a little distracted, picturing her and Jared in bed without condoms.

Oh God...

The door opened, and the nurse returned with a large cart with some equipment on it.

"This is a sonogram machine. We can take a quick peek at your baby and record any activity."

Numb, Felicity sat still while the nurse prepared the sonogram and vaginal wand, slipping a condom over it and covering it with lube.

"Ready?" the nurse asked as Felicity lifted her legs and spread them apart. The position and knowing that wand was going in her left her feeling shaky and vulnerable.

"I guess so," she whispered, clenching her fingers in the hospital bedding.

"You're going to feel some cold and pressure," the nurse warned.

Then the nurse slowly inserted the wand inside her.

Felicity stared at the black screen as it began to show gray-and-white shapes. A black circle appeared in the center of the screen. The nurse pressed the wand deeper into Felicity, and an odd little shape appeared in the center, like a gummy bear with little stubs and a bigger shape at the top.

"That"—the nurse smiled and pointed at the shape—"is your baby. This is the head." She pointed to the bigger part. "And the arms and legs." She pointed a finger at the center of the shape, which was fluctuating. "The baby's heart."

The world shrunk around Felicity as she stared at the small flashing shape. It was...amazing...terrifying.

"Want to hear it?" the nurse asked.

Felicity nodded, beyond the power of speaking as she

gazed at the gummy bear shape. *My baby and Jared's.*

"Here we go." The bottom of the screen lit up with a pulsing pattern, and the speakers made a fast *thump-thump-thump* sound.

"One hundred and sixty-five beats per minute. That's good." The nurse pressed several keys. "I can make a copy of this and email it to you if you put your contact info on the forms before you leave."

"Thank you." Felicity finally found her voice. "The pills, the birth control..."

The nurse's smile faded. "Stop them at once. And when you get home, check in with an ob-gyn to have more tests run. You want to make sure it's healthy and safe. I've got pain pills that are safe to take for your back and hip. You'll be sore for about a week, so it's okay to take it easy. And no sleeping for the next four hours. I want to make sure you don't have a concussion."

Felicity watched as the ultrasound screen turned off and the view of her baby vanished. The nurse removed the wand and cleaned it up before she rolled the machine to a corner of the room.

"You want me to send in your boyfriend? He's wearing a hole in the waiting room rug with his pacing."

Jared, right... How she going to deal with this?

"He doesn't know about the baby—please don't tell him," she begged the nurse.

"I won't. I can't, technically, since we didn't have any medical release forms for him. He can't get access to your records."

Relief flooded Felicity at the same time that guilt swamped her. She would have to tell Jared, but not over Christmas, and not when she was around his family. The last thing she wanted to do was upset everyone, especially Jared. Springing a "Hey, I'm pregnant" announcement on him while his parents were there was a bad idea.

She placed her palms on her stomach, knowing she wouldn't feel anything, but she couldn't get the image of the baby out of her head. Suddenly tears were forming at the corners of her eyes and fat teardrops trailed down her cheeks.

"Oh, honey, don't cry," the nurse murmured and picked up one of her hands, giving it a squeeze. "Your baby is fine, and that man out there is crazy about you. It won't be bad when you tell him. Trust me. I've seen plenty of couples in this hospital. Your man has been pacing by the nurses' station for the last two hours since they brought you in. Now," the woman said, "dry your eyes, honey, and I'll go get him."

The second the nurse was gone the tears got thicker. She could barely see and was choking down sobs when Jared appeared in the doorway.

"Princess, oh God, honey, what's wrong? The nurse said you would be okay with some rest." His warm body curled around her as he sat on the side of the hospital bed. She buried her face in his neck, choking on her pain and her fear.

A baby. How could she have a baby? She had so much to do, and a child wasn't part of her life plan. Not yet. And with her and Jared likely parting ways in the spring, she'd be a single mom with a tight income.

She could give the baby up...no. The thought of losing a baby created out of a moment of love between her and Jared was impossible. She would keep it and do whatever it took provide for her child.

"Hey...Felicity, please look at me." Jared's voice was a soft masculine rumble that soothed her enough to look up at him.

"I'm sorry," she gasped. "I don't feel so good, and my body hurts pretty bad." She winced as she shifted on the bed.

"What did the nurse say about your injuries? They didn't tell me much except that you were going to be okay." He cupped her cheeks and used his thumbs to wipe away the tears coating her face.

"They…" She swallowed and fought for control. "Gave me some pain pills. I hurt my back and my hip, so no more skiing."

"When can you go home?" Jared asked.

"Today. Could you go find the nurse and ask?"

"Sure, sweetheart." He pressed his lips to her cheek and slipped out of the room.

The second he was gone she buried her face in her hands. *A baby. I'm having a baby. What am I going to do?*

Fifteen minutes later, Jared returned, smiling. "You're free to leave. I pulled a few strings and assured them I'd serve your every need while you rest. The nurse will come and help you change while I pull the car up to the front doors."

"So soon?" She was surprised.

"Yeah." Jared's face flushed. "I really convinced them I'd spoil you, and since your injuries aren't that bad and you just need rest, it makes sense to take you home."

"Wow. Okay." How was she going to tell him? She couldn't tell him now, but she'd need to soon before she started to show.

"I'll see you downstairs in a few minutes."

She nodded and watched him leave just as the nurse returned carrying a plastic bag.

"Your clothes. I'll help you get dressed."

Felicity eased off the bed and changed out of her hospital gown and into her ski clothes. The nurse returned and helped her into a wheelchair.

"I think I can walk," she said.

"Hospital policy, honey. Enjoy the free ride." The nurse winked. "Now, I've got your paperwork ready. You should buy some prenatal vitamins and make sure you eat. Your boyfriend mentioned you'd been suffering from an upset stomach in the last two days. I'm sure it's morning sickness."

"But I wasn't sick in the morning," Felicity noted.

The older woman chuckled. "It's just an expression. The nausea can strike at any time."

The nurse wheeled Felicity out of the hospital room and to a nurses' station, where they signed the paperwork.

"As long as you're here in Steamboat, come back immediately if you don't start to feel better or if you think something might be wrong with your pregnancy, okay?"

"Got it." Lucy scribbled her name all over the forms and then dug into her pockets for her cell phone. She had to talk to someone about the situation. She texted Layla.

Felicity: *I need help. Something happened.*

Felicity and the nurse had reached the elevators when Layla's response text came back.

Layla: *You okay? What's up?*

Her fingers hesitated above the keys.

Felicity: *I'm in trouble.*

Layla: *Trouble?*

Felicity blew out a frustrated breath.

Felicity: *I'm pregnant. Jared doesn't know yet. Apparently I messed up the birth control pills somehow. I'm at eight weeks.*

She stared at the screen with a frown, waiting to see what her friend would say.

Layla: *Okay. Breathe. We can handle this. I know a great gyno who I can help get you on her list for an appointment. You want to keep the baby, right?*

There was no hesitation in her response.

Felicity: *Yes.*

Layla: *Okay. Good. When are you telling Jared?*

She glanced up and watched the distant SUV that was coming toward the hospital entrance from the far end of the parking lot.

Felicity: *After New Year's. I need time to figure this all out myself before I tell him.*

Jared parked the SUV and climbed out of the driver's seat. He opened the passenger door and then headed toward her. She didn't miss how the nearby nurses were eyeing Jared with hungry appreciation.

Her phone vibrated with a new message.

Layla: *I'm here for you. Whatever you need.*

Felicity: *Thanks, that means a lot to me.*

Then she put the cell phone back into her pocket and eased out of the wheelchair. Her bones protested, and her muscles twitched.

"Ow," she moaned and hobbled toward Jared.

He caught her by the waist and helped her get in the car.

"I think you need another night in the hot tub."

She grimaced, hot tubs were a no-go for pregnancy. "I think I'd just like to cuddle on the couch." And she placed a hand over her abdomen for a brief instant. When Jared got into the driver's seat he looked away, a muscle in his jaw clenching.

"Felicity, I'm so sorry this got all fucked up." He clenched his fingers around the steering wheel hard enough that his skin turned white. "I just wanted you to have a nice vacation, do some skiing, be with me." He closed his eyes, exhaled, and then looked over at her again. Pain laced his gaze.

" I *am* having a nice vacation." She reached over and kissed him, letting her mouth linger against his lips.

"Are you sure?" The intensity of his searching stare left her feeling edgy and exposed, as though he could see all of her secrets.

He can't see the truth in my eyes. He can't know that I'm pregnant or that I'm scared as hell that I'll lose him.

"I'm sure. You're wonderful, and this trip is wonderful, snowboarders aside."

A slow smile spread across his lips, and a wicked gleam she recognized all too well glinted in his eyes.

"I still plan to make this all up to you tonight in the hot tub. I'm thinking of a back and neck massage. Maybe even a foot massage." His voice turned whiskey-rough, and she shivered.

"Then why aren't you driving us home? I want these promises fulfilled."

"Good. My parents have Christmas all planned out for tomorrow. Some relatives will be in for the day and will be leaving by the evening. You'll get to meet all my cousins, aunts, and uncles."

She blinked in surprise. "Will there be a lot?"

"Oh, about a dozen, but don't worry, they'll love you."

Felicity resisted the instinctive urge to cover her abdomen with her hand again.

Oh boy...

CHAPTER TWENTY-THREE

Christmas with the Redmond family was nothing short of magical. The cousins, aunts, and uncles descended upon the house in a storm of happy, familial chaos. She was introduced to no less than nine people and received half a dozen hugs as though they'd been a part of her life forever. It didn't matter that she was a stranger. The moment Gerald had introduced her as Jared's girlfriend, everyone had been all smiles and friendliness.

Now all the women were in the kitchen whipping up a feast while the men played billiards in the upstairs entertainment den. Jared hung back with her and was resting on the couch, watching the female family members cook. He was stretched out on the couch with her leaning back against him, so she lay cocooned in the warmth of his arms. His cheek pressed against the top of her head as he played with her hands where they rested on top of the blankets in her lap.

"You don't have to stay here with me if you want to play billiards," she said.

His low, throaty chuckle sent a shiver of delight through

her. "Uncle Bill's a bit of a windbag. I'm happy to miss out on his antics. He'll talk your ear off and then try to cheat at whatever game you play."

Felicity laughed softly. If there was one thing she'd learned about Jared, it was his preference for honesty. He didn't have to win like a lot of guys, but he wanted a fair game to be played.

"Which one was Bill again?" All the men were tall and had dark hair like Jared's father.

"The one with the thick mustache, a little heavyset."

"Oh, yeah." She did remember him. He was a little brash, but not completely unlikeable.

"Do you still want me to go off and hang with the guys?" he asked as he dipped his head down to feather his lips on the shell of her ear. She bit back a moan.

"No…definitely not. You should stay right here and keep doing that." She curled her toes and clenched her hands when he bit the lobe of her ear.

"Why don't we sneak away upstairs for a bit?" he suggested huskily.

"Okay." There was no way she could argue with him when he was touching her and kissing her like that.

She and Jared slipped off the couch and crept out of the living room. He stifled a laugh as they ducked behind the banister so the men in the den wouldn't see them. She loved this side of him, the playful man, the family man, the man who still wanted to sneak away to a secret place with her. But even as it filled her with joy, she was strangled by a heavy sadness. This perfect dream wouldn't last because they wouldn't stay together. This family, this house—it would all vanish come spring.

Even if he wanted to be part of the baby's life, she didn't know how he would handle raising a child. She might be like so many young women she'd graduated high school with. A single mother raising a child, getting child support checks in the mail.

Don't think about it. She forced a smile onto her lips as she and Jared entered his bedroom. He shut the door behind him and leaned against it. He looked so sexy in his blue jeans and a red flannel shirt, a sexy woodsman with a shadow of stubble along his jaw. It made him sexy, rugged, a little dangerous in the best way.

"I want to give you your present early." He pushed away from the door and came over to her.

"Now? What about your family? Surely they want to open gifts at a certain time tonight."

"This isn't one they should see." He walked over to the bed and retrieved something flat and rectangular from underneath the bed. It was wrapped in brown paper and tied with a dark-blue ribbon. He set it down on the bed and beckoned her over with one finger.

"What is it?" she demanded, her heart racing.

"And deprive you of the surprise?" He waggled a finger at her, a flirty smile on his lips that made her hungry to skip presents and tackle him flat on the bed.

"Fine." She reached for the large package and began to unwrap it. The brown paper fell away, and she gaped at what lay beneath.

"How…when?" She lifted her eyes to his, speechless.

He slid his hands into his pockets and gazed at her, as though bashful. On Jared—the masculine, too sexy, powerful lawyer—it was devastatingly charming.

"I may have seen it at your apartment that first week we met. I had Layla sneak it out of your sketchbook so I could have it framed."

Felicity lifted the framed sketch. It was one of her favorites. She had drawn herself as Cleopatra and Jared as the handsome Antony bent over her where she lay on the couch, the seductive pose she'd fantasized about. And he'd framed it.

"Are you mad?" he asked.

She said her head. "No...I'm...Oh, it's beautiful." She admired the expensive framing and matting job.

"It's not really for you—at least, I was hoping you'd want to give it back to me so I could hang it in my bedroom back in Chicago."

Felicity's throat tightened. "Of course." She couldn't say no. What if it was the only thing he'd have left of their relationship when she moved away?

I will not cry. Not on Christmas.

"But I have a real present for you." She set the sketch down and rushed over to her bag. Digging through the side pockets she found a small blue velvet rectangular box and held it out to him.

"I only had a little bit of money, but I wanted to get you something that mattered."

She'd saved up for this particular gift, hoping he'd see the value and know how much she'd cared about him to save to afford it.

Jared took the box, his eyes strangely dark and full of emotions as he gazed at her, and then he cracked open the lid. A gold pen was nestled inside with two ink cartridges.

"You could use it to sign contracts on the new hotel," she suggested. Her heart thumped wildly. Would he like it? Why wasn't he saying anything? Her palms began to sweat.

Jared closed the pen box and set it on the corner of the bed. His face was unreadable. Felicity's heart sank. He didn't like it.

"If you don't like it, you could exchange it—"

He reached for her, cupping her face and drawing her close. "Shut up and kiss me," he growled. And then his mouth was on hers. Honey and fire, sweetness and raw carnality all dueled for dominance in that kiss. His tongue sought entrance between her startled lips. She melted into him. Her fingers dug into his soft flannel shirt, and she moaned, needing more. She could never get enough of this man. He knew just how to hold her, how to touch and kiss her to make her feel alive and loved.

When they finally broke apart minutes later, she found they'd moved to the bed and she was straddling his lap. He caressed her cheeks with his thumbs, and their foreheads touched as they both caught their breath.

"I love it," Jared whispered. "I love you." The words sent her flying and then crashing.

Every minute she kept silent about the baby was one more minute she was lying to him. She didn't want to lie to someone she loved. Felicity opened her mouth, and the confession about the baby was on the tip of her tongue. Jared's eyes were full of love and warmth. What would he do about a baby? What if he didn't want a child? What if he was furious because she would have to take the baby with her when she left?

I could stay in Chicago…but I'd have to give up my dreams. What if she did, and missed a huge opportunity in LA because she stayed here and risked breaking up with Jared? Babies could wreck relationships of people who weren't prepared to be parents. She'd seen it happen.

"Maybe no one will notice we're up here." Jared chuckled, and his hands dropped from her face down to her waist.

Felicity swallowed down the words that could destroy their fragile happiness and kissed him, hard, desperately fighting back tears.

"Hey," he whispered. "What's the matter?"

"It's nothing," she lied. "Christmas always makes me a little emotional."

His smile was big enough that it crinkled the corners of

his eyes. "I love that about you." He turned his body so they fell back on the bed with her beneath him. "Let me give you a reason to smile." He rocked his hips against the cradle of her thighs, hitting just the right spot to kick her arousal into overdrive. He nipped her chin, her throat, and her collarbone. It felt so good.

"Stop teasing me, Jared," she gasped. "Take me to bed."

"Anything you want, princess."

Felicity threw her head back and surrendered to him and the fire of his touch. Christmas dinner could wait.

"Your dad isn't the type of man to greet his daughter's boyfriend with a shotgun in his hands, right?" Jared asked as he eyed the little one-story white painted brick house that belonged to Felicity's parents.

He and Felicity stood on the sidewalk of the narrow street, and his heart beat wildly. He'd dealt with some of the most powerful men and women in Chicago in his law offices, and yet here he was in a small town in the Midwest, nervous about meeting a mechanic and a nurse.

Because they are Felicity's parents, and I need them to like me.

He gave Felicity's hand a little squeeze. She'd been quiet on the long drive from Colorado to Nebraska. Ever since the skiing accident she seemed...different. At times intensely happy and then distant and a little sad. Jared tried to tease the blues out of her, but she didn't respond the way he'd hoped. What smiles and laughter he could win from her quickly faded.

"Don't worry." Felicity met his gaze solemnly. "Dad

doesn't even have a shotgun."

He exhaled in relief.

"But he does have a Colt revolver." She added this with a sudden twinkle in her eyes.

"Jesus," Jared muttered. "Let's get this over with." He tugged her hand as they started up the sidewalk to the house.

"I promise he won't shoot you." She giggled when he threw her a suspicious look. Halfway up to the house, Felicity tugged him to a stop.

"Is it okay that we're staying here in my bedroom and not a hotel? I'm sorry we don't have an extra bedroom and my bed is small." She fiddled with the buttons of her coat as she waited for him to respond.

"It's fine—a tiny bed means being closer to you, and that won't ever be something I'll complain about." He knew she needed reassurance, and he was determined to prove to her that she shouldn't be embarrassed by her modest background. He loved the woman she was, and this house, this town, and her parents had made her the wonderful woman he'd fallen in love with.

"You're too perfect." She shook her head, and he saw a hint of a smile on her lips.

"I doubt that, but for you, I'll certainly try."

When they reached the front door, Felicity pressed the doorbell and shifted nervously on her feet. He knew her now, knew she was afraid for him to see what her life was like compared to his. He never once wanted her to think the difference in their background mattered, because it didn't matter to him.

"Janet and David." He murmured the names again as a way of calming down.

"Now you know how I felt when I had to meet your parents." She nudged him in the chest with one elbow.

"But you weren't dating someone's precious baby girl. If

I had a daughter and was meeting her boyfriend, it wouldn't matter if she was fifteen or fifty. I'd want to know who the guy was and scare him into treating my baby girl right."

Felicity suddenly sniffed, and he glanced at her. Her eyes were a little too bright...with tears?

"Princess—"

The front door opened, and a woman appeared. She was thin with dark hair laced with silver, her face lined with a few premature wrinkles, but her smile was warm and inviting.

"Felicity, honey." She embraced her daughter and then turned to Jared, her eyes sweeping him from head to toe, not critically, but certainly with curiosity.

"And you must be Jared." She held out a hand, and he shook it.

"Hello, Mrs. Hart."

"Please call me Janet. David is outside on the patio getting the burgers ready. I hope that's okay?" Janet glanced between him and Felicity, a little nervous.

"Burgers sound great. What can I do to help?" He followed Felicity and her mother inside.

The house was small, but it felt lived in. The couch in the family room looked a little worn in places, and an old box-style TV sat against one wall. Behind the couch there were photos of Felicity and her family. He wanted to look at them more closely, but Felicity blocked him by holding her arms out.

"Oh no, you aren't going to see those. I look horrible. My awkward teen years were *really* awkward." Her palms flattened on his chest, and she attempted to push him away from the photos.

"I'll look later. You got to see me. It's only fair." He kissed the tip of her nose, and she sighed in exasperation.

"Fine, later." Felicity turned to her mom. "What can we do to help?"

Janet waved them deeper into the house. "If you want, you can set the table. I'll let David know you're here." Janet slipped out of the kitchen and into the backyard. The weather wasn't bad, which was good. He'd grown up in Nebraska and knew how heavy snow could be in the winter, but there was no snow on the ground, and the temperature for New Year's was actually mild, in the upper forties.

Jared trailed Felicity into the kitchen, where she opened cupboards. He accepted plates and glasses as she handed them over, and then he arranged them on the small walnut wood kitchen table. It was obvious they didn't have a dining room or a bigger table. He set the plates, glasses, and silverware and was in the act of folding napkins when the patio door opened and Janet returned with Felicity's father.

David Hart was a tall man, close to Jared's height, with dark hair and features that were friendly, and Jared knew he must've been a good-looking man when he was younger. His gray eyes fixed on Jared, a quiet but nonthreatening measuring-up, just as Janet had done.

"Jared, is it?" David set the tray with the burgers on the stovetop and wiped his hands on a faded dishtowel. Then he walked over and shook Jared's hand.

"It's nice to meet you, sir," he said.

David broke into a smile and went to Felicity. "Sir? I like him, honey." David smacked Jared's shoulder and then nodded at the fridge. "Want a beer? We got Corona and Coors. Nothing fancy, but—"

"A Corona would be great." Jared smiled back. Felicity was watching him and her dad interact. He nodded at her when David's back was turned, and her shoulders visibly relaxed.

"So you kids went skiing, I hear?" David retrieved a pair of Coronas from the fridge and then opened them before handing one to Jared.

"We did," Jared continued.

"Felicity has always wanted to go," Janet explained before turning to her daughter. "How was it?"

"Cold." Felicity laughed. "Very cold. I get why people go skiing in the spring."

Her laughter made Jared relax.

David leaned in to Jared to whisper loudly, "Well, was she any good?"

"Quite good after some lessons." Jared enjoyed seeing the blush on Felicity's face when he said this.

"Everyone help yourselves to burgers. I made some coleslaw." Janet set a bowl out, and everyone gathered around the food, filling their plates before they sat down at the table. It was nice to sit down to a quiet dinner. His own family could be large and loud at times.

"So...Jared." David sipped his beer. "You're a lawyer?"

Jared swallowed a bite of his burger. He was thirty years old, but sitting here at a table with the parents of the girl he was in love with made him feel like he was sixteen.

"Yes. I practice real estate law."

"Hmmm." David grunted and bit into his own food. "How did you meet Felicity?"

The second the question was out of her father's mouth, a foot kicked Jared's shin under the table, and he met Felicity's frantic gaze. *Right—edit the story.*

"Uh...well, my brother, Tanner, was hosting a Halloween party, and we met there...at the party. We've been dating since then." The truth. It was just missing a lot of the details that would send David Hart running for his Colt revolver, like the fact that they'd shared Jared's bed and Felicity had slept in his clothes. Everything they'd done after that...

Felicity kicked him again under the table, and he flicked his gaze away. She stared at him meaningfully, but he had no idea what she was trying to tell him.

"Felicity and I are working on a project together," he said.

"Oh? She didn't mention it." Janet scooted forward in her seat. "What sort of project?"

Felicity's cheeks were still pink. "Jared's firm is helping to complete a real estate transaction on an old hotel from the 1920s. My boss's art gallery been hired to do the interior design."

"That's wonderful, honey," David said, his voice full of pride.

"It's been great to work with Felicity. She's very talented." Jared finished his Corona and smiled at Felicity. He couldn't begin to tell Felicity's parents how amazing their daughter was.

"She is." Janet agreed with a happy little laugh. "Ever since she was a child, I've never seen anyone so gifted."

"So you spent Christmas with your folks, Jared?" David helped himself to more coleslaw and passed the bowl to Jared, who accepted it and added more to his own plate.

"We did. My family usually goes to the Bahamas for Christmas, but this year they chose the cabin, and we couldn't resist getting Felicity out on the slopes."

"The Bahamas?" Janet's eyes brightened. "How lovely! I've always wanted to go there." She paused, blushing. "We can't get off work, and it's a little out of our budget."

Jared knew what she meant. Felicity had told him that neither of her parents had ever left the state of Nebraska. It was something he'd considered when he'd spoken to his parents in Colorado before coming here.

"My parents have some flight miles they're not using in March, and they were looking to give them to anyone who wanted to fly out and spend some time at the Bahamas house. If you're interested, they'd love for you to go. It wouldn't cost anything except the food to stock the fridge for as long as you're there." *Please let them say yes.* He wanted so desperately to give something good to Felicity's parents, to show them that he was looking out not just for their daughter but for them too.

"Mom, you should really consider it," Felicity urged.

Janet and David exchanged silent glances, and then David smiled. "That would be nice. Thank you, Jared. We could certainly use a real vacation, couldn't we, honey?" he added, a little twinkle in his eyes as he met Janet's delighted gaze.

Felicity smiled, but her face was suddenly ashen, and her lips parted as she drew shallow breaths.

"Felicity?" he asked, his heart jumping into his throat. He shoved his chair back from the table and rushed over to her.

"What's wrong?" David asked.

"I'm just..." Felicity struggled to her feet and shoved past everyone. Jared was right on her heels as he got to the bathroom and she fell to her knees by the toilet, throwing up.

It tore him up inside to see Felicity like this. He pulled her hair back from her face and waited beside her on the floor, wishing he could do more.

"What's wrong with her?" Janet asked, her nurse side taking over.

"She's been sick since we got off the plane about five days ago. It seems to be just nausea. She did have an accident while skiing, with a minor concussion, back and hip injuries, but she was able to leave the same day. Her nausea started before then," Jared explained.

"Right." Janet knelt by her daughter and searched in the cabinets beneath the sink for towels and handed some to Jared. "Wet these and put them on the back of her neck. I'll get some water for her to drink."

Jared soaked the cloth with cold water and placed it on Felicity's neck. David watched them from the doorway, a small sound curling his lips down. "I'll go help Janet."

Once they were alone, Felicity started to cry. Her sobs broke his heart, and he made soft shushing sounds.

"Hey, honey, it's okay. Just calm down and relax," he urged.

"I've ruined our vacation," she moaned. Her tone was so full of misery he suddenly laughed.

"No, you haven't. This is *not* the worst trip I've ever been on."

"Really?" She turned her face away from the toilet, eyeing him skeptically. He could tell he had her full attention now. It was a gamble, but the best he could do to take her mind off her nausea.

He settled in beside her, rubbing a hand on her back as he started to talk.

"When I was twenty-one, Angelo, Thad, and I went on a float trip. We flew out to Arkansas and spent four days attempting to float the rivers. Have you ever been on a float trip?"

She shook her head.

"Right, well, the way it works is you drink a ton of beer, do cookouts, and sit on rafts that float several miles down the river over a period of days. The weekend we went?" He could not stop chuckling at the memories. "There wasn't a river to float on. It had dried up completely. So picture the three of us, too drunk, hauling heavy rafts across dry river bottoms for miles with no real water to float on. We kept getting sick because it was hot and we drank too much beer as we were trying to haul those heavy rafts. That was my worst vacation ever." When he looked her way again, her breathing had calmed and she was sitting back a little.

"I think I'm okay." She glanced around and exhaled as

her mother appeared in the door with a glass of water.

"If you're feeling better, some fresh air might be best. You could show Jared Harmon Park. The weather is still warm enough for a walk."

Felicity got to her feet. "It sounds like a good idea. Thanks, Mom." She turned to Jared, but he was already standing.

"I'll go get our coats." He left the bathroom and headed for the front door, where Felicity had left their jackets. He tried not to think about what was wrong with her and how sick she looked whenever these bouts of nausea hit her. It wasn't natural. When they got home to Chicago, he was taking her straight to the doctor to get her properly checked out. She was his woman, and he would do anything to care for her. *Anything.*

CHAPTER TWENTY-FOUR

"How far along are you?" Felicity's mother asked, her voice a whisper.

Felicity froze over the bathroom sink where she'd been getting another glass of water. Her mother stood behind her, brow furrowed. Their eyes met in the mirror. Felicity closed her eyes, trying to quell the wave of shame and panic inside her that her mother had discovered she was pregnant.

"You are pregnant, aren't you?" Janet asked, a little uncertain now.

There was no point lying to her mother, and she didn't want to. The idea of having a baby when she wasn't ready was terrifying, and as silly as it felt, she needed to have her mother's support and guidance right now.

"A little over eight weeks. I only found out a few days ago when I got into a skiing accident and was taken to the ER. I was on the pill, but the nurse thinks I didn't use condoms long enough after starting and the pill wasn't effective yet." She couldn't finish as she met her mother's gaze.

A mixture of emotions flashed in Janet's eyes. Disappointment, concern, and resignation were the strongest. Each one hit Felicity like a wrecking ball.

"Jared doesn't know." It wasn't so much a question, but rather a keen observation.

"I'll tell him we get back to Chicago, after seeing a doctor to make sure things are fine with the baby." Her heart gave an erratic thump-thump as she asked the question that scared her the most. "How'd you know I was pregnant?" What if it was obvious she was pregnant? It would be a matter of time for Jared to figure it out before she was ready to tell him, and she could ruin everything more than she already had.

A rueful smile twitched her mother's lips. "I threw up constantly the first two months I was pregnant with you. I'd be totally fine one minute and suddenly sprinting to the bathroom or the nearest sink the next. It didn't matter what time of day. I found food smells, typically meat, made me sicker."

Felicity would have laughed if her stomach hadn't turned at the thought. She'd gotten sick after she'd eaten a bite of her cheeseburger.

"Fresh air will do you good." Her mother paused, strangely hesitant before she spoke again. "You know…your father and I weren't married when I discovered you existed. It was scary and exciting. I knew I wanted you, no matter the cost." When her mother admitted this, Felicity reached out, touching her mother's arm to show she wasn't upset by hearing this. Janet covered Felicity's hand with hers before she continued.

"So I told your father, and we got married." She looked away, her eyes distant as though recalling something from many years ago. "Things were different then. A child meant giving up everything. But now…with Jared, you might have a chance to have children and your dreams as well. I don't want you to think this means the end of what you've dreamt of doing with your life." Janet met her shocked stare. "You're the hardest working person I know. If you want a life and children with him and dreams for yourself, you can find a way to have both."

Felicity couldn't stop the rush of tears that followed, and she flung herself at her mother, hugging her. Her mother held her tight, an unusual display of emotion that made both women weepy.

"Everything will be fine. Jared seems to be crazy about you. Besides, your father and I will help in whatever way we can." Janet brushed a hand over her hair in a gesture she hadn't made in many years, and it made Felicity feel like a little girl again. Safe and loved.

"Thanks, Mom." Felicity squeezed her mother for a moment longer and then let her go.

Janet rubbed at her eyes. "Now go walk. It will help." Her mother shooed her out of the bathroom, and Felicity found Jared by the front door, buttoning up his coat. When he saw her, he held up her coat, and she slipped it on and then pulled her gloves on.

"Ready?" he asked.

"Ready." She reached for his hand, needing to hold it as they left the house. "The park is only a block away."

She and Jared walked in companionable silence, their hands linked. When they reached the park, she saw a flash of appreciation in his face. Harmon Park wasn't just a field with a playground. It had a rock garden, a pond that during the summer boasted a large stock of goldfish, and even a set of tennis courts. Flowerbeds lined the sidewalks, the buds dormant now. But the park would be glorious in late spring and in summer with flowers and kids everywhere.

"This is an amazing place. Did you ever come here as a child?" Jared asked.

"All my life, actually. This park is a place for the whole town to come together." She pointed to a flat field backing up to the rock garden. "My high school graduation happened right there." She then pointed to the open fields. "And I played soccer there in middle school. We even had a small theater troupe that did 'Shakespeare in the Park' every June."

She couldn't contain the smile at the memory of those late-summer nights, the crickets stirring with an orchestra of wings rubbing against legs, the stark scent of bug spray mixed with freshly cut grass. The way the sky was dotted with stars as the men and women in vintage costumes paraded around on the flat mats from the school gymnasium. They recited some of the most beautiful verses ever written by man. Sure, it hadn't been a troupe of actors on the London stage, but the emotions were there, the raw, gut-wrenching tragedies and humorous cracks that made Shakespeare such a genius.

At the other end of the park, a group of children were huddled by the soccer field, seemingly undeterred by the lack of green grass. She and Jared watched silently as the older kids, who looked to be about twelve or thirteen, helped marshal the younger ones into a game of kickball. The littlest of the group had to be about five years old, and he trundled along in a thick winter coat and pants with a cap covering everything but his eyes.

When Felicity looked at Jared, she saw he was smiling as he studied the children playing in the park.

"Jared..." She held her breath an instant before she spoke. "Would you ever consider having kids? You know, in the future." They paused in front of the small pond where frost clung to the lily pads and ice dominated the water's surface. Jared could be like a frozen pond. Quiet and calm on the surface, but still holding life beneath. It was the lawyer in him, she had come to realize. He had developed an ability to control his reactions.

He slid his hands into his pockets, and their gazes locked.

"At the right time with the right woman, absolutely. But I'm not ready yet. Once I've been a partner for a few years, I'll feel more settled, and I'd be able to add to the responsibilities in my life. What about you?"

Felicity's chest crushed in on her heart, squeezing painfully. *He's not ready. But I don't get a choice.* She struggled to compose herself.

"I want kids, with the right guy, someone who would be a partner with me."

"Me, too." He squeezed her hand and they came to a stop for the frozen rock waterfall.

Jared opened his mouth to speak, as did she, but the hum of Jared's cell phone vibrating silenced them both. He dug around in his pockets until he found the cell and answered.

"Redmond," he said, his voice suddenly deep and businesslike, but when he stared at her, his eyes were bright with mischief. He raised one of her gloved hands to his lips, but she cupped his jaw playfully before he could kiss it, making him catch her wrist and hold her hand to his cheek as though enjoying the way she stroked his face.

Seconds later, however, the light of Jared's good mood faded.

"Yes sir, of course. I need to get a ticket for my girlfriend —" He was apparently cut off and shot her an apologetic expression then spoke again. "Right. Thank you, Mr. Pimms. See you this evening." When he hung up the call he sighed, the sound world-weary.

"Work?" she asked. Just when her mother had said things were different now...but they weren't. There would always be work in the way of life. She might get used to being second, but it wouldn't be fair to her.

"Yeah, how'd you guess?" He sighed again. "I'm sorry about this. This was not how I planned to end our holiday."

She nodded, resigned, already thinking.

He raked a hand through his dark hair, mussing it up. "It's the hotel. The closing is moved up to two days from now, so I need to be back since it's my account."

She didn't say anything, but she knew there was no choice in what they had to do.

He grabbed her hands, capturing her attention so she looked at him. "You're a part of this too, actually. Sabine will be involved much more once the closing is over. I'd love for you to come back with me so I don't have to work the holidays alone, if that's okay?" He paused, searching her face. "Unless you want to stay?"

She thought it over, and realized she needed to be back in Chicago in case Sabine needed her. It would also be possible to get the baby checked out much sooner. Yes, she did want to go back. The thought of getting a doctor's appointment so she could see the baby again—it was too tempting to resist.

Maybe I can find a way to tell him soon.

"I should go back to Chicago, too." She let out her own sigh. The vacation they'd vowed to have and enjoy had been burdened with the news of her pregnancy and she couldn't stand being around Jared and his parents while keeping a secret like that. She would have to tell him sometime soon, but not right now.

"I'll let my boss know. Did the walk make you feel better?" Jared asked as they turned back toward home. He had already pulled his cell out to text his boss back about flying home, clearly distracted.

"Yes," she lied. Her nausea was gone, but in its place was now a deep-seated fear for her baby and herself, all because she would be one step closer to losing him.

Was this how the rest of her life would be if she stayed in Chicago and had the baby there with Jared? Just one more distraction for a man who was a workaholic? She didn't want to put herself or the baby through that, but she loved him and didn't want to leave.

What am I going to do?

It was raining when their flight landed in Chicago, and Felicity couldn't help but think the dreary cold wet matched her mood. The entire flight back, Jared had been immersed in work, with his laptop on with contracts and spreadsheets on his lap. Part of her had wished she'd changed her mind and stayed in Nebraska a few more days. She could have talked to her mother about the baby, the dos and don'ts, and everything else a newly-pregnant woman needed to know.

Now here she was, back in a city with hundreds of thousands of people, and she felt more isolated and alone than she'd ever been in her life. A whole other human now depended on her, was *growing* inside of her, and she was terrified that she wouldn't do all the right things to give the baby the life it deserved.

"I've got to go to the office for a few hours. I'll have a cab come pick you up and bring you to my place for a movie, among other things." Jared leaned over and kissed her. For the first time in three hours he was paying attention to her, and she hated that it filled her with joy.

Felicity wanted to do that more than anything, but she knew she needed some time to figure things out and think about the baby.

"I'm too tired. What if I see you tomorrow night?"

The look of disappointment in his eyes would haunt her forever, but she needed space and time to think about everything. She wasn't ready to tell him about the baby, even though she knew she'd have to tell him soon.

The cab they caught from the airport dropped Jared off at his office first and Felicity at her apartment building twenty minutes later. He'd kissed her before he'd gotten out of the cab, and she clung to that memory, knowing she'd sleep alone tonight. She hauled her duffel bag over her shoulders, wincing as her body screamed at the movement. It would be weeks before her body got back to feeling normal after getting crushed by that snowboarder.

She *hated* that she had to come home to this small apartment with its cramped rooms and dark halls. For the last month and a half, she'd spent half her nights in Jared's bed. Her small apartment felt less and less like home and more confined than ever. But she had to get used to it. If she ended up going to Los Angeles, she'd be facing the same issue of small living quarters. It would be even more confining once the baby arrived.

Felicity touched her stomach for the hundredth time. Would it be a boy? Or a girl? For the first time since she found out she was pregnant, she was excited to think about the baby. If it was a girl, she'd buy all the cute dresses in bright colors; if it was a boy, he'd be in natural colors. She smiled a little. Colors. As an artist and a person who'd studied art most of her life, she was always focused on colors. What would she do with the baby's room? She'd have to paint the walls with something wonderful. She could just picture it. A little boy with dark hair and expressive eyes like his father, or a girl with her father's sense of sweetness and mischief. A pit formed in her stomach at the thought of having to figure this out on her own if Jared didn't want to be involved with the baby.

Her apartment building was dark as she entered the lobby. The overhead lights were not working, as usual. It was so different from the light, clean lobby of Jared's apartment building. She climbed the stairs, her bag hitting her back in the same sore spot the entire way up before she reached her floor. The hall was quiet, except for the muted sounds of the couple next door who always argued and the TV in the apartment by the stairs. Felicity dug her keys out of her purse when she reached her door.

The moment that the key slid into the lock it wouldn't turn. She tried again, muttering, and when she fiddled with the knob the apartment door eased open.

It had been unlocked already…

Maybe I forgot to lock it when I left for Colorado?

No. She'd never forgotten to lock it before. A tingling sense of unease crept up her spine, making her shudder.

She nudged the door open with her foot, and it creaked loudly as it opened farther. She walked a few steps into her apartment and then froze. Her couch was ripped to shreds, stuffing puffed out at odd angles between clear slash marks. Her bookshelves were upended, the textbooks crumpled on the floor, their pages bent and torn. All around her was destruction and ruination. She dropped the duffel bag to the floor, her heart stuck in her throat.

"I've been robbed…" she whispered brokenly. The truth of her situation hit her fully when she heard a shuffling step and a crash in the kitchen. She whirled and screamed at the sight of a man rooting through her cabinets. He stopped moving and stared at her through a black ski mask. All she could see was the whites of his eyes. Never in her life had she faced a nightmare like this. Everything inside her seemed to speed up while all around her the world slowed down.

Baby, must protect baby. It was strange that an instinct she had never possessed before was now suddenly screaming inside of her.

Felicity ran for the bathroom, which was closer to her. The outside hall was too far away, and he could catch her, kill her… Her feet skidded as she hit the tile in the bathroom. Her shoulder slammed against the doorframe as she struggled to turn and slam the door shut. When the lock clicked, she backed away from the door, her heart smacking against her ribs so hard she could barely breathe. Her ears strained to pick up any sounds outside the door.

Boots stomped past the bathroom, more crashing. Something shattered, and then there was nothing but silence.

Felicity was shaking so hard she clutched her hands together for several long seconds before she crumpled to the floor and reached for her purse. She pulled her cell phone out and dialed 911.

"911, what's your emergency?" a calm female voice asked.

"Please help me," she whispered. "There's a man in my apartment, robbing me. I'm locked in the bathroom. Please… I'm pregnant and I'm scar—ed." Her voice broke at the last two words she uttered. Her mind was racing, but not a single thought was rational. Sheer panic flooded her.

"Stay calm, ma'am. What's your location?"

Felicity whispered her address and waited. "*Please hurry.*"

The woman on the phone spoke again. "Stay on the line, honey. Officers are en route to your location."

Felicity stayed on the phone listening to the sounds outside. Her blood pounded in her ears, making it hard for her to distinguish any other noises beyond the bathroom door.

Please…let him leave me alone…

She held on to the cell phone and waited.

CHAPTER TWENTY-FIVE

After ten minutes of hiding in the bathroom, Felicity heard footsteps and a click followed by fast chatter on a police radio.

"Ma'am, it's the police. We've entered the premises. Remain in the bathroom until we knock."

"Okay." She pressed a hand to her stomach.

It seemed to take years before somebody knocked on the door.

"It's all clear, ma'am. It's safe to come out. I'm Officer Winston, and my partner Officer Bowen is standing beside me."

"Ma'am, the officers are at your location. It's safe to hang up," the 911 dispatcher said.

"Thank you," Felicity breathed and disconnected the call. Then she got to her feet, her knees knocking together as she unlocked the door.

Two uniformed officers stood there, frowning.

"Ms. Hart?" the older one asked. He looked to be in his midforties.

"That's me." She stepped out of the bathroom.

"Whoever was here when you arrived is long gone. We need you to file a report and list anything that's missing."

She nodded numbly.

"Do you have anyone you can call?" the second officer asked. He was younger, probably in his early thirties. Both of the officers were looking at her in concern. "We were told you're pregnant," the younger officer continued. "My wife's four months pregnant, and if she'd gone through a scare like this, I'd be worried about her being alone."

"I can call my boyfriend." She would call Jared and then she would call Layla.

"You should call him and have him come over to help you pack a bag. I would urge you not to stay here tonight. It's unlikely for burglars to come back, but the dispatcher said you saw him, even though he was masked. It's still a risk I wouldn't advise taking."

"Right..." She dialed Jared's number and waited, watching the cops move about the apartment doing one last examination.

Jared answered on the fifth ring, sounding frustrated. "Felicity? What's up? I'm in the middle of something—"

"Jared..." she whispered, her voice cracking again with another unwelcome flood of emotions.

"Honey? What's wrong?" His tone changed instantly to concern.

"I was robbed. I got home and I came in and there was a man and I walked in on him, and I saw him." Her heart was still pounding, and she couldn't stop shaking. It took a second for her to collect herself and continue. "I locked myself in the bathroom. I called 911. The police are here, and they told me I shouldn't stay here tonight."

"Fucking hell! Of course you're not staying there! Are you okay?"

"Yeah, just shaken up." She glanced at the two cops, who were now standing by the door.

"I'll be there in twenty minutes." Jared hung up.

While she waited for Jared to arrive, Felicity had called Layla and told her everything and assured her that Jared was coming to take care of her. Then she'd filled out the police report and tried to go through room by room to see what was missing. Her secondhand laptop and a tiny TV had been stolen. Other than that, everything was completely destroyed, but nothing else was missing. Broken dishes littered the kitchen floor, and everything in the bathroom was scattered on the tile. She felt numb as she stared at the pieces of her life that lay damaged and broken.

That could have been me lying on the floor...with the baby...

Raw emotions swept through her, leaving her vulnerable and rattled. There was no way she could stay here in this apartment, not after this. For her baby's sake, she had to move out of here as soon as possible.

She was standing by the bathroom door, hands clenched into white-knuckled fists, her eyes darting to the front door. She jolted when Jared burst into the apartment. His hair was mussed as though he'd been clawing his hands through it, and his tie was loosened, his jacket hanging off one arm as though he hadn't even stopped to put it on before rushing out of his office to come to her.

"Felicity, honey?" His voice was low, harsh, and full of worry.

"Here." She rushed to him, throwing herself into the safe cocoon of his arms. The floodgates opened, and she was crying. *Again.* Since when had she become so weak that she cried at the drop of a hat? *No, I'm not weak. This is just hormones and stress and trauma.*

Jared wrapped his arms tighter around her, pressing his

lips against the crown of her hair. "I'm here. You're safe." His low murmurs soothed some of the panic. He was warm, strong, and holding her like a sturdy rock, immovable against even the mightiest of storms.

"Sir, we had her complete a report and will get it filed. We advised her to stay somewhere else tonight."

Felicity didn't look at the cops as they came over to her and Jared.

"I'll take her to my place."

"Good. Try to have a good night," the older cop said.

"You too," Jared replied. When the cops left, he pulled away from her enough that she had to look up at him. He cupped her chin.

"Hey, it's going to be okay. You're safe now." The way he said it, with his strong arms and tall, muscled body cradling hers, she felt it had to be true.

Safe. She was safe. The baby was safe.

A startling burst of clarity struck her in that moment. She couldn't wait another minute to tell Jared about the baby. If something had happened to her tonight, he might not have known about the baby until it was too late. She couldn't keep the truth from him any longer. It was time to tell him and face whatever may come.

"We have to talk," she said, her voice stronger now that she knew what she had to do.

"Ok—ay." He drew out the word slowly as though sensing whatever she had to say was important, and that seemed to worry him. "It can wait until we get to my apartment, right?"

She bit her lip and nodded.

"Good. Pack a week's worth of clothing. I'm not letting you stay here until I feel it's safe for you to come back." He released her after one more kiss to her forehead.

Felicity packed clothes and took all the items she was

afraid to leave behind, including her sketchbook and the family photo album she'd brought from home. Jared collected the textbooks she needed for the week, and together they left her apartment. Jared whistled for a cab and helped her inside. Even though he was there, she still couldn't stop the slight shaking of her body. The adrenaline that had spiked when she'd seen the burglar was still pumping through her system. It would probably take a few hours to totally calm down.

Jared's phone buzzed, and he slipped it out of his coat pocket, cursing. He texted something back and shoved the phone into his pocket.

"Work?" she asked.

"Yeah, they'll be fine without me for another half hour."

"I'm sorry you had to leave work," she said just as the taxi pulled up in front of his apartment.

He shrugged as he climbed out of the cab. "They can be without me for a few hours. I'll go back once I have you settled."

Felicity didn't reply. She couldn't help but dread what she had to do. By the time they got up to Jared's apartment, her stomach was doing cartwheels and she was afraid to open her mouth in case she threw up. God, it was too silent in here, so quiet she half expected him to hear the racing thoughts that screamed through her head. She was getting ready to tell him he was going to be a father. Was there any good way to spring this news on a man?

"Is Tanner here?" she asked quietly when Jared set her bags down by his bed.

"No, he and Layla won't be back for another couple of days."

Good. She had time to talk to him without any interruptions.

Jared approached her and impulsively pulled her into his arms. "When you called me, I thought I was going to have a heart attack." He kissed her forehead, and then his lips moved down her cheek, then to her mouth.

If I don't say it now, I'll never tell him.

Felicity pressed a hand to his chest, separating them.

"Jared..." She lifted her lashes and tilted her head back.

"What is it? Talk to me," he urged.

"In Colorado, when I fell..." She frowned and paused, struggling for words. "They can't do X-rays on certain people because of conditions..."

"Okay." He'd crossed his arms and was watching her intensely, his brows drawn together.

"But I wasn't conscious, so they couldn't ask me about those conditions, you see?"

"All right..."

When he continued to stare at her, she could feel the tears ready to spill, but she fought to control them.

"So they did the tests to figure out if I had those conditions in order to do the X-rays." He still said nothing. *What the hell, here it goes...* "Jared, they gave me a pregnancy test. I'm *pregnant.*"

The space between them was covered in a cloak of silence. They stared at one another, and she could see the words were slowly settling in.

"Jared? Are you all right?" She bit her lip, trying to figure out how to get through his shock. "Jared, I'm having a baby. *Our* baby." His hands, which had been holding her waist, dropped away and he stepped back, his jaw going slack.

"Pregnant?" He uttered the word roughly. "But...you were on the pill, and we used condoms." He turned away from her, his hands digging into his hair as he began to pace the floor of his apartment.

"The nurse in Steamboat Springs told me that I might have needed to wait longer to have sex without condoms for the pill to be effective."

He paused in his pacing, like a jungle cat sensing danger. Every muscle in his body appeared to tense.

"How far along are you?" He stared at her belly and she put one hand over herself.

"A little over eight weeks. We must have…"

"Eight weeks." He whistled softly. "God, a baby," he muttered and started pacing again. His face was lined with worry.

What if he didn't want the baby? Her throat went dry at the thought, but she had made her decision long ago and would raise the child alone if she had to.

"I'm keeping it, Jared. I don't expect anything from you if you don't want to—"

"What?" He froze and stared at her, mouth agape. "Of course I want to be a part of this. I just need a minute to adjust." He stopped pacing and faced her, his eyes heavy with concern and shock. "You've known for days," he muttered.

She flinched at his tone and backed up, giving him space if he needed to pace again.

"I wanted to tell you at the hospital, but it was all too much, and then I didn't want to ruin the holiday. And then it all made sense—the throwing up because of morning sickness, not bad plane food or altitude. And I just needed to process and think and figure things out…" God, she was rambling. Felicity wrung her hands together.

Jared slowly walked into the kitchen and grabbed a bottle of scotch from the cabinet. He poured one glass and glanced her way. "Sorry, princess, but I really need this." He downed the glass and rubbed his closed eyes with his thumb and forefinger. She collapsed on the couch and wrapped her arms around her chest.

"This whole time you've been sick, it was the *baby*?" He said the word *baby* carefully, as though hesitant.

"Yes. I didn't know until the accident, but that's what it

was."

He stared at the bottle of scotch before he put it away and came toward her. She was rooted to the spot, too afraid that now was the moment he'd decide he didn't want her or the baby and would tell her to leave. He reached out and cupped her cheek, his thumb caressing her lip. His eyes were fathomless depths that swallowed her whole. Felicity's body trembled and her spine tingled as she waited for him to speak. He lifted her chin and then very slowly lowered his head. One of his hands touched her lower back, his palm heating her through her thin sweater. His touches were light, easy to escape, yet somehow he made her feel trapped, in a good way that made her belly quiver and her womb clench.

"Are you mad at me?" Felicity whispered. It was the one question she had to ask, even if the possible answer scared the hell out of her. She curled her fingers into his shirt, keeping him close.

Jared stared at her lips, arching one brow as he spoke. "Mad? No. Shocked? Yeah. It knocked me on my ass, but..." He licked his lips, his voice low and husky, the sweet scent of scotch teasing her nose. "I'm scared out of my goddamned mind," he admitted, and her heart jolted in fear until he spoke again. "But I'm happy, too. So happy, princess."

At long last, he kissed her. The slow burn of that kiss melted away the icy-cold fears that had been clawing at her for days. The hollow fluttering panic that she might be facing parenthood all alone had been crushing her. Now, at long last, she could breathe. Jared lifted her up by the waist, and she wrapped her legs around his hips. She continued to kiss him as he carried her to the bedroom. He dropped her on her back and climbed over her. When she was caught beneath him on the bed, his hips wedged between her thighs, he gazed down at her.

"A baby," he whispered.

She bit her bottom lip and nodded.

"The nurse in Colorado emailed me a video of the heartbeat and some pictures. Do you want to see?" Hope fluttered like nervous doves inside her chest.

"You have that?" His eyes widened. "Of course I want to see." He slid off her body and lay beside her as she pulled her phone out of her pocket. She scrolled through her videos until she saw the heartbeat label and then tapped the screen, handing it to him. They both lay there, her head on his chest while he watched the screen flicker to life.

"That thing fluttering there, that is the heart beating," she explained. The rapid pulse thumped through the speakers, and it made her own heart race. She lifted her hand, resting her chin on his pectoral muscles so she could see his face.

He was gazing in rapture at the photo screen, and she saw his Adam's apple bob as he swallowed thickly when the screen went dark.

"Do we know the sex of the baby?" he asked, his voice rough with emotions.

She shook her head. "Too early to tell."

"God, it's beautiful," he said.

Felicity laughed. "I thought it look like a grayscale gummy bear."

He was silent for a second before bursting out laughing. "Congratulations, princess. You just nicknamed the baby. Gummy bear." He chuckled to himself.

"You can't tell me you didn't think the same thing."

"All I thought was that it was perfect. Just like its mother." He set the phone down and rolled her over again, his mouth slanting over hers as he threaded a hand through her hair. She arched her back, but winced from the pain of the skiing injury. It was still a little tender.

He broke the kiss, and she was startled by the fear in his eyes. "You could have been killed tonight. You and the baby.

God, Felicity, I don't know what I would've done if anything had happened to you."

"But I'm fine. *We're fine.*" She touched her abdomen, and he covered her hand with his, lacing her fingers through his.

"You're never going back to that apartment again." His tone brooked no argument.

"Jared, that's my place. I have a lease—"

"I'm a fucking lawyer. I can break a lease in a heartbeat," he growled.

"And just where would I go?" she demanded.

Jared brushed his fingertips along her jaw, impossibly tender, completely at odds with the fiery expression in his eyes. "You're moving in here tomorrow, first thing in the morning."

"But that's not a permanent solution," she reminded him. "We have to talk about what we're going to do."

"What do you mean?" The genuine puzzlement in his face surprised her.

"About us. And the baby."

His eyes narrowed. "You aren't going to give it up—"

"No!" she gasped. "It's ours. I could never give it up or…" She shook her head. "What I meant is what happens in May? I sent off my application to the Los Angeles County Art Museum, and I'm waiting to see if they want to interview me."

She knew the moment when he put two and two together. The hand that had been stroking her cheek stilled.

"You still want to go to California," he guessed.

"And you still want to stay here," she guessed. That awful hollow pit was back in her stomach.

"And I want you and the baby." He closed his eyes and breathed slowly. Felicity held her breath and studied the fan of dark lashes on his cheeks until he opened his eyes again.

"We can be smart about this," he said slowly. "When will you know about the job in Los Angeles?"

"In a few months."

Jared resumed stroking her arm. "Then let's not worry about the future until we know that this is what we have to choose from."

She knew what he meant. It was a real possibility she wouldn't get the job. Museum curators' positions were highly sought after. She would be in tough competition against other candidates who had more degrees than she did, like PhDs. And if she didn't get the job? She guessed she could stay in Chicago, but she'd be slim on job possibilities.

He caught her eye and gave her a reassuring smile. "I know how self-sufficient you are, but just know this. I can support you and the baby if you choose to stay here and can't find work immediately."

She tensed. The idea of not paying her own way rankled, but he was sweet to offer to support her. She was a firm believer in women standing on their own two feet, but for the sake of the baby, she would be willing to consider his help. It also meant more time with the man she loved, something she had not thought possible even with the baby. She had honestly expected him to freak out more or be upset, but he'd wholeheartedly embraced the idea of being a father.

"The important thing is that you're here with me, and now you and the baby are safe." Jared curled his fingers under her chin, lifting it up, and she leaned into his kiss.

I can worry about the rest of this tomorrow.

CHAPTER TWENTY-SIX

I'm going to be a father.

Jared stared at the stack of papers in front of him, not really focusing on his work. He'd come into the office early since he hadn't returned last night. The whole baby-bomb-dropping had been a huge distraction. He couldn't stop thinking about the ultrasound video he'd seen last night. The little shape that vaguely looked like a gummy bear and the fluttering heart, that rapid sound. It had changed everything. Just like the night he'd walked into his room and seen Felicity asleep in his bed.

I'm having a kid.

Sure, it was years before he'd planned to be a dad, but now he couldn't stop smiling. The woman he loved like crazy was having a baby…with him. He couldn't wait to tell his parents and Tanner.

"Jared."

He glanced up from the Worthington closing documents and found his boss staring at him.

"Mr. Pimms. I was just reviewing—"

"Jared, I need to see you in my office." Pimms's no-nonsense tone knocked the breath out of him.

Whatever it was, he didn't think it involved a raise or good news.

"Okay." He pushed away from his desk and followed his boss into the corner office.

Pimms straightened his suit and sat down, as regal as a king, and then he motioned for Jared to sit in front of him.

"It's been made clear to me that you and my daughter are no longer together. I'll admit, I was disappointed. But your work *up until now* has been excellent."

The phrase *until now* had been emphasized enough that Jared suspected he was about to get reprimanded for something. He wisely kept his mouth shut. Pimms pushed a few papers idly across his desk.

"We conducted background checks for the Worthingtons on all known employees at Sabine's before we signed contracts with Sabine's company to have them do the interior design. Last evening, after you left, a secretary who was expensing plane tickets to get you home from Nebraska pointed something out to me." He lifted unamused eyes to Jared's face. "Your girlfriend works for Sabine. That's a clear conflict of interest that you should have immediately declared to our clients. You failed to disclose the relationship, and we've been working on this deal for two months. You're playing with the lines of ethics, Redmond. It's also affected your work. Last night when you left, we found a lease in the title report on the hotel. It's an old lease, but we need a release of that lease or it could cloud the title and delay the closing. We could lose the Worthington business. You and I both know how important it is to keep them as a client."

Throughout Pimms's speech, Jared felt his throat closing with panic. It was true. He'd failed to disclose his and Felicity's relationship to the Worthingtons. Thad had known, but his dad didn't. They should've been notified and asked to sign an agreement allowing Jared to continue as their counsel while dating someone with a business connection to them. Instead, he and Felicity had been hiding in their own private world, relishing the joy of a semi-secret love affair that clearly put his job at risk.

"I'm sorry, Mr. Pimms. You're right. I should have declared my relationship to the client. And I can fix the lease-release issue immediately." He slipped a finger under his collar and loosened it a tiny bit. Damned if he wasn't having trouble breathing.

"Take my advice, Jared. A woman who makes you forget about work may be fun for a while, but she isn't the sort of girl a man marries."

Jared kept his mouth shut. He knew full well how Pimms viewed marriage. Love wasn't necessary and certainly wasn't preferred if it interfered with work. It was why he and his wife had divorced years ago.

"So have your fun and move on. If it interferes with your work again, I'm not much for third chances. That means no more running off when I ask you to work late nights, on weekends, or on holidays."

Jared bristled, his control slipping. "Mr. Pimms, I have been a loyal employee. I've worked here since law school, and I love my job. My personal life is not a distraction."

Pimms fixed him with a stare. "You can't let every passing fancy ruin your career trajectory."

"I left last night because my girlfriend was robbed. She was hiding in the bathroom, praying to God the man burglarizing her apartment wouldn't hurt her. We only just found out she's pregnant. She was upset and frightened, and I couldn't refuse going to her." He paused when he realized his voice had deepened and his tone was much louder than it should've been. He lowered his volume as he continued. "I love her, and I won't just leave her alone when her life and the baby's are in danger. I'm not a bastard."

He didn't regret the outburst. But he did regret that it could very well cost him his job, the job he told Felicity last night that he'd have to support her and the baby.

Pimms, as enigmatic as the Sphinx, stared at him for long seconds before speaking again. "Every man should have a fire in his gut, Jared. I'm glad you finally found yours. Just don't let this interfere with your performance."

Jared rose from the chair and halted halfway to the door.

"Is the partnership offer still on the table if I seal this transaction for the hotel?" His heart beat hard as he waited for Pimms to answer.

"Yes. I made a promise. But I want that release by tonight, Jared. I mean it." The implied "or else" made Jared's stomach turn.

Fuck. He could lose everything he'd spent seven years working toward. He could lose his job.

Jared nodded and left Pimms's office. When he was back at his own desk, he called Felicity.

"Hello?" Her sweet voice made him ache to just leave and go home to her, but he was stuck here, fighting through paperwork for the rest of the night.

"It's me. I've got to work late tonight."

"But what about the doctor's appointment? It's at four o'clock." He didn't miss the worry in her voice. She'd told him last night she didn't want to go to the appointment alone, and he'd promised her.

Hell. He'd forgotten all about the appointment. There was no way he could go, not after Pimms put his job on the line.

"I can't go. I got raked over the coals by my boss for not telling the Worthingtons that I'm seeing you. It's a potential conflict of interest." He pressed the heel of one palm into his forehead as he leaned over his desk.

"You got in trouble for dating me?"

She had no idea how thin a line he'd crossed by dating her. Most people thought lawyers were grade-A assholes. No one knew that lawyers policed themselves pretty harshly on ethics, and dating someone on the other side of a transaction was a huge liability if he didn't get his clients to consent to it in writing.

"I can't even afford to talk right now. If I don't get a problem with the title on the hotel cleared up, I'm done. Consider my ass fired." Frustrated, he slammed his hand on his desk.

"Jared?" Her voice was heavy was concern, but he wasn't in the mood to explain in detail how he was fucking everything up. It wasn't exactly the sexiest of things to own up to in front of the woman he loved.

"Look, I've got to go. I'll talk to you later." He hung up without waiting to hear her reply.

There was a lot he had to do in the next four hours or else he'd be in deep shit. He dug through the folder of the first title report, hunting down the troublesome lease. The paper was tucked in between two other documents. The date of the lease was old: 1938. Jesus, that was ancient. Why the hell did Pimms think it still mattered? The hotel had been closed since 1983. He scanned the document.

The hotel had apparently leased out the first floor to an Italian bistro, and the lease had an auto-renewal clause. That was why they needed a release. Even old, it could cloud the title and destroy the closing, just like Pimms had said.

"Fucking hell," Jared muttered. How was he supposed to find someone to sign off on a release for a restaurant that probably went out of business in the 1940s?

He spent the next three hours scanning every major website containing public land records, but he couldn't find a trace of the bistro's owner. His nerves were frayed, and he felt sick. Pimms had made it pretty clear he was toast if he couldn't get a release signed tonight. He rubbed his face in his hands.

I have to think of something. Felicity and the baby needed him. *I have to get my shit together and figure this out.*

"You okay, Jared?"

He glanced up and saw Shana leaning in his doorway. They'd been friends a very long time, and he'd never had a problem sharing his concerns about things before, but now he hesitated over what to say.

"Seriously, are you all right? You look like hell," she said.

"I've got to find someone to sign a release for a bistro that used to be in the first floor of the hotel we're working on for the Worthingtons."

"Okay, well, we can make some calls tomorrow." Shana stepped further into his office, placing her hands on the back of one of his client chairs opposite his desk.

Jared closed his eyes and rubbed them with his thumb and forefinger.

"This is serious, Shana. Your dad gave me an ultimatum. He's pissed that I'm dating someone else. He thinks it's affecting my work because I had to leave early yesterday."

"I remember. What happened?" She came around the chair and sat down.

"Felicity walked in on a man robbing her apartment. She needed me to come over. She's pretty shaken up. Because she got a look at the man, the police advised her to stay somewhere else."

"Okay, I understand that," Shana said. "But you didn't come back?"

"I could have come back after I took her home, but she sort of dropped a bombshell on me—she's pregnant. I was so unprepared. We've been careful. And I *really* am letting it affect my job. If I don't fix this lease release, I'm out."

Shana waved a hand. "That's wonderful news about the baby, Jared. I'm happy for you." Her eyes were shining, but he saw that her sadness was not out of jealousy, but a desire for her own family. "You need to ignore my dad. He's being an idiot. Finding out that someone you love was in danger and then adding a baby to that? I'd be a mess too. Let me help with the lease. What info do you have?"

He handed the lease to her, knowing that her intentions were good, but she wouldn't have any new strategies that he hadn't thought of before.

Shana furrowed her brow and then tapped the paper as she set it down his desk.

"It looks like the bistro is a family-owned restaurant, so any heirs could sign, right?"

"Possibly."

"Then you need to find an Italian family in Chicago, right?" She raised her brows, and then it hit him, the solution she was hinting at.

"Angelo," he breathed.

"Angelo," Shana echoed with a chuckle. "If this family is still around, he will know how to find them." Angelo was a font of information about the other restaurants in Chicago, especially the Italian ones. He'd know what had happened to the bistro owners, or he'd know someone who would know.

Jared leaped out of his chair, the release papers in his hand as he came around the desk and impulsively hugged Shana.

"You saved my ass," he called out before sprinting down the hall to the elevators.

For the first time in a long time today, he felt he could breathe.

Everything was going to be okay.

Felicity stared at the screen of her cell phone long after it went dark. Jared was going to get fired because of her relationship with him.

It's my fault.

Tears stung her eyes, but she held them at bay. She'd been a fool to think she and Jared were ready to become something more permanent. His career needed his full-time commitment, and a pregnant girlfriend was an unnecessary burden. She loved him with all of her heart, and she knew how much he cared about his job at the firm. It wasn't fair to destroy his future by staying here and complicating his life.

She touched her belly, her heart shattering as she faced the only real option left. She needed to stay away from him long enough to let things cool between them. He could and would be a part of the baby's life, but he couldn't be a part of hers, not in the way she'd dreamed about.

"I have to fix this," she told the baby, even knowing it couldn't hear her, not yet.

She texted Thad telling him she needed his help. He called her a few seconds later.

"Felicity?" Thad's voice was rich and soft, but it made her miss Jared's voice all the more.

"I made a mistake. Jared and I didn't disclose our relationship officially to your father or you."

"We don't have a problem with it," he replied immediately.

"Thank you, but I think Jared's boss needs some sort of signed document."

"A consent and waiver document, that'd be my guess," he said. "I can have one drafted, signed, and sent to Pimms's office this evening."

She exhaled in relief. "Thank you, Thad. Really."

There was a pause on the other end of the line. "Is everything okay? You sound as though you've been crying."

"I...um...I need a new place to live for a few months. My apartment got broken into last night, and I've decided I can't go back there to live." She knew what he was going to ask next, but there was no avoiding it.

"You were robbed? Are you okay? Have you talked to Jared?" Thad's questions came out hurried, and his tone was rough, as though he was angry at what had happened to her.

"I'm fine. Jared came over and took me to his place for the night. But I can't stay at my old apartment anymore."

"And you're not moving in with Jared?"

"No. He made it pretty clear that I'm in the way and a threat to his job security. So I'm leaving. Tonight while he's at work. I just need some time to myself to heal." She was not about to tell him she was pregnant.

"But he's crazy about you. He nearly killed me that night I took you out to Club Amazon. He's never been like that with any other woman." There was a note of puzzlement in his tone.

"I know he cares, but we're at different parts of our lives. I don't want him to get hurt because he's with me." She held her breath, waiting for him to say something.

"I don't want to help break the two of you up, but if there's any other way I can help, I will. What do you need?" Thad asked.

She steeled herself to ask him the question she dreaded. It was not in her nature to ask for help. But the truth was, she needed a new place to stay, away from Jared. She considered rooming with Layla, but that meant seeing Tanner and then thinking of Jared.

"I need to get an apartment that's in my budget and not

in a scary part of town. I figured you know a lot of real estate people around town, so maybe you could help me find a place? Something small, no amenities." More silence, then Thad surprised her.

"I'm not having you stay anywhere but at the Gold Circle."

The Gold Circle? That was one of the world's most exclusive hotels. She couldn't afford one night there—it was the equivalent of her monthly rent. It was also where the closing party was going to be held in two weeks.

"Thank you, but I can't afford it."

"It's my hotel. You get the 'friends discount,' and by that I mean you don't pay anything. What's the point of owning a hotel if I can't offer a room to a friend in need? Consider it a bonus for the services you and Sabine are rendering to me and my father."

He had to be joking.

"Thad, I can't—"

"I'm afraid I'm insisting on this. Jared is my best friend, aside from Angelo. It's a man's duty to protect his friend's woman. So until you and Jared sort out your issues, you should stay somewhere safe."

It touched her heart that Thad was such a good friend that he would offer this, but she couldn't accept.

"I mean it, Felicity." His tone was firm, and she knew he wasn't going to let her say no. "You're going to be somewhere safe. I have an excellent suite at the hotel, and you will go straight there. I'll tell the doorman that you're coming. Anything you need will be provided."

"But—"

"If you don't arrive in two hours, I'll come get you."

She sighed. "Okay, but I want to find a way to pay you back."

Thad chuckled. "How about I hire you in the future for a

side decoration and art project? I'm thinking about buying a beautiful brownstone, and it needs some interior makeovers. We can talk in a few weeks."

Free art advice and interior design? Yeah, that was a bargain she could make.

"That sounds good to me." She felt calmer, more relaxed. It was going to be okay.

"Excellent. Two hours, remember, or I'll come get you," Thad warned and hung up.

What was it about pushy, dominating men? A new ache blossomed in her heart for Jared. How was she going to live without him? Somehow she'd have to.

She let her cell phone fall into her lap and tucked her knees up against her chest on Jared's bed. She would have to reschedule her doctor's appointment. There was no way she was going alone. She'd wait for a day when Layla could go with her. There was so much to do. She had two hours to pack up and leave the place she'd come to love and view as her real home because it was a place she'd shared with Jared. They would never make love in this bed again, or share a glass of wine on the couch, or eat dinner and talk about their day at the table. The life they'd been pretending to build together was just that, an illusion. She was always going to go her own way, especially when the job would take her far from him, but she hadn't wanted to face that reality. She wanted to cling to that bit of illusion just a little while longer.

One tear escaped and rolled down her cheek, dropping into a spot on her jean-clad knee.

She would find a way to make everything okay. She had to, for the baby. Picking up the pieces of her shattered heart, she walked over to Jared's closet and opened the door. In the corner of the closet she saw the gown—the Tudor gown she'd worn. He had made her wear it once, and they'd gotten carried away in a playful role play game that night. It had felt wonderful and wicked and sweet all at once. So much had changed from that first night she'd fallen asleep in his bed. She remembered how she felt the first night she'd come in here during the Halloween party.

The allure of the mysterious Jared Redmond. The glint of his expensive watches, the neatly rolled ties with elegant designs, and the feel of his business shirts when she rubbed them against her cheek. Her imagination then had nothing on the reality of the man now. The way he'd made love to her that first time, as if anxious to be inside of her, but also as if he would have years to explore her every fantasy. From the drugging kisses and the flirty smiles, to the hint of dominance when he pinned her wrists into the bed sometimes, she'd always felt like she was the center of his world, even when they simply drank wine and cuddled on the couch.

Being with Jared made her feel like more than just herself. It wasn't that Felicity had felt empty before she met him. She'd had hopes and dreams and a life all her own, but after meeting him, after being with him, she knew exactly what sort of joys she would miss out on by leaving his apartment tonight. Before she could stop herself, she slipped into his closet and removed one of his black T-shirts. The soft cotton was like velvet in her hands, and she pressed it against her cheek. It carried his scent, that natural, clean male scent. He didn't use cologne, and she liked that. He was exactly who he wanted to be and didn't need anything to enhance that raw sex appeal that rolled off him in waves.

I shouldn't...

She clutched the shirt and carried it to her bag, which she'd put on his bed, and tucked the shirt inside. One little piece of him was all she could keep.

When she looked up, she saw the framed drawing of her and Jared as Cleopatra and Mark Antony. That would be his bit of her to keep.

Felicity packed quickly, cramming her old duffel with everything she could squeeze into it, then using her backpack for schoolbooks. She'd need to get a new laptop since hers had been stolen, but she didn't have the money right now. Once she was packed, she paused in the doorway of Jared's apartment, already missing him. She wouldn't think about him, not how she would miss his kisses, his touch, his whispered words of love, or the way he'd made her feel like she was capable of anything. She wouldn't cry, not until she was far away from here.

Here I leave my heart and the dreams I never had before I met you.

The door closed behind her with a finality that made her almost push it back open and run inside again. Instead, she lifted her chin and shouldered her bags, heading to the elevator. All the while she reminded herself that this was for the best. But it didn't stop the shattering of her heart. The ride down the elevator was quick, and the doorman was distracted with another tenant and could only spare her a friendly nod. When she hailed a cab in front of the building, she'd almost convinced herself she was all right.

Fifteen minutes later the cab pulled up in front of Thad's luxury hotel. The lobby windows facing the street glittered in the winter night like the open doors of a grand palace. Felicity climbed out of the cab after paying the fare, and headed for the swirling glass doors. A bellboy rushed out to meet her, prying the duffel and backpack from her body and making her jump.

"You must be Ms. Hart. Mr. Worthington had us watching out for you." He led her to a set of private elevators at the back of the lobby and used a key card to access them. "You will get one of these cards. The elevators will take you to the private floor on level ten." He flashed the card at her.

"Seriously?" *Jesus*, Thad hadn't been kidding about the

private suite.

"He said only the best for you during your stay."

The elevator carried them to the tenth floor. The bellboy took her to a room at the end of the hall and swiped the card to the door. Then he opened it and entered to set her bags down.

"The card will operate the elevators and the door. Room service is completely on the house."

"But I don't—"

"The boss's orders," the bellboy said, clearly suspecting there was something between her and Thad. There wasn't, but she bet that if she tried to explain, he wouldn't believe her.

"If you need anything, you just use the phone in the room and dial zero," the man said and then handed her the card and left.

Felicity stared around the opulent suite, with a California king bed, the extended kitchen and living room, plus a master bath. It was overwhelming. The whole afternoon had been like that. She shivered and headed to the shower. Maybe it could warm her up and relax her.

She stripped out of her clothes and got in when the water was hot enough to steam the room. It burned her skin in a good way, and she pressed her forehead to the wall of the shower and closed her eyes. She'd gotten used to—no, *addicted* to—showering with Jared. The way his body bumped up against hers, how they touched, teased, and talked inside the glass doors. They'd been together, and she hadn't ever felt alone, even when they were working side by side in his apartment on their own projects. It had been a glimpse into a life she knew she couldn't have.

Our own private world. It was one more thing she'd lost. Felicity pressed a palm to her belly, seeking support from the baby within, but it was no use. She was falling apart inside. Her heart was as fragile as a spiderweb in the midst of a rainstorm. She slid down to the floor of the shower, tucked her knees up under her chin, and cried. The sobs ripped her apart, and she couldn't hold back the sweeping waves of pain that threatened to obliterate her from the inside out. Her dreams were dying, dreams she should never have pretended might be real. Her grief was choking, and her heart couldn't slow down as she wept for her broken heart and the man she loved.

Jared was on top of the world. The executed release of the lease sat on Pimms's desk, and the older attorney had conceded that his reaction that morning to Jared's news had been overly harsh.

"You are a damned sight better at your job than most people, and I don't want to lose you." His words had been music to Jared's ears.

It was almost nine o'clock by the time Jared rode the elevator up to his apartment. He was going to order pizza, and he and Felicity were going to cuddle together on the couch and watch a movie, even a sappy one if she wanted to. There was still a tightness in his chest at the thought that he'd missed the doctor's appointment, but he vowed he wouldn't miss the next one. Felicity and the baby were his world—he wasn't going to let either of them down.

Humming softly, he unlocked his door and walked inside. The apartment was quiet. His briefcase slid off his shoulder, and he let it drop quietly onto the kitchen table. She must be asleep, the poor darling. He was going to go in and surprise her, wake her up for a few kisses, and then let her go back to sleep.

His bedroom was completely dark, the shades drawn over the windows. He stumbled through the blackness before he found the side of the window and flipped the switch to pull the curtains back. His heart froze as the glowing light from the city outside revealed an empty bed.

Where was Felicity? He hastily turned the room light on, and it was then he saw the folded piece of paper on his pillow.

For a few seconds his body simply didn't move, couldn't move. By the time he reached for the note on his bed, his hands were shaking. The page unfolded and he stared at the words.

Jared,

I love you too much to have you sacrifice everything you've worked so hard for. I knew going into this that your job is your life, and I don't resent that now. I just need time to heal, to process that the life we let ourselves think we could have can't ever be. I've moved into somewhere safe tonight, so please don't worry about me or the baby. I just need some time to heal on my own. After that, we can see each other and raise the baby as best we can. I promise I won't take up valuable time and put you in a position where you lose your job, but I can't stay with you, not when it hurts us both so much.

Thank you for loving me,

Felicity

He couldn't breathe. Black dots momentarily covered his eyes as he tried not to panic. After sucking in a lungful of air, he glanced down to see that he'd crumpled the note in his hand.

Felicity was gone. Gone from his bed and his life.

But not my heart.

He wasn't going to let her walk away. She loved him. He loved her. They were going to have a baby. He wasn't about to let Pimms and his threats ruin the only real happiness Jared had felt in years. He would quit first. If Pimms made another threat, Jared would walk away and start over at another firm. Another firm would want him. His client list was extensive, and his work was excellent.

Fuck Pimms. He didn't need that partnership, not if it cost him his very heart and soul.

Jared dug his cell phone out and dialed Felicity's number. It rang and rang, finally going to voicemail.

"Princess, you need to come home to me, *please.*" He knew there wasn't enough space on voicemail to say all the things he needed to. He hung up and dialed Layla.

"Yeah?"

"Where is she?" he demanded.

"Who?" Layla asked, her tone softened in concern. "Jared, what's wrong?"

"Felicity," he growled. "Where did she go?"

"She's gone?" The genuine surprise and Layla's tone scared the hell out of him. Layla was her best friend. Why wouldn't she tell Layla where she went?

"Jared, calm down. I didn't know she left. Maybe she had a night class?"

"She doesn't. I know her schedule." He paced across his bedroom. "And her clothes and books are gone."

"Then maybe—"

"She's left me, Layla. There's a goddamned note and everything. She's breaking up with me because..." He swallowed thickly. "Because I'm a fucking prick who made her think work is more important than her."

"I can't blame her for leaving you if you didn't put her first." There was a long pause on the other side of the phone. "Do you know she's..." Layla didn't finish, but he knew what she was going to say.

"Pregnant? Yes. I want her, Layla. I love her so much it's fucking killing me. And the baby...I didn't know I could feel more love in my heart now than before, but I do." As he spoke, his eyes burned and his nose itched. He choked on the words he spoke. "I can't go back to how things were. I need her, Layla. *Please*, just tell me where she is." He would beg, grovel on his damn knees if he had to.

"She didn't call me. I didn't know about this, I swear." Layla's voice was thick with emotion. "Tanner and I are close to her apartment. We'll go see if she went back there. You stay at your place in case she comes back. I'll call you if we find her."

"Thank you," he whispered brokenly, and hung up.

Jared collapsed into his desk chair, his body vibrating with anger and hurt. How could she leave him? How could she go somewhere alone? What if she needed him because something happened to her and the baby and—

He swept a hand across his desk, sending files, papers, notes, and a dozen other things crashing to the floor. He slammed his elbows onto the desk surface and plowed his fingers through his hair, pulling hard enough to hurt. That pain was more welcome than anything else. He focused on breathing slowly, but it didn't help the mad race of his heart. He'd been furious and panicked when Pimms had threatened to fire him, but this, the choking, stark fear of losing the only thing that truly mattered to him?

It was far, far worse.

Come back to me, princess. Please.

CHAPTER TWENTY-SEVEN

Felicity stood at the foot of the large bed in the hotel suite, a towel wrapped around her body and hair wet. Her skin was warm from the shower, but it hadn't erased the chill from within. She opened her bag on the bed and sifted through her clothes until she found underwear and slipped them on. Her hands paused as they touched the black T-shirt of Jared's. She lifted it to her face, burying her nose in the soft cotton again. It carried a hint of him, just enough to make her heart shudder. She slipped the shirt over her body and let the towel drop to the floor.

A small flashing green dot on her cell phone caught her eye from where it lay a few inches away from her bag on the bed. She flipped it open and saw three missed calls from Layla and one from Jared…and a voicemail.

I shouldn't…

She pressed the Play button and lifted it to her ear.

Jared's voice, rough with pain that came through as he spoke and ripped her heart into even tinier pieces. "Princess, you need to come home to me, *please.*"

If only she could go home to him. She didn't delete the voicemail. A tiny part of her refused to give up the sound of his voice. Sitting down on the edge of the bed, she dialed her mother's cell phone number. She was probably working, but Felicity needed to talk to her.

"Hello?" Janet's voice was a welcome relief to Felicity's broken heart.

"Mom, do you have a minute to talk?" she asked, shutting her eyes to keep the tears from rushing down her cheeks.

"Felicity, what's wrong? Is it the baby?" Her mother's voice was hushed now.

She sniffled and opened her eyes. "No. The baby is fine. I broke up with Jared."

"What? Why, honey?"

Wiping her eyes, she tried to draw in a slow breath. "It's a long story," she warned.

"I've got time. It's slow at the hospital tonight, and I'm on my break," her mother said.

Felicity told her mother everything about the robbery, the police, Jared leaving work and getting in trouble because he'd been focused on her and the baby, and how she'd decided to leave.

"Honey, men aren't the best at big life changes. Trust me. Your father almost fainted when he learned I was pregnant with you. But he adjusted. It takes time. They get a little irrational, more than us, even though we're supposed to be the hormonal ones." Janet chuckled gently, but then she grew serious again. "Give him a few weeks, let him see how much he wants to fight for you. He'll come around. I saw him with you—he loves you. That kind of love doesn't fade or falter, not when it really matters. I know you need some space and time, but don't close your heart to him, honey, not yet."

She couldn't imagine Jared finding a way to juggle being a father and his job. It would never happen, no matter how hard he fought.

"Why don't you get some rest? I know you'll have trouble sleeping, but try, okay? It's important for you not to let your own work and school suffer, remember?"

"You're right." Felicity sniffed again. "Thanks, Mom."

"Sweet dreams, baby," Janet soothed.

"Good night." Felicity hung up, and with shaky hands she combed her fingers through her wet hair and lay back upon the bed, not sure how she'd ever get to sleep.

Jared's ringing cell phone woke him up before his alarm. He reached for the phone and groggily stared at the screen.

Thad's name flashed at him. He was tempted to throw the phone across the room. His head pounded in a violent headache, and he glanced down to see he'd fallen asleep in his clothes and hadn't bothered to get under the covers. With a low groan, he swiped the screen and answered.

"What?"

"Jared, get your fucking ass out of bed."

"No way in hell." He was going to stay right here. Fuck work, fuck Pimms. He wasn't going anywhere today, not when the woman he loved was still gone, his bed still cold. His heart couldn't fucking stand a minute of facing a world outside when she wasn't with him.

"You will get up and shower and dress. You want to know why?" Thad snapped.

"Why? So I can kick your ass?" Jared was only half-joking.

"So I'll tell you where Felicity is."

He shot up in bed so fast his head swam a little. He hadn't drunk anything last night, but he'd been tossing and turning for hours worrying about Felicity and the baby, and it had left a hangover as if he'd downed a bottle of whiskey.

"Where is she?" he demanded.

"Get up and take care of yourself and meet me at Sabine's in half an hour."

"Fine," he growled and hung up.

In the next fifteen minutes he showered, shaved, and dressed. He felt like shit, but at least he didn't look like shit. If he was going to Sabine's, it was likely that Felicity would be there. She didn't have classes in the morning. His heart gave a hopeful leap as he left his apartment and rushed to catch a cab.

By the time he arrived at Sabine's, Thad was standing in the main gallery with Sabine, talking and drinking coffee. There was no sign of Felicity.

"Ah, Jared, I had some additions to the contract with Sabine. I wanted you to look them over. Sabine's just got to make a quick call, and then she'll join us in the conference room."

Sabine smiled at Jared and stepped into her office.

Jared turned and jabbed a finger into Thad's chest. "Start talking. Felicity is the *only* reason I'm here."

Thad stared down at the finger poking his chest until Jared dropped it. "She's safe. She called me last night hoping I'd help her find a new apartment within her budget. She said she'd broken up with you."

"We're not broken up. This is a minor road bump. One I intend to get over fast. Where is she? I thought she'd be here."

"Sabine said she's actually giving a few tours at the Art Institute today, but you should know she's staying in my suite at the Gold Circle."

"What?" Jared knew exactly what suite he was talking about. Thad's private suite. He clenched his fists.

"Get that jealous rage out of your eyes. I'm not staying there with her. You owe me, Jared. I talked her out of going anywhere else. She's staying there as long as it takes."

"As long as it takes for what?"

Thad smirked. "For you to win her back, of course. I hope you have a good plan to do that."

Jared tugged at his tie, feeling it choking him as he met his friend's stare. "I fucked up, Thad. Big-time. I let her think work matters more than she does, and it doesn't. But I don't know how to prove it. She said she needed time and space and…" He trailed off, his voice breaking.

His friend's eyes narrowed. "Then give her time and space. I'll keep her safe and sound for you at the hotel until you've got a game plan mapped out. She won't go anywhere without me knowing, and she'll be safe. I've got maids who watch that private floor around the clock."

For the first time in his life, he realized how much his friends Thad and Angelo had his back. They'd helped him more than they could ever know.

"Thank you," he whispered.

Thad nodded. "She's worth fighting for, Jared. Stand up to that dick Pimms. Don't let him take her away from you. If you want to go out on your own, Dad and I have agreed that we'll go with you. We can keep you busy and paid until you build another client list if you can't bring other clients with you."

Leave Pimms & Associates? He'd never considered it, not when he'd been on track for partner, but the thought of losing Felicity made him face it. He would leave the firm if they wouldn't give him fair hours and some leeway for his personal life. He could stand up to Pimms, because Felicity was his first priority.

Sabine popped her head out of her office. "You boys ready to talk shop?"

Jared and Thad glanced at each other before they replied in unison. "Yes, ma'am."

"Great." She waved them to her office.

Jared's heart felt a little lighter, a hint of hope on his horizon.

I will fight to get you back, princess. I'll prove to you I'm the man you deserve.

"I can do this," Felicity whispered as she stood at the foot of the steps leading up to the Art Institute of Chicago. The bronze lion, now tinted green, stood a few feet from her, staring stoically out at the street before it. She climbed the steps, her heart pounding.

She couldn't believe she was here—well, at least here as a worker of sorts and not a visitor here to admire the pieces. Sabine had called her early this morning, asking if she wanted to spend a few hours giving tours to exclusive art patrons who were interested in private viewings of some of the currently closed European galleries. Felicity had jumped at the chance. It was huge to get asked to provide tours to these upper-end donors who gave money to the major museums. It would part of her duties if she ever became a curator. Donors liked to have face time with the top staff at museums and institutes and get special treatment, since they donated a lot of money to keep the exhibits open. And it was a joy for the staff to share their love of art.

When she entered the institute, she headed to the

information desk and asked for the woman Sabine had told her she was to meet, a Mrs. Burroughs. The man in the information booth got on his phone and dialed a number.

"Mrs. Burroughs, Ms. Hart is here, and she says she has a meeting with you this morning at eight thirty." After a pause, he continued. "Very good, ma'am. I'll send her up." The man hung up and pointed at the elevators. "Second floor. She'll meet you once you get off."

"Thanks." Felicity tugged her purse higher up her shoulder and walked toward the elevators. It would be so wonderful to work here. She'd come here for her undergrad and her master's hoping to work here, but Sabine had told her the job openings were slim to none and that LACMA would be a better try.

She got into the elevator and focused on staying calm while she rode up to the second floor. A woman in a dark-blue business suit, who looked to be in her early forties, greeted Felicity as the doors opened.

"Ms. Hart. Welcome!" She shook Felicity's hand. "Sabine is a dear friend of mine, and when I told her I had board meetings today and couldn't conduct my patron tours, she recommended you. I was thrilled to have you come. She's told me you're quite wonderful." Mrs. Burroughs was smiling warmly, and all sense of nerves fled as Felicity followed her to the closed European wing. A group of fifteen or so well-dressed men and women were drinking champagne and chatting with a security guard who was watching over them next to the gallery entrance.

"Ladies and gentlemen, this is Ms. Felicity Hart. She'll be giving you the tour today. She's a specialist in European paintings and sculptures." Mrs. Burroughs gave her a gentle nudge toward the crowd and made introductions to all of the patrons before she quietly slipped away and left Felicity to start the tour.

Still a little nervous, but also excited, Felicity dove into her task and set thoughts of the baby, Jared, and her broken heart aside.

After the tour was over, Felicity felt as though she could fly. It had gone so well. She'd been comfortable talking about every piece in the gallery, and she'd answered all of the questions put to her by the patrons. By the time she headed back down to the front of the museum to leave, Mrs. Burroughs caught up with her and thanked her.

As she walked down the steps to find a cab, her cell phone rang. She checked the name, her heart dropping when she saw it was Layla and not Jared, not that she would have answered. It would have been hard, but she would have fought the urge to do that.

"Hey, Layla," she said with a sigh, unable to hide her disappointment.

"Hey, so I thought we could do lunch today? I'll meet you at Sabine's. Sound good?"

"Yeah, okay. See you in a few minutes." She hung up and stopped a cab that was ready for a passenger and climbed in.

She stared at the screen of her phone for a long moment, and then against her better judgment she scrolled through the photos from Christmas break. Her favorite was a photo that Jared's mother had taken of the pair of them in front of the fireplace, cuddled up and warm, and laughing at a joke that his father had made. Her body quivered with a hundred emotions too strong to stay bottled up.

By the time the cab reached Sabine's gallery, Felicity was feeling completely low again. She paid her fare and climbed out, her mind far away, lost in memories of kisses by a warm fire in a Colorado cabin. When she saw Layla standing there outside the gallery doors, her face pale, Felicity's pulse leaped.

"What's wrong?" she asked as she reached Layla.

"Um, we should go to lunch right now. Like *now*." Layla tried to grab her arm, but Felicity saw what her friend had been afraid for her to see.

Jared was sitting in a chair inside Sabine's office, just visible through the glass doors of the gallery entrance. She soaked up the lines of his profile and ached to rush inside to throw herself at him.

It has to be the hormones, me wanting him when I know it will only hurt, right?

"You're right," she said thickly. "Let's go." She turned to Layla. "I don't care how cold it is outside, I want ice cream. A lot of it. Right now."

Layla's sad smile echoed her own feelings. "I do, too."

With one last look at Jared, Felicity left her aching, beating, hurting heart at the doors of Sabine's gallery.

How will I ever stand to be around him with the baby and not be with him? She didn't know the answer, and that terrified her.

CHAPTER TWENTY-EIGHT

Two weeks. Somehow Felicity had survived fourteen long days without Jared. She timed her work at the gallery to avoid any meetings with the Worthingtons in case Jared was there. She'd not gone back to her old apartment, either. Thad had sent men to pack her things up and put most of them in a storage facility until she found a permanent place to live for the rest of the semester. Since then, she'd hidden from the world except to go to classes. At first she'd expected Jared to be there, waiting to see her. It was something she feared and hoped for at the same time. But he was never there.

Part of her knew logically that she should be grateful he'd accepted the breakup and that he was leaving her alone so she could adjust. But her heart protested. It wanted him to fight for her, to seek her out, and it demanded that she give in, not push him away.

The door chime on the hotel suite broke her loose from her dark thoughts. She rushed to the door, knowing who would be there.

Layla stood in the doorway wearing a black-and-red flapper dress, and she was holding a second dress in a bag.

"You are so lucky you know me. I got a killer deal on these vintage dresses. It's going to be perfect tonight." Her friend slipped past her into the room and whistled. "Damn, girl, this is Thad's suite? Why the heck haven't I been over before now?" Layla eyed the rooms with open appreciation.

"Because I didn't want you to see that I emptied the fridge of the Magnum ice cream bars." Felicity was only half-teasing. She hadn't wanted Layla over because whenever she was here, Felicity tended to dissolve into sobs. It wasn't home, and it wasn't where Jared was. She didn't want her friend seeing her like that.

"Thad is really letting you just stay in this place for free?"

"Yes, he insisted I stay here. Something about having a brother code to Jared." She nearly avoided flinching at saying his name. "How is he?"

The sympathetic look Layla shot her said she knew Felicity meant Jared.

"I've never seen him like this. Tanner says he hasn't, either. You ripped his heart out, girl." Layla's eyes darkened with sorrow.

I ripped my own out, too.

"He kicked Tanner out of the apartment, by the way. I was going to tell you tonight anyway, but Tanner and I have moved in together. I suppose it was about time." Layla smiled, but it was cloaked with sadness.

"Wait, what? Jared kicked Tanner out?"

Felicity collapsed onto the edge of the bed. Layla set the dress bag down beside her. "Get dressed. The party's already started. I don't want to talk about anything else depressing."

The party. The one to celebrate the hotel deal closing with the Worthingtons was tonight in just a few hours and a few floors below in the grand ballroom.

Her stomach flipped at the thought of running into Jared. He was bound to come. He'd known for a week that she was here. Thad had warned her he had to tell Jared because Jared was frightened enough to call the police if she didn't turn up. But Thad had assured her Jared wouldn't come to see her, that he respected her wishes to stay away and give her space.

"I really don't think I'm up to it tonight," Felicity said.

"You are going." Layla planted her hands on her hips.

"But—"

"No," Layla snapped. "Put on your big-girl pants, Felicity. You have moped around for two weeks. Get over it or go back to him. No more crying and eating ice cream, got me? You need to be emotionally and physically healthy for your own sake and for the baby."

Felicity gaped at her friend. Guilt smothered her as she realized Layla was right. She hadn't wanted Jared to come after her—at least the sensible side of her didn't. She wasn't a damsel in distress. That didn't erase her desire to be loved or to wish someone would fight for her. Her friend was right. She needed to stop hiding out here and go down there and live her life. She'd worked hard at Sabine's to make this closing happen, and she deserved to celebrate at Thad's party.

"Here." Layla opened the dress bag and lifted out a glitzy black-and-gold flapper dress worthy of the Roaring Twenties. "This is yours. Now go to the bathroom and change." Layla pointed imperiously at the master bath.

Felicity took the dress and went to the bathroom. She left the door open a crack.

"Layla?" she called as she started stripping out of her clothes.

"Yeah?"

"Tanner really moved into your place because Jared threw him out?" She couldn't picture it. Jared loved his brother.

"Oh yeah, it was a whole big thing. He told Tanner to move in with me because he needed the apartment all to himself. Apparently he has plans for the room, not that he told Tanner. Tanner said he overheard Jared on the phone with some furniture companies."

Furniture companies?

"Is Jared doing okay otherwise?" She was desperate for any news of him she could get. Layla didn't answer her right away.

"He...well, he gave his boss an ultimatum. Partnership or he walks. I don't know what else. That was all that Tanner found out."

"He did? Did it work?" Mr. Pimms was a jerk as far as she'd heard, and she couldn't picture him accepting an ultimatum.

"Yeah, as far as I know. Jared said he was coming tonight. I don't think he would if he wasn't working at the firm any longer."

Felicity bit her lip, happy for him, but she was sad that it had all come too late for them.

She slid the gown up and opened the door. "Zip me up?" she asked her friend.

Layla tugged the zipper up the dress and handed Felicity a pair of beautiful diamond earrings.

"Remember the shoes with the bows? You should wear those."

Felicity almost said no. Those were special shoes she wore only for Jared. *But he's not my man anymore.*

"Come on, put the shoes on. You look so good in them! Let's make all those men downstairs jealous. And yeah, I know you can't drink, but I'll buy you some Shirley Temples from the bar," Layla encouraged.

"It had better be a lot of Shirley Temples with extra

cherries." Felicity slipped her shoes on and peeked at herself in the mirror.

She had a tiny bit of makeup on, but she didn't see the point of going all out. She retrieved the shoes from her closet and slipped them on.

I will not think about him or how much I miss him.

She grabbed her purse and followed Layla to the door. Her friend was already spinning around in a mock dance, and Felicity couldn't help but laugh. Maybe tonight would be fun after all. They rode the elevator down to the grand ballroom floor. Jazz music boomed out of the speakers, and gold was everywhere and on everything. The opulence of the Roaring Twenties was everywhere in the ballroom. There were towers of glasses of champagne, chocolate fountains, and glitzy professional dancers who whirled on special tables throughout the room.

"Wow," Layla said. "I'm so glad that Thad let Tanner and me come to this. Can you believe this?" She twirled in place, the beads on her gown dancing in the sparkling light.

"Where is Tanner?" Felicity asked, looking over the hundreds of faces in the room. Thad said about two hundred people were on the guest list. He hadn't been kidding. It would be easy to hide out here and avoid Jared if she stayed on the fringes.

All I have to do is see Thad and thank him for inviting me and for letting me stay in the suite.

"I left Tanner at the cash bar, and he should still be there waiting for me. I'll grab him real quick, and the three of us will hit the dance floor."

"Sounds good."

Felicity watched Layla slip into the crowd. She didn't follow her. Her heart still wanted her to run back upstairs and hide from the world and the pain. When she walked away from Jared, she tore a hole inside her heart, one so big she was afraid it might never heal.

What do you do when the love of your life can't be in your life?

The music changed from jazz to a swelling orchestral piece. The people closest to her left the dance floor to get in line at the bar. The slowly rotating lights bounced off the shimmering chandeliers, creating the effect of falling stars on the people below.

And there *he* was.

A tall, well-dressed man with his back to her. Just beyond him stood Thad, who met her gaze and said something to the man, who turned. It was Jared. His eyes fixed on her, his hands in his pockets. He looked dangerous with a heavy shadow of stubble, and his full lips were set in a determined line. The man had that brooding, sexy expression down to perfection.

Jared. My Jared. Her heart was bleeding, but her soul was shaking off its dust and starting to sing.

Don't go to him, don't...

Her feet moved at the same time his did. When they were only a few feet apart, Felicity held her breath. Jared slid one hand out of his trouser pockets and reached for her, but he stopped short of her cheek. His eyes burned as he stared at her.

"Felicity." Her name escaped his lips like a prayer whispered fervently at midnight. "How are you...and the baby?" His eyes stayed locked with hers.

"I'm okay. We're okay." She touched her abdomen. *I miss you.* "You?"

A rueful smile crossed his lips. "Awful." He glanced away, and then when he finally looked at her again, she saw the ghost of tears in his eyes. The expression was shattering and crushing all at once. They were in this beautiful place, and here they were, falling apart in front of each other.

"Would you give me one dance, princess? For old times' sake?" He held out one of his hands, palm up.

The world seemed to collapse around her, leaving only the two of them standing there. His hand was a lifeline, and she couldn't say no.

"One dance." She could barely get the words out. She took his hand, and he pulled her into him until they fit like two halves that had never been separated. They began to sway, slowly at first, and she couldn't believe how wonderful it felt to be back in his arms.

They began to dance as a singer crooned about being loved when she was no longer young and beautiful. Jared's strong arm curled around her back, and she pressed her cheek against his chest. For a few minutes she could relive the dreams she'd once had.

"Felicity, would you let me tell you something?" he asked in a low murmur, his lips brushing the shell of her ear, making her shiver.

"Yes," she whispered. *Please don't break my heart any further,* she begged him silently.

"After you left, I threatened to quit my job at the firm."

"Jared, no—"

"Pimms gave me my partnership interest instead." He smiled down at her.

"That's wonderful! Everything you worked so hard for. Congratulations. I'm happy for you." She was thrilled for him, but it didn't heal the broken pieces of her heart.

"I'm not done, princess."

She glanced up and tried to pull away from him a little, afraid of what else he might say. "Jared, I—"

He held her tighter. "I told him I wanted him to consider opening a branch in Los Angeles."

Her lips parted, and she sucked in a breath. Did he mean what she was too afraid to hope he could mean?

"He seems warm to the idea. He'd set me up with a location, I'd recruit the other lawyers." He paused, licked his lips, and rubbed a hand along her back. "I have some money saved up. We could buy a house. With a yard, near a park with a playground."

Felicity couldn't breathe. The air had been sucked out of the room, and all she could do was focus on the way the blood roared in her ears and how she was glad he was holding her so she wouldn't pass out.

"What I'm trying to say is..." His hold on her tightened as though he was afraid she would pull free. "Would you give me another chance? Let me prove to you that I'm your man, the one to care for you and the baby? I want to be there for you when you're in pain, and I want to be there to see that first smile, to help our child learn how to walk, and to argue with you over who gets to pick the baby up from daycare and..." He trailed off, his voice catching.

The baby. He was doing all this to help with the baby. She blinked back tears.

"Jared, you don't have to do all this for the baby."

He cupped her chin, and she had to look at him.

"It has nothing to do with the baby, princess. I have wanted you from the beginning, and the baby is just a happy accident." He brushed a lock of hair behind her ear. "When we were at my parents' house over Christmas, I asked my mother for my grandmother's ring. I was planning to propose to you in the spring. I just wanted time for you to finish school and for me to work on my plans to move to Los Angeles with you if that's what it took."

Her throat burned, and she couldn't breathe. "You wanted to marry me?" She'd ruined everything. There was no way he still wanted to marry her.

"*Want* to marry you." He reached for one of her hands and got down on one knee and pulled a small velvet box out of his coat pocket.

Oh God, what's he doing? Why is he kneeling? Surely he's not going to—

"At the risk of having you crush my heart a second time, Felicity Hart, *my heart*, would you marry me?"

She couldn't get the word *yes* out. She simply dissolved into tears and pulled him to his feet so she could hug him.

"That's a yes, right? Please say it's a yes—people are staring," he asked her in all seriousness.

"Yes, God, yes," she murmured, wiping at her tears. She was crying so much she could barely see him through blurry tears. "It's these damn pregnancy hormones. I cry at the drop of a hat." She hated crying, but in that moment she didn't care. She threw her arms around his neck and dragged his head down to hers for a kiss. Fourteen days without him... and her memories hadn't lived up to the reality of his kisses. He ravaged her mouth as though he was starved, and she opened up to him, letting his tongue duel with hers. The smattering of applause nearby made her blush and pull away from him, ducking her head shyly. It was so easy to lose herself in the moment when she was with him.

"And you were worried she'd say no." Thad chuckled as he walked over and slapped Jared's shoulder.

"You knew?" she asked, one eyebrow rising.

Thad smirked. "Yeah. Why do you think I kept you in my suite? I didn't want you running off so he couldn't find you when he was ready to ask you."

"Thanks." Jared chuckled and cuddled Felicity closer.

Thad smiled and walked over to where Layla and Tanner were standing at the edge of the crowd. Her friend gave her a thumbs-up and mouthed, "We'll talk later," before she pulled Tanner out to the dance floor.

She was smiling and couldn't stop. "Why do I think I was somehow played here?"

"You weren't. Thad let me know you were safe. I just had to get everything ready and give you time to miss me."

She had missed him. So much. She'd taken to sleeping in the black T-shirt because she couldn't lose that last bit of him. More than one night she'd woken up dreaming he'd slipped into her bed and was making love to her only to discover it was all a dream.

"Wait. What did you have to get ready?"

He kissed her forehead before meeting her gaze. "I got my job sorted out, and Tanner's room is now a nursery. I got a few hints from Layla and your mom, so I believe I got it right. Anything you want to change we can. I left the walls blank, though. I thought you might want to paint them."

Felicity bit her lip, tears coursing down her cheeks. "So that's why you kicked Tanner out? Layla told me, but I couldn't believe it."

Jared shrugged. "He wanted to move in with her. I just sped things up a bit."

"Felicity!" someone called, and they both turned to see Sabine striding toward them. She wore a dark-green slim-fitting gown that shimmered, with gold strap sandals completing the look of a forest goddess.

"Hey, Sabine." She released Jared and faced her boss.

"I just heard the good news from Thad that you're engaged, but I wanted to add some extra good news. Mrs. Burroughs at the Art Institute called me this morning and said the tours you did with the patrons really impressed her. She asked for your résumé and looked it over and wanted to know if you'd be interested in an assistant directorship. You'd be working right under her. She knows you can start work in May after school. Do you want the job?"

Felicity glanced at her boss, then Jared, completely shocked.

"It's your dream, princess. I'll follow you anywhere."

In that moment life was simply too full, too good, a dream within a wonderful dream. She couldn't contain the joy that was bursting out of her at the seams.

"Tell the institute I'll start May first." She took Jared's hand and squeezed it.

Her boss grinned. "Excellent. And congratulations, sweetie." Sabine kissed her cheek and went off to greet a group of guests who had walked into the ballroom.

Jared spun her in his arms so she faced him. He curled his fingers around the back of her neck in a gentle, possessive grip.

"You make me happy, Felicity. Happy beyond imagining." He swallowed hard and smiled so broadly it made his eyes sparkle.

"You really want to marry me?" she asked, smiling enough to make her cheeks hurt. She still couldn't believe it.

His gaze sobered, and he looked at her intensely as he stroked her bottom lip with his thumb. "I realized there was nothing for me in a world without you, and I'd do anything to win you back."

Felicity felt the same way, that life without him was no life at all. Like a taste of Eden before being banished, she'd been adrift without him, and he without her.

"Tell me our life will be wonderful?" she asked.

He lowered his head, and when their mouths were inches apart, he whispered, "I won't tell you. I'll show you." And then he kissed her. She shivered at the tender ravishment of his mouth and the sweet promise of the shared life and love that awaited them.

EPILOGUE

Felicity stood in the nursery of her and Jared's apartment, putting away the naptime books and collecting the recently washed onesies to put away in the dresser. The crib was empty which meant Jared had taken the baby for her breakfast. The morning sun made the walls glow with light. It was a fine Saturday morning, and she had all day to spend just as she wished. After a long but enjoyable week at the Art Institute, she was glad it was the weekend. She smiled as she let her gaze drift from wall to wall. She'd painted stories that had made her childhood happy.

There was a rotund yellow bear snoozing beneath a tree, a hive full of honey far out of his reach. The next wall showed a young girl perched on a window seat, white curtains billowing into her room. A distant star above a London skyline shimmered, and the silhouette of a boy who could fly covered part of the window, a tiny fairy above his shoulder. The next wall showed a boy wizard riding in a boat toward a distant castle, a distinctive scar on his forehead in the shape of a lightning bolt. The last wall showed a sleeping princess and a prince on one knee beside her bed, inches away from giving her love's true kiss.

"Somebody is hungry for her bottle." Jared's sleep-roughened voice made her turn toward the door. He stood there bare-chested, wearing flannel pajama pants. In his arms he cradled their three-month-old daughter, Hayley Hart Redmond.

Felicity walked to them and reached up to take her baby, but Jared stepped back, smiling.

"My turn. You go back to bed, princess. Gummy bear and I will be just fine, won't we?"

He bent his head to nuzzle the baby's cheek before he kissed Hayley's brow. Hayley unfisted one of her tiny hands and placed it on Jared's chiseled jaw, her gaze so serious.

"She's giving me that look again," he said with a laugh. "I wonder what she's thinking about?"

Felicity giggled. "I think she's trying to show her displeasure at being called *gummy bear*."

Jared took Hayley's little hand in his and kissed it. "Don't look at me, gummy bear, your mom is the one who named you that."

"I did not," Felicity protested, still laughing as she followed Jared into the kitchen to warm up a bottle. He held the baby in one arm, easily cradling her as though he'd been around children and babies all his life.

Felicity came over to him and leaned against his back, hugging him.

"How did I get so lucky to have you in my life?" She'd whispered this almost every morning since Hayley had been born.

Jared, just like every morning, met her gaze and replied, "A princess deserves nothing less than a prince, and for you I'd do anything and be anything. I love you."

"I love you, too," she murmured.

He held the baby between them, and Hayley cooed and wriggled her tiny hands, exploring Felicity's loose hair and tugging gently. This world held love, beauty, and hope. It was a world where a woman could have all her dreams come true.

Thanks for reading *Legally Charming*. I hope you enjoyed it!

Want a free romance novel? Fill out the form at the bottom of this link and you'll get an email from me with details to collect your free read!
Claim your free book now at:
http://www.laurensmithbooks.com/coming-soon/, follow me on twitter at @LSmithAuthor, or like my Facebook page at https://www.facebook.com/LaurenDianaSmith. I share upcoming book news, snippets and cover reveals plus PRIZES!

Reviews help other readers find books. I appreciate all reviews, whether positive or negative. If one of my books spoke to you, please share!

You've just read the first book in the Ever After series. I plan to write more books about Thad and Angelo soon!

Want to read the first chapter of ANY of my books to see if you like it? Check out my Wattpad.com page where I post the first chapter of every book including ones not yet released!
To start reading visit:
https://www.wattpad.com/user/LaurenSmithAuthor.

If you'd like to read the first three chapters from *Forbidden: Her British Stepbrother*, the first book in another fun, steamy contemporary romance series of mine, please turn the page.

CHAPTER ONE

"Tonight is the start of my grand adventure. And since it's my birthday, you guys are welcome to join in the fun." Kat Roberts grinned as she spread out the folded piece of paper on the table so her friends Lacy and Mark could see.

They were nestled in the corner of the Pickerel Inn just outside Magdalene College in Cambridge, catching a brief break from studying for exams. The pub was full of other students, all enjoying the relaxed atmosphere and the fish and chips the pub served late into the night.

"What on earth is that?" Lacy asked as she brushed her hair back from her face and peered at the list.

Kat tapped the paper. "A list of ten things every undergraduate should do while studying and living in Cambridge. Number one? Drink a glass of Nelson's Revenge at the Pickerel Inn pub on Magdalene Street."

Mark, Lacy's boyfriend, chuckled. "Have too many Nelsons and he'll definitely get his revenge. You Americans aren't used to our stout ales."

Kat was only half-listening as she studied the list, contemplating the other suggestions it gave. She'd moved to England in August to start college while her dad worked in London, and now more than ever she wanted to do something wild, something fun and crazy. Her parents had divorced when she was a kid, and she'd been living with her father, whose job entailed frequent corporate moves. She'd been too afraid to get close to people and break out of her shell. She didn't want to make connections with people only to have to leave and never see them again. It reminded her too much of when her mother had left.

But that's all changed. I'm finally living in one place for three years. I'm making friends here. Roots. For the first time I can really live.

Now she yearned for an adventure. She wasn't used to being wild and crazy or doing things out of her comfort zone, but she wanted to be that way.

Baby steps, she had to remind herself. That's why she'd picked this list from an online article about attending school in Cambridge. It had fun things for her to do. Things she might not have otherwise tried. Now that she'd settled into her classes and schoolwork, she could focus on enjoying the whole college experience. She'd picked an easy item from the list first—drinking a pint here at the Pickerel—but she'd work her way up to the bigger items soon.

Mark leaned forward, his elbows propped on the old wooden table. "Is this really all we get to do to help you celebrate your nineteenth birthday?"

"He's right, Kat. We should be doing something really fun tonight. Like going clubbing!" Lacy curved her lips in a charming but teasing smile that under other circumstances would've made Kat laugh.

"Clubbing? Lacy, you know I can't dance. I'd fall flat on my face. Maybe if I drink enough you can talk me into it."

Kat winked at her friend and gulped down more of the cider and beer blend she had ordered. It wasn't strong, but she wanted to get warmed up before going for the Nelson's Revenge.

Lacy grinned. "You're officially nineteen, and as this is your first semester at college, we need to make something amazing happen. Leave high school behind. This is your chance. Let's go dancing, meet some hot guys." She jerked her head suggestively toward a nearby table where a group of decent-looking men were watching them, pints in hand and friendly smiles on their faces. She nudged Mark in the ribs. "Right?" She winked.

Mark put an arm around Lacy's shoulders and shook his head, silently laughing. "You have a hot guy right here for you, no need to find a new one," he teased.

Lacy rolled her eyes. "You know what I mean, *for Kat*. She needs some action."

Kat couldn't disagree. She'd never really dated in high school since she and her dad had moved every couple of years. Maybe Lacy was right. Now was the time to give it a try.

"First I'll drink my pint, then I'll work my way up to meeting hot guys. How's that?"

Mark shook his head. "I think you're underestimating your appeal. British blokes like me would love to date an American. You'll have no trouble getting a guy." He nodded at the same group of men his girlfriend had pointed out. "Start with them. They look nice enough, and if they aren't, I'll beat them up for you." Mark put up his fists with a silly, goonish expression that made Kat and Lacy giggle.

Kat adored her new friends. She'd only known them since August, but something about them, their natural warmth, the way they opened up to her, made her feel like she'd known them for years.

Maybe it was the magic of the city, too. Ever since she'd

come here for university, this little Elizabethan-era town had captivated her. Between the shops tucked in crooked, wandering alleys and the tolling bells of the various colleges throughout the day, Kat had been bewitched by this tiny part of the world. It was more of a home for her than any other place she'd ever lived.

"Well, don't tell me you're afraid to give it a go?" Mark laughed.

His brown eyes were dark and full of brotherly mischief, offering a friendship Kat hadn't thought she'd find again since she'd left her last high school boyfriend behind. She and Ben had been good friends, more than she'd ever thought possible with a guy. Like him, Mark was easygoing, with a ready smile and a playful attitude that put her at ease.

She and Ben hadn't been serious, and calling him a boyfriend was really more of a stretch. They'd hung out but never even kissed. When she'd confessed this to Lacy, her friend had gasped and immediately informed her that what she and Ben hadn't been a "real" relationship.

Kat jerked herself out of the spiral her thoughts had taken and focused on her friends. She tipped back her drink and finished it. She couldn't believe it was close to the end of November, and the term was winding down. As much as she'd enjoyed her classes, she was glad for the upcoming winter break. What better way to start the holidays than getting a jumpstart on her "Operation Adventure."

When the front door of the pub suddenly opened, an icy wind cut through the cozy atmosphere of the building. Despite the dim gold light cast by the fixtures in the pub, Kat could see more than one person at the surrounding tables muttering, clutching at their coats and glancing toward the front door.

"Oh my," Lacy murmured, her brown eyes all soft and dreamy as she stared at something behind Kat.

Mark coughed, catching Lacy's attention, but Kat was already turning around in her seat. For some reason all of the breath left her body and she blinked, completely spellbound.

There, framed in the doorway, was a living, breathing god. When he closed the door behind him, snowflakes swirled and eddied around him, clinging to his dark hair and his black knee-length pea coat. He made her think of Hades, the dark god of the Netherworld, in search of his sweet, innocent lover Persephone.

Kat would never have thought she'd describe a man in such terms, but this man...oh yes, the description was perfect. So perfect it almost hurt to look at him. The kind of gorgeous that made a woman's body respond instantly. A slow wave of heat overtook Kat as she stared at him, and she clamped her thighs together when a slow throb began to build in her lower abdomen.

Now that's the sort of man I want to get involved with. One who would sweep me away, make me forget who I used to be, and show me who I might become. A woman who lives life on the edge, who explores dark passions and truly experiences life. The thought of being with a man like him...it felt right to want him.

The decent-looking guys a few tables away had nothing on this man. And that was just it: He was a man. Nothing about him screamed "college student." The way he walked, in an almost predatory, graceful movement, sucked her in, and she couldn't look away. He was the sort of man who would stop every woman in her tracks as he strode past, demanding their attention, *their desire...*

His eyes swept over the room, not even noticing her.

No surprise. She was just another undergraduate student bundled up in jeans, a thick sweater, and boots.

Not like him.

A pinch of pain in her chest made her set her cider down

and blink rapidly. She'd never minded being invisible before, but looking at this sexy god of a man…she wanted to get his attention. It was a stupid, girlish feeling, but she wanted him to look her way, see her. The pull he had on her was strange, magnetic, like nothing she'd ever felt before. It was as though something inside her was pulling her toward him, erasing everything else around him.

Look my way, she silently begged.

But he didn't. A knot of disappointment tightened in her chest. There was no way he'd ever notice her.

He's way out of my league. We're in different galaxies.

Even knowing this, she couldn't stop looking at him. This man looked expensive, from his shiny, black boots to the sleek look of his trousers and coat. When her gaze locked on his face, she was lost in a study of him. His aristocratic features were stunning. The man had a jawline that looked like it had been cut from marble, and a straight patrician nose that created an aura of entitled ease. He knew he was attractive and exactly how his mere presence could affect a room.

The hint of an arrogant smile played upon his full, sensual lips, so faint that she wondered if she was imagining it. And there was something about how he surveyed the room, like a ruler among his subjects. It wasn't surprising. Like King Arthur, but with dark, chocolate hair rather than fair. He was tall and lean with wide shoulders, and she could tell there were muscles beneath those fine clothes by the way the fabric clung to him. As he strode over to the bar and leaned against it to order a drink, the focus of the room went with him.

A stir of whispers started up a table behind Kat, Lacy, and Mark. A group of college students, three girls, were watching the new stranger, too. Their heads were bent together, and their hushed voices carried just enough that Kat caught snippets of their conversation.

"I think that's....yes, I'm sure it's him. You go, Talia, ask him..." one girl suggested.

"No way, if that's who he is...He'd never...Too hot though right? I'd let him do anything to me..." More giggles. "Can you imagine having sex with him? I heard he's a god in bed. I'd like Mr. Sexy to take me home."

The third girl fanned herself. "He's got a bad reputation, though...total heartbreaker. Never dates, only fucks them, you know...but I'll be damned if I don't want to..."

The conversation was muffled when a waiter delivered the girls more beers, and Kat couldn't hear anything else. So whoever Mr. Sexy was...these girls knew him or knew *of him*. And he had a bad reputation? What kind of bad reputation?

Kat turned her focus back to him, gazing longingly, watching him slide his black leather gloves off to reveal long fingers and elegant but masculine hands. A gold signet ring gleamed on the little finger of his left hand. She swallowed hard as a wave of heat rippled through her so fast beads of sweat gathered at her temples. She reached for her empty glass of cider again, never taking her eyes off the gorgeous man.

"You should probably go get your pint of Nelson's Revenge," Lacy said. "I really want to go clubbing, so get that drink, check it off your list, and let's go!"

Her friend's voice seemed to break through the odd sort of fog in her head. She didn't want to leave this little pub and go dancing, not when a man like *him* was here. She could have watched him all night.

Clubbing was definitely not on the list of things she'd like to do, but it would get her out of her shell. Of course, it would really help if she had that drink. And getting that drink meant a chance to get close to the beautiful stranger.

"Okay, be back in a second." She pushed her chair and headed toward the bar. The crowd was thick around the bartender, and Kat could barely see him over the heads of the students laughing and talking as they leaned against the antique wood bar. The only empty spot against the counter was next to Mr. Sexy…

Raising her chin, she started to walk in his direction, attempting to play it cool, like she wasn't going to get turned on just by standing so close to this god of a man.

He probably won't even look at me…but what if he does? Gotta be cool….I can handle this, right?

A second before she reached him, her right foot slipped in a spot of melted snow.

"Ahh!" Kat gasped as she tried to catch herself, but she careened straight into the beautiful stranger. Normally she wouldn't have been so clumsy, but she'd been too focused on him and hadn't been watching the floor. Plenty of people had been slipping all night.

"Oomph," he grunted and threw his arms out, pulling her to his chest.

Kat's head fell back as she clung to his shoulders. He was tall, deliciously so, and her head only just reached the bottom of his chin. His hair was swept back from his face, but it fell across his eyes as he stared down at her, and the light kissed the dark brown strands with a faint hint of gold. The color of his eyes was…stunning and made her almost dizzy when she stared. Like losing herself in a kaleidoscope of blue and green in endless splintering shafts.

Her knees wobbled, and she dug her hands harder into his shoulders, trying to stay on her feet.

What is wrong with me?

"Hello, darling, are you all right? Bit of a slick spot, eh?"

That rich voice, such decadent, sinful syllables uttered in that oh-so-perfect English accent, made Kat quiver inside. What was it about accents? They made a girl think strange, silly things, like asking him to talk dirty to her. Oh, the things he could say that would melt her into a puddle just like the snow at his feet. It might kill her with pleasure. The thought was so unlike her that she blinked. There was something about this man that made her want things she'd been hesitant to want before now. Like hot, sweaty sex. She was still a virgin, and yet this man was making her want to strip down naked and jump into the nearest bed with him.

"I…"

His hands were still holding her waist, his body pressed against hers. She couldn't think; her brain short-circuited. His hands on her, so hot to the touch…They were standing so close, faces mere inches apart, and the world around her seemed to burn with a heat along her skin. Her breath quickened.

Kat struggled to think logically, but all she could think about was how much she wanted to kiss him.

"Are you able to stand on your own?" He smiled, the single flirty twist of his lips making her knees buckle again.

What the heck? She'd never had a problem with her legs working before.

"Er…yes," she finally managed to say.

"Good." His hands dropped, but the movement felt reluctant. He trailed his hands down her body, the light but suggestive skimming of his palms over her waist, then her hips, sent little throbbing pulses throughout her entire body. He didn't step away, either, but kept close to her, his eyes still fixed on her face. "I'm glad to have prevented a nasty fall."

Before she could reply, the bartender leaned over the counter and spoke. "What can I get you?"

Mr. Tall and Sexy shifted slightly, allowing Kat to slip into the space next to him, their shoulders and arms touching as she answered.

"I'll have a pint of Nelson's Revenge, please."

The stranger next to her chuckled. "Are you sure about

that?" he asked. "That's a stiff drink and likely to bring tears to your eyes." There was a hint of teasing in his tone, and Kat couldn't resist responding.

"I'm sure. Besides, I'm more likely to start crying at the sight of a butterfly than a stout ale." She laughed, then realized what'd she said and blushed.

The man angled his body toward her, propping one arm on the counter as he stared down at her.

"Butterflies make you cry? What on earth for? Don't tell me you're afraid of them." Humor heated those blue-green eyes of his, and she felt an answering heat sweep through her body.

"I…well, it's silly really…" She hedged. She didn't normally open up to people, let alone strange, beautiful men in pubs. But there was something about the way he was watching her, his intense focus on her and his interest in what she was saying, that gave her courage to continue.

"I used to live in Texas with my dad, and we saw monarch butterflies when they migrated. But now with their habitats dying out, I rarely see them. When I do get lucky and one flies past me, it's beautiful…and sad." She shrugged her shoulders, glancing away. "I know that sounds silly."

"Not at all," he murmured softly. "No sillier than how I feel when I look at stained glass windows. It's the same for me, that mixture of melancholy and beauty. It's not often I meet someone else who thinks about things like that." His intense scrutiny tore her in two directions, between the need to squirm and to go very still.

The man possessed an overpowering, seductive and masculine presence. She caught the scent of pine and something clean and crisp that sparked her other senses to life. It encompassed her like some dark spell, leaving her with a desperate need to stay close to him. The things those girls had whispered about him came rushing back…"*bad* *reputation"..."god in bed"...*Whoever he was didn't matter, she just *wanted* him. Wanted to curl her arms around his neck and get as close to him as possible.

"I think about that stuff all the time," she said, unable to tear her gaze away from his.

He lifted his glass to his lips and sipped. It wasn't ale he was drinking but something else, a dark, warm gold color, probably Scotch. She realized she must have been staring at his mouth when he licked his lips and spoke again.

"Keep staring at me like that and I'm liable to kiss you."

CHAPTER TWO

Desire and hunger lit up his eyes, heating the strange mixture of blue and green. It almost made her forget that she was talking to a stranger. It *really* was possible to lose yourself in someone's eyes. Maybe the poets weren't wrong about love at first sight. She didn't love this man, but she was...captivated by him, which felt like love, in a strange sort of way. The lightness of her head, the wobbly knees, the fascination with him.

"There's nothing stopping you from kissing me," she breathed. Her heart was pounding against her ribs as excitement skittered through her. Would he accept the challenge and kiss her?

His eyes softened, but there was a dangerous glint to his expression, one that warned her that if he kissed her...it wouldn't be chaste, wouldn't be sweet. It would be the sort of kiss that made a girl forget where she was and moan helplessly for more.

They were mere inches apart now…When had she leaned into him? Somehow she had shifted closer, fixated on his mouth, the full sensual lips. The bit of the cider ale she'd been drinking earlier made her thoughts a bit muddy. Well, all but one thought.

I want him to kiss me. If he won't, I'll kiss him first.

Before she let herself think better of it, she seized the chance to be reckless and rocked up on her tiptoes, curling her fingers into the lapels of his coat as she kissed him. *Hard.* It was wild, the way she let go and just gave herself into kissing him. Her own sexy stranger…

His hands gripped her waist, fingers digging in slightly, making tingles of excitement shoot down her spine, clear to her toes. His lips were soft and warm, moving against hers hungrily. When he angled his face, he caressed her lips with his tongue. The startling, erotic feel of it had her mouth parting, and he thrust inside. The little teasing strokes of his tongue against hers created shivers deep in her belly. He overwhelmed all of her senses, and Kat couldn't catch her breath. There was no escaping his strong hold, and she didn't want to. His lips were a drug, and she couldn't get enough.

Every cell in her body pulsed and hummed to life when the kiss turned slightly rough, as he nipped her bottom lip. She rocked her body into his, desperate to get closer, to feel him completely surrounding her.

All mine. She smiled against his lips just as their bodies separated a few inches and she gasped for a breath. Blood pounded against her temples, and she panted and glanced up at him. Stark, raw lust burned like coals behind his eyes as he stared down at her, an almost animal ferocity in his expression.

"That was—"

Before she could finish, he curled an arm around her waist and pulled her flush against him for another kiss. The touch of his lips this time was feather light…as though he were savoring her. A simple, almost innocent brush of mouths, before she shivered, and a little moan of longing escaped. Suddenly he rotated her, pinning her against the bar, his mouth taking her hungrily, seeking entrance to hers. She parted her lips, more from surprise than anything else. When his tongue slid in and teased hers, she whimpered. The bare hint of stubble rasped against her skin as he kissed her, making her sensitive to every sensation.

More, I need more of this…

No one she'd dated in high school had kissed like this, as though he had all night to taste her, explore her, excite her. Nothing else mattered, nothing but this man and his life-altering, seductive lips.

When his mouth parted from hers, she blinked and stared up at him, wondrously dazed.

"You were too tempting to resist. Makes a man hungry for more when a woman looks at him like that." He brushed the pad of his thumb over her swollen lips, his eyes tracing the shape, along with his finger.

"Like what?" she asked, fascinated by his words just as much as his hands and the way they touched her.

His laugh was dark and rich like a pint of Guinness. "Like she needs to be kissed, to be *taken* by a man who knows just what to do to make her moan with pleasure."

Taken…the word was heavy, dark, forbidding and yet it filled her with a secret thrill. She could picture this man taking her, doing a thousand erotic things that would blow her mind and her body apart.

She struggled to respond, but what could she say to the man who'd just changed her life with one mind-blowing kiss and talked to her about how he could make a woman moan with pleasure? Had she really just made out with a complete and total stranger? She needed to do something, *anything*, to lessen the suddenly awkward moment.

She thrust out her hand and said, "I'm Katherine Roberts, but everyone calls me Kat." It felt silly to introduce herself after the kiss they'd shared, but she did it anyway.

The man stared at her hand and then took it, raising it to his lips rather than shaking it. He brushed his mouth over the backs of her knuckles in a caress, like an old world prince greeting a lady. Her heart fluttered inside her chest at the little romantic act. She'd never met a man who'd done that before, and it made her imagine what it might feel like to have his lips on other parts of her body.

"Tristan Kingsley. It's been quite the pleasure meeting you." The blue-green of his eyes rippled with glints of light like a summer lake at noon. "I'd like to kiss you again—"

"Tristan! There you are!" A light, feminine voice shook Kat out of her hazy daydreams of being wrapped in his arms again.

A tall blonde with stunning, classical features and a killer sense of style stood in the pub's doorway, watching Tristan and Kat. Her pink lips were curved up in an excited smile, and her blue eyes were bright and merry.

"So sorry I'm late. The snow is quite wretched on the roads," she said as she strode over in her too perfect high-heeled boots and skinny jeans.

Kat wanted to melt into the floor but shuffled her own scuffed boots instead. Her face heated when Tristan released her hand and glanced at the blonde woman. Just like that, Kat was forgotten as he stepped around her. So much for her dreams of a man like that paying attention to her. She was just another passing fancy while he waited for his girlfriend to show up. A wave of nausea mixed with anxiety rolled through her stomach. This was why she was afraid to take risks. Because rejection hurt like hell.

"Celia!" Tristan grinned, as he opened his arms to

embrace the beautiful woman.

Oh, God. She really is his girlfriend. Of course she is. Tristan looked perfect with Celia. It was obvious they were a couple. A couple of beautiful, sophisticated people. Like a pair of models from a Burberry ad. She'd never had a snowball's chance in hell with a guy like him.

Kat slipped away, her pint of Nelson's Revenge in her hands as she left Tristan and headed back to her friends. Mark and Lacy were watching her when she dropped down into her seat and covered her face with her hand.

"Wow, Kat, that was…" Lacy reached out and gave Kat's shoulder a pat.

"Mortifying? Pathetic?" Kat supplied, as she finally dropped her hand from her face and set her glass down next to Mark, nudging it in his direction. Drinking the pint seemed to pale in comparison to the adventure of being kissed by Tristan Kingsley.

"Well, the kiss was kind of hot…until that other girl showed up," Mark observed with a smirk, but he had a point.

She'd been totally on fire and hadn't wanted to stop kissing Tristan. It was as though her life had depended on touching him, on feeling his muscles move beneath her hands, and his mouth exploring hers. There had been nothing else in the world she'd wanted more than him in that moment. She'd *never* felt like that before about anyone or anything.

"I know, right? What kind of guy kisses someone like that when he has a girlfriend?" Lacy said, crossing her arms over her chest.

Mark laughed. "Obviously that guy."

Kat winced. "Do you mind if I just go back to the dorm? I think I've had enough of this place tonight."

"But it's your birthday." Lacy pouted.

Kat shrugged. This was the first time she wasn't

celebrating with her father. They'd moved from Chicago to London in August and neither of them had thought about what it would mean when she was two hours away at Cambridge for her birthday. Somehow celebrating without him didn't feel right.

"What about cake?" Mark asked before drinking some of his pint.

"No, thanks." Kat shook her head and brushed some dust off the table, avoiding looking in Tristan's direction.

How was it possible to still feel his lips on hers when he was a dozen feet away?

"Are you sure?" Lacy asked, her brows knit together in concern.

"Yeah, I'm sure. I'd rather just go back to the dorms. I have a lot of studying ahead of me in the next couple of weeks before final exams."

"Well, drat," Lacy said. "All right, you go home, then." She nudged Mark. "Go pay for the drinks. It's on us tonight, Kat."

"Thanks, guys." Kat stood and tucked her chair under the wooden table. "See you both tomorrow?"

"Bright and early," Lacy laughed. "Did I ever say how much I hate 8:30 a.m. classes?"

Mark leaned over and kissed Lacy's cheek. "That's why I'm the smart one. My first class is never before 11 a.m."

"That's right, rub it in," Lacy grumbled, but she was smiling at him.

"Bye, guys." Kat was still laughing as she exited the pub. She didn't want to think about the mysterious Tristan Kingsley or how he kissed. Better to just forget it and move on. It had been a fun adventure, even if a short one.

The snow blew in thick currents around her, and the dim streetlights looked like glowing golden orbs in the darkness. It was a bewitching sight.

Most of the small shops around the pub were closed, but one was still open. Its merry lights called to her as she approached. A bakery. Cakes, breads, and other sweets filled the windows. Behind the glass counter, a plump woman was checking a tray of cookies, the front of her blue apron dusted with small white splotches of flour.

"Maybe just one," Kat murmured, entranced by the sight of the small chocolate cupcakes with elaborate swirls of icing. It was her birthday, after all. Kat entered the shop and the brass bell above her head tinkled.

"Hello, dearie," the woman said and wiped flour-covered hands on her apron. "Come to get a late-night snack? You're just in time, I was ready to close up early due to the weather."

Kat peered through the glass cases, trying to decide which one of the little cakes would taste as good as the man she'd kissed only minutes ago. She doubted anything could come close.

Tristan. Tristan who had a girlfriend. Kat mentally kicked herself. She'd pretty much thrown herself at him and begged to be kissed. Maybe he didn't normally go around slipping his tongue between a girl's lips and setting her on fire inside. Then again...if he'd been a good guy, he wouldn't have done more than a chaste peck on the cheek.

Focus on chocolate, not hot Brit you'll never see again. She went back to studying the contents of the case. When the entry bell clinked again, she didn't turn around.

"Have a need for something sweet?" A rich, decadent voice, smooth as chocolate, filled her ears.

She spun to find Tristan standing there, snow dancing about him as he let the door close behind him. He walked toward her with lithe, graceful steps. Her body trembled with a little wave of excitement at the mere sight of him. *I shouldn't be happy to see him, he has a girlfriend...* But that didn't change the rapid beat of her heart.

"Evening," the baker said merrily.

"What are you doing here?" Kat sputtered. The moment the words were out, she slapped a hand over her mouth.

His chuckle made a warm flush creep down her cheeks. "I saw you left the pub and…" He paused, his brows drawing together. "Well, I didn't want you to go off on your own. I saw that your friends remained behind." It was a lame excuse, and they both knew it. For some reason that made her want to smile.

"So you're protecting me from snowflakes?" She couldn't help the partly amused and partly sarcastic tone of her voice.

Tristan shrugged and joined her at the counter, peering at the desserts. "Snowflakes can be treacherous buggers."

This time she couldn't stop her laugh. "I'll bet. Death by ice fractals sounds horrifying."

He quirked a brow. "Ice fractals?"

God, I'm an idiot. Sure, Kat, show him what a nerd you are. "They're the mathematical phenomena of a repeating pattern that displays on every scale. Snowflakes are one of nature's fractals." She wasn't a science wiz, but learning was something she enjoyed, no matter what subject. Ben had always teased her about it. Not that she'd minded being called a nerd. There were worse things than being addicted to learning.

Tristan glanced over his shoulder at the dancing snow, then turned back to her. "I'm surprised you know what fractals are. Most people don't." He leaned forward then and caught a lock of her hair, playing with the strands. Kat held her breath as every nerve in her tingled to life. He was touching her again, and she could feel every cell of her body humming with excitement.

Please kiss me again.

When he didn't, her mind attempted to return to reality, and she remembered Celia.

"What about your girlfriend?" she blurted out.

"Girlfriend?" He let her hair drop from his fingers and met her gaze.

"That woman in the pub..." *The one he looked so perfect standing next to.*

"Celia?" The responding smile that lit his face filled her with envy. Would a man ever smile like that when he thought about her? Something about Tristan and the way he smiled, she couldn't help but wish one smile was for her.

"Right, Celia," she echoed. Her heart twinged a little at the mention of the other woman.

"She's my cousin, not my girlfriend."

Kat stared. This total stranger had abandoned his cousin to chase after her? Tiny flutters of excitement stirred in her stomach.

"You seem surprised." His sensual lips—lips she couldn't get out of her mind—twitched, as though he was fighting off a smile.

"Why ditch your cousin when you don't even know me?" This entire evening was surreal. God-like men coming in from snowstorms to kiss her senseless...What next? Winning the lottery and moving to the Bahamas?

Tristan's gaze dropped to her mouth.

"When a lovely woman kisses me and runs off into the snowy night...well, the temptation to go after her is irresistible. I don't let lovely women escape, not until I've tasted them properly." He licked his lips and everything south of her waist throbbed to life.

What? Was he kidding?

"So here I am, in a bakery with you. Is there a reason we're staring at cakes?" He moved a step closer, even though he was facing the desserts again.

His arm brushed her right shoulder. The man was tall, but not too tall. Just enough to make a girl feel small, in a good way, like he could protect her if she needed it. A masculine scent, warm and clean, filled her nose. *His* scent. It was an enticing one she could've inhaled forever.

Focus, Kat. Try to be normal and have a normal conversation. Do not keep starting at Mr. Sexy.

"It's my birthday today. I'm nineteen."

At her reply, he looked at her again.

"Well, we must get you a cake. Chocolate, I presume?" He leaned one elbow on the glass counter as he waited for her to answer.

She nodded mutely.

Tristan turned back to the woman behind the counter. "What's the best chocolate cake you have? The richest, most decadent one." His words were as decadent as his statement. She could practically feel the chocolate melting on her tongue.

"The Devil's Triple Layer Cake." The woman pulled out a small cake for two people. Raspberry sauce was drizzled over the top of the simple yet elegant icing design.

Tristan took out his wallet and slid a black credit card across the counter.

"We'll take it. And a small candle, if you have one."

CHAPTER THREE

"**B**ut—" Kat's protest died when the woman took the Devil's cake from the counter and started to box it up. She didn't like feeling indebted to him, and he'd already made her feel off balance with his kisses.

"Consider it a thank-you." He laughed.

"For what?" Her tone was a breathless as she watched his dark hair fall into his eyes. Her hands twitched to brush it back from his face, to touch him back the way he'd so boldly touched her earlier. Everything about this man drew her in—his face, his eyes, his rich voice speaking of kisses and passion.

"You surprised me tonight. It's been a long time since anyone has done that." He scrubbed a hand over his jaw, and she saw the hint of stubble there and remembered the way it had tickled her when she'd kissed him.

I surprised myself, kissing him like that.

"Allow me to escort you home. Is it a long walk?" Tristan asked Kat, when the woman had returned with the boxed cake.

"Only a block. I'm staying in a dorm at Magdalene College." She shouldn't be telling him something like that. What if he got the wrong idea?

"A student at university? Excellent. So am I." He smiled. "I'm not an undergraduate, though. I'm earning a Master's degree in business." He thanked the baker and collected the box with the cake. "I'll walk you home." It was a statement this time, not a question, and she didn't want to argue with him, not when it meant spending more time in his presence. She'd just have to be sure he didn't think she'd...well, she'd worry about that when they got to her dorm.

"You're a student? How old are you?" Kat could've smacked herself for being so rude. "I'm sorry, I shouldn't have asked."

"I'm twenty-five." He held the door open with one hand, and she had to slide past him to exit the bakery. A gust carrying fresh snow hit her face, and she braced against the frigid air. Her first instinct was to turn around and bury herself against Tristan. He was so warm, she remembered from kissing him at the bar. The way his body had enveloped hers with heat, and the way his hands had gripped her hips.

"So what brings an American to Cambridge? Is this a semester of study abroad?" He walked alongside her as they went down the street, snow crunching beneath their feet. Kat stayed closer to Tristan than she would have normally, telling herself it was because she was afraid she'd slip on the ice. But the truth was that she wanted to be close to him, feel his warmth, smell that piney scent of his that made her senses come alive. She struggled to focus on their conversation, given how her thoughts kept drifting into dangerous territory.

"I'm a full-time student. My father travels for work, and he's living in London for the next couple of years."

Tristan made a little hum of interest. "And what does your father do?"

"He's an investment banker at Barclays. He's at their London office, and I wanted to be close to him." It was so easy to talk to Tristan. Maybe it was because she knew she'd likely never see him again after tonight. But it wasn't just that. Something about talking to him just clicked.

It reminded her of a day when she'd been a young girl, crawling through her parents' attic searching for treasure maps and wardrobes that opened to snow-swept worlds lit by solitary lampposts. She'd come across a large, weather-beaten, locked trunk. After hours of digging through boxes, she'd found an ornate key in an antique lacquered jewelry box heavily covered with dust.

Eyeing the lock and the key, she'd given it a chance. The satisfying click-click of the key in the lock had made her heart pound and her hands tremble as she'd opened the trunk. It had contained old books, the very best kind, of course. But she'd never forget the moment of fitting that key into place, and the feeling of connectedness it had made. Being near Tristan, talking to him, was like fitting that key into the lock all over again, and she couldn't fathom why that was, only that it was true. It scared her a little, but she wasn't the kind of woman to turn her back on something amazing just because it sent her nerves skittering inside her.

"And your mother?" Tristan paused as they reached the main door to her college grounds. The massive, ten-foot-high door had a smaller door built into its frame that everyone used to enter the grounds. It was a bit like a scene from *Alice in Wonderland*.

The smaller door to the college was unlocked, and Kat entered, Tristan following behind her. A cheery porter came out of his booth to greet them.

Tristan caught her arm, halting her in the middle of the snowy courtyard so she had to face him. The hold was firm, and the subtle sign of power rippling through that touch made her shiver. She remembered how he'd grabbed her in the pub, kissing her, forcing her to enjoy his kiss without escaping. It was madness to desire that, to let him take control and allow her the freedom to just...feel. But that was the thing about this man she couldn't get out of her head. If he could affect her in public, in a pub, what would it be like when they were completely alone?

"You didn't answer my question about your mother." There was a gentle reprimand in his voice. Their warm breaths billowed out in soft, white clouds in the Magdalene courtyard.

Those unique eyes of his held her spellbound. It was like watching the tide pulling out to sea and being sucked deeper into the water.

"I...my mother isn't part of my life, hasn't been for quite some time." For some reason, admitting that out loud stung. Thinking about the woman who'd abandoned her hurt, but saying it aloud made it too real, too painful. She and her father never talked about her mother and how empty her leaving had left Kat feeling. No one to talk to, bake with, laugh about boys with, see mushy romantic movies with... those were all the things mothers and daughters were supposed to do. *But not me.*

"I didn't mean to open old wounds, darling." Tristan's eyes softened, the colors changing yet again, and she was lost in their depths. The way he'd called her *"darling,"* that intimate word surrounded her heart with a cottony warmth. This beautiful stranger was offering her comfort, and she wanted it, wanted him. And that need scared her. She'd needed her mother, and her mother had left. The only person who hadn't let her down was her father. Kat couldn't let herself need Tristan, not when it might lead to more heartache.

He cupped her cheek, the gesture tender. How could he

be such a contradiction? Bold and seductive, then tender and compassionate.

"They're divorced?" he asked. That focused intensity only seemed to deepen as the snowfall muffled the world around them. Like they were cocooned in the shelter of a snow globe holding only them and the falling white flakes.

She licked her lips. "Yes. For a long time now."

Tristan nodded. "My parents are divorced, as well. My father is an overbearing, pompous arse." He chuckled, but there was a bite to the sound that caught her attention.

"You don't like your father?" she asked.

The flash of cold in his eyes made her shiver more than the snow falling around them. He continued to stroke her cheek with one of his hands, which softened the hard look in his eyes.

"I don't like to talk about him." It was clear from the steel in his voice that she wouldn't get anything else from him about his father. But she wanted to know more about this mysterious, seductive stranger whose kisses burned straight through her. There were hidden depths to him, dark, deep, flowing underground rivers and she wanted to dive in and discover who he really was.

"What about your mother?"

The defensiveness evaporated as he grinned. "One of the best, as far as mothers go."

"That must be nice, to have a mother around, I mean." A part of her still felt like maybe *she* had been the cause of her parents' breakup. Maybe she'd been too much for her mother to handle.

"It's not your fault, you know. Sometimes it feels like it is, but it isn't." His hand on her cheek moved to her hair, threading through the wild strands that were slightly damp with melted snow. The heat in his eyes burned slowly, like a fire in a hearth.

Kat's body responded, her thighs clenching together and her nipples hardening. From a single hot, tender look, she was melting for this intense, handsome stranger. A shiver racked her, and he chuckled. Did he know how much he was affecting her? He had to, with that pleased look gleaming in his eyes, and his lips twitching in bemusement.

"Let's get you inside so you can warm up and eat your birthday cake."

She came back to herself and realized they'd been standing inside the courtyard, unmoving, just standing so close, breaths mingled and almost whispering as they opened up about their lives.

They walked up to the front of the red brick dormitory, and he followed her up the small set of steps to her door on the first floor. She turned, ready to thank him for walking her home, but he caught the door, preventing it from shutting.

"May I come inside?" He tilted his head toward the door, and she saw he was still carrying the cake.

"I..." she swallowed down the nervous lump in her throat. She wasn't ready to say good night, or good-bye. But she didn't want him thinking she was the sort of girl who slept with someone she just met. He seemed to sense her indecision.

"Just for cake," he said. "You have my gentleman's promise." He used his index finger to draw a cross over his heart.

A gentleman's promise? She remembered the things those girls had said back in the pub. Was he the sort of man to break a promise? Or just a girl's heart?

Take a chance, a little voice whispered inside her head. *He's a risk worth taking, at least tonight.* If she did let him inside, she'd get to spend more time with him. She didn't want to let him out of her sight, not until she'd figured him out. She'd always loved puzzles, and this strange, sexy man was more of a puzzle than anything she'd ever seen.

"Okay. But just for a few minutes." She let him follow her inside. It was large for a dormitory room, with a tiny kitchen counter against one wall and a small bathroom. Flicking on the one overhead light, she took the bakery box from Tristan and set it on her desk before turning around to face him. She couldn't help but wonder what he'd think of the world she'd built in the few short months she'd lived here.

The walls were a pale, eggshell white, and she'd covered most of them with posters of famous British people. Tristan eyed one above her bed.

"Lord Nelson? Good God, that sure explains your drink tonight at the Pickerel." He burst out laughing. "What is it like to wake up to that each morning?" The rich sound of his amusement warmed her insides all over again, and she started laughing, too.

"My father got it for me as a joke, and I loved it. I thought he deserved a place of honor."

The throaty laugh that escaped his lips was husky this time. "Above a woman's bed is certainly a place of honor." His gaze roved over her full-sized bed, with its dark royal blue and white fleur-de-lis pattern.

Simple and elegant. *Just like him. He'd look so good on my bed.* The thought made her blush.

It was the first time she'd really let herself go there. When she'd dated in high school, she'd never let herself think about sex. It was pointless to build that connection with someone when her father might be transferred to a new location at any time, and they'd have to pack up their lives again. But she wasn't going to be moving for the next three years. Maybe now was the time to give it a chance.

Tristan stripped off his coat and laid it over the back of her desk chair. She had a brief moment to admire his body from behind, the lean lines of his legs, the broad, muscular shoulders outlined by his sweater, before he would notice her staring. The man was gorgeous. Too gorgeous. It was intimidating, yet she didn't want to look away.

She was still staring when he straightened and faced her. Oh, what he could do to her with that body...Tristan was making her feel a little crazy. Okay, really crazy. She wanted to touch him, to put her hands on his chest, feel that heat she remembered from the pub, and kiss him again. God, she wanted to kiss him, and it almost made her hurt with hunger.

"How about we taste that cake?" He grinned almost lazily, as if he'd known she'd been thinking sinful thoughts.

"Uh...right." She dug through her cabinet and found a pair of blue plates, a knife, and two forks. She cut two slices and held one out to him.

He didn't take his plate right away, instead reaching into the bag from the bakery and retrieving the little packet of candles. He nestled one on the top of her slice.

"You don't need to—"

"Of course I do." He produced a small lighter with a silver crest embossed on it and flicked it on, the flame sparking as he put it to the wick of the candle. The crest matched the one engraved on the gold signet ring on his left hand.

Another part of the mystery. What sort of man wore a signet ring? Given what she knew about history, especially English history, she had to wonder if he might be...No that was silly. He couldn't be royalty. She knew enough about the current monarchy to know he wasn't related to Prince William or Prince Harry. Was he titled? A lord? If so, what was he doing studying at Cambridge? It wasn't unusual for nobles to send their children to study at Oxford or Cambridge, but after they'd gotten their undergraduate degree they didn't normally pursue graduate studies. Of course, the simpler explanation was that he was simply wearing the ring as a fashion statement. A lot of British movie stars wore signet rings to give themselves an aura of mystery.

"What's the symbol on your ring?" she asked, nodding at his hand.

A shadow flickered across his eyes, and he glanced away before he replied. "A family heirloom."

That only created a hundred other questions, but she was prevented from asking anything else because he'd successfully lit the candle.

Once the wick caught fire and burned steadily, he pocketed the lighter and took the plate from her hands.

"Now make a wish and blow it out." Tristan's eyes locked with hers, and that enchanting blue-green was now bright with fire. They were so close, only the plate separating them, as he watched her, waiting.

She leaned down, closed her eyes.

I wish... What did she wish for? A funny thought popped into her head, and she felt strange enough to go with it.

I wish to have an adventure. She was tired of reading about them between the pages of old books, she wanted to live one. Standing here with Tristan and kissing him tonight was the start, and she wanted more, so much more. With a puff, she blew out the candle, and smoke curled up from the blackened tip of the wick.

"Happy birthday, Kat," Tristan whispered.

"Thank you." Kat meant for more than just his sweet words. She meant for the cake, for the kiss in the pub, for setting her down a path of living. She flicked her gaze up to his again as she removed the candle from the slice of cake and set it aside on the counter.

A slow smile curved his lips as he handed back her plate and collected his own. Then he walked over to her bed and sat down.

Tristan tasted his cake, and she wished he were tasting

her. She wanted to be back in his arms, kissing him. And part of her was curious to know what made him so notorious that women were whispering about him in pubs.

I have to be smart about this. There was no way she could ask him to kiss her again and open that door to more intimacy. Not after he'd made a promise to behave like a gentleman and just eat his cake. But she was torn. Wanting him to stay, wanting more, and being afraid of that desire and where it could lead. After just a short while of being around him, she could see that heartbreaker side to him, the one that would hurt her if she fell for him. He was full of charm, sex appeal, and mystery. There wasn't a woman in the world who wasn't intrigued by that, or seduced by that...

"Mmm...The baker wasn't lying. This cake is sinful." He patted the bedside next to him. "Come sit."

Kat tried to ignore her confusion about Tristan and the way he made her feel. Hesitant, excited, off balance, fascinated. He was too handsome to be in her room and on her bed. And his simple presence on her bed made her mind go to wonderful places. The images he put in her head with just a thought should have scared her. She wanted to do things with him that she'd never thought about before. Like having him push her flat onto her back and pin her wrists on either side of her head while he kissed her, ruthless, seductive, hard, as she wriggled beneath him, desperate for more. His eyes promised that and so much more as he licked his lips and watched her.

She was finally nineteen, but he made her want to be twenty-five, worldly and experienced. Being around Tristan, she wanted to be someone interesting. Which brought her back to a question that plagued her: Was he pretending to be interested, wanting another notch on his bedpost and thinking she'd be an easy target?

Or does he really like me? A nervous flutter stirred in her stomach again.

"Why did you really follow me to the bakery?" she asked.

For a man like him to come after her when the pub had been filled with plenty of pretty college girls, there had to be a reason. She wasn't exactly the type of girl guys flocked after. She was a size twelve, definitely curvy, with brown hair and gray eyes. Not a stunning model or even like the prettier girls she'd seen on campus, those tall leggy British beauties who were similar to his cousin Celia.

Tristan bit into a forkful of cake, sucking chocolate off the prongs.

Kat stared at his mouth, remembering all too well how his lips had felt on hers.

"You've caught my attention, Kat." He set his plate on the table by the bed and folded his arms over his chest.

"Your attention?" She avoided the bed and sat at her desk, where she nibbled on the cake. The flavors were decadent. The zing of the raspberry, the dark, almost erotic taste of the semi-sweet chocolate. *Sinful.*

"Yes." He reached up to stroke his jaw. "Very few things attract my attention. But *you* did." His brows drew together.

What did that mean? Kat had trouble swallowing. Maybe if she drank something…Kneeling by her fridge, she retrieved a small carton of milk.

"Want something to drink?" she offered.

"Yes. Thank you." He rose from the bed and came up behind her. The warmth of his body seared hers as he reached around her to grab one of her mugs and fill it himself.

A shiver rippled down her spine, and she closed her eyes a brief moment, until he stepped back again. Then she raised her glass to her lips and hastily drank, trying to quench the thirst chocolate always created, and this newer thirst for the man not two feet from her. He was like a drug—one hit and she needed more. To feel that giddy rush when he pinned her against a wall, his hands exploring her curves, his mouth possessing hers…She was supposed to be playing it cool, and not letting him think he could get her into bed, at least not tonight. The fact that this was exactly what she wanted was very…very bad.

ABOUT THE AUTHOR

Lauren Smith is an Oklahoma attorney by day, author by night for Grand Central Publishing, who pens adventurous and edgy romance stories by the light of her smartphone flashlight app. She knew she was destined to be a romance writer when she attempted to rewrite the entire *Titanic* movie just to save Jack from drowning. Connecting with readers by writing emotionally moving, realistic and sexy romances no matter what time period is her passion. She has won multiple awards in several romance subgenres, including New England Readers' Choice Awards, Greater Detroit Booksellers' Best Awards, Amazon.com Breakthrough Novel Award quarter-finalist and a semifinalist for the Mary Wollstonecraft Shelley Award. To connect with Lauren, visit her at www.laurensmithbooks.com or Twitter at @LSmithAuthor. For news of her latest releases and upcoming stories, be sure to sign up for her VIP Reader Group and Mailing List through her website!

CPSIA information can be obtained
at www.ICGtesting.com
Printed in the USA
LVOW11s0752051117
555072LV00001B/76/P